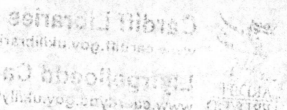

LEGACY

TAMARA McKINLEY

LARGE PRINT

Oxford

First published in Great Britain 2009
by
Hodder & Stoughton

Published in Large Print 2010 by ISIS Publishing Ltd.,
7 Centremead, Osney Mead, Oxford OX2 0ES
by arrangement with
Hodder & Stoughton
An Hachette Livre UK Company

British Library Cataloguing in Publication Data
McKinley, Tamara.
    Legacy.
    1. Man-woman relationships - - Australia - -
    History - - 19th century - - Fiction.
    2. Gold mines and mining - - Australia - - History - -
    19th century - - Fiction.
    3. Australia - - History - - 1788–1900 - - Fiction.
    4. Historical fiction.
    5. Large type books.
    I. Title
    823.9'2–dc22

ISBN 978–0–7531–8540–7 (hb)
ISBN 978–0–7531–8541–4 (pb)

Printed and bound in Great Britain by
T. J. International Ltd., Padstow, Cornwall

My journey through this trilogy has been a roller-coaster ride. The hardest part of any journey is the first step, but having taken that, and reached my goal, I feel an enormous sense of achievement. I didn't really know if I was capable of such an ambitious project, but I have come to really appreciate just how much I owe to the people who love and encourage me even when the going gets tough.

It is to those people — and they know who they are — that I dedicate *Legacy*. Without them, I wouldn't be so blessed.

Author's Note

I have taken liberties with the timeline of Kumali's tragic story, placing it several years before the era of the "lost generation", and hope the historians among you will forgive me. Kumali is a fictional character, but I could not finish the Oceana Trilogy without showing the legacy she — and her people — inherited.

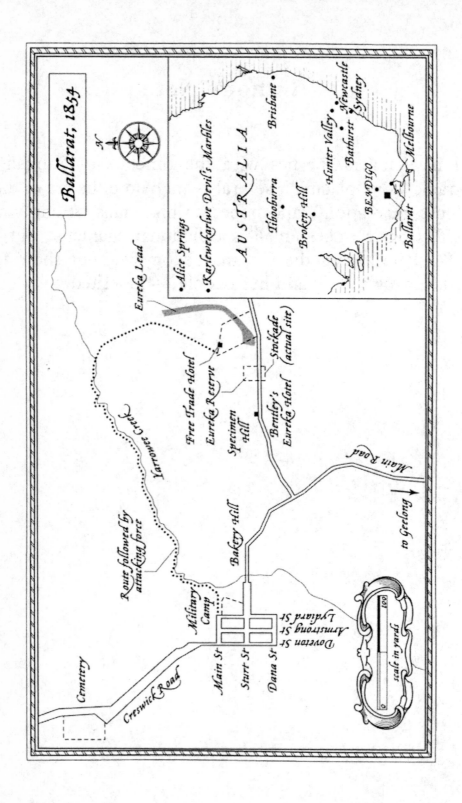

Ballarat, 1854

N

AUSTRALIA

Alice Springs
Karlwekarlwe Devil's Marbles
Tibooburra
Broken Hill
Brisbane
Hunter Valley
Newcastle
Sydney
Bathurst
BENDIGO
Melbourne
Ballarat

Eureka Lead

Yarrowee Creek

Free Trade Hotel
Eureka Reserve
Specimen Hill
Bentley's
Eureka Hotel

Stockade
(actual site)

Route followed by
attacking force

Military
Camp

Bakery Hill

Main Road

to Geelong

Cemetery

Creswick Road

Doveton St
Armstrong St
Lydiard St

Main St
Sturt St
Dana St

scale in yards
100

The legacy of heroes is the memory of a great name
And the inheritance of a great example.

Disraeli

PROLOGUE:

The Ties That Bind

Moonrakers Farm, New South Wales, 1835

Nell Penhalligan held her granddaughter's gaze and tried, unsuccessfully, to maintain a fierce expression. Ruby was a darling child and aptly named, for her hair was red, her temper fiery. She was as inquisitive and bossy as her mother, Amy, had been at five, and it was difficult not to smile under such determined scrutiny. "It's rude to stare," she said mildly.

"You're very old today, Grandma, aren't you?" The head was tilted, the blue eyes speculative.

Nell puffed out her generous bosom. "I'm seventy," she said proudly.

"That's nothing," interrupted Alice Quince. "I'm seventy-four."

Nell eyed the little woman next to her. "Yeah, but I'm in better health," she retorted. "And I still do a full day's work."

"Hmph." Alice tucked stray wisps of white hair beneath her bonnet. "A bit of washing and ironing isn't

1

work," she said dismissively. "I still help at the shearing."

"Get in the way more like," muttered Nell.

The child was listening avidly. "Why do you fight with Aunt Alice, Grandma?"

"Because she talks nonsense most of the time," puffed Nell, pulling the thin shawl more tightly around her plump shoulders. Despite the blazing sun, she was cold, and should have brought her thicker shawl, but she wasn't about to ask for it — Alice would no doubt make some scathing remark about her lack of stamina.

"And you don't?" Alice snorted in derision. "You fill that child's head with all kinds of rubbish — things she couldn't possibly understand."

Nell winked at Ruby, who beamed back. "Me and Ruby understand one another perfectly," she replied. "Better she hears the stories from me than some garbled version from strangers."

"I hardly think telling her about your convict past is appropriate," muttered Alice, her bony shoulders stiff with disapproval. "Especially considering the reason for your transportation." Her glare spoke volumes.

Nell's life as a London whore had ended the day she'd landed here. "You know I don't tell 'er them sort of things," she snapped.

Ruby clambered on to Nell's capacious lap and snuggled against her. "I like Grandma's stories." She gazed up at Nell. "Tell me how Aunt Alice nearly got eaten by a dingo and how you shot it dead. That's a scary one."

2

Alice snapped open her fan. "I tell that story much better than you," she muttered. "After all, the dingo was chasing *me*."

"Yeah, but you wouldn't be 'ere today if I wasn't such a good shot," fired back Nell. "Isn't it time for your afternoon kip?"

Alice's brown eyes narrowed. "Not *everyone* snores their way through half the day," she countered. She struggled out of the chair, her skirts rustling, gleaming blue-black in the sunlight. "I'm not sitting here while you fabricate the whole incident. Your daughter Sarah needs help serving tea."

Nell watched her friend hobble across the clearing and carefully negotiate the steps to the homestead. They were both getting frail, although neither of them would dream of admitting it. Yet, despite their constant bickering, their widowhood had drawn them close over the years and now they were like sisters. She felt the child move on her lap and winced. Her joints were painful and even Ruby's light weight made them complain. "Give me a kiss for me birthday, Rubes, then go and help your mum."

"But I want a story," she said, pouting.

"Later," she promised.

"I love you, Grandma, and I love Aunt Alice too. Please don't be cross with her, 'cos she's really, *really* old and Bindi says he can hear the Spirits singing to her." The child frowned. "I can't hear singing. Can you, Grandma?"

As Ruby flung her arms round her neck and kissed her cheek, Nell felt chilled. She would have a word with

3

Bindi. How *dare* the Aborigine worry the child with his superstitions? "Darling Ruby," she muttered, "the only singing you'll hear today is for me when I cut me cake." Nell clung to her, revelling in the vitality of the little girl she adored. "Now, run along," she murmured distractedly.

She watched the child scamper away, bright hair glossy, ribbons fluttering as her bare feet danced through the grass. The adventure of life awaited Ruby, and Nell felt a pang of sadness for her own lost youth. Where had the years gone? How had they managed to slip away, leaving her with only dream-like memories of a life lived by a Nell who bore little resemblance to the old woman who sat here feeling sorry for herself?

Cross at letting her thoughts stray and determined not to allow Bindi's superstitions spoil the day, she leant back into the cushions and watched the bustle as tables were set in the shade of the trees, and the native children were shooed away with bribes of stick candy.

Bindi was squatting by the river with the other native men, their women chattering like galahs as they splashed in search of the crayfish they called *yabbies*. The little boy whose life had been saved by her husband Billy's last heroic act was now a man — a man with silver in his hair. She gave a sigh as she took in the scene.

Gum trees bent pale trunks over ochre banks, their leaves trembling as bright finches darted back and forth. The sky was clear, the blue leached by the heat that shimmered on the horizon, and in the distance she could hear the chortle of a kookaburra and the sad caw of a crow. The scene depicted the essence of this ancient land she now called home. It was familiar and dangerously deceptive, as beneath the serenity lay a cruelty that had, at times, brought her and Alice to the edge of despair. Yet, as she looked at her family, she felt contentment, for the trials of taming this primal landscape had given her many blessings despite the price she'd had to pay.

Her son Walter would have looked more like his father if he hadn't got that dark red hair, but her heart twisted as she noted the lithe strength in her son's wiry figure and the same glint of silver at his temples that Billy had once had. Despite the resemblance, Walter didn't possess his father's careless approach to life and took things far too seriously. He still had a temper, though thankfully it had waned with maturity, but once roused, the family had learnt to keep their distance. Widowed for four years, he kept a firm hand on the reins of Moonrakers and seemed disinclined to remarry.

Walter's four boys were charging about getting in everyone's way, and Nell smiled as their little cousin Ruby stood, hands on hips, telling them off. Those boys were as restless as colts — it was a good thing their father put all that energy to use about the place and kept them out of mischief.

Her gaze settled on the homestead. Moonrakers hadn't changed much, and although she and Alice had moved into Jack's cabin by the river once Walter had married, it was still the heart of the property. The homestead was raised on pillars to avoid flooding and termites, and had been extended several times to accommodate Walter's family. A broad veranda ran along the front, screens and shutters kept out the flies, and roses clambered up the posts and sprawled along the roof. The old pepper tree was gnarled, its branches and drooping leaves giving added shade.

The shearing shed was sturdy, and although some of the barns had been rebuilt, and the pens extended, the essence of home remained. As she sat there, an island of stillness amid the chaos, Nell could still see the past as she watched the present unfold. The early years had brought hardship as they'd struggled to clear the land, build shelter, grow their crops and tend the sheep, but she and Billy, and Alice and her husband, Jack, had never lost the belief that one day they would have the best farm in New South Wales. She felt the familiar ache as she remembered the bushfire that had taken Billy and Jack, and the awful flooding that had been swiftly followed by a lengthy drought. She and Alice had survived it all, their initial animosity buried along with their husbands as they turned to one another for comfort and support.

She forced her thoughts to happier times. Her gaze settled on Niall and she smiled. The young Irishman had come courting her eldest daughter, Amy, many years ago. How awkward and shy he'd been in his patched clothes and worn boots — a youth, really, but with the experiences of a tortured man in his eyes after his years as a child convict. He was so different to the prosperous man who stood talking to his brother-in-law Walter as their children played around them. There had been joy and sadness visited upon him and Amy over the years, but love and hard work had seen them through, and now they lived in the fine house Niall had recently built behind his new forge in Parramatta. Niall had proved that the human spirit, however battered, could not be quenched.

Her gaze followed her grandchildren. There were ten in all, quite a brood, but it assured the future of Niall's forge and Walter's Moonrakers, and brought life back into this old place. She watched Ruby, the youngest of Amy's six surviving children. She knew she shouldn't favour her, but there was something about the child that warmed her heart. Perhaps it was because she loved hearing the stories Nell and Alice told her, or the way she seemed to appreciate the time they had for her when her parents were busy. Either way, the child had brought Nell and Alice a great deal of pleasure.

"Are you all right, Mum?"

Nell, startled from her thoughts, looked up at Sarah. "Just counting my blessings," she replied. "But I wish I had their energy." She saw the shadows in her youngest daughter's eyes as she watched the children race around the clearing, and understood her regrets, for Sarah had never married. She looked after her widowed twin brother and his boys, and now, at forty-two, would probably never know the joy of having her own. "Where's Alice?"

Sarah ran her hands down her apron, her blue eyes narrowed against the sun. "She's issuing orders from her kitchen chair like a sergeant major," she said with a giggle. "I'm surprised you haven't stuck your pennyworth in as well. You usually do."

"I shouldn't be expected to work on my birthday. But if Alice is getting in the way, I'll gladly sort her out."

Sarah laughed again. "Stay where you are, Mum. We don't need another argument when there's so much to do."

Nell settled once again into the cushions. She didn't really have the energy to argue with Alice, and it was pleasant sitting here in the dappled shade. "Get me my thicker shawl, love. The wind's a bit nippy."

The fleecy shawl was soon placed around her shoulders, and Nell was about to ask for a cup of tea when there were shouts from the other side of the river. Niall's family had come on horseback or in wagons, a great gaggle of them, accompanied by the sounds of pipes and fiddles. She cheered up immediately, as the Irish always had a story to tell, a song to sing or an instrument to play, and she loved their enthusiasm for a party.

She watched them cross the bridge over the river, which had become sadly depleted during this latest five-year drought. Niall had never forgotten his mother or his sisters, and had sponsored them and his brothers-in-law by paying their passage to Australia and finding them work. Most of them had stayed in or around Parramatta and were regular and very welcome visitors to Moonrakers.

"Help me up," she ordered. "It's my party and I'm stuck out 'ere on me own."

8

She struggled to her feet and took a moment to catch her breath and adjust her bonnet. It was an old one, but she'd replaced the ribbons and added a few sprigs of wattle so it complemented her green dress. Old she might be, but that was no excuse for letting standards slip. Not for her the black bombazine and plain bonnets Alice favoured, but then Alice never did have an adventurous eye. She waited for Sarah to retrieve her fan and crocheted gloves from where they'd fallen, took her arm and headed for the table.

"That's your third piece of cake."

Nell paused mid-munch. "At least I've still got enough teeth in me 'ead to eat what I want."

"Which is why you're so fat." Alice drew in her lips.

"Hmph. Anything's better than being scrawny — it's so ageing, and a breath of wind would blow you away."

Alice pulled a face. "It would take a hurricane to shift you," she muttered. "I'm surprised that chair hasn't collapsed."

"My Billy made things to last." She finished the slice and contemplated another.

Alice surprised her by not retaliating. "Yes," she sighed. "Billy certainly knew the worth of good craftsmanship. As did my Jack, of course. Our little place by the river will stand long after we're gone."

"Now you're getting morbid," said Nell, rather unsettled by Bindi's talk of "singing" and by the faraway look in her friend's eyes.

Alice appeared not to have heard. "Do you remember that first argument we had, over the sheep?"

9

Nell wasn't quite sure where this was going. That first row had started within minutes of Alice arriving at Moonrakers and had served as a forceful reminder that they were women of very differing backgrounds. The animosity it caused had lingered for years. "It was a humdinger, that's for sure," she replied hesitantly.

"You were an uppity piece back then," Alice mused. "Still are, most of the time." Her brown eyes twinkled as Nell bristled. "But I reckon we've got each other's measure, and I have to admit I've enjoyed our spats."

Nell raised an eyebrow as she brushed crumbs from her bosom. There was still a hint of the younger Alice in those eyes, but her face was lined from too many years in the merciless sun, her hands were gnarled, and her slenderness was emphasised by the looseness of her dress. Age and the elements had wreaked havoc on both of them. "You're not going soft on me, are you?"

Alice shook her head, the faded ribbons bobbing on her straw bonnet. "Just thinking how lucky we've been to have each other — and of how much we've achieved together." She nodded towards the cheerful cacophony of chatter and laughter at the other end of the table, where Ruby was happily perched on her cousin Finn's knee, gazing up at him adoringly. "Thanks for sharing your family with me. It would have been a lonely old age without children of my own."

"Now I know you're getting sentimental," said Nell crossly, disturbed by Alice's unusual show of emotions. She was in the act of pushing back her chair when Alice clasped her arm.

10

"You are my dearest friend," she said softly. "For once in your life, Nell, don't argue with me."

Nell could feel the beat of her heart thudding against her ribs. Alice was acting very strangely, and there was a sense of urgency in her voice she hadn't heard for years. It was as if she was aware of time running out, that she must make her peace before it was too late. Perhaps Bindi's superstitions weren't as foolish as she'd supposed.

Yet the thought of losing her friend was a sobering one. She gently took the crippled hand, aware of how the arthritis pained Alice even though she rarely let it show. "I don't know what all this is about," she said softly. "You and me have always argued — it's what's kept us going. Don't think that because I call you a silly old fool I don't love you." She swallowed the lump in her throat and forced a smile. "But don't you dare tell anyone I said so, or I'll tell 'em how you went to pieces when Henry Carlton died."

Alice reddened and snatched her hand away. "I didn't."

Nell nodded, satisfied Alice was restored to her usual brusque self. "I heard you," she said triumphantly. "Sobbing into your pillow like a lovesick girl."

"Despite your outrageous flirting with him, Henry was *my* beau, not yours. I had every right to mourn him." Alice glared at her, but couldn't maintain the furious expression for long and broke into a smile. "Oh, but he was handsome, wasn't he?"

Nell grinned. "That he was. Clever too. We wouldn't have done 'alf so well without him."

They lapsed into comfortable silence as the sounds of the party faded and memories took over. Henry Carlton had brought new warmth to their lives after they had been widowed, and his absence was still keenly felt. His friendship and guidance had been invaluable, his supply of breeding merinos from South Africa ensuring the quality of their stock after the terrible drought that had brought others to their knees.

"I sometimes think we've lived too long," said Alice, on a sigh.

"Stuff and nonsense," blurted Nell. "How can anyone live too long?"

"We're almost the last of that generation, Nell, and with every year comes news of another death. It seems unfair."

Nell had had enough. She grasped the arms of her chair and hauled herself upright. "Well, I ain't planning on turning up me bloody toes just yet," she snapped. "You can sit 'ere in your misery if you want, but while I've breath in me body, I'm gunna have some fun." She rapped on the table to get everyone's attention. "Let's have some music," she ordered. "I wanna dance."

"Don't be ridiculous, Mother," barked Walter. "It's not seemly for a woman of your age, and your heart isn't up to it."

She eyed her son. He was in danger of becoming pompous and the need to take him down a peg was irresistible. "Seemly or not, this old ticker's still thudding away. Do it good to get some exercise — and it wouldn't 'urt you neither," she snapped, eyeing his midriff. She turned to Niall's nephew, a handsome youth of about fifteen, with blue eyes and curly jet-black hair. "How about it, Finn?"

Finnbar Cleary took Nell's hand, his eyes bright with laughter as he sketched a bow. "It would be a pleasure to dance with the birthday girl, for sure. And I have me in mind that a waltz should suit the occasion. 'Tis all the rage in Europe." The others quickly picked up fiddles, pipes and the large, plate-like drum that would be beaten with a bone-shaped stick to set the rhythm.

"Mother! I forbid it!" Walter's face was puce.

"You can forbid all you like. I'm old enough to do as I please." Nell winked at Finn and stepped into his embrace. "Take no notice of 'im," she murmured. "Walter always was a stuffed shirt."

It had been many years since she'd danced, and the feel of a strong arm around her, and the warm hand clasping her fingers made her forget the inconveniences of age, and as he slowly guided her into the dance, she breathed in the scent of his freshly laundered shirt and felt young again.

The fiddles played their lilting tune to the haunting notes of the pipes as the drum stirred the feet and heart, and when the dance was over, Nell was breathless and giddy. She allowed Finn to guide her back to her chair and eased herself into the cushions. "That was fun," she gasped, as she fanned her hot face and tried to catch her breath.

"It was my pleasure." He bowed once more and a lock of dark hair fell over his eyes. Smoothing it back, he winked at her before leaving to join the others in a wild jig.

"He's lucky you didn't have a heart seizure," muttered Alice.

"At least I gave it a go," retorted Nell, who was still battling to get her breath. "I notice you're not joining in."

"I have more sense." Alice pulled her wrap more firmly around her bony shoulders. "You won't catch me making a fool of myself with a boy young enough to be my grandson."

"Good thing he didn't ask you to dance, then."

"Too old for all that nonsense," replied Alice. Her expression softened as she watched Finn swing Ruby into his arms for a fast polka. "But he's a handsome young fellow, I'll give you that."

"He's so like Billy, even though they aren't related," Nell sighed. "Right down to the way his hair falls in his eyes."

Alice was silent as she sipped lemonade. Her foot tapped in time to the music, and her gaze followed the dancers for a while before she turned her attention back to Nell. "I'm glad you've enjoyed your party, and I do so envy your vitality. If the truth be known, I would have loved to dance." She smiled, her expression soft with affection as she got to her feet and planted a kiss on her cheek. "Happy birthday, Nell."

"Where are you off to? The party's not over yet."

Alice patted her shoulder. "I'm tired," she said. "Time for my bed. It has been a lovely day, Nell, a really lovely day."

Nell was tempted to follow her to make sure she found her way in the darkness, then accepted that Alice knew the way as well as she, and that her old friend needed some peace and quiet after the long, busy day. She watched until Alice was lost in the deepening shadows, before turning her attention back to the dancers. They were getting rowdy, the prodigious amount of rum and beer adding to their enthusiasm, but not necessarily to their skills, as they twirled and stumbled across the grass. Even Walter had loosened up enough to take off his jacket and clap in time to the music.

"I'm tired, Grandma," said Ruby, as she came to lean against Nell's thigh some time later. "Tell me a story."

Nell gathered her into her lap. Ruby's curls had become a tangle, the ribbons long lost, and her fingers and mouth were sticky with cake. She smiled as she held the little girl close. "Once upon a time, long, long ago, when I was younger than your mummy, I went on an adventure," she said softly. "I sailed in a big ship which had lots of masts where sailors would climb right to the top like possums. That ship brought me from England to this land where no white man had lived. It was a frightening place back then, thick with trees and strange creatures, and black men who threw spears. There were no houses, and we had to clear the ground to grow our food." She eased the child into a more comfortable position as her joints complained. "But none of us knew 'ow to grow wheat, and after two years we was all starving. Billy was in charge of government stores, but it made no difference, and we 'ad to make do with what we could catch or forage."

15

"Tell me about Grandpa Billy," mumbled the child around her thumb.

"Billy was tall and 'andsome. With a twinkle in 'is eye and a strong arm to guide me," whispered Nell, her voice soft with love as the memories sharpened.

"Just like Finn," the child murmured. "I'm going to marry Finn when I'm a big girl. Then we'll be like you and Grandpa."

Nell smiled. Ruby had declared her love for Finn many a time. "That would be lovely," she replied. "But I was telling you about Billy. He rescued me when there was a terrible fight on the beach the day me and the other women landed, and we stayed together for years and years. He and Uncle Jack built Moonrakers, and it was 'ere that your mummy was born."

"She's asleep, Mum," murmured Amy, as she kissed Nell's cheek. "I'll put her to bed."

Nell touched her daughter's face and smiled. "The thought of bed is enticing," she admitted. "I think I'll turn in too."

Amy took Ruby and hoisted her on to her hip, her copper hair tangling with Ruby's and gleaming in the candlelight. "Stay here and I'll take you when I've got this one settled."

"No need. I know me way." She kissed Amy, caressed the soft, slumbering cheek of her beloved Ruby and smiled. "Thank you for the party. I've had a wonderful time."

Amy chuckled as she glanced across at Niall, who was regaling them all with an Irish song. "There will be some sore heads in the morning, but yes, it's been a good day."

Nell took her proffered arm and hauled herself out of the chair. As Amy headed towards the homestead with Ruby. Nell took a lingering look at the gathering before she turned away. The party showed no sign of flagging, but the little shack by the river and the comfort of her bed awaited her.

The sounds of the party echoed in the stillness, growing more distant as she tramped along the riverbank. Even after all these years it felt strange not to be returning to the homestead and the bedroom she had shared with Billy. She paused for a moment to catch her breath as she saw the moon's reflection on the water. The same reflection had inspired Billy to call this place Moonrakers, and she smiled as she remembered the former smuggler laughing uproariously at his cleverness. "Oh, Billy," she murmured, "how I miss you."

A rustle in the scrub made her start. "Who's there?" she rasped.

"Bindi, missus." The Aborigine stepped from the shadows, his wild mop of hair glinting silver in the moonlight.

"What on earth are you doing lurking about, giving me a fright?"

The broad brow creased, and the amber eyes were puzzled. "Bindi alonga missus. Take alonga *gunyah*, safe, safe."

"I know me way home, thank you, Bindi. Gawd knows I've done it enough times." She smiled, regretting her sharpness with him. She had known him all his life and he was as much a part of Moonrakers as she. "Go back to the party," she said. "And no more talk of singing to Ruby. It's unsettling and she doesn't understand."

The amber gaze was mesmerising. "Missus understand," he said. Then he nodded as if to confirm this statement before melting into the darkness.

Nell's heart was beating too rapidly, and her breath was laboured. Bindi had given her a fright and no mistake — why the hell did he have to spoil everything by looking at her like that? She shivered, blaming the sudden chill on the night breeze as she continued on her way. She was angry with herself for being so easily upset, and angry with Bindi for talking nonsense. The native superstition that death came with a song from the Spirits was thought by some to be rather romantic, but at her age it was unnerving, and although she didn't believe a word of it, she caught herself listening to the night sounds just in case the Spirit Voices could be heard whispering in the darkness.

As expected, there was no lamplight to guide her up the shallow steps, but as she hauled herself on to the veranda, she realised Alice was sitting in her usual chair. She paused to catch her breath. "I thought you said you were going to bed." There was no reply. "Come on, Alice, you can't sleep here. It's cold and you'll get a chill." She took the other woman's hand and, with a sharp cry of distress, sank into the adjacent chair. Alice's sleep was one from which she would never wake.

Nell's heart thudded as she gripped the lifeless fingers and tried to accept what had happened. "You knew, didn't you?" she muttered. "Just as Bindi knew. All those things you said, the memories we shared. It was your way of saying goodbye." The tears ran unheeded down her cheeks as she blinked at the moon, which was now floating high in a sea of stars. "Oh, Alice," she sobbed, "who the 'ell will I fight with now?"

She lost all sense of time as she held her friend's hand and watched the moon drift across the sky. Her heart was hammering, and she was still short of breath after that long walk and the scare Bindi had given her. She and Alice had shared so many years, had squabbled and celebrated like an old married couple, their love and respect for one another never faltering, even in the darkest days. They had lived and worked as one, and it wasn't fair of Alice to slip away, to abandon her to this awful silence, this emptiness.

Yet, as the moon dipped lower, and her tears dried, she thought she heard the faint sound of singing on the night breeze. It was beautiful in the stillness and a great sense of peace washed over her as she realised she was being called home. "Jack's there with you, isn't he, Alice? Can you see my Billy?"

"I'm here, darlin'." The soft voice came from the shadows. He emerged into a patch of moonlight, his dark hair flopping in his eyes as he smiled the same slow, sweet smile she had never forgotten. "You didn't think I'd leave you on your own, did you, Nell?"

"Billy." She sighed as she rose from her chair and took his outstretched hands.

"Come, Nell. It's time."

She glanced over her shoulder towards Moonrakers, where her family slept.

"We'll watch over them together," Billy said, as he drew her close, "'cos I know you'll want to keep an eye on young Ruby."

Looking into his eyes, she felt the purest joy, and when he led her into the blinding glow, she walked with the lithe step of a young woman in love.

PART ONE

Homeward Bound

CHAPTER
ONE

On the tracks, October 1849

Ruby pulled the collar of the oilskin coat up to her chin and shivered as the mare splashed through the mud. This was not the most romantic way to begin married life, and although she could sense the warmth of her grandmother Nell's spirit travelling with her, she hadn't expected to feel quite so downhearted.

The latest drought had broken with devastating ill timing, for there were still many miles to go before they reached the valley beyond the Blue Mountains, and as the rain hammered on Ruby's hat, it bowed the brim so the icy water ran down her neck and soaked her to the skin. The downpour was the only sound to be heard as the four oxen plodded through the valley, for even the roar of the nearby waterfall was muffled in its thunder. Talking was impossible, and anyway, the six of them had nothing to say to each other in the misery of trying to ignore sodden clothes, keep the sheep and string of horses together, and the overladen dray from getting bogged down in the mud.

Ruby had met James Tyler a year ago, and it had been love at first sight for both of them. He'd arrived at

23

Moonrakers looking for work, bringing with him an energy and hunger for adventure that matched her own. He'd swept her off her feet with his charming ways, good looks and roguish smile, and when he had expressed his desire to follow Blaxland, Lawson and Wentworth's route through the Blue Mountains to the endless pastures and plentiful water that were so perfect for rearing sheep, she'd known she had to go with him. Her childish passion for Finn was exactly that, and James — kind, sweet-natured James — was the man she'd been waiting for. When he had proposed six months later and slipped the ring on her finger — when he had kissed her for the first time and held her close in the moonlight — she had known without doubt that this was the man with whom she would share the rest of her life.

Her father, Niall, had at first refused to countenance her marrying an English Protestant when there were good Catholic husbands to be found among the ever-increasing Irish community. He'd been further disturbed by the young couple's intention to travel into the wilderness, where frequent native attacks were being reported ever more regularly by the squatters. Yet he'd eventually yielded to her unswerving determination to follow in her grandmother's pioneering footsteps, and Ruby had married James three weeks ago on her nineteenth birthday. Niall's gift to the newly-weds was the lease for several thousand square acres of prime grazing land.

Niall, whose keen eye had yet to fail him, had exploited both the market crash five years before and new legislation by buying offloaded sheep at sixpence a head, cattle that had once cost six guineas each for seven shillings and vast parcels of land for pennies. His forward thinking meant that as long as the demand for wool continued, Ruby and James's futures were secure.

The four oxen lumbered along as they pulled the enormous dray, which was loaded with supplies. The sheep had lost their skittishness and formed a bedraggled mob as they were chivvied along by the young Scottish shepherd and his dogs. The three ticket-of-leave men — convicts who'd been freed to earn a wage for the remainder of their sentences — led the string of horses through the rain, ready to put their shoulders to the wheels if they got stuck again, and James had abandoned his seat on the dray to grasp the leading ox's harness and encourage it to keep going.

As the rain fell in a blinding curtain, the surrounding trees trembled beneath its force and Ruby huddled deeper into the oilskin coat. The oxen managed twelve miles on a good day but only three or four on days like this, and she was beginning to wonder if they would ever reach the valley, for the precipitous mountain trail still lay ahead. Yet the dreams she'd nurtured since listening to the stories from Grandma Nell and Aunt Alice remained, as did the yearning to experience her own adventure. Her imagination had been fired by those stories, and although the reality of experiencing the hardships and battles of the pioneer was daunting, it nevertheless strengthened her resolve. With the spirit of Nell to guide her, she and James would survive this trek into the unknown and would raise their flock and their children in a landscape far from the crowded settlements that now surrounded Sydney and crept along the coast.

She was startled from her thoughts by a shout and peered out from beneath her dripping hat-brim. James had brought the oxen to a halt. "What's the matter?"

"The river's about to run a banker," he shouted back. "We have two choices: stay here and get flooded out or cross and risk getting drowned." He took off his hat and ran his fingers through his fair hair in frustration.

Ruby eyed the swiftly flowing river, noted that it seemed shallow enough a bit further upstream and looked back at her husband. "We can't stay here. The land isn't high enough to give protection if it floods, but if we take the dray further up, there's a way across."

James regarded her, his brown eyes thoughtful as he tugged on the hat and turned to the others. "What do you think?"

It seemed the men agreed with her, and James climbed back on the dray and took up whip and reins. With grumbling unwillingness, the animals headed upstream to where the water tumbled over a bed of rock and shale, and offered dubious passage to the other side.

Ruby dismounted as the shepherd and his dogs brought the mob of sheep to the riverbank. The oxen bellowed in fear. She understood how they felt, as it was a daunting prospect. The river raced over glossy shale, eddying around boulders and dragging at tree roots and reeds that clung to the banks. Broken branches and clumps of weed raced past, and in the rapidly dwindling light she could see the bloated corpse of a wallaby that had become stuck between two rocks.

"I'll cross first and find a way," shouted James. He handed the reins to Fergal, the sturdiest of their hired men. "When I signal, bring them over."

His wink to Ruby before he waded into the water was one of bravado and her heart began to thud as she realised he was as scared as she. Step by step he found purchase on the slippery river bed and countered the force of the water. It reached his hips and then his waist, but still he ploughed on.

Her heart hammering, Ruby's mouth dried as she willed him to reach the other side.

And then he was gone.

Ruby screamed and would have plunged in after him if the shepherd, Duncan, hadn't hauled her from the edge. "James," she yelled. "James, where are you?"

"There!" shouted Fergal. "He's over there."

James was clinging to a boulder downstream, but he was still in danger. Ruby's breath was a sob as James strained against the current to drag himself clear. She urged him on, every muscle tensed as if she too was battling for survival. James grappled with the slippery boulder and, with inexorable slowness, began to gain leverage. Inch by inch he dragged himself up until he was slumped on what appeared to be a rocky outcrop. Scrambling and slipping, he used this natural causeway to gain the other side. Ruby burst into tears as he waved from the opposite bank.

LEGACY

"Och, there's nae time for tears, lassie," muttered Duncan, the shepherd. "I have tae get these sheep across yet."

Ruby was so relieved James was safe she lost her usual reticence with the dour Scot and gave him a beaming smile. "Then you'll need all the help you can get," she said. "What do you want me to do?"

He glowered and mumbled something she couldn't hear above the rain, then turned and began to marshal dogs and sheep. Ruby shrugged. Duncan Stewart was a tree man and a skilled shepherd, but he'd never win prizes for his manners. She turned to the most senior of the ticket-of-leave men, who was checking the ropes that tied their possessions to the dray. "What's the plan, Fergal?"

The Irishman surveyed the river. "James has signalled that there's a sharp dip where he lost his footing, so I'll have to be taking the beasts midstream and then south to those boulders." He nudged back his hat, eyes narrowed against the rain as he gloomily surveyed the river. "The sheep are another matter," he muttered, scratching the stubble on his chin. "If the flow's strong enough to sweep away your man, then a woolly stands no chance."

"We can take the lambs on horseback," she replied.

Fergal glanced at the milling sheep and shook his head. "You'll have your hands full with the packhorses. I'll get the dray across, unload it and come back for the sheep. It's the only way."

Ruby gathered up the reins of two of the extra horses and climbed back into the saddle as Fergal told

28

Duncan his plan and the others followed suit. Fergal clambered on to the dray, and, with a crack of the whip, set the oxen lumbering towards the water. They baulked and snorted as it sucked at their legs, but the sting of the whip and the shouts of the men kept them moving and the dray was soon up to its axles in water.

Ruby nudged her mare out of the shallows, and as the chill swirl rose beyond the stirrups, she had to fight to keep the horses calm. Their ears were back, eyes rolling with terror as their necks arched and they yanked on the leading reins. The mare's hoofs slithered over the shale, and at each shout and crack of the whip Ruby felt her flinch.

"Steady girl," she murmured, as she struggled to maintain a grip on the leading reins and her purchase in the saddle. The water reached her thighs, the packhorses were being buffeted by the current, and the heavily laden saddlebags threatened to drag them down.

"Gerrup there!" yelled Fergal, as the oxen stumbled and bellowed and almost came to a halt. "Gerron, yer bastards."

The oxen strained as the dray's wheels scraped over the treacherous rocks that littered the river bed and threatened to sink in the soft shale. The tightly sealed barrels at the bottom of the load were soaked as the dray approached midstream, and with each jolt of the wheels the precious cargo began to shift. Ruby knew there was nothing they could do if it came untied, and as she and the two men urged the oxen on, she prayed it would hold until they reached the other side. The whip cracked repeatedly as Fergal used every oath he knew to keep the beasts going. As they scented the sanctuary of the far bank, they at last began to pull their burden willingly.

Ruby was soaked, her hands numb with cold as she urged the horses on to firm ground. As she slid from the saddle and searched for James, she realised he'd gone to help the others, who were still fighting to get horses and bullocks ashore.

One by one the men reached the bank and the spare horses were hobbled so they wouldn't stray. Fergal's voice was gruff from yelling as the bullocks dragged the dray away from the water. "Hurry," he rasped to the men, as he jumped down. "The river's rising every minute."

In silent desperation their numb fingers fumbled with sodden ropes, and the bundles, sacks and casks were carried into the trees. Tools, seed, furniture and clothes were quickly unloaded and placed beneath the oiled canvas that had kept most of it dry thus far.

Ruby helped Fergal unhitch three of the bullocks and get them hobbled, and then adjusted the harness so the remaining beast could pull the dray. She glanced repeatedly across to the far side of the river, where Duncan waited, surrounded by sheep, the faithful dogs panting at his feet. The river seemed higher and swifter — the bullock would take time to cross and would then have to make the journey back. It was a huge risk, but they had no choice.

"I have an idea," shouted James. "Take off the wheels, tie the ropes to the rear corners and lash them round these tree trunks. We'll float the dray but guide it with the ropes so it can be pulled across the flow."

The sturdy hubs were swiftly knocked away, and the iron-rimmed wooden wheels were hauled off the axles. Once the ropes were secured, James sat astride the bullock as it dragged the dray through the mud and into the water.

Ruby added her meagre weight to the ropes as the men used the tree trunks for leverage and slowly eased them out. They held their breath as the current began to batter and tug at the dray, but the ropes kept it steady and it floated neatly behind the bullock. As the beast finally reached the other side, they gratefully released the ropes and James reeled them in, lashing them round the nearest tree. It would be up to him and Duncan to pay them out on the return journey.

Peering through the rain, Ruby could just make out the two men who were coaxing the bell-wether, the lead ram, on to the dray. She was about to get back in the saddle when Fergal stopped her. "Stay here," he ordered.

"You're going to need every pair of hands if we're to get them safely across," she retorted.

"James doesn't want you at risk again," he shouted over the thunder of rain and river. "Do as you're told and stay here." Without waiting for an argument, he took his horse back into the water.

Ruby clenched her fists. Fergal might gain his freedom in less than a year, but he had no right to order her about, and it was infuriating to be made to feel useless when she was perfectly capable of helping.

She stood on the riverbank, burning with frustration as Fergal and the others headed for the other side.

Duncan's dogs worked swiftly, nipping and nudging the reluctant sheep until they followed their leader on to the wooden flat-bed. With the two smallest lambs tucked safely in the vast pockets of his coat, and one tethered by its feet round his neck, Duncan stepped on to the dray as the bullock was hurried back into the water.

Ruby held her breath. The sheep were tightly packed and beginning to panic, and the makeshift raft was fast becoming unstable. Two of the rams locked horns as the ewes jostled, their lambs in danger of being trampled as they bleated in terror. The dogs ran across their backs, nipping and snarling to bring them to order, but they were too badly spooked. One of the ewes took a flying leap, landed in the water and was swept away, to be swiftly joined by a second.

Fergal managed to grab its fleece, haul the beast out of the water and dump it across his saddle. The others positioned their mounts to form a barrier on either side of the dray, preventing more of the stupid creatures following suit. The riders had to contend not only with terrified horses but the pull of the current, and the sheer instability of the makeshift raft that seemed destined to drown its cargo.

Ruby swung into the saddle. The ewes were bumping and boring, and unseen by the men, a lamb had been knocked into the water. Digging her heels into the mare's flank, she set her in a gallop along the bank. The lamb was bleating piteously as it was swept along by the

32

current, and Ruby knew her only hope was to head it off further down.

The current was stronger now, the mare whinnying with terror as it was forced to swim. She could see the lamb being tossed and spun by the raging eddies. The mare was struggling against the tide, but Ruby clamped her thighs, let go of the reins and reached out. Her fingers touched sodden wool and she grabbed the lamb by its neck. Hauling the terrified creature out of the water, she stuffed it down the front of her voluminous oilskin coat and snatched up the reins. Now all she had to do was get back to the bank.

The river tugged and pulled and almost knocked the mare off her feet as Ruby coaxed her to keep going. The lamb struggled and bleated, its little hoofs battering her chest as it tried to escape the coat, but Ruby ignored the discomfort, determined to get the three of them to safety.

They emerged to shallower water and at last gained higher ground. Ruby was trembling so badly from cold and fear she couldn't dismount. She sat there in the teeming rain, the lamb quieter now, its head peeking out of her collar as the bullock finally dragged the dray out of the river. She began to sob with relief as the sheep skittered off into the bush, the dogs giving chase. James was safe, and although they had lost a ewe and two lambs, the majority of the mob had made it. Her tears were a release, for until now she hadn't fully digested the very real danger they had all been in.

She handed over the lamb to Duncan, who glared at her and turned away without a word, and as she was gathering enough energy to dismount, she was yanked from the saddle by James.

He clasped her to his chest. "Don't you *ever* pull a stunt like that again," he said fiercely. "I thought I'd lost you."

She clung to his sodden coat as the rain battered them and was soothed. There were still hundreds of miles ahead of them, but no matter what dangers lay in wait, Ruby's faith remained unwavering. As long as she and James were together, they would survive.

Kumali knew the *gubbas* — the white people — couldn't see her, for she was camouflaged by the surrounding trees. She remained in the gloom as she watched the antics in the river. The woman was brave and strong, and although her man was angry, he obviously cared for her, and Kumali sensed they were good people.

Kumali was of the Gundungurra, whose tribal lands encompassed the Wollondilly River to the south, the Nepean River to the east and the caves of Binnoomur to the northwest. Mandarg, her great-grandfather, had told stories of the *gubbas*, and these had been passed down to her mother's people. He had known that these white invaders would soon find a way over their sacred mountains. He had spoken of the good men he had met during his time in Warang, yet had warned them of the savagery of others, and the carelessness with which all whites plundered the sacred Dreaming Places and Songlines. His wise counselling had been heeded, but none of them had really understood the devastating effect the *gubbas* would have until it was too late.

They had come many moons after Mandarg had gone to the Spirits in the sky, and now the hunting grounds beyond the mountains were forbidden to her people. The white men had brought their women and cattle, their sheep and their labourers, and had stolen the Gundungurra's traditional lands. Their firesticks had cleared the forests and chased away the possums, koalas and birds, their ploughs had ripped up the grass where kangaroos and wallabies had once come to feed, and their guns and poisoned flour had murdered the starving Gundungurra.

Kumali's heart was heavy. It had become a battle between the *gubbas* and the few survivors of her tribe, but the stealing of cattle, sheep and grain was punished by hanging or, worse, a rout by the squatters and their black stockmen, who seemed to take pleasure in slaughtering even the youngest of her people. As her mother's grandfather had foretold, the enmities between the tribes had been used by the white man to clear the land, and the choices left to her people were stark: remain free, starve and be hunted, or live with the white man and be at his mercy.

Kumali grimaced. She was free for the moment — had walked many miles to escape the boss who beat her and forced her into his bed — but she knew from experience that he would send one of his black-fella trackers to find her and take her back to his farm in chains, for this was not the first time she'd run away.

As the travellers became lost behind the grey curtain of rain, Kumali emerged from the trees. The river was fast and deep, and although she was a strong swimmer, she was reluctant to cross. The Elders had told her about Mirringan and Gurrangatch, and she feared that Gurrangatch, who was part fish and part reptile, might have been swept from his lair in the Wingeecaribbee River into these waters and be lurking in the depths to ensnare her.

She hesitated, her fingers plucking at the thin cotton dress the missus had given her. It was her only protection from the chill, and it clung wetly to her like a second skin. Kumali blinked against the rain and stared down into the water. Gurrangatch was still angry from being chased by Mirringan, the tiger cat, and Kumali shivered as she thought she saw a flash of silver in the tumbling waters. She chewed her lip, weighing up her options.

Her life had begun in a mission compound, where initiation rites and the Elders' teaching had to be carried out in secret, as the minister had forbidden them. She had grown up with little understanding of the Ancient Ways the Elders talked about, for life in the *gubbas'* compound had a way of destroying independent thought or action. Hunting was banned; their meagre food allowance came from the mission. New laws denied them the right to have a meeting of more than two people, so there were no more *corroborees*, and although they were permitted to build *gunyahs* for shelter, these could be ransacked at a moment's notice should the minister suspect there was rum hidden inside them. Women and children were taken from their families and forced to work in the *gubbas'* houses and fields, often sent many miles away so they were never seen again. Kumali knew their fate, for it had been her own.

She stepped back from the river and squatted in the shelter of a tree. She had been taken three years ago, when she was twelve, and she could still remember her mother's screams, could still hear her father pleading with the man to release her. Ropes were tied round her neck and wrists, and she was hauled away, her mother's cries echoing long after she'd lost sight of her. Her innocence had been taken brutally on that first night, and as the long journey progressed, she had learnt that this was her future.

Kumali fought back the tears, refusing to give in to the hurt and bewilderment that still sometimes threatened to overwhelm her even though she was now fifteen summers. Her new master, a cattle farmer, was cruel, and his beatings had left their mark, not only on her body but on her soul. She was worth nothing, and if she died today in the river, no one would sing the ritual songs and mourn her passing.

The rain's thunder eased and she looked out from her meagre shelter. The clouds were clearing, the sun struggling to break through. Kumali eyed the river, but still she hesitated. The thought of death was terrifying, and although she knew what awaited her at the cattle station if she was caught by the tracker, surely it was better to experience this fleeting chance of freedom —

to live as the Ancient Ones had done, and try to learn how it must have been in the old days.

The thought was dismissed almost immediately. She didn't know how to survive in the bush, had no hunting skills, no intimate knowledge of her surroundings, no spear or knife. She had heard of the big cities that sprawled further south and east, but suspected life there would be just as harsh, for they were populated by the *gubbas*. The same held for the coastal plains, where she would be even more vulnerable, for the black-fella tribes there were traditional enemies. With a deep sigh she wrung the water from her dress. All she knew of life had been learnt in a mission compound or on a cattle station — it gave her little choice.

As the rain ceased and the clouds drifted apart, a shaft of sunlight fell on the opposite bank. It pierced a path through the trees as if pointing the way. Kumali stared at the golden beam and realised it was a sign. All hesitation gone, she waded into the shallows. If she survived the crossing, then she would follow the tracks of the bullock cart and the woman who had been so brave.

At sea off Tahiti, October 1849

Hina Timanu stood on the deck of the whaler, *Sprite*, and looked towards the misty smudge on the horizon. It had been almost two years since he'd seen his homeland, and although they were still several leagues from her shores, he thought he could already detect the aroma of cooking fires, frangipani and hibiscus.

38

Hina was twenty-eight, a gifted linguist and a seasoned whaler. He wore the standard-issue canvas trousers and serge shirt of the deckhand, but his height, muscular girth, long black hair and blue eyes set him apart from the Europeans he sailed with. It was something he'd become inured to over the years, for his own people were brown-eyed and short of stature, but the legacy of his mother's white great-grandfather lived on in him, and far from being shameful, he carried his difference with pride.

As the smudge began to take shape, Hina felt a thrill of expectancy. The months of hunting in the icy Southern Ocean had become a distant memory, and as the heat danced in waves over the far-off volcanoes, he wondered if *Sprite* had been spotted yet — and if Puaiti would be on the beach to welcome him. Her name meant "Little Flower", and her beauty put the hibiscus to shame, but she was the youngest daughter of a chieftain who demanded a sizeable offering in return for his daughter's hand. Hina experienced the familiar surge of mixed emotions — hope that his wages from the trip would be enough, doubt that it would and the suspicion that her father would find another excuse to keep them apart.

"You're thinkin' about that *wahini* again. I can always tell." The speaker was Bones, a runt of a man whose real name had been forgotten long ago. "I don't blame you neither," he said with a lascivious wink, "and I for one can't wait to get me 'ands on a woman."

Hina's bare feet made little noise as he strode along the wooden deck to follow Captain Jarvis's orders, thereby saving him from having to reply. Bones was like the rest of the crew: eager to lie with the *wahinis* and take what they freely offered without a second thought. After his years at sea, he could understand their reasoning, for few other ports offered such enticing and beautiful entertainment, but Hina had witnessed the sickness they left behind, and the distress it caused, and although the children of these brief couplings were seen as blessings, the missionaries made it clear they didn't approve, and would harangue the women at every opportunity.

The dark cones of the volcanoes rose from the lush canopy of palms that grew down to where the black sand shelved gently beneath the turquoise water. Shoals of brightly coloured fish darted away as turtles poked up their heads to eye the intruder before lazily swimming off to make way for a pod of dolphins that streaked through the water ahead of the bow.

Hina watched them, smiling at their sheer exuberance, as he waited for the order to furl the sails. Then a shout came from shore and he squinted into the blinding sunlight, searching for the beloved faces of his family, and for Puaiti. And there they were, clambering into the dug-out canoes — the bright sarongs and garlands of flowers as dazzling as the sun.

He swiftly furled the sail and lashed it down. The anchor sank with a splash as the first canoe came alongside. Hina climbed the bow-rigging, tore off his shirt and dived into the water. It was like cool silk against his skin, and as he surfaced, he was almost submerged again by the small body that hurtled against him and clung to his neck like a limpet.

"Puaiti," he gasped.

"Hina, oh, Hina, I have missed you so." Her words were punctuated by kisses.

He held her close as he trod water. Her eyes were as dark as night, the lashes long and bejewelled with droplets. Her lips were soft and warm, yielding beneath his kiss, her firm, young body pressed so tightly to him he could feel her breasts against his ribs. "It has been too long," he murmured.

Her eyes were misty with desire as she ran her hand down his chest and cupped his erection. "I too am impatient, but we have only to reach the beach," she sighed, "and then we will be one again."

He acknowledged the greetings from his brothers and sisters with a wave of his hand, knowing they understood they would see him later, much later. To the sound of their encouraging shouts and happy singing, and with Puaiti still clutched to his chest, he struck out for shore.

The glade was far from prying eyes, deep beneath the canopy of palm trees. The pool was fed by a stream and sat in the basin of dark rocks, where it trickled through a narrow fissure into another stream. Bright birds flitted above them, dipping occasionally for a drink, their melodious songs filling the air.

Hina's heart was racing as they stood in that cathedral of green light and music. Puaiti was more beautiful than he'd remembered, but now they were alone he was content to wait, to look at her and allow the desire to build, for the pleasure would be even greater, and now they had all the time in the world.

Puaiti seemed to understand this, and she stood before him, her dark gaze never leaving him as she loosened the belt of his trousers and eased the canvas down. Her small hands moved with almost unbearable softness as they cupped and stroked and caressed.

Hina touched her tawny cheek, reverently tracing the delicate brow, the curve of her cheekbone and the swell of her lips. His fingers followed the column of her neck and the sweep of her shoulder to the tangle of wet hair that reached almost to her hip. It was as black as the most precious pearl, and the hibiscus that was tucked behind her neat little ear exuded a perfume that heightened the sensuality of the moment.

Puaiti's eyes darkened as she reached for the knot in her brightly coloured sarong. With one graceful twist the material slithered to her bare feet. She eyed him through her thick, dark lashes. "Puaiti is still beautiful?" she whispered. "You still desire her?"

Hina could only nod, for he was transfixed. Her skin was golden, the swell of her hips in perfect symmetry with the narrow waist, taut belly and ripe breasts. The nipples were dark and swollen, thrusting from those golden orbs like exotic flowers, and he couldn't resist brushing them with his fingers.

She stepped closer, her eyes drowsy with desire as she arched her back to his touch. Hina could scarcely breathe as his hands slowly travelled down her stomach to the glistening black triangle of hair. His fingers

42

gently entered the warm, welcoming core that was Puaiti and he heard her gasp with pleasure. Falling to his knees, he drew her hips closer and kissed her belly, revelling in her musky perfume and the silken softness of her skin. His tongue flicked inside her and he tasted her essence.

With a groan of desire she pressed her hips towards him, urging him to take her, to bring this moment to the conclusion she wanted, needed, had waited for, for so long. Hina drew her to the valley floor, his need just as great, and as he kissed her trembling thighs, she opened up to him. Sliding over her, he resisted for a heartbeat and then entered her. He was home at last.

The night was warm and scented with woodsmoke as they sat around the fire. Hina heard the sigh of waves lapping the shore, and the rustle of palms in the sea breeze. They were the familiar and much-loved background sounds to which he'd been born, and as the talk flowed around him, he drew Puaiti closer, wanting never to leave again.

"When will you speak to Puaiti's father?" Oriata's eyes showed a mother's concern for her son.

The mood broken at the thought of Vainui, Hina tried to look confident. Vainui's name meant "Big Water", and he lived up to it — leading the fishing canoes to the furthest reaches, diving the deepest for the black pearls, thereby guaranteeing his powerful position on the island. He was daunting, and Hina dreaded approaching him. "I will ask for a meeting tomorrow."

Oriata eyed him thoughtfully, then nodded. "You are a good son and have worked hard. Vainui should be proud to give you his daughter."

Hina noticed there were strands of silver in her long hair and felt a great sadness. He'd been away too long. To dispel the gloomy thoughts that threatened to overshadow this joyous homecoming, he turned to his grandmother Manutea. Her hair was as white as the ice in the Southern Ocean, but her eyes still burnt with the fire of youth. "Tell me one of your stories," he coaxed.

"You have heard them all many times."

Hina smiled, not taken in by her dismissive tone. "You know you love telling stories," he pressed, "and it's been a long time since I've heard them."

She eyed him, her lips twitching in a smile. "Then I will tell you of the golden gift my father once had, and of how it was lost because my mother was tempted by coloured glass."

Hina rested against the log, his arm round Puaiti. His grandmother knew this story meant more to him than most, for it explained his blue eyes and the red teardrop birthmarks on the skin of his nape.

"A long, long time ago there was a beautiful young *wahini* called Lianni. In those days Tahiti was a peaceful island, with few ships and even fewer missionaries." Her wrinkled face showed her displeasure at the current state of affairs before she carried on. "There was a ship, a fine ship with many important people sailing in her. They came to build the large stone place on the hill, so they could look at the sky through strange things they called telescopes. It was said they wished to watch the sun darken a part of the sky, but no one really understood what they were doing, or why it was so important."

Silence had fallen, and even the youngest stilled to listen, for Manutea was a great storyteller.

"A young man travelled on this ship. His name was Jon." She stumbled over the unfamiliar word, took a sip of coconut milk and continued. "He was a fine fellow, with dark hair and eyes the colour of the Tahitian sea. There were red marks here" — she pointed a gnarled finger at her temple — "as if his blood was crying, for they took the shape of teardrops." She nodded as if to affirm this was an apt description. "He saw Lianni and they fell in love. Lianni knew he would leave — just as all the men do when they come on ships — but she was happy to love him for the time they could be together — just as you and Puaiti are happy."

Hina returned his grandmother's smile. "I am not leaving," he said. "This is my home, and once Big Water gives his consent, we will be married."

The old woman's doubts were clear in her expression. "Let us hope your wish comes true," she said softly. "But for Lianni and Jon, it was a love meant only to last until his ship set sail." She took a breath and another sip of coconut milk. "On that final day he gave Lianni a gift — a very fine gift — which she promised to treasure. She did not know what it was for, but from my father's description, it was probably a pocket watch. It was round and gold, with a fiery white stone set at its heart. There was a tiny clip at the side, and this opened to reveal the treasure inside."

She lowered her voice and everyone drew nearer. "Inside was a white disc, with gold numbers all round it and two tiny gold hands, but best of all were the images painted on either side. They were of Jon and Lianni." She smiled as if she had memories of this extraordinary gift. "He looked fine and proud, with his strong face and blue eyes, and the artist had even painted in the red teardrops, so there could be no mistaking him. Lianni, of course, looked beautiful — as beautiful as all the women in my family."

Hina smiled as she looked round the circle, defying anyone to disagree. "You are still beautiful, Manutea."

"My hair was not always this colour." Her eyes grew misty. "I remember when —"

Hina realised she would drift from the story if given half the chance and hurried to interrupt. "So he sailed away and Lianni kept the watch. What happened next?"

"She cried many tears after he had gone, for she had not told him she carried his son, but now she had his special gift to give to the boy when he was old enough to understand its importance."

She paused and stared into the darkness beyond the campfire. "Tahamma was a strong baby, with his father's eyes, and the same red teardrops. Lianni was a good mother, and she loved Tahamma more than her life, but sickness had come to Tahiti from one of the sailors and our people were dying. Lianni was close to death and begged her aunt, Tahani, to take the boy to another island before he too fell ill. She made Tahani promise to keep the watch for Tahamma and guard it well. She was not to know Tahani would give her life for it." An uneasy stillness settled over the listeners as they saw tears glisten in the old woman's eyes and trace her wrinkled cheek. "Tahani's husband, Pruhana, was a bad man. He had been banished for beating Tahani and trying to steal the watch, but he came back in the night and killed her. Tahani must have known he would return, for she had given the watch to her brothers to keep safe, and Pruhana never found it."

She wiped away the tears and settled more comfortably on the rush mat. "Tahamma was given the watch on his marriage to Solanni, but my mother did not understand the importance of this gift, and when a ship came and she saw the merchant's sparkling wares, she exchanged it for a jewelled knife. My father was very angry and banished her for six seasons. She was very afraid, for she had to live alone and not eat at the communal fire. Those months were very hard, for she had me and my brother, and there was no one to help her. My father, Tahamma, forgave her in the end, but never forgot his lost inheritance, and that is why the story has been passed down to each generation. I think he hoped fate would one day bring the watch back to where it belongs."

"It is probably destroyed after so many years."

The old woman eyed Hina and shook her head. "I think it was worth much money, and such things are not lost for ever. It is somewhere, out beyond the sea, waiting for the tides to bring it back to our sacred island. One day it will come, I am sure of it."

Hina dipped his chin so she couldn't see his smile. His grandmother might think she had the gift of foresight, but there had been little proof. If the watch did exist, it was probably just a cheap memento that legend and myth had built into a treasure. Finding it after all this time was as improbable as catching moonbeams.

Kernow House, Watsons Bay, near Sydney,
October 1849

"Frederick, where are you?" Gertrude Collinson's voice held a note of anger as she repeated her question for the third time. "Frederick Cadwallader, I know you're hiding. Come out this instant."

Freddy realised his father's half-sister was at the edge of her formidable temper and he reluctantly emerged from the crawlspace he'd discovered in the abandoned nursery. He'd stumbled on it quite by accident, and the cleverly masked dovetail joint in the panelling had slid open as if in an Arabian adventure. He'd been hesitant at first, for it was narrow and dark, and spiders' webs had got trapped in his hair, but his courage had been rewarded, and now, as he looked at the treasures he'd found, he knew they were worthy of any pirate.

"If I have to come upstairs, there will be trouble," barked Gertrude.

He hastily stuffed the booty back into the darkness, checked the secret door was firmly shut and ran down the stairs. The treasure was a delicious secret, and he would examine it properly tonight.

His aunt was in the entrance hall, arms crossed, face like thunder. "What on *earth* have you been doing? Just look at your filthy knickerbockers, and your hair, your face." She grabbed his ear between finger and thumb as if afraid he would mark her pristine grey dress and dragged him back to the bottom of the stairs. "My brother and his wife are due to arrive from England today. How *dare* you get so dishevelled? Go and wash immediately, and change your clothes. I will not have you disgrace me."

Freddy rubbed his ear as he took the stairs two at a time. He did wish his aunt would attack another part of his anatomy when she was angry, for his poor ear had withstood so many tweaks it was beginning to stick out like a flag.

As he poured water into a bowl and began to wash away the dirt and cobwebs, he thought of their guests' imminent arrival with little enthusiasm. The house had been in uproar for the past three months with builders and decorators swarming all over it, his mother taking refuge in her drawing room, his father spending more and more time in his city office. Aunt Gertrude had turned into a harrying, flustered bully who ordered maids, gardeners and stable-hands to work from dawn to dusk in preparation for this important visitation. Yet no matter how hard everyone laboured, it never seemed enough. Gertrude Collinson seemed determined to show her sister-in-law that, despite living in the colonies, her management of the household was as gracious as any in England.

Freddy suspected his mother, Amelia, was in awe of Lord and Lady Cadwallader, just as she was of Gertrude, which didn't bode well, for Amelia would become very grand — like she did when they went to visit Governor Fitzroy at Parramatta — and that meant he'd have to mind his manners even more than usual.

He changed into the fresh clothes laid out by the maid, and carefully plastered his dark hair with water before combing it back from his forehead. It was a trial being eleven, he decided, for although he'd escaped the strictures of the nursery, he was still regarded as too young to have any say in his life. This visit from his uncle heralded a new beginning — one he wasn't at all sure about — as when it was time to return to England, Frederick would go with them. His father had enrolled him in a boarding school in London, and his future holidays would be spent at the family seat in Cornwall.

"I just hope I fit in," he muttered. His smile returned as he realised there was a good side to those future plans. There would be an entire ocean between him and Aunt Gertrude.

"Frederick! Your mamma is waiting. Hurry up."

With a sigh he put down the comb, eyed his reflection in the mirror and hoped he would pass his aunt's fierce scrutiny. He cast a longing look out of the rain-spattered window to the tree house. It was his refuge, his pirate ship and treasure store — a perfect place for the bounty he'd discovered earlier. Frustration burnt. If only Gertrude would give him a few more minutes . . .

"Frederick, come down this instant."

With a groan of despair he snatched up the top hat and hurried out of the room.

His mother, Amelia Cadwallader, was resplendent in one of the new dresses the local seamstress had sewn from a series of fashion plates imported from London, the effect of which was spoilt by her flustered expression. She stood beside Gertrude, her gaze darting back and forth as she twisted the furled parasol and smiled nervously at her son.

Gertrude's gaze swept over him, the blue eyes missing nothing. Freddy stood to attention, not daring to meet the glint of humour in his father's eye, knowing that to do so would have him burst into laughter, which would mean another tweak of his ear.

"I suppose I should be grateful you have at least removed the cobwebs," Gertrude sniffed. "But you still resemble a ragamuffin. I despair."

Amelia cast him a pitying look before she swept out of the front door and down the steps to the enclosed carriage, her wide skirts and shoulder flounces billowing like a ship running before the wind.

Freddy risked a glance at his father as they followed in her wake, and grinned as Oliver Cadwallader winked at him.

"You look very handsome," murmured Oliver, grimacing as he eased his tight waistcoat. At forty-eight, he had become portly, his brown hair and moustache liberally sprinkled with grey. "Don't mind your aunt, son. She doesn't really mean to be harsh."

Freddy suspected otherwise, but was astute enough not to argue. If only his mother would stand up for him more often, he thought wistfully. Since Gertrude's arrival three years before, she had become less attentive to his needs — almost a shadow of the mother who had once been sweet, amiable and loving.

"My half-sister merely wants to make a good impression on our brother and his wife," said Oliver quietly, "but she will soon realise that neither Harry nor Lavinia care a fig for appearances."

"Are you looking forward to seeing your brother again, Father?" They were waiting on the veranda for Amelia to settle into the carriage, her voluminous skirts taking up all of one seat and most of the floor.

Oliver smiled. "Of course. I haven't seen Harry for years, and letters don't really give the full picture, do they?"

Freddy didn't know — he'd never received a letter. "It must be strange to have a brother you rarely see. Still, I suppose it's better than not having a brother at all."

Oliver must have heard the wistfulness in his voice, for he smiled down at him and softly knuckled his chin. "You will soon have your cousin Charlie to fill the void. But be warned, Freddy, brothers aren't always the best of friends. They fight and argue, and the competition between them can get quite heated at times. Harry was a likeable chap, though, a good chum when we were boys." He stared into the distance. "I've missed his company."

"Why are you standing about?" barked Gertrude. "You're late enough already."

"Yes, do hurry. I fear I shall catch cold if I sit here much longer," added Amelia fretfully.

Freddy and his father exchanged knowing glances. It was going to be a very long day.

CHAPTER
TWO

Sydney Harbour, October 1849

Harry Cadwallader, the Earl of Kernow, stood on the deck of the *Elizabeth Ann* and eagerly awaited his first sight of Sydney Town in thirty years. It was the homecoming he'd longed for, but now, as the ship slowly made her way towards port, he found his initial excitement laced with unease. There were memories here — dark memories that had been locked away but never truly forgotten — and there would be no sign of his beloved mother and stepfather waiting to greet him, for Eloise and George Collinson had perished several years ago on a sea voyage to the Americas, where they had planned to celebrate their long and happy marriage. He gave a deep sigh. There were so many regrets, few of which he could remedy.

"You look troubled, my dear," said the soft voice at his shoulder. "I thought you would be overjoyed to see Sydney again."

Harry determinedly pushed away the dour thoughts and smiled down at his wife. At forty-nine, Lavinia was still a beauty. With fair hair and blue eyes, skin as pale as milk and a trim figure, he had fallen in love with her the moment their eyes had met across the ballroom. He still loved her, with a deep and abiding passion that had never waned, despite the passing years. "You look lovely," he murmured, as he took in the pretty bonnet, the curls framing her face, and the pale blue gown.

She smiled, but her expressive eyes remained concerned. "You didn't answer my question, Harry. What's worrying you?"

"Memories," he said gruffly, as he stared towards shore.

"The past will always be with us," she replied, "no matter where we are, but it is the way we deal with it that is important, and thus far it has not hampered our progress."

Harry squeezed her fingers. Despite her knowledge of his family's past, could she really understand what this return meant to him — what memories it evoked? Coming home to a land that held memories of his father Edward's madness, the murder of his elder brother, Charles, and the heartbreak of his mother was harder than he'd expected. And yet, as he gazed out at the city that sprawled along the harbour and into the hills, he felt a glimmer of hope. The change in Sydney was startling, and in that change lay the opportunity to set aside that dark past and remember only the good.

"I do understand," she said quietly.

He looked into her blue eyes and realised that indeed she did. He held her hand and they lapsed into the silent, comfortable closeness that had been their strength throughout their marriage.

The light shower had ended and the sun streamed from a cloudless sky, and as the shoreline became clearer and the flotilla of small boats guided them towards the dock, Harry scented the aromas of boyhood. The familiar, almost forgotten smell of warm, damp earth mingled with pine and eucalyptus, the sharp tang of freshly cut timber and the delicious hint of baking bread and cut grass drifted on the light breeze as they reached the shore. He could hear the shouts of seamen, the cries of gulls and chatter of galahs, could see the fine buildings that had sprung up since his departure, and the way commerce had expanded the number of warehouses strung along the quayside.

"It is not quite what I expected," said Lavinia, opening her parasol against the fierce sunlight. "But of course the docks in any city are rather rough places, so one shouldn't judge." She dabbed her face with a scrap of lacy handkerchief, her bright expression not really masking the worried frown as she watched a chain gang unload a nearby vessel.

"If you think this is rough, you should have seen it in the early days. I remember when the streets were a danger to life and limb, with dark, narrow alleyways and hovels squeezed into every available, filthy corner. The old convict laundry used to be over there, and it was a common sight to witness public floggings and brawling natives. But look at those new buildings, the parks and gardens, the fancy shops and bright awnings. The old place has at last begun to look respectable."

"You love it, don't you?"

56

He nodded. "I suppose I do. But then, I was born and raised here. The unhappy times had little to do with the place itself, and I've never lost my affection for it."

"There's nowhere like home," murmured Lavinia.

Harry knew she was homesick for Cornwall and the two daughters they'd had to leave with her sister. Neither of them was strong, and it had been deemed unadvisable for them to travel so far. "I remember my stepfather, George, telling me many years ago to look on every journey as an adventure," he replied. "Australia differs from England in so many ways that it cannot be compared, so please don't judge her until you have seen beyond this harbour."

"Mamma! I have seen my first kangaroo. Look! Over there."

Harry glanced across at the grassy area that swept almost to the shore and ruffled his son's hair as he dutifully admired the grey kangaroo. Charlie George Cadwallader was the child of their late middle age, and had been named in memory of the uncle he would never know. The heir to the House of Kernow in Cornwall had his mother's fair hair and blue eyes, and possessed the enthusiasm that only a boy of thirteen could engender.

"I get the sense you'll find Australia most invigorating," Harry said, with a smile.

"I can't wait to meet everyone, and see the house by the shore, and go exploring. Do you think Freddy will come with his parents to meet us?"

"We have made good progress after the doldrums and are prompt in our arrival," he replied. "I do hope Oliver and his family will be waiting, for I sent a letter from Cape Town, and I see the ship that carried it is already in port."

They turned back to watch ropes flung ashore and sailors scramble to furl the sails as the anchor was dropped. Harry regarded the sizeable crowd gathered on the dock, noting the carriages, the plethora of top hats and brightly decorated bonnets and the quality breeding of the horses. It was a forceful reminder that New South Wales was rapidly evolving into a wealthy, settled colony, and he envied Oliver's luck to be at the very forefront of this expansion.

Life in Cornwall had not been easy since the Industrial Revolution, and he was waging a constant battle to keep the farms and mines manned as the workers sought higher wages in the factories and mills. The unwanted mantle of his title and legacy weighed heavily still, as did the debts his father and grandfather had left behind, and although Harry had worked tirelessly to regain honour and solvency to the family name, he had never stopped yearning for the freedom to do as he pleased.

"Harry!"

The booming voice carried above the excited babble and Harry's gloomy thoughts were dispelled by the sight of the portly figure on the quayside. It was a shock to see his younger brother looking so middle-aged, and was that grey in his hair? Harry grinned and waved. No doubt Oliver was thinking the same about him, for the passing years had taken their toll on both of them. With his wife and son trailing behind him, Harry joined the surge to disembark.

"Welcome back," shouted Oliver, as he pushed through the mêlée.

Harry embraced his brother. "It's good to see you," he said, as they drew apart. "By Gad, Ollie, you've put on some winter condition, but you look positively well heeled."

Oliver grinned sheepishly and tugged at his colourful waistcoat. "It's good living, Harry. I don't get the exercise now I'm stuck in the office." His brown eyes studied his elder brother. "You look fit enough, though. The sea voyage obviously agreed with you."

"You should have seen me during the storm as we left the Cape. I was practically green!" Harry laughed. "George would have been horrified to see me thus." He clasped Oliver's hand, his expression sobering. "It really is good to be back." Their eyes met and they grinned in delight, oblivious to everyone around them.

"Lord Kernow, I do apologise for my husband's lack of manners." Amelia dipped a flustered curtsy and introduced herself and Freddy.

"There's no need to stand on ceremony, Amelia," boomed Oliver. "Not among family."

Harry suddenly realised he'd left his own wife and son behind and swiftly bowed over Amelia's proffered hand before he turned to find them. "Ah, there you are," he said cheerfully, as Lavinia and Charlie appeared.

While the introductions were being made, he watched the interaction between the two women. Amelia's attempts to pretend she was every bit as high-born as his wife made for almost painful viewing, but Lavinia, bless her, didn't appear to notice the other woman's strained vowels and simpering manner as she greeted her like a sister and admired her gaudy bonnet. As for the boys, they had already wandered off to the other end of the quay to watch the sailors unload a consignment of horses.

"Reminds one of you and me at that age," muttered Oliver, as he followed his gaze. "I know Freddy has always longed for a brother, and it's good to see how well they've taken to one another on such short acquaintance. I suspect there will be plenty of mischief afoot over the coming months."

They shared a knowing smile and turned back to their wives.

Jessie Searle was also waiting to disembark the *Elizabeth Ann*. She placed her battered bag at her feet as she stood on the tin trunk and watched the swirl of activity on the quay. Her excitement was laced with trepidation, as she had never been so far from home, and although the colours of this southern colony were glorious, the welcome enthusiastic, she had scant knowledge of what awaited her at the country school.

She had convinced herself that it wouldn't be very different from the one in Cornwall, where she had stayed on to pass the teaching examinations, and that the Church School Board wouldn't have engaged her and paid passage if they didn't think she was capable. Nevertheless she was barely past her nineteenth birthday, and once her brothers had departed for the southern copper mines in Kapunda, she would be alone, and at the mercy of strangers.

"It's a rare sight, this Sydney," said John Searle, as he used his height and bulk to push his way to her side.

Jessie looked up at her eldest brother and tried to smile, but the fear of what lay ahead made it impossible. "I wish you were coming with me," she said, in a rare unguarded moment.

His large, labour-roughened hand lay on her arm. "You know we can't." A frown drew his dark brows together, and he scratched his bushy black beard as he surveyed the quay and the sprawl of the town. "Me and Daniel have got to get to Port Philip. The mine-owner won't be pleased if we're delayed." He cast her a sharp look. "It's too late to change your mind now, Jess. I warned you —"

"Our ship doesn't leave until tonight," interrupted Daniel, as he joined them. "We've got time to make certain Mr Lawrence is trustworthy." He gave Jessie an encouraging smile.

She experienced a surge of loving exasperation for these two big men who had protected her ever since she could remember. "I hardly think a member of the Church will prove dishonourable," she replied.

"We'll see," said John darkly.

She eyed her brothers and realised that no matter what she said they would judge for themselves. With a sigh, she looked back at the bustle on the quay. Their love and protection had, at times, become a handicap, especially now the three of them were alone in the world. No wonder she was unwed, for any beau she'd ever had had been frightened off.

When Daniel and John had gained assisted passage from the mining company in the south, Jessie had secretly replied to an advertisement in the newspaper. The interview had been held in Truro, and although she had been warned she would be living far from civilisation among the natives and farmers, she couldn't help but feel excited at the prospect. When the post had been offered to her, she'd leapt at the chance. It was an opportunity for adventure, far from the poverty and strictures of Cornwall, in a land that promised a new way of life.

Her brothers had baulked at the idea, refusing to allow her to take such risks, but she'd worn them down with logical argument and determination. The three of them were the last of their family now Grandmother Rose had passed away, so how much better it was to live in the same country, Jessie had argued, than be parted by thousands of miles of sea. They had given in, but not gracefully, and she prayed fervently that her new employer was old, married and ugly, for only then would her brothers allow her to go with him.

John plucked her from her perch on the trunk and set her on the deck. "Time to go, Jess." He and Daniel grabbed a handle each and began to carry the heavy trunk towards the gangplank.

Jessie's heart was racing as she followed them, her weighty bag dragging on her arm, palms damp with anxious perspiration. The freshly polished button-boots were not the most sensible attire for clattering down a steep ramp, and she discovered as she reached the quay that she could still feel the rocking of the ship beneath her feet.

"I can't see no-one who looks like a minister," growled John.

Jessie, who could see very little because of her lack of height, adjusted her bonnet and smoothed the creases from her dress with nervous fingers. She knew she looked dowdy in the plain brown dress, but it was appropriate attire for a schoolmistress, and the posy of cream fabric roses on her bonnet was surely not too flippant. It was imperative she gave the right impression, and she was beginning to have doubts.

"Stay here while me and Dan try to find him," ordered John.

Jessie was an island in the swirl of activity, the trunk beside her, the bag at her feet. She couldn't have moved if she'd wanted to, for she was almost rigid with fear.

"Miss Searle?"

The voice, coming so close behind her, startled her, and she whirled round. He was of average height, with thick brown hair drooping over his collar, a broad smile, which showed even, white teeth, and amused grey eyes that were darkly lashed. His complexion was weathered beneath the broad-brimmed hat, as were his dusty brown trousers, shirt and long, loose coat. His figure, although lean, held the promise of strength and vitality. Jessie met the laughing grey eyes and gave a tentative smile. If this was Mr Lawrence, then there would be a fearful row when her brothers returned.

"You are Miss Searle?" His eyes widened as he regarded her from boots to bonnet.

She drew herself up to her full five feet and a quarter inch and held his impudent stare. "That I am," she said haughtily. "Who might you be?"

He seemed unabashed as he swept off his hat and grinned. "Abel Cruickshank at your service, and may I say it's a pleasure to meet you, miss."

Jessie reserved judgement on whether this feeling was to be reciprocated. "Well, Mr Cruickshank, perhaps you had better explain yourself, for I have no idea why you have accosted me." She knew she sounded rather fierce, but she had been taken unawares and he could be anybody. Where were her brothers when she needed them?

"Sorry, missus . . . miss . . . Miss Searle," he stuttered, all at once uncertain. "Mr Lawrence asked me to meet you when I came into town for supplies. He sent this by way of introduction."

Jessie took the rather grubby piece of paper and read the copperplate flourish of a practised hand. Mr Lawrence apologised for not meeting her, but his work at Lawrence Creek Mission could not be left. Abel Cruickshank was a trusted friend who would provide protection and company on the long journey, and she was not to dawdle in Sydney Town.

She carefully folded the letter and looked up at him. Their eyes met, and in that moment she felt an easing of her anxieties.

"Who's this?" John pushed his way between them at that moment, Daniel right behind him.

Jessie introduced Mr Cruickshank to her brothers. "Mr Lawrence has written a letter of introduction." She thrust the letter at him as the men glowered at one another.

He scanned the letter and handed it back. "Have you got proof you're who you say you are?" growled John, his nose an inch from the other's face.

Abel stood his ground and drew a parcel of letters from his coat pocket. "These are all I have," he said quietly. "I picked them up from the trading office this morning. You will see they are addressed to Mr Lawrence."

John riffled through them and then handed them back with a grunt. "Where is this school, and how long will it take to get there?"

Jessie was about to intervene when John stopped her. "Let him speak, Jess. Anyone could lay claim to those letters."

"The school is at the Lawrence Creek Mission, which is about ninety miles north-west from here in the Hunter Valley," replied Abel, a spark of anger at last showing in his eyes. "It will take over a week to get there because I have a wagon full of supplies, two milk cows and a string of horses to look after along the way." He looked down at Jessie, his expression kindly. "Rest assured, Miss Searle, you will be quite safe with me."

"Let's see this wagon, then." John and Daniel picked up the trunk and, with Abel leading the way, headed off.

Jessie watched them go, realised she'd been forgotten in her brothers' quest to protect her honour and, with a sigh of impatience, picked up her bag and followed them. It seemed that her brothers were determined to dislike Mr Cruickshank, but then they didn't approve of any man under the age of sixty getting anywhere near her — and Mr Cruickshank was decidedly too young and handsome.

The wagon was indeed loaded with sacks, barrels and tools, and the horse in the traces eyed her belligerently as he ate from a nosebag. A chicken pen had been fashioned out of wood and was placed behind the driver's seat, the cockerel and his harem of five hens fussily pecking at seed. Two cows were tied to the rear wheel. A string of eight horses stood nearby, tethered to a tree where a black man lounged in the shade smoking a clay pipe.

Jessie came to an abrupt halt as this rather frightening individual stood up and came towards them. He was wearing clothes similar to those of Mr Cruickshank, but his blackness almost masked his features, his hair was wild and tangled, and she noted he wore no shoes.

"This is Tumbalong," said Abel. "He's my offsider, and good mate." He grinned at the native. "Say hello, Tumbalong. This is the new schoolteacher."

Before Jessie could return the black man's shy smile, her brother intervened. "There was no mention of travelling with savages," he rasped. "Come on, Jess, we'll find you work elsewhere."

"Now look here, mate," growled Abel, as he grabbed hold of John's arm. "I don't care much for your talk of savages. Black he might be, but Tumbalong is a fine fellow with good Christian learning. He's my mate, and if I say he's right, then he is. Understood?"

There was a terrible silence as each man tensed.

Jessie stepped around her brothers and held out her hand. "Good day to you, Tumbalong," she said, with as much courage as she could muster.

"G'day, missus," he muttered, his amber eyes watching the men warily as he fleetingly returned her handshake.

"Jess, it's not safe. You're coming with us."

She turned to her brothers. "No," she said firmly. "I will travel with Mr Cruickshank and Tumbalong, and fulfil my duty at the mission school, where I will no doubt meet many more of the native people."

John grabbed her arm and hauled her out of earshot. "But you'll be alone and unprotected — who knows what that savage might do. I forbid it."

She pulled from his grasp, furious with his unreasonable behaviour. "Mr Cruickshank has assured me I will be safe — from him and Tumbalong — and Mr Lawrence would certainly not have sent either of them if he thought they were a threat. I will proceed as planned, and I would prefer it if you could at least give me the courtesy of allowing me to make my own decisions."

"You're barely nineteen," he hissed. "And I've yet to meet a woman who can make a sensible decision when her mind is set on stupidity."

"Tell you what," interrupted Abel's drawl. "How's about I give Miss Searle one of my rifles? She can keep it by her side day and night if that will put your mind at rest."

"That sounds an admirable idea," replied Jessie with asperity. She gingerly took the rifle, felt the weight of it and followed Mr Cruickshank's instructions on how to check it was loaded. She turned back to her brothers. "There, now I am fully armed and ready for anything. Satisfied?"

John and Daniel exchanged glances. "Not really," John muttered. "But since you refuse to come with us, we have to accept your decision. Grandmother was right — you are impossible."

"Now that's settled, it's time to go. Load up that trunk, Tumbalong, and un-hobble the horses while I sort out the cows." Abel began to tether the cattle to the side of the wagon. "Say your goodbyes, Miss Searle. We're leaving."

Now the moment of departure was upon her, she forgave her brothers their faults and clung to them, fighting tears. "Stay safe," she murmured, as she kissed them. "Write to me at the school, even if it's only a line, just to let me know how you are."

"God keep you safe, Jess," murmured Daniel. "It's a fearsome journey in front of you by all accounts."

"For you too."

"I still think you should come with us," said John stubbornly, as he lifted her and held her to his chest. "At least we'd be able to keep an eye on you."

"Let me have my adventure, John," she pleaded.

He solemnly set her on her feet again. "Only if you promise to stay in touch and to let us know if you want to leave."

She nodded and turned away. Abel Cruickshank was already in the wagon, the reins in his hands. Tumbalong was astride one of the horses, the rest of the string firmly held by leading reins. She placed her foot on the wheel-hub and grasped the side of the wagon, drawing herself up on to the seat. Abel slapped the reins and the wagon rumbled over the cobbles. Jessie looked back at her brothers and forced a brave smile. They waved back, and when they were finally lost from sight, Jessie lifted her chin with determination and looked at the track ahead.

This was her chance to prove herself, to make a new life far from the poverty and starvation of a Cornwall that had suffered so much from the recent failure of the potato crop and to take the opportunities of advancement that would surely come in this brave, bright colony. After all, she reminded herself silently, her grandmother had held the firm belief that they were descended from nobility — to show any sign of regret now would be seen as weakness.

She smiled as she tucked a stray dark curl beneath her bonnet and clung to the side of the wagon as it rolled and pitched over the rough ground. Her grandmother had been a woman of great imagination and told many a good tale, but none of the family had lent them credence. As for the teardrop birthmark that she and her grandmother had shared — it was a common enough thing and certainly nothing to ponder over or question.

Sydney Town to Watsons Bay, the same day

Harry and Oliver supervised the loading of the trunks and bags into a wagon as the others repaired to a nearby hotel for afternoon tea. When, at last, everything was satisfactorily stowed and tied down, they gave instructions to the drayman and the two families began the journey to Kernow House.

Harry blocked out the sound of chattering women and boys, and gazed at the familiar panorama as they bowled along the coastal path. The rocky bays were sheltered by towering cliffs that plunged into churning water, and behind him he could see the sprawl of Sydney Town. It was an imposing sight. As they passed Rose Bay and approached Watsons Bay, he felt a tightening in his stomach.

"The house is much changed," said Oliver, as if he'd read his brother's anxiety. "When Mamma married George and rented out the house, the tenants made several alterations. Amelia and I have added to these, and I think you will find very little to remind you of the past."

"I was always amazed you wished to live in it at all," said Harry, unable to keep the bitterness from his voice. "If I'd had my way, the place would have been burnt to the ground."

"It was Mamma's legacy to me," Oliver said quietly, "and although she never lived in it again, she realised I had few memories of what had happened there. Don't forget, Harry, I was only a little boy when Papa . . ."

Harry looked away. They had all been boys, but Oliver had not gone boar-hunting that fateful day, had not witnessed the death of their elder brother, Charles, by the bullet fired from their drunken father's rifle, or seen their mother's face as she tried to comprehend what had happened. For Harry, though, those images lived on, and he wondered if he would ever be rid of them.

As the carriage crested the final hill and began the descent to Watsons Bay, Harry waited almost fearfully for sight of the house. And there it was, standing as it always had, well back from the beach. To his great relief he discovered Oliver spoke the truth when he'd said it had changed.

The original building had been square, but in recent years wings had been added and a columned portico had been built above the front door. Stone steps led down to the sweeping lawns and manicured flower-beds, and the wrought-iron lace of the balcony railings glowed white in the gathering gloom. The old wooden stables had been torn down, and in their place stood a line of impressive sandstone loose boxes complete with clock tower and neatly cobbled yard. More sandstone had been used in the wall that sheltered what he suspected to be a kitchen garden, and several wooden cottages had been erected on the edge of the paddock, which no doubt housed the servants.

Trees had been cleared from the surrounding pastures where horses and cattle now grazed, and as the carriage rattled along the gravel driveway, he caught a glimpse of fishing boats down on the beach. "Don't tell me you have your own fishing fleet," he teased.

Oliver laughed, obviously relieved the awkward moment was over. "That's a chap named Doyle," he explained. "He set up shop down there about four years ago and sells his fish straight from the boat. Quite the entrepreneur — he plans to open a restaurant soon."

"Reminds me of Cornwall," replied Harry, as he caught a whiff of fish and watched the gulls squabble over the scraps.

"That's no bad thing," said Oliver. "And it's convenient to have fresh fish for the table without having to send one of the maids all the way into town."

The carriage came to a halt, the loaded wagon drawing up behind them several moments later. Harry was astounded by the number of servants pouring out of the house to fetch the luggage. Compared with the poorly staffed house in Cornwall, Oliver's palatial home and numerous servants were proof that being the younger son and unencumbered by a title was no barrier to making a fortune.

After helping Lavinia down from the carriage, he turned towards the house again, where he saw a slender, still figure standing in the doorway. Her beauty was apparent despite the severely parted hair, dull grey dress and lack of any feminine adornment. The blue eyes that had once shone with laughter were narrowed as she watched the bustle with an air of disapproval.

"Gertrude?" He couldn't believe this was the half-sister he and Oliver had adored from the moment she'd been born to their mother, during the sea crossing from Cornwall to New South Wales — for where was the happy smile he remembered? It seemed to have vanished in the tightly buttoned-up little person who waited for them.

"Come and greet me, then, Harry. I can't stand about all day when there's so much to be done." Her voice would have been the pride of a sergeant major, and Harry meekly obeyed. "It's good to see you at last," she said, after kissing his cheek.

Harry embraced her awkwardly and found her unyielding, the stiffness not, he suspected, entirely due to creaking whalebone and corsetry. He could smell camphor in her clothes and a hint of lavender water, but there was no jewellery, lace or ribbons to alleviate the dour grey, only a waist-chain jangling with keys.

She eased from his embrace, folded her hands, her beautiful eyes critical as she regarded him. "You've aged better than Oliver," she said in clipped tones. "I'm always telling him not to eat and drink so much." She looked over his shoulder. "Aren't you going to introduce me to your wife and son?"

He actually blushed, and felt as foolish as a boy in front of a daunting nanny. With the introductions over, they were ushered into the hall, where he didn't dare catch his wife's amused gaze.

"The servants will see to your luggage," said Gertrude. "I must check supper arrangements with Cook." Without a glance at Amelia, she hurried away, the keys clanking with every purposeful stride.

As the others followed the servants upstairs, Harry looked at his brother. "What on earth has happened to Gertrude? And why has she taken on the role of housekeeper?"

Oliver sighed. "Gertie's certainly not the pretty little thing you'll remember. She's positively overbearing at times, and poor Amelia is terrified of her." He led Harry into a side room that had been furnished as an office. "I could do with a drink," he muttered.

"Not for me."

Oliver raised an eyebrow, shrugged and poured himself a generous whisky before he sank into a deep leather chair. "I didn't realise you'd joined the Temperance Brigade."

"Never touch the stuff," replied Harry. "You were telling me about Gertie."

"Before Mamma and George left on that fatal last journey, Mamma asked Gertie to look after us all until she came back. I'm afraid she took that maternal endearment rather too literally and she moved in with us." Oliver sighed. "I had hoped to marry her off, but she rejects all suitors and seems to prefer being single."

"But Gertie's only thirty-five — still young enough to find a husband, instead of hiding away here, playing at housekeepers."

"Gertrude doesn't 'play' at anything, Harry, I can assure you," he said wryly. "She takes her duties very seriously — almost to the point of usurping Amelia." Oliver drank deeply and poured another measure. "I'm afraid our little half-sister is determined to remain a spinster, and now she has discovered her talents for keeping my house, nothing short of an explosive charge would shift her."

"How sad." Harry surveyed the book-lined room that had once been their mother's drawing room and realised there was nothing of her left in here — not even the memory of her perfume. "When I think of all that promise . . . She could still be so beautiful if she took care of herself. Mamma would be heartbroken."

"That's why I feel it is my duty to care for her. But I'm finding it increasingly hard to placate Amelia. The two women don't see eye to eye, and it can make for some heated moments."

Harry regarded his brother, saw the slump of his shoulders and the deep lines round his eyes, and realised that, despite his wealth, Oliver possessed little contentment in his life. With a consoling pat on his brother's shoulder, Harry went in search of his darling Lavinia.

Freddy had lain in bed in a fever of impatience, waiting for the house to fall silent. The adults had lingered over dinner, and it seemed an age before they came upstairs and he heard the bedroom doors close. When the grandfather clock in the hall chimed midnight, he gauged it safe enough, and having donned dressing gown and slippers, he lit a candle and opened the door.

The knowledge that Gertrude might still be awake and alert for every sound made his heart thud. She didn't approve of boys — especially boys who crept about in the night — and he didn't want another ear-tweak for his pains, but all was still. He carefully shielded the candle from the draught as he tiptoed along the narrow landing. He had thought to tell Charlie about the treasure, for he liked his cousin, but as he'd had little chance to examine what he'd found, he'd been loath to share it.

The attic stairs were hidden behind a door at the end of the corridor and climbed steeply upward to the disused nursery. His slippers made little noise on the wooden treads, but as he pushed through the last door and closed it behind him, he realised he'd been holding his breath.

The nursery still retained reminders of childhood, with the rocking horse gathering dust in the corner, the tiny chairs and tables stacked away beside boxes of toys and books. There were trunks and cases scattered about, the contents of which had provided many hours of exploration when the weather was inclement, or he was hiding from Aunt Gertrude.

Freddy set the candle firmly into a dish and looked about him. The attic room was even more mysterious in the flickering light, and although he wasn't afraid of shadows, and didn't believe in ghosts; the vast chimney stacks looked rather daunting. He swallowed his fear and turned his attention to the secret panel. It slid back with a loud click and Freddy glanced over his shoulder, certain someone must have heard, but the silence remained, thick and laden with trapped heat and the dust of years of neglect. Bringing the candle closer, he began to retrieve the treasure.

"I say, how exciting."

Freddy banged his head as he whirled round. Charlie was standing right behind him. "You shouldn't creep up on people like that," he hissed.

"Sorry." Charlie didn't look a bit repentant as he knelt beside him. "I couldn't sleep, and when I heard you leave your room, I followed you."

Freddy was about to inform him he had no right to follow people about when they weren't invited, but realised it would be rather impolite. "You can stay only if you take an oath to keep this secret," he whispered.

"I swear I will tell no one," replied Charlie, eyes gleaming with excitement.

"Cross your heart and hope to die?"

Charlie nodded and performed the necessary ritual.

"Then spit and shake on it," ordered Freddy.

Wet palms were clasped and quickly smeared clean down dressing gowns.

"Come on, Freddy, let me see what you've found."

"There's to be no touching — not until I say so," Freddy ordered. As a single child, he'd become used to having his own way and wasn't about to relinquish that right even though Charlie was a guest, and two years his senior.

Freddy reluctantly made way for his cousin and they looked down at the things he'd already retrieved from the secret crawl-space. He could barely breathe for the thrill of it, for there was a military sword, complete with scabbard, belt and tassels, a pair of duelling pistols with ivory handles nestling in an ebony box, a spyglass and an old leather saddlebag stuffed with maps and notebooks.

"We must keep this from our parents," muttered Charlie. "Father will not abide guns in the house, and there will be a fearful fuss."

Freddy nodded. "My father doesn't like them either," he replied. "As for Aunt Gertrude, I dread to think what she'd do if she found them." He thought for a moment and then came to a decision. "We'll keep them up here in one of the trunks until we can smuggle them out to the tree house. She never goes up there."

The boys looked at one another with barely contained excitement. The tree house had been explored that afternoon and Charlie had agreed it was the perfect place to hide from the grown-ups. The battered tin trunk that was stored up there would serve as the ideal home for their treasure.

"Is there anything else?" asked Charlie, peering into the cavity.

Freddy saw there was indeed something lying in the shadows and brought it out.

"It's only an old book," said Charlie dismissively, his gaze returning to the pistols.

Freddy agreed it wasn't half as exciting as the pistols or sword — or even the maps, which certainly begged a second look — but he was determined to examine everything closely and in his own good time. He forced open the rusting clasp and riffled through pages brittle from their incarceration and covered in spidery handwriting.

He couldn't make any sense of it, but wasn't about to admit it. "It's in code," he declared. "I suspect it is linked with the maps, and probably the journal of a pirate captain who wanted to keep the whereabouts of his treasure secret."

Charlie shot him a look that was condescending and disbelieving. "Let me see."

While his cousin was busy turning the pages, Freddy reached for the ebony box. He felt the weight of one of the pistols before inspecting it more closely. It was beautifully wrought, the ivory handle cool in his palm, the silver casing gleaming dully in the candlelight.

"I don't think this is in code," said Charlie thoughtfully. "There are no hieroglyph's or numbers. It looks more like foreign writing."

"Well, it's not Latin or French," retorted Freddy, who had been forced to study both subjects by his tutor and was certain he would have deciphered at least the odd word here and there. He carefully replaced the duelling pistol in its bed of silk.

"It's not Greek either," said Charlie, dismissing the book by snapping it shut. "It's probably just an old journal someone hid away and forgot about."

Freddy allowed his cousin to examine the pistols and the sword, but his gaze kept returning to the book. It was thickly bound in leather, with a silver clasp that had once held a tiny key. Whatever its contents, the thought that someone had written it and meant it to remain hidden intrigued him.

He waited until Charlie was fully engrossed in the sword and scabbard, and returned the book to its hiding place. Solving the mystery of its author and what it contained would be his secret quest, but for now he would revel in the real treasure he'd found and be content.

CHAPTER
THREE

The Blue Mountain Trail, a week later

The rain had petered out after a few days and, in the spring sunshine, Ruby could appreciate the beauty of her surroundings as they slowly traversed the rough tableland track. The blue haze that had given the range its name came from the mist of eucalyptus oils emanating from the gum trees that smothered the craggy peaks and deep canyons. Waterfalls plummeted down dark ravines, their spray casting rainbows in the sunlight. Creeping ivy entwined glossy green tendrils through giant ferns and delicate wild flowers, and stands of pale-barked eucalyptus vied with the blood-like gashes of the red gums and the rough brown bark of the pines.

Ruby felt quite light-headed as she breathed in the delicious scents and watched the light dance on the waterfall. This sense of freedom, of the wildness beyond the orderly structures in Parramatta and Sydney was all she could have hoped for. She looked at James, her heart swelling with love as she smiled. "It's worth the anxiety, isn't it?"

He mopped the sweat from his brow. "We have a long way to go yet, and it will be just as treacherous going into the valleys as it was climbing up here." His eyes were warm with love as he smiled back at her. "But you're right. It is an amazing sight."

"It makes me feel very small," she said, returning to the majestic vista. "How brave the explorers were to come all this way and find a path through." She shivered at the thought of being lost out here. "But it's a lonely place for all its grandeur."

James took her hand. "Not having second thoughts, are you?"

Her pulse raced at his touch. "Not for a minute. I'm just thankful I have you and the others with me." She glanced towards a clump of bushes.

"Is she still following us?" murmured James.

"Since we crossed the river."

James frowned. "Do you think it's wise to encourage her by leaving her food? There could be warriors with her, waiting to attack."

"She's on her own, I'm sure of it, and I leave her food because she's very young and far too thin."

"But what does she want? And why is she wandering about on her own?" James peered into the shadows. "By the way she's dressed, she's obviously been in contact with settlers or missionaries, but the nearest civilisation is miles away."

"Don't glare like that," she reproached him softly. "You'll frighten her."

James gave a sigh of impatience as he gathered up the reins. "That soft heart of yours will lead you into trouble one day, but I suppose you're going to insist she travels with us?"

"We can't just ignore her. You don't think the others will mind, do you?"

"It's not their decision to make. But it could cause trouble, especially with the Pentonvillians."

Ruby hadn't given this any thought, but on reflection she accepted it might pose a problem to have bailed convicts in such close proximity to a young girl. Then again, she argued silently, James would protect them.

James tugged his hat. "If you're determined to give her half your food, then she has to earn it. No one gets free passage on this journey."

She watched her husband take up his usual place ahead of the bullock cart. James had come to Australia as a free migrant, the youngest son of poor tenant farmers. Like many others, he had believed Aboriginals to be savages. Ruby had tried to change his attitude, and although he'd asked the Elders who lived near Moonrakers for advice on the journey they planned, she sensed he had never learnt to fully trust them.

As the dogs chased the last of the ewes into line and the cavalcade slowly merged into the shadows of the overhanging trees, she realised it was time to make a decision. She gnawed her lip as she remembered her childhood playmates — dark-skinned boys and girls who were as much a part of Moonrakers as she. They had grown up together, worked in the shearing sheds and paddocks, and celebrated the wool-clip cheque that ensured their security for another year. Her grandmother Nell had taught her to respect their beliefs, nurture their progress and understand that their knowledge of this ancient place was invaluable to the white settlers —

how could she now ignore the girl who'd followed them so doggedly?

And yet James had a point. The "Pentonvillians" — two of the ticket-of-leave men who'd started their prison sentences back in Pentonville Gaol in England — were not to be trusted around such a young girl, and she fretted that she might be putting her into danger by being kind.

Ruby dismounted, tied the mare to a tree and, after a moment's hesitation, plucked the waterbag from the saddle and walked to a flat boulder jutting out of the ground a few feet from the girl's hiding place. She took off her hat, ran her fingers through her auburn curls and let the breeze chase away the dust and sweat. "My name is Ruby," she said calmly. "What's yours?"

There was a rustle among the ferns, but no reply.

Ruby repeated her question in the language of the Moonraker natives. It was unlikely the girl would understand, for there were hundreds of dialects and she was probably from another tribe, but it was important to establish some kind of contact. "My guess is you can speak English," she said, after a long period of silence from the undergrowth. "My name is Ruby, and I want to be your friend."

"Alonga me Kumali," came the timorous voice.

Ruby smiled. "Hello, Kumali. Why don't you come and sit with me?" She edged to one side of the boulder to make room.

The leaves rustled and the girl emerged, poised to flee at the slightest danger.

84

Ruby guessed she was fourteen or fifteen. She saw fear in those amber eyes, and the grime from many days' travelling. Her heart went out to her, and she delved into the capacious coat pocket for the stale bread and tough mutton she'd kept for lunch. Kumali flinched and backed away.

Ruby drew out the parcel and opened it. "You must be hungry," she said softly, as she placed it on the boulder. "Please take it."

The girl eyed the meagre offering and licked her lips, but she remained at a distance.

Ruby nudged the parcel along the warm slab. "It's yours," she said gently. "Take it and eat."

Step by cautious step Kumali approached, her gaze darting between Ruby and the food. She came within reach, snatched up the food and ran back to the shadows, where she tried to stuff it all into her mouth at once.

"Poor Kumali," murmured Ruby. "You're starving, aren't you? I wish I had more, but it's all there is until tonight." She watched as the girl struggled to chew and swallow, amazed she didn't choke. "I have water too," she said, as the girl wiped her mouth with the back of her hand. She took the stopper from the waterbag, drank from it and held it out. "Water," she said. "Drink."

This time Kumali was less hesitant. She took the bag from Ruby and didn't back away. "Watta?" At Ruby's nod she took a long drink. "Ta, missus. Kumali tirsty. Much walk."

Ruby smiled and encouraged her to sit. When Kumali warily perched on the edge of the boulder, Ruby nodded. "There," she breathed. "That wasn't so hard, was it?"

The amber eyes looked back at her, the curiosity and wariness still evident in the way she plucked at her garish dress. "Kumali alonga you, missus?" she mumbled. "Boss 'im like?"

"The boss won't mind," Ruby replied with a certainty that belied her doubts. "He realised I would take you under my wing." At Kumali's frown, Ruby smiled. "Don't worry. The boss is a good man. He won't hurt you."

Kumali still frowned. "Other boss-men. Alonga Kumali no beat 'im?"

"No one will beat you. You have my promise."

As Kumali shifted on the rock, her dress slid from her bony shoulder to reveal a network of scars. The weals were interlaced on her back, some still purple and raised, others pale reminders of previous beatings, and Ruby experienced a rush of sick fury that anyone could be so cruel. She reached out and the girl cowered. "Who did that?" Ruby demanded.

Kumali dragged the dress back over her shoulder and edged away, the wariness returning as a solitary tear clung to her eyelashes. "Boss alonga Kumali. Make 'im angry. Much beat. Kumali bad black-fella."

"Dear God," breathed Ruby. "Who is this boss? Where does he live?"

Kumali shook her head so determinedly Ruby knew she would never reveal his name for fear of recrimination.

"You've run away, haven't you? That's why you're out here on your own." She took the girl's hand, felt it tremble and drew her close. The rage against the unknown man who'd done this terrible thing was so great she could barely speak. "It's all right — you're safe now. You are coming with me, and no one will beat you ever again."

The girl finally calmed enough for Ruby to release her and unhitch the horse. It took a while to persuade Kumali it was perfectly safe to climb into the saddle, and as the girl clung to Ruby's waist, they set off.

They reached the others as the sun began to sink over the craggy mountains. The golden glow touched the peaks and danced in the cloud of dust that trailed behind the men and beasts. Ruby could feel the girl tense as they drew near. "It's all right, Kumali," she murmured. "I'll take care of you."

The men were unhitching the oxen, while Duncan was rolling out the calico that would pen the sheep. No one noticed as they dismounted and led the horse to a nearby stream. Kumali stayed close, her gaze darting to the men, her fear tangible.

"Come," Ruby said a while later. "It's time to meet James and the others." Taking her by the hand, and with a smile of encouragement, she led her into the clearing. "This is Kumali," she said, as the men turned and stared. "She will be travelling with us."

James pushed his hat from his brow, his expression disapproving. "I hope you know how to cook," he said, "because you'll have to earn your keep like the rest of us."

"Kumali alonga tucka good," mumbled Kumali, eyes downcast.

"That's Duncan," said Ruby, nodding towards the dour Scot, who glared at them. "Don't mind him. He's not as grumpy as he looks," she fibbed. There was little point in telling her that Duncan seemed to dislike women in general.

Kumali giggled behind her hands as Duncan grimaced and stomped off.

"This is Fergal," said Ruby, introducing the Irishman, who tipped his hat and carried on hobbling the packhorses. As she was about to introduce the other ticket-of-leave men, she saw them nudge one another, their hot eyes devouring the girl with naked lust.

"Kumali is under my protection," she warned. "If I catch you anywhere near her, you'll be sent back to Sydney."

Bert Grayson's gaze slid away and he shuffled his feet, but his companion, Wally Simpson, was more belligerent. "She's only a gin," he muttered. "You can't punish a man for looking, and I ain't 'ad a woman in years."

"She's a child! You're to stay away from her," she snapped. "Is that understood?"

His eyes were defiant despite his shrug, and as he turned away, she heard him muttering. Ruby bit her lip. James was right. There was trouble ahead. Wally and

Bert would have to be watched and Kumali closely guarded.

The track to the Hunter Valley, October 1849

Jessie had become inured to the rattle and roll of the wagon now that they were deep into the countryside, but she had yet to appreciate sleeping on the ground beneath that wagon every night, and in consequence seemed to suffer from a permanently stiff neck and aching back.

Abel Cruickshank had proved as good as his promise, and he and Tumbalong — a man of few words, and most of those unintelligible — had kept their distance, sleeping on the other side of the fire, rolled in blankets, using their saddles for pillows. Jessie had come to realise that the possession of a rifle to defend her honour was ridiculous, for neither man paid her much attention during the day, preferring to chatter to one another or ride in silences that would sometimes stretch for hours. It was as if she didn't exist, and it was beginning to annoy her.

She surreptitiously studied Mr Cruickshank as they trundled along. His rolled-up sleeves revealed sturdy arms lightly sprinkled with fair hair that glinted in the sun as the muscles worked beneath the tanned flesh. The stubble on his chin was just as golden, flecked here and there with the same hint of copper that threaded through his long, untidy hair. His mouth, occupied at that moment with a clay pipe, always seemed to be on the verge of a smile, as if he found the entire episode rather amusing — which irked her even more.

"I reckon you must know my face better than I do," he said mildly.

Mortified, Jessie blushed and quickly looked away.

He laughed. "I hope you like what you see, Miss Searle, 'cos you and me will be travelling a fair few miles yet."

Jessie's blush deepened. She had indeed liked what she'd seen, but she was certainly not about to bolster Mr Cruickshank's ego by telling him so. "It is not your looks that interest me, but your character," she said stiffly. "I am of the opinion that you are a chameleon, Mr Cruickshank, for your manner since the start of our journey is very different to that of our initial meeting."

He raised an eyebrow as he turned to face her. "I don't know what a cham — what manner of thing that might be," he said quietly, "but if you're referring to my lack of sociability, it is only because I am aware of your delicate sensibilities and would not wish to offend you with my rough talk."

His grey eyes were laughing at her, and Jessie noticed how the irises were ringed with black, and how thick and dark the lashes were. She hastily looked away. "Your silences make me feel like an intruder."

He gave a deep sigh and returned to smoking his pipe. "Then I apologise, Miss Searle. What would you like to talk about?"

Jessie had many questions, but her thoughts were in such a whirl she had to search for something to say that might breach the awkward moment.

He gave a deep chuckle. "Now who's lost for words? See, it's not easy to have a conversation with a stranger, is it?"

"Then perhaps that's where we should begin," she said, taking charge of her wayward thoughts. "Do you work at the mission, Mr Cruickshank?"

"No. I've got my own place in the valley."

Jessie waited, realised there was to be no expansion on this statement and, with barely concealed impatience, tried again. "You have a farm?"

"Yeah."

She glanced at him and knew from his expression he was being deliberately obtuse. "What kind of farm? Cattle, sheep or crops?"

"Vines," he replied.

"Vines?"

"Yeah, you know — those plants that grow grapes."

"I know what a vine is, Mr Cruickshank," she retorted.

"Thought you might. You being a teacher."

Jessie saw he was trying not to laugh. Deciding this was infinitely more interesting than sitting in silence, she pursued her questions. "And what kind of wine do you make, Mr Cruickshank? Are you a successful vintner?"

"Middling successful," he said, his jaw clenching on the pipe-stem. "The vines are still too young to get a good vintage, but in the next couple of years they should be right. That's if the drought or the kangaroos don't get them before the frost, the rain and mould kill them off."

It was the longest sentence he'd spoken since the start of their journey, and Jessie pressed the advantage. "What's the Hunter Valley like?"

"It's beaut," he replied. Then, as if he realised the game had gone far enough, he turned to her and smiled. "The valley is enormous, and sheltered by great granite outcrops — the perfect place for grazing and vine-growing. There are rivers and streams and enough space for everyone. It was discovered about thirty years ago, and although the Lower Hunter is fairly well settled, the Upper Hunter, where we're going, is less populated."

"Why is that?"

He shrugged. "People like to have other people around them, I suppose, but a few of us prefer the isolation of the Upper Hunter," he replied. "There's a good sense of community throughout the valley, though. We poor folk work for the rich tending their vines during the day before we cultivate our own plots in our spare time. The best month is February, when everyone helps bring in the harvest."

"It sounds as if growing vines is a rather risky enterprise."

"It is, but if you have enough belief and passion for what you're doing, you grit your teeth when things go wrong and work in the Newcastle coal mines to earn enough to start again."

"Coal mines? I didn't know they had discovered coal out here."

"You don't seem to know much for a schoolteacher, Miss Searle." He stuck his pipe in his pocket, a smile once more twitching his lips. "Coal was found back in the early years of settlement, and a penal colony was set up in Newcastle around 1804 to mine it. The port is now one of the busiest in New South Wales," he added proudly.

"Thank you, Mr Cruickshank, for your lesson in local history. I shall make a point of remembering it." He eyed her suspiciously, but she kept her gaze averted. Two could play his game, and it would certainly make the journey more entertaining. "If coal-mining is a good source of income, then why choose to farm vines?"

"If you'd ever worked in a coal mine, you wouldn't ask such a question," he muttered.

"I am familiar with copper and tin mines," she retorted. "My brothers and I come from Cornwall."

"There you are, then."

There was no reply to that, and Jessie broached another subject, which had been worrying her ever since she'd left England. "What is Mr Lawrence like?"

"He's a pompous little fellow, with a monocle, and a moustache like a brush. He wears a black suit even on the hottest day and always carries a Bible." Abel shot her an amused glance. "What he'll make of you I don't know."

Jessie bristled. "What is that supposed to mean?"

He shrugged. "I think he was expecting a more matronly person to help him run his school." His gaze travelled from her bonnet to the tips of her dusty boots. "You're a bit young and green, and will cause a stir in the valley — not something that will endear you to Mr Lawrence, who is a stickler for all things proper."

"The Church Board hired me knowing my age and circumstances," she retorted. "Mr Lawrence should count his blessings that *anyone* should want to come all this way to teach in his school." She took a deep breath. "As for conducting myself in the proper manner, I doubt Mr Lawrence will find fault with me on that score."

"No good getting on your high horse with me, Miss Searle," he drawled. "I was just trying to put you right."

Jessie's misgivings were returning fourfold. "Just how isolated is this school?"

"It's on the northern rim of the Lower Hunter," he replied. "The mission house and school are well placed, although there isn't a town nearby. As more settlers come into the valley, the school has become an important place."

"I assume Mrs Lawrence will be assisting me in the classroom?"

Abel frowned. "Mr Lawrence is a single man." He smiled down at her worried expression. "Have no fear — the spinster ladies of the valley have done their best to alter that condition with little success, and we all reckon he doesn't like any of us very much, especially the women. He might wear the clothes of a minister and preach from the pulpit every Sunday, but his love of the Church doesn't extend to his parishioners."

That wasn't comforting news, and Jessie suspected her employer might expect her to keep his house in order along with his school. "Does Mr Lawrence employ a housekeeper?"

He glanced at her, eyes twinkling. "There was talk of him hiring a local widow, but she wasn't installed when I came to collect you."

"I was led to understand I would have my own accommodation," she said nervously.

"Yeah. There's a room at the back of the school. Me and my mates finished it a few weeks ago." His grin widened. "We put a sturdy lock on the door."

Jessie's relief was tempered with the knowledge he was teasing her again. Then another thought struck as she glanced at Tumbalong. "Are there many natives in the area?"

"Not since we've managed to kill most of 'em off with colds and measles. Tumbalong is from the Wanaruah tribe, and there's a few Kamilaroi still around, but they don't cause trouble."

"Do their children attend the school?"

Abel grimaced. "The government doesn't hold with educating the black-fellas, but a bit of schooling along with the Bible-bashing wouldn't go astray — especially for men like Tumbalong, who's as sharp as a knife."

"Why do you call him Tumbalong?"

"That's not his real name," he said, with a wink to the man riding alongside the wagon. "His tribal name is unpronounceable, so I called him Jimmy. Then he came with me to Sydney a couple of years ago and took a liking to an area the local natives called Tumbalong. He prefers that to Jimmy, so I oblige. Ain't that right, mate?"

95

"Yeah, boss. Tumbalong betta." He smiled to reveal yellow teeth and kicked his horse into a gallop.

As he rode away with the string of horses to set up camp for the night, Jessie turned back to Abel. "You speak with an intriguing accent, Mr Cruickshank. It is not from any county that I have heard, and yet I discern the urban dialect of London and the lilt of Ireland."

There was a long silence and Jessie was beginning to think she'd spoken out of turn when he finally answered her.

"The first convicts were mostly from the East End of London. Then the Irish, the Scots and Welsh came, and to confuse those in charge at the time, they developed a 'flash' language only they could understand." He tipped the brim of his hat and kept his gaze on the track ahead. "I reckon my generation just picked it up."

"So you were born here?"

"Yeah. And I'm a free man — always have been."

She realised she'd touched a nerve, and although she suspected he was descended from convicts, and longed to ask about his family history, she knew better than to pursue it. "Have you always lived in the valley?"

He brought the wagon to a halt as they reached a clearing where Tumbalong was digging a fire-pit. "I was born in Sydney, and we lived in a place just outside Windsor." Dropping the reins, he jumped down and went round the wagon to help her alight. His eyes were crinkled with amusement as he set her on her feet. "For a little body you possess a vast curiosity, Miss Searle. But I think that's enough for today, else we'll have nothing to talk about tomorrow, and I know you hate too much silence."

Jessie's face burnt as she looked up into those laughing grey eyes. She swiftly turned away to shake off the dust and adjust her bonnet. Mr Cruickshank could be amusing company, and was an intriguing, rather handsome man in an uncouth sort of way, but he had an irritating knack of making her feel foolish, and as she was unused to such an emotion, she found it most unsettling.

Kernow House, Watsons Bay, October 1849

"Oliver is taking me to see his latest venture this morning," said Harry, as he finished dressing.

Lavinia eyed her reflection in the glass, tweaked a curl and turned to face him. "It strikes me your brother has many irons in the fire. What with the whaling fleet, the Burra copper mine and his interests in imports and exports, I would have thought he had enough to occupy him."

Harry smiled as he smoothed his moustache. "He's always had an eye for profit. I remember when we were boys and we first visited Treleaven House. I saw a pile of rubble and a yoke that would hang round my neck for the rest of my life. Oliver saw beyond that, to what it had once been and could be again. In his hands the estates would have flourished. I just don't seem to have the touch, Lavinia."

She smoothed the lapels of his jacket and smiled up at him. "You have succeeded where many would have failed," she soothed. "The estate farms are productive, the house is almost back to its former glory, and now they've found copper in Cornwall, we can at last see less red in our account books."

He kissed her forehead. "Ever the optimist," he said fondly.

Lavinia kissed his cheek. "The new steam engine and winding gear will soon pay for themselves now copper production is in full swing. You worry too much, Harry."

Harry didn't reply. The newfangled machinery that was so necessary to dig out the copper, tin and coal had been outrageously expensive, and he'd baulked at spending so much. It had seemed that for every two steps he took towards solvency something came along to halt his progress. But Lavinia was well versed in the trials of mine ownership, for her father's vast estates encompassed at least half the Kentish coal mines, and she had advised him to invest the last of her dowry to make the most of this new boom. He was pleased he had, for the account books told their own tale, and at last something seemed to be going right.

"So what is this new venture?"

"He wants it to be a surprise. I must present myself at his office in Sydney within the next two hours." He saw his wife raise an eyebrow. "I know it's all a bit mysterious, but Ollie is like a dog with two tails, and I don't want to spoil his surprise by asking too many questions." He pulled the silver pocket watch from his waistcoat. The melodic chimes filled the silence. "Why don't you come too? I'm sure he wouldn't mind."

Lavinia sighed as she picked up her hat. "Amelia has arranged another of her little outings. I declare, Harry, it is far too hot, and I find I'm quite drained after a day of listening to her prattle." She must have seen his frown, for she hurried on. "Amelia is very sweet, but I do wish she would leave me to read or sew, and not feel she has to entertain me every day."

"I'm sure she means well, Lavinia," he murmured.

"Of course she does, and her hospitality cannot be faulted. It's just a pity we have so little in common," she added, sitting on the bed.

"There must be something you can talk about?"

"She hasn't read Byron or Shelley, though knows of their reputations, and she only has a fleeting knowledge of Shakespeare. Her interest in politics is negligible, and apart from discussing the servant situation, the latest London fashions and Sydney gossip, she has few opinions on anything."

Harry's concern deepened as his wife unleashed the pent-up frustrations that had obviously been building over the past week.

"I know I've had the advantage of a good upbringing and education, and that I was fortunate to have a father who believed women should be fully conversant with current politics and commerce, but I really cannot abide another endless morning of idle chit-chat. It is so *boring*." She finally paused for breath, caught her husband's eye and giggled. "And as if that isn't bad enough, why does she persist in wearing every bit of jewellery she possesses? Diamonds during the day are so *vulgar*."

The bed dipped as Harry sat next to her and put his arm round her waist. "Oh dear, you are cross, aren't you?"

She gave a great sigh. "Not now I've had my say. I'm sorry, Harry. It was unfair to be so rude."

"I do understand," he said, a smile crinkling the corners of his eyes. "Amelia can be irritating, especially when she puts on airs, but you have to remember she's the daughter of a minor military officer, and I think rather overawed by our titles. Give her time to get used to you and I'm sure things will improve."

"I hope so," muttered Lavinia. "I'm getting rather weary of being paraded about Sydney like a prize exhibit."

"At least it gives you some respite from Gertrude," he replied, with a wry smile.

Lavinia's frown turned to laughter. "My goodness, she's a dragon," she whispered. "No wonder Amelia is constantly on edge. Poor woman, I do feel sorry for her, despite her irritating ways."

"My sister, or Amelia?"

"Amelia, of course," she hissed. "I wouldn't stand for it, Harry, not in my own home. Gertrude has simply taken over, and even Oliver is in awe of her. If I was Amelia, I would put her very firmly in her place. She wouldn't boss me around."

Harry kissed her forehead and smiled. "She wouldn't dare," he teased. "You are quite formidable when roused, and even I have cause to tremble when you play lady of the manor."

Lavinia gave him a playful dig in the ribs.

He gathered her into his arms, kissed her thoroughly and then reluctantly let her go. "Do you want me to have a quiet word with Amelia and see if you can be let off this proposed outing to come with me and Ollie?"

"No," she said firmly. "I am a guest in this house and will fulfil my duty to Amelia. She has enough to put up with without me being uncooperative. You go and enjoy some time with your brother."

"What about the boys? Have any plans been made for their day?"

She smiled. "Charlie and Frederick seem to be fully occupied one way or another. If they're not in the tree house, they are out riding, or up in the old nursery. I cannot imagine what they find to do for so many hours, but having seen the condition of their clothes, one imagines it involves more than a peck of dirt." She giggled. "Gertrude gets absolutely furious with them. You should have seen her face when I told her firmly to let them be! It screwed up so tightly it reminded me of a lemon!"

"You are naughty," he scolded fondly. "But you're right," he added wistfully. "Boys will be boys, and a bit of dirt never hurt anybody." He envied them their freedom and wished he was still young enough to climb trees and race along the beach at a gallop. Yet the memory of his boyhood riding days brought back sharp images of his elder brother, and unwilling to return to those days before tragedy had changed everything for ever, he forced them away. The past was gone, and he was determined to focus on the future.

★ ★ ★

Sydney Town, the same day

Oliver's office was in the heart of the business district, and as Harry tied his horse to the hitching post, he eyed the building with wry amusement. It was a monument to his brother's vanity; proof, if it were needed, that Oliver Cadwallader was a force to be reckoned with. As he took in the marble portico and the many windows, he noted the coloured glass in the elaborately carved front door and the highly polished brass knocker. He ran up the steps and was about to announce his presence when the door was thrust open.

"You're late," said Oliver, bustling past, the door slamming behind him. "Come on, come on. I promised to meet Niall Logan, and he's not a man to be kept waiting."

"Niall Logan? That name sounds familiar . . . I seem to remember him from Mother and George's wedding. Isn't he the convict who married one of the Penhalligans?"

"One and the same." Oliver was becoming red in the face as he hurried along. "But Amy was a Penhalligan only through her mother Nell's marriage to Susan's brother, Billy."

"And Susan was George's mother . . . so that must make him almost a relative."

"Only in a very vague and distant way. Really, Harry, you should keep up with the family tree."

Harry cheerfully acknowledged he had always found the history of the Penhalligans, Collinsons and Cadwalladers confusing, and had long since given up trying to remember just who was related to whom. "I didn't think you 'exclusives' did business with convicts," he teased, "much less worried about keeping them waiting."

Oliver came to an abrupt halt. "Balderdash!" he snorted, as he tried to catch his breath. "Niall might have been a convict once, but this colony would fail if it weren't for men like him. He has a canny mind, and a good head for business. You don't want to listen to Amelia prattling on about exclusives and the convict stain — it's pure snobbery."

Harry was rather taken aback at his brother's vitriol. "Keep your hair on, Ollie. I was only making fun."

"Hmph." Barely mollified, Oliver began to walk again. "I admit it is rather irksome to have a convict in the family — even if it is a tenuous link — and that it is sometimes frowned upon to do business with men such as Niall, yet one can't help but admire him. He's made his money through hard work and an eye for opportunity. His forge now employs at least eight men, he owns hundreds of square miles of pasture in the hinterlands, and he has expanded his business to cope with the growing demand for carriages and wagons. I'm hoping he'll agree to join the syndicate and invest in our project, and I'd appreciate it if you kept all talk of convicts out of the conversation."

"So what is this project? And why do you need outside investment? I'd have thought you were prosperous enough."

Oliver came to a halt again and mopped his brow, his breath coming in shallow gasps. "Prosperity is in the eye of the beholder, Harry. You see the fine house, the servants, the horses and carriages, and the frippery Amelia insists upon — all that costs money, and as fast as I earn it Amelia spends it."

"What about the whaling interests and the import and wholesale market George set up? My share of the dividends is healthy: yours should keep you in comfort for many years."

"It would if I didn't have Frederick's education to think about, Gertrude's allowance to pay and Amelia's sister to keep. On top of which, the banks charge extortionate interest on my loans."

"Why are you paying for Amelia's sister? Surely that is her husband's duty?"

"Proved unreliable," muttered Oliver, as he took a swig from the silver flask he'd hidden in his pocket. "Got into debt and, instead of finding work, went off to Adelaide and hasn't been heard of since. Good riddance I say. The man was a wastrel."

"You've lost me, Oliver. Where on earth's Adelaide?"

"North-west of Melbourne. It's in one of the new colonies," replied Oliver. He must have noted Harry's frown, for he continued, "Melbourne was named back in 1837; you'll remember it as Port Philip. Perth, on the western shores, was founded in 1829, South Australia in 1834." He took another drink and popped the flask back into his pocket. "Things have changed considerably in the past three decades, so I'm not surprised you're confused. There has even been talk of self-government, which I heartily agree with, but doubt we'll get. Queen Victoria seems determined to keep us tied to her London Parliament."

The history lesson was all very well, but Harry had more pressing concerns. "I still don't understand why you pay an allowance to Amelia's sister. I thought her family had money."

"They did, but it all went during the recession in 1842. They lost the land and all their stock, packed up and went home to England to eke out his army pension in some dreary London suburb."

Harry was still finding it difficult to digest all he'd heard, and as Oliver set off once more, he tugged his arm and brought him to a halt. "Why are you borrowing from the banks if they charge such high rates?"

"Never invest one's own money, Harry. Surely you know that?"

"But it's more prudent than borrowing from banks."

"Not necessarily," replied Oliver, his gaze sliding away.

"But if you have the capital, why pay bank charges when you don't need to borrow?"

"I didn't realise you were a wizard at finance, Harry," he said, with a hint of asperity. "Since when have you understood the ins and outs of ledgers?"

"Since I was forced to take on the estates in Cornwall," he snapped. "Don't take me for a fool, Oliver. I can do the mathematics."

"Then you will know that to risk your own money is foolhardy," his brother retorted. "Far better to persuade others to venture their capital — the profit may be smaller, but so is the loss if it all falls apart. That is why there are four of us working on this particular scheme."

"And if Niall comes on board, that will make five?"

"Correct," snapped Oliver. "Now, if you've finished quizzing me, we need to get on."

Harry walked beside him, his thoughts in turmoil. Oliver was holding something back, he could always tell — it was the way his ears went pink and he avoided eye contact. Could it be possible that the trappings of wealth were a smokescreen? If so, then yet another venture was foolhardy in the extreme.

He glanced at Oliver as they approached Devonshire Street Cemetery and felt a tingle of apprehension as he noted the reddened cheeks and heavy jowls. It seemed Oliver had inherited the worst traits of their father, for not only was he drinking too much, he was gambling with his family's future — and they both knew where that could lead.

Cleveland Fields, Sydney, the same day

The man waiting for them bore little resemblance to the one Harry remembered. Gone was the whip-thin figure, the dowdy clothes and untidy hair of the callow youth he'd encountered at his mother's wedding, and as Niall strode towards them, Harry realised just how much the Irishman had achieved in the intervening years.

Niall had matured into a sturdy, upright man of about sixty, with thick white hair, trim moustache and goatee beard. The trousers and coat were of the finest cloth and cut, and his top hat had been brushed to a gleam. His eyes were very blue, his gaze direct with the confidence that only came with success.

The introductions were made and Harry approved of the firm handshake. "It's my fault we're late," he said, noting the way Niall checked his pocket watch.

"No matter, no matter," Niall muttered, the Irish brogue still strong even after all these years. "But I do have to be elsewhere in a while."

Oliver took the Irishman's arm and began to steer him round the perimeter of the rough clearing. "I expect you wonder why I have asked you here," he boomed. He didn't wait for a reply. "You see before you an opportunity to change the character of Sydney Town for ever. Look at these fields, ideally placed just outside the centre of town, with Devonshire Street on its northern boundary, and over there" — he pointed towards some trees — "is Parramatta."

"I have lived in Parramatta long enough to know its whereabouts, and I think you should know that —"

"Of course, of course, dear chap," interrupted Oliver. "You have also either had to ride into town on horseback or in a wagon, which is not the most comfortable way to travel. What would you say to being carried on your journey in style, to be able to sit back at your ease and watch the world pass by?"

"I would say that I already —"

"I know you make carriages," interrupted Oliver again. "They are the finest mode of transport one can currently buy in Sydney Town, and an excellent example of your workmanship." He leant towards Niall,

107

his voice lowered conspiratorially. "But the steam engine is coming, Mr Logan, and with it the opportunity for a man such as yourself to make your mark on history."

Harry saw the amusement in Niall Logan's face as he gave up trying to get a word in edgeways, leant on the ivory-handled cane and watched Oliver puff out his chest as he extolled the virtues of the steam engine. It seemed the Irishman was of the same opinion as he, for Oliver's sales pitch was bordering on the theatrical.

"There will be a track running the whole thirteen and a half miles to Parramatta," Oliver continued. "There will be a platform with a waiting room for the ladies to shelter from the elements. The steel for the rails is due to arrive within the month from London, and my fellow investors and I are very keen you should be given the opportunity to join us in this most prestigious venture."

Harry agreed that steam railways were certainly the answer in a country that was so vast. They had opened up England most satisfactorily, and had encouraged trade and commerce during the Industrial Revolution that was sweeping the country. The endless possibilities in Australia were an exciting prospect, and if he'd had the spare money to invest, he could have been persuaded to do so. Yet, as they both waited for the other man's reaction, Harry could see the tension in his brother and wondered why that should be so.

108

"It is a pity you did not reveal the reason for this meeting earlier, Mr Cadwallader," said Niall. "If you had, you would have realised I am fully aware of the plans for Cleveland Fields."

Oliver's eyes bulged. "How so?"

"I was approached many weeks ago by the other members of your syndicate." He frowned at Oliver's bewilderment. "I apologise, Mr Cadwallader. I thought you knew."

Oliver's bluster was gone, the colour drained from his cheeks. "They approached you?" he wheezed. "But if you had agreed to join us, I would have had to sign the contracts, and I have seen no such papers."

"The contracts I signed were not for joining your syndicate, Mr Cadwallader, but for agreeing to provide the workforce and skills needed for making and laying the track."

"How much are we paying you?" Oliver clenched his fists and Harry swiftly stepped forward.

Niall's gaze was steady, his expression giving nothing away. "The details are in the contracts, Mr Cadwallader. Suffice it to say, there will be a deposit paid when the steel arrives, and further regular payments each week until the work is completed. Should there be a shortfall and my men aren't waged, then all work will stop."

"Of course you'll be paid," roared Oliver, now thoroughly roused. "How *dare* you insinuate otherwise?"

"I am merely looking after my men, Mr Cadwallader," said Niall softly. "There have been other schemes that have fallen through due to lack of capital, and it is always the working man who suffers."

"There is capital enough to build many more lines than this," boasted Oliver.

Niall cocked his head, his blue eyes thoughtful. "So you didn't ask me here today because you thought I might invest in this scheme?"

Oliver's mouth worked like that of a fish out of water; he couldn't seem to breathe. Niall's silence spoke volumes as he tipped his hat and strode away.

"Insolent bounder," spluttered Oliver. "I should have known better than to offer an ex-convict the chance to be on equal terms with gentlemen."

Harry would have protested at his brother's about-turn, but he didn't like his colour, or the wheezing in his chest. "Convict or not, Niall Logan has proved he's no fool," he said, as he led Oliver out of the field. "Instead of risking his money, he's making a profit — regardless of whether the scheme fails or succeeds. You can't blame him for that, surely?"

Oliver's face was grim as he watched the retreating figure. "I need a drink," he muttered.

"I think you should sit down, draw breath and tell me the truth," retorted Harry. "It's not the syndicate that's short of capital, is it? It's you. And you thought you could persuade Niall to put in enough to carry you into this scheme so you wouldn't have to go to the bank for another loan."

"It's none of your damned business," snapped Oliver. "I will thank you to keep your nose out of it." With that, he strode off.

Harry let him go. There would be time enough to talk, but talk they would, for Oliver was on dangerous ground, and he had to be made to see sense before it was too late.

CHAPTER
FOUR

Hunter Valley, November 1849

Jessie stared in awe at the endless panorama. This was like no valley she'd seen before, and as they trundled on, she compared it with Cornwall. She was used to undulating hills plunging into narrow valleys that followed meandering rivers, to windswept fields running along granite cliffs that reared up from crashing seas and to the soft green of the moors, vibrant with yellow gorse. But this . . . this took her breath away.

Distant mountains rose smoky-blue against a brilliant sky, endless lines of vines disappeared into the shimmering horizon, and bronzed sandstone cliffs poked their heads through forests of beech. As Abel brought the horse to a halt, she gasped with delight as a flock of brightly coloured parrots swooped towards the trees. Their colours seemed to have been taken from the entire spectrum of the rainbow.

"They're so beautiful," she breathed.

"They're a pest," said Abel. "They eat everything in sight and make the most fearsome racket."

She felt he was being a bit harsh. How could something so beautiful be regarded as a nuisance? "Oh, look over there," she said excitedly, as she saw a tiny bird with an oversized tail. "What is it?"

"It's a blue wren."

"How sweet," she sighed.

"Vicious little ba— devils. Always fighting."

"No, they're not!"

"Sentimentality has no place out here." He puffed on his pipe as he took up the reins again and urged the horse into a walk. "Parrots eat seed and fruit, kangaroos and wombats trample vines, and those sweet little wrens cause havoc when two hundred of them turn up at once."

Jessie had no reply, and as she watched the parrots rise with a thunder of beating wings, their cries sharp in the somnolence of the beautiful valley, she realised she'd had her first lesson in the brutal reality of life out here.

"I'm sorry, Miss Searle. I didn't mean to spoil it for you."

She saw his apology was honest, and gave a tremulous smile. "I can still admire their beauty, even if they are a nuisance." She looked out at the vista. "I never imagined it could be so . . . so vast, or so magnificent."

He beamed with pleasure at her praise. "Yeah, it's a beaut place all right, but it's taken hard labour to tame it and nature has a way of fighting back. It's a constant battle."

"I don't doubt it," she murmured, as she regarded the endless rows of vines, the rich, dark soil and the neat, whitewashed houses with their corrugated-iron roofs.

They fell into a companionable silence as they moved further into the valley and Jessie narrowed her eyes against the glare. It was hot, almost unbearably so, and her stays were chafing where the perspiration soaked through the material. She would have liked to remove them, but of course that was not possible — Mr Lawrence would be horrified if his new teacher arrived in such a disgraceful state of undress. Yet she yearned to be free of them, longed for a chance to wash and change her clothes, to brush her hair and feel clean again.

"You'll see the mission soon," Abel said some time later. "First glimpse you'll get is when we are through this pass." He glanced at her, his eyes crinkling in a smile. "You'll be right. For all his fussiness, Mr Lawrence ain't a bad cove."

Despite the reassurance, Jessie felt the return of uneasiness. She had become used to Mr Cruickshank's company, to the unfolding scenery, but now the journey was almost at an end, she didn't feel at all prepared for what was to come.

"Do you think we could stop?" she said, as she spied a stream running close by. "I would like to make myself presentable before I meet Mr Lawrence."

Abel pulled the horse to a standstill, told Tumbalong to go ahead with the horses and cows, and climbed down from the wagon. He helped her down with her bag. "I reckon you look all right as you are," he drawled, "but then I'm not Zephaniah Lawrence."

His gaze held her and she blushed. "Zephaniah? Is that really his name?" Her voice was breathy and high-pitched.

He grinned. "Yeah, but most people only dare call him that behind his back. His parents were God-fearing missionaries who came out thirty years ago, and actually the name suits him." He tugged his hat-brim, then reached for the bag of chicken feed. "I'll tend the chooks until you're ready to leave."

She hurried down to the stream and sank on to the cool grass of the bank. With a hasty backward glance, she confirmed she was out of sight before she unbuttoned her boots, drew off her stockings and wriggled her toes. Gathering up the hem of her skirt and petticoats, she gingerly dipped her feet into the water and sighed with pleasure.

As she watched the water swirl round her pale ankles, she took off her bonnet, unpinned her hair and ran her fingers through the tangles. She could feel the gritty dust of the miles they'd travelled and wished she had time to wash it, but a good brushing would have to suffice. Having finished with her hair, she pinned it up again and loosened the buttons of her dress so she could wash her face and neck. Kneeling on the bank, she scooped up the clear, cold water, splashed it liberally on to her hot face and realised she had never experienced anything quite so wonderful.

The movement was tiny and at the very edge of her vision. She froze, then slowly turned her head. The creature stared back at her, the eyelids multi-layered and reptilian in a triangular, scaly head. Long claws gripped the stone it sat upon, and a ruff of skin slowly swelled and darkened around its jaw as the mouth opened to reveal lethal teeth and a thick tongue.

Jessie screamed and scrambled up the bank, her bare feet scrabbling for purchase in the lush grass. She ran blindly through the trees, her cries echoing around her. "Mr Cruickshank! Mr Cruickshank!"

His bulk stopped her flight and she collapsed against him. "Oh, Mr Cruickshank," she sobbed, "there's a fearsome beast in there."

He roughly held her away and gave her a shake. "You haven't been bitten, have you?" he barked.

She stared at him, bewildered by his reaction. "It spat at me," she wailed. "It had teeth and big claws, and a horrible fan thing that swelled and went black."

He threw back his head and roared with laughter.

Jessie blinked in disbelief. "It's not funny," she rasped. "That monster could have killed me."

"That monster was a bearded dragon," he spluttered. "Won't do you no harm, and I reckon you scared him more than he scared you."

"It's not dangerous?" she breathed.

He shook his head, the laughter still in his eyes. "Not unless you try and catch him. Those claws can be deadly if he's cornered." His gaze travelled from her face to the unbuttoned bodice and down to her bare feet, the colour deepening in his face as he hastily looked away. "I'll fetch your things," he muttered.

Jessie realised what he'd been looking at and quickly did up the buttons. Running her fingers distractedly

116

over her hair, she discovered half the pins had come out and it was again in disarray. The embarrassment was too much, and when he returned, she couldn't look at him.

"I'll wait by the wagon," he said, the laughter still in his voice. "Don't worry, the dragon's nowhere to be seen."

Her fingers fumbled with the buttonhook as she did up her boots. She silently cursed her stupidity at having been so frightened, at the foolish way she'd thrown herself into Mr Cruickshank's arms. So much for decorum.

Yet this was a country of conflicting enigmas, where beauty was regarded as a nuisance, and the ugly — like that dragon — was harmless. Would she ever understand it? She finished making herself presentable, grabbed her bag and clambered on to the seat beside Abel. Without a word or a glance, he set the wagon rolling.

"You asked if I had been bitten," she said after a while. "What did you mean?"

"There are snakes out here," he replied, his gaze firmly fixed on the horizon. "Spiders, too, and most of them have a venomous bite that will kill you. If you make enough noise, the snakes will get out of your way, but if you tread on one . . ."

Jessie shivered and made a silent vow never to go into long grass again.

"The woodpile's the worst place for snakes, and you should always shake out your boots before you put them on, 'cos the spiders like getting in them." He

117

glanced across at her, his expression kindly. "It's not all bad," he drawled. "Just keep your wits about you and you'll be right."

Jessie wasn't reassured. Life out here seemed fraught with danger and difficulties, and she experienced a sharp yearning for Cornwall. Unbidden, she felt the onrush of tears, and furious with herself for being so pathetic, she blinked them away and forced herself to remain calm and focused.

"There's the mission," he said a few minutes later. "We're almost home."

Home. It was an emotive word, and alien in the context of her surroundings. Jessie stared out at the sprawling fields of vines, which looked so green against the dark earth and brilliant sky. She saw the house, which seemed to be a part of the hillside, the plain wooden building that was probably the school, a second, much smaller house and the whitewashed church with its modest bell tower. There was a large barn and numerous sheds dotted about, but apart from two horses in a corral, there was little sign of life. This isolated place was her future, and although she acknowledged its beauty, she couldn't help but compare it to the tightly packed cottages and close community of the Cornish fishing village she had left far behind.

"My place is about ten miles out that way," he said, pointing off to the west.

"Are you the nearest neighbour?" Her voice held a note of wistfulness she couldn't disguise.

"Just about," he replied. "The Prestons live nine miles out, but most of the vintners are spread further across the valley."

Jessie's mouth was dry as they approached the buildings. Now she was nearer, she realised that all but the barns were built on stilts, and guessed this was to protect them when the valley flooded. She could now make out the clearing that spread to one side of the schoolhouse, and the trees that had been left for shade. The main house was square, with two windows, a door and a stone chimney, and over the veranda that ran along the front there clambered a cavalcade of pink roses. On the steps watching their approach was a squat figure dressed in black.

"There's Mr Lawrence," said Abel. He cast a glance at Jessie. "Nervous?"

She nodded. Her hands were tightly clasped to stop them from shaking, and her heart thudded. "What if he doesn't like me?" she breathed.

"You'll be right," he muttered.

She was tiring of that particular phrase, for although he meant well, it did nothing to ease her concerns.

The wagon came to a halt and Zephaniah Lawrence closed his pocket watch with a snap and came down the steps. "You made good time, Cruickshank." He put the monocle to his eye and his beady gaze raked over Jessie. "Miss Searle?" His mouth puckered beneath the bristling moustache. "You are much younger than I was led to believe," he noted. "Still, you're here now, so I suppose you'll have to do."

119

Stung by this lack of welcome, Jessie waited as he took the mail from Abel, fussily ordered where he wanted the supplies stacked, looked at his watch again and, with a cluck of annoyance, turned back towards the house.

Jessie looked into Mr Cruickshank's eyes as he helped her down. There was sympathy and understanding there, and she took strength from it. "Thank you, Mr Cruickshank," she said, as he hauled the trunk from the back of the wagon and placed it on the veranda.

He tipped his hat. "I'll be coming this way in about a month," he drawled. "By then you should be nicely settled."

"Come along, Miss Searle. There is no time for gossip."

Jessie reluctantly climbed the steps, and when she looked back, Abel Cruickshank was already lost behind a cloud of dust. With a deep breath she lifted her chin and followed Zephaniah Lawrence into the house.

Her boot-heels rapped on the wooden floor as she walked down the short hallway and glanced into the rooms on either side, trying to gain some measure of her new employer. Mr Lawrence had few sticks of furniture, no rugs, curtains, pictures or ornaments, and this lack of home comforts gave the overall impression of neat austerity — combined with his dismissive welcome, it didn't bode well.

"Come in, Miss Searle." He beckoned from behind the vast desk that dominated the room. "Take a seat."

Jessie perched on the edge of the straight-backed, uncomfortable chair. Like the rest of the house, the study was barely furnished, but one entire wall was lined with books, and he'd lit a lamp to dispel the gloom.

"Your duties will begin tomorrow morning," he said, his left eye magnified grotesquely by the monocle. "Lessons start at eight, but you must be in the schoolroom at least an hour before to prepare for the day. You will make the fire and keep it tended throughout winter. The classroom is to be swept daily, the windows washed and steps scrubbed."

Jessie tried not to look at that eye, but found her gaze repeatedly drawn to it.

"The children bring their own food and are to eat it in the shade at eleven-thirty. There is water in the well for drinking. Classes will resume until two, when the children will leave for home. They come on horseback, and I have provided a yard to accommodate their animals. The dung is to be collected each night and added to the heap you will find close to this yard. Once rotted, it proves to be an excellent fertiliser for my roses," he added smugly.

Her eyes widened in disbelief. "You want me to shovel horse manure?"

"It will keep you fit, Miss Searle. Hard work and exercise will give you a good night's sleep and prepare you for the coming day." He laced his fingers over the generous belly that was testament to the fact he didn't practise what he preached. "Besides," he added, "you will have little else to occupy your evenings."

"And what would you like me to do at weekends, Mr Lawrence?" she asked tartly. "Dig your rose beds, chop wood, or perhaps do repairs to your house? I noticed the veranda railings need attention."

The monocle popped from his eye socket. "Sarcasm is not attractive, Miss Searle, and I abhor impertinence."

She realised there was little point in pursuing the subject and gritted her teeth as he proceeded to catalogue her duties.

"Of course," he finished, "I will expect you to conduct yourself with utmost modesty. There are to be no followers, and certainly no 'walking out', as the young so vulgarly put it. I realise you have had the unfortunate experience of travelling alone with Cruickshank and his black servant, which was unavoidable, but be assured, Miss Searle, you will not be placed in such a position again. As a teacher of young minds, you must be the epitome of high moral fibre, and any hint of scandal would mar your reputation."

Jessie stared at him in astonishment.

He seemed unaware of her reaction, for he continued without taking breath, "You may entertain other ladies of course, and I shall expect you to participate in my church services and play your part in the good works I organise in the parish."

"I am but nineteen, sir," she protested. "My wish is not to end my days as a spinster."

"Then you have chosen the wrong profession, Miss Searle," he retorted. "If you disobey this most important of rules, you will be dismissed without reference."

"There was no mention of this at my interview."

"This is my school and my church," he snapped. "If you are unhappy, then I suggest you find yourself another position."

Jessie held his furious glare, her thoughts churning. "Are you not aware my reputation may already be damaged by the fact we are alone?"

"You may rest assured, Miss Searle, that you are in no danger from me, and my housekeeper, Mrs Blake, will be a suitable chaperone."

Jessie was relieved to hear about the housekeeper, for so far there had been no evidence of one, and hope ignited that she might prove friendlier than her employer. Yet the rule barring her from socialising still infuriated her. "I understand your parents were missionaries," she replied, with a calm that belied her fury. "Did your mother teach?"

"Things were different then," he said dismissively, his gimlet eyes narrowing. "This was a godless place in those early years, and my mother's saintly self-sacrifice meant that many of the native children were brought to God. My father baptised them in the creek, and was honoured to have it named after him."

He had an answer for everything and Jessie knew she was beaten. It was so isolated here she probably wouldn't see anybody for months, let alone find another post. "I agree to your terms," she said stiffly. "Now I would like to see the classroom and my accommodation." She rose from the chair with as much dignity as she could muster.

He snatched up his Bible and a bunch of keys and led her back outside. Jessie noted how he circumnavigated her trunk and didn't offer to help carry it, so she ignored it as well.

"That is Mrs Blake's cottage," he said, pointing. "You will meet her this evening. The church is locked when there is no service, but of course you have permission to use this key should you wish to pray."

Jessie clutched the key, eyed the church and hurried to catch up as he picked his way over the rough ground, the monocle swinging from the black ribbon.

"There is a native camp beyond those trees, but they are permitted on the property only to work or attend church. I do not encourage fraternisation, and you are never to go there alone. It is an unsavoury place, and entirely unsuitable for a white woman."

Jessie saw the downturn of his mouth and realised that, despite his position as minister and missionary, he didn't approve of the Aborigines.

"The schoolhouse was rebuilt five years ago, and since then we have seen the number of children rise every year," he said proudly, as he unlocked the door.

It was a large single room, with lines of desks and benches neatly placed to face the blackboard, which was propped against the wall. A fireplace was on one side of the room, a line of pegs on the other, each with a name printed above it. Her desk sat on a low platform, with an uncomfortable-looking chair beside it, and on the wall was an enormous map of the world — the British Empire coloured in pink. A rather stern Queen Victoria watched over the room; the Union Jack was draped over the picture frame.

The light from the four windows was diffused by the trees outside, and cast cool green shadows across the scuffed floor and exposed roofbeams. She eyed the iron roof and suspected that when it rained, it would be almost impossible to make herself heard.

"We have slates and plenty of chalk, and each new child is presented with a Bible. They are kept in here," he said, as he opened a cupboard. "I hope you remembered to bring the books I ordered?"

"They are in the trunk, which is still on the veranda."

He eyed her sharply, then strode the length of the room and unlocked the back door. "This is your accommodation. It is to be kept in order at all times."

Jessie was pleasantly surprised by its generous size. The sunlight streamed through the window and pooled on the freshly planed floor. There was an iron bed, a washstand with a plain white bowl, jug and chamber pot, and a chair and table had been placed beneath the window. Pegs for her clothes had been put on the back of the door, there was a small chest of drawers in the corner, and on the wall were shelves lined with pretty paper that held china and cutlery.

She eyed the mattress and the neatly folded linen that had been placed on the end of the bed along with a patchwork quilt. "Thank you, Mr Lawrence," she said. "It is most pleasant."

He hovered in the doorway. "The quilt was made by the ladies of the parish, and it was they who advised me on how to furnish the room."

"Where am I to find washing facilities?"

He cleared his throat, obviously ill at ease. "The other offices are outside, Miss Searle." The monocle dangled against his barrel chest as he checked his watch. "I will leave you to settle in. Dinner will be at six in my dining room. Don't be late."

Jessie stood in the centre of the room watching the dust motes dance in the sunbeams. A fly was buzzing somewhere, and she could hear birdsong in the distance, but the heat and silence were oppressive.

"You'd better make the most of it, Jess," she muttered, "because this is it." The thought was depressing — the longing for home, and the company of her brothers, almost unbearable. "Get on, Jess," she hissed. "There's nothing like work to stop you thinking."

She placed her bag on the chair, took off her bonnet and rolled up her sleeves. Throwing open the windows, she saw Mr Lawrence's roses and, with a smile, turned away. He would soon discover that shovelling manure was not on the school curriculum.

The mattress was clean, if a little lumpy, the pillow thin, but the linen was cool and crisp with starch. Eschewing the blanket, for it was far too hot, she finished making the bed, covered it with the quilt and stood back to admire the effect. With a nod of satisfaction, she returned to the veranda and unpacked her clothes from the trunk.

Her clean dress, two skirts and best jacket were placed on the doorhooks, petticoats, blouses and underwear tidied away in the drawers with the tiny bag of lavender she'd brought from home. Her spare pair of boots was neatly placed beneath the washstand; her brush, comb and box of hairpins went on the top next to the bowl and jug.

At the bottom of her carpet bag she found the leather writing case her mother had given her when she'd been accepted as a student teacher, and she ran a loving hand over it, breathing in its scent, remembering the woman who'd died too young only five years before. Placing it on the table, she pulled out the last but perhaps most precious possession of all.

The bright blue shawl was deeply fringed and finely embroidered with flowers and butterflies of every hue. The quality of the material and the stitching could not be denied and not for the first time Jessie wondered where on earth her grandmother had got it. She didn't believe it had been a gift, for despite the old lady's talk of noble ties, they didn't mix with people who could afford such things.

With the shawl draped over one corner of the table, Jessie blinked away the tears and went to explore. The cooking arrangements consisted of an open fire, with a rusty iron grille perched on top, and a separate pot-bellied stove for baking. There were no walls to this outdoor kitchen, the corrugated-iron roof being attached only to four sturdy poles. This edifice stood some way from the other buildings, and she assumed it was because it posed a fire hazard. She grimaced as she noted the cobwebs, the rusting pots and pans. Remembering Mr Cruickshank's warning, she warily eyed the woodpile.

127

The solitary wooden shed turned out to be the water closet. Jessie peered at the hole in the ground and the single wooden seat, and slammed the door on it. She'd seen worse in Newlyn, but dreaded to think of the poisonous things that might be lurking in the darkness.

The key turned smoothly in the church door and she stepped inside. It was plainly furnished with lines of benches, and a simple cross stood on a table at the front. There was no stained glass or ornate hassocks, no flowers to decorate the altar — just the trapped heat of the day, the familiar hush and soft shadows cast by the wooden shutters.

There was still no sign of the elusive Mrs Blake, and although Jessie hesitated outside the second cottage, she didn't feel brave enough to knock. With a glance towards the trees, she saw a wisp of smoke rise through the green canopy and wondered how many natives lived there and what they did all day.

Returning to her silent room, she sank on to the chair, gazed out of the window at Mr Lawrence's roses and beyond to an endless vista of sky and land. The isolation and loneliness pressed in, and as the tears came, she gave herself up to them.

Jessie had cried herself into an exhausted sleep, and when she finally opened bleary eyes, it took a moment to remember where she was. Then the reality of her situation pressed in and she slumped back into the pillows.

The knock on the door was soft, and if she'd still been asleep, she wouldn't have heard it. "Just a minute," she called, hastily covering herself in a loose peignoir and tidying her hair. The hated corset had been tossed over the back of the chair, along with the travel-stained dress, but there was no time to get them back on and she hoped it wasn't Mr Lawrence on the other side of the door.

"Who is it?" she called.

"Only me, dear. Sorry to wake you, but dinner's in half an hour and I didn't want you to be late on your first evening."

Jessie saw lively brown eyes and a round face as she opened the door. "Mrs Blake?"

"That's me, ducks, but you can call me Hilda when 'is lordship's not about." She swept into the room like a galleon, her prow of a bosom leading the way.

"I'm Jessie."

"Yeah, I know," replied the older woman with a smile. "I've been looking forward to meeting you ever since I heard you were coming." She looked around the room. "You've made it nice," she said, with an approving nod. "I like the shawl."

"It was my grandmother's," murmured Jessie, who was rather overawed by this bustling cheerfulness. "Thank you for waking me. I was so tired I might have slept right through until morning."

"I know, dearie." The brown eyes regarded her kindly. "It's a long way to come for one so young, and I admire your courage."

"Mr Cruickshank might argue with you on the subject of my courage." She giggled and went on to tell Hilda about the dragon.

Hilda's face was wreathed in smiles, her eyes knowing as she listened. "It seems you have made a friend in Mr Cruickshank," she said, her head cocked like an inquisitive sparrow. "He's single, you know, and quite a catch with his vineyard."

Jessie blushed. "He is good company, that is all," she protested.

"Handsome, though, you got to admit that." Hilda nudged her arm. "No good 'iding it from me, ducks, I can spot romance a mile off."

Jessie realised this conversation was getting out of hand. "There will be no romance, Hilda," she said firmly. "Mr Lawrence has forbidden it, and although I was reluctant, I have agreed to his terms of employment."

"Hmph." The arms were tightly folded beneath the bosom. "Mr Lawrence and 'is stupid rules. He'll find it impossible to hide you away once the young bloods of the valley catch sight of you, and when they do, your feet won't touch the ground for all the attention you'll be getting."

"Oh dear," fretted Jess. "That isn't why I came all this way, and I don't want to cause trouble. If Mr Lawrence gets it into his head that I'm wayward, he'll dismiss me without references and I will have nowhere to go."

"You let me deal with Mr Lawrence," Hilda said darkly. "Not that I'm condoning no improper behaviour — I got my standards too, you know." She grinned as if to let Jessie know she wasn't too particular. "You're young and pretty, and it's only right you should be courting. So if the opportunity arises, you grab it, ducks."

"I doubt it will," Jessie sighed. "I will be far too busy, but thank you for your support."

Hilda pulled a face and shrugged off her thanks. "I've lived round here for years, there's always dances and harvests and celebrations of one kind or another," she said. "Isolated this area may be, but we make sure we have plenty of opportunities to meet and exchange gossip. It's when folk arrange christenings and weddings, and encourage the youngsters to mingle, and like it or not, Mr Lawrence will be expected to permit you to attend."

Jessie had a fleeting image of dancing with Mr Cruickshank and firmly blocked it out.

"Have you had the lecture about the horse manure yet?" At Jessie's nod, Hilda laughed. "Ignore it," she advised. "I haven't paid no heed in the short time I've been in his employ. Let him shovel his own muck. He could do with the exercise and that's a fact."

Jessie laughed with her, grateful for her friendship and cheerfulness after the awful welcome from Mr Lawrence. "Thank you for coming to see me, Hilda. I was feeling very sorry for myself."

Hilda nodded in sympathy. "It's all new and very strange for you at the moment, and there will be times when you feel lonely and out of sorts." She smiled. "I felt just like that when my Patrick died and left me all alone out here, so I do understand."

"I'm sorry to hear about your husband," Jessie murmured. "Do you have children close by?"

Hilda's expression saddened. "They flew the nest a long time ago," she replied. "The eldest is in Sydney, the other two down in Melbourne. I never get to see them, but they write occasionally." Her eyes were warm as they regarded Jessie. "But I get the feeling you need a friend right now, and although I'm old enough to be your mother, I think we will get along famously."

"So do I." They exchanged smiles, and Jessie realised Hilda yearned for her children and saw in her a chance to mother again.

"I'd better get on," muttered Hilda, checking the tiny watch pinned to her bodice. "Mr Lawrence is very particular about having the evening meal on the table at precisely six o'clock."

"It won't take long for me to get dressed," Jessie assured her.

"The best thing you can do with that is put it in a drawer and forget about it," she said, eyeing the corset. "And I advise you to leave off some of those petticoats and your stockings. No one will notice — not out here."

Jessie's eyes were wide as she looked at her new friend. "But it isn't proper."

"In this heat you'd be a fool not to," said Hilda stoutly. "You have a neat figure and there's no need to be trussed up like a chicken ready for roasting — and roast you will, mark my words."

"But Mr Lawrence . . ."

"He won't notice. Never looks beyond a woman's eyes." She patted Jessie's arm. "I'll leave you to get ready, ducks, and remember, you ain't alone out 'ere. You got me now."

Jessie was close to tears again as the older woman closed the door. Hilda's kindness had eased the longing for home, but it had also reminded her of the loss of her mother and grandmother. Determined not to allow her emotions to get the better of her, she tossed the corset aside, stripped off some of her petticoats and firmly laced up the bodice of her clean dress.

Brushing the tangles from her hair, she pinned it up and glanced at her reflection in the small mirror she had propped up on one of the shelves. Hilda was right: she felt better already; the lack of heavy underclothes made not a jot of difference to her appearance, but gave her an unfamiliar sense of ease and freedom. Refreshed by this discovery, and heartened by Hilda's friendly presence in this isolated place, Jessie headed for the main house, her steps light, her hopes for the future brightening the way.

CHAPTER
FIVE

The Blue Mountain Trail, December 1849

They had been travelling for many weeks and Kumali's initial fear of being among the *gubbas* had been quelled. She was mostly ignored by James and the man they called Fergal unless they needed a chore done. Duncan was surly, but she preferred that to the leering Bert and Wally, whose hot eyes always followed her. She had made a point of never being alone with them during the day, and sought safety at night under the wagon with Ruby and James.

Preferring to walk rather than ride, Kumali strode along next to the wagon and listened with amusement as Fergal cursed and snarled at his oxen. He sounded very fierce, and it still made her flinch every time he cracked his whip, but she'd soon understood that Fergal took great pride in his beasts, and she'd noted how well he tended them.

Kumali felt content for the first time since she'd been torn from her mother's arms. The old dress had been cut down and roughly sewn by Ruby so it fitted properly, and she wore one of Ruby's battered hats. She had refused the offer of boots, for the unfamiliar chafing made her clumsy and less sure-footed, and the under-drawers Ruby had insisted she wear felt very odd, but it was a small price to pay for her freedom and Kumali supposed she would eventually get used to them.

As they emerged from the cool shadows of the surrounding trees into the harsh sunlight, Fergal drew the oxen to a halt. They had crested the final hill and everyone gathered to look at the valley spread beneath them. Green and lush, the grassland seemed to go on for ever in the sheltering arms of the granite outcrops. Glinting water meandered through it, pooling into vast lakes that reflected the haze of distant hills and the soft grey-green of the gum trees.

"We're almost there," said Ruby excitedly. "We should have first sight of our selection within the week."

"We'll be after gettin' the beasts and wagon down first," muttered Fergal.

Kumali looked at the steep, winding track and the unstable edges that gave little protection from the plunging canyons that lay far below. She eyed the broad wagon and the heavy beasts and shivered. It would take fearsome strength and courage to get them down safely.

"Well, we can't stay here," said James. He squinted up at the sun. "There's at least six hours of light left. Better make a start."

Kumali and Ruby waited while the oxen were reharnessed, with one at the front and three at the back. The lead ox would pull, and the others would be used as brakes to counter the slope and the weight of the wagon. The horses were each burdened with at least two of the smallest bundles, which meant everyone but Fergal had to walk. Duncan would follow with the dogs and sheep later.

"Alonga me?" Kumali asked Ruby fearfully as she took the horse's reins. She'd never been placed in sole charge of a horse before.

Ruby patted the chestnut neck. "He's the quietest of the lot. You should be right." She must have seen the uncertainty in Kumali's eyes, for she smiled encouragement. "I'll be here behind you. Just don't let go of the reins and keep away from the edge."

"Ready?" shouted James. He glanced at each of them, then signalled to Fergal.

The leading ox was coaxed forward, the wagon rumbling behind him, the other beasts firmly lashed to the back. Kumali waited until the others had formed a line behind the wagon before she and Ruby followed.

The bulky packs forced Kumali's horse into the middle of the track, and as the path steepened and his feet slid on the shale, he yanked on the reins and snorted in fear. Kumali's grip tightened as the packs buffeted her. She hugged the side of the hill and didn't dare look beyond the horse to the sheer drop on the other side. She was terrified the heavy beast would trample her feet, but Ruby trusted her to make it safely down and she was determined to prove she could do so.

Apart from a few curses, and the snort of a horse or an ox, the only sounds were the crunch and slither of hoofs and the creak of the wagon. The wheels jolted over the scree, their rims sometimes on the precipitous edge of the track.

As the path steepened and the load's weight began to shift, Fergal had a fight on his hands to keep the lead ox on the move and the rear ones far enough back to act as a counterbalance. "I need help," he shouted to James.

James took charge of the three oxen at the back. They were heavy beasts, but they found it hard to keep their footing, for they weren't used to having a weight in front of them. Kumali could see that James had to use all his skills to slow them up and keep the ropes taut.

Inch by tortuous inch they made their way down the serpentine track as the sun travelled west.

Just then a bird clattered with a shriek of alarm from its nest in the rocks.

The horse in front of Kumali's reared up in terror. Wally cursed and clung to the reins as the animal's hindquarters threatened to slam him into the rocky hillside.

Kumali's horse whinnied and pranced, ears tight to its head. She instinctively placed her hand on its soft nose, tightened her grip on the reins and brought it to a trembling standstill.

Wally's horse would not be appeased. It kicked out as it twisted and scrabbled over the rough ground, and Wally was almost knocked from his feet as he fought to control it.

Kumali backed away from the flashing hoofs, and Ruby did the same.

With a jerk of its powerful neck, the horse swung Wally towards the edge.

He scrabbled for purchase, throwing himself backwards until he was curled in a tight ball beneath the deadly hoofs.

The horse reared up, eyes rolling in terror as it pawed the air inches above Wally's head.

Wally cowered, waiting for the death blow.

But the packs were unstable and the rearing horse lost its balance as the weight of them pulled it backwards. Wally let go of the reins an instant before the horse plummeted over the edge.

Kumali whimpered as she huddled against the hillside. The animal's terrible scream echoed through the shocked silence until it was brutally cut short.

"For Christ's sake, Wally!" James was red-faced and furious. "I told you to watch out. Now you've lost me a horse and at least a month of supplies."

Kumali saw Ruby flinch as James continued to bellow at the poor man, who was now trembling with shock. She pressed harder against the rocks, pulse racing, dreading that anger being turned upon her.

"The horse was spooked, James. It wasn't Wally's fault." Ruby's voice was unsteady.

"Of course it was," he retorted. "The bloody man should have taken more care."

Ruby paled at his rage and turned to Wally, who was trying to get to his feet. "Are you all right?" She asked tremulously.

Wally nodded, but his face was drained of colour and he could barely stand he was shaking so much.

"Sort yourself out and be quick about it, Wally," snapped James, his expression grim. "Give Fergal a hand, and this time take more care. Any more losses and they come out of your wages."

"That's not —"

James glared at Wally. "You lost my horse and a month's supplies — don't you dare answer me back." He finally glanced towards Ruby. "Are you all right?"

"We're fine," she replied, eyes wide with shock at his unaccustomed temper as she edged closer to Kumali.

"Then let's get off this mountain," he said crossly. "Keep more distance between you in case another horse gets spooked, and check those packs are firmly tied."

Ruby nodded and lowered her gaze. "Come on, Kumali, we'd better do as we're told."

Kumali found she was so terrified she could barely walk, but she tested the ropes, saw they were firm and followed the others. Anything was better than living on her own in the bush — and certainly an improvement on her life with the cattle-farmer boss — but she longed for this terrible journey to be over, and for James to return to his usual sunny nature.

Kernow House, Watsons Bay, December 1849

It had been nearly two months since the meeting with Niall Logan, and although Harry had tried repeatedly to get his brother alone, Oliver had been evasive. He seemed constantly occupied with business meetings

139

and, when he was at home, made certain Amelia or Gertrude was with him.

Harry had pondered long and hard how to approach Oliver with his concerns. Oliver already knew he was uneasy — it was the reason he was avoiding him — but Harry couldn't just ignore his suspicions. It had been many years since they'd resided under the same roof, and to all intents and purposes they were strangers, and this estrangement made it difficult to know where to begin without causing offence.

The sun sparkled on the water as he watched Doyle's men unload the day's catch. Gulls swooped and screamed overhead as the women gutted and cleaned the fish at the tables. Taking in the scene, Harry experienced a deep and unsettling yearning for Cornwall. Confused by his emotions, he tramped up the beach towards the house.

His love for this land had been all-encompassing — or so he'd thought until today. Now he was here, he realised he didn't really know or understand it at all, that he no longer felt the intrinsic sense of belonging. The years of exile — for that was how he saw them — had distanced him from the almost savage urgency of the pioneers to make their mark and their fortunes in this vast country. He'd forgotten the rawness of it all, and the harsh light and loud voices merely emphasised the isolation and breadth of a land that had yet to be fully explored and tamed.

He reached the gate and contemplated the house and grounds, his emotions in turmoil. This house and all it stood for had haunted him, but now he found he could regard it with the air of an outsider, and the knowledge that that was what he was saddened him.

He'd left here at twenty-one, and the ensuing years had set him adrift from his boyhood and the way of life in Australia he'd once taken for granted. Now he was used to the customs and rituals of England, where the seasons were more forgiving, and life was ordered by centuries of civilisation. He felt comfortable in the presence of nobles and industrialists, and had come to accept the position thrust upon him. And that was the most surprising revelation, for until this moment he had considered it a burden.

He dug his hands into his pockets and strolled across the lawn, lost in thought. The change in his half-sister saddened him, for she had shown such promise as a girl — now the beauty and vivacity were drowned in bitterness. His brother, too, seemed to have lost his way, and the weight of responsibility pressed down as he moved towards the house. The return to this country had been longed for and eagerly planned despite the memories he knew it would evoke. At first he'd been enthralled as he sought out favourite boyhood haunts and caught up with friends and family, but the stark reality was that, despite his continuing love for this colonial backwater, and the adventure to be had here, he didn't belong any more.

His home and daughters were in Cornwall, where the estate workers and villagers depended upon him for their livelihood and welfare. He'd strived to be honest and fair in his business dealings and in his management of the estate, and although it had proved an uphill struggle at times to keep his head above water financially, he hoped his efforts had earned him the respect for which he'd fought so hard. Now it appeared his brother was repeating their father's mistakes, and Harry knew it was up to him to steer him back on track.

Harry grimaced at the unintentional pun, for this railway Oliver had become involved in was already proving an expensive enterprise. With the in-fighting among the syndicate, the lack of investors and the race to complete it before the one in Melbourne, the scheme had disaster written all over it. He gave a deep sigh and went into the house.

Silence greeted him. Lavinia and Amelia were out on one of their interminable jaunts, the boys were in the tree house. Gertrude was upstairs somewhere, and the servants were busy in the kitchen. Of Oliver there was no sign. Thinking he was probably shut away in his office, Harry crossed the hall.

The door was ajar and he could see Oliver slumped in his chair, staring into space. His mood was plain in that defeated demeanour and Harry felt a pang of pity. He drew back, not wanting to witness such misery, or be caught doing so, for Oliver's pride was at stake.

He went back to the hall, slammed the front door and called out as he strode towards the study. "Oliver? Are you in there?"

"Come in, come in." Oliver rose from the desk, forcing a smile. "I was just enjoying a moment of peace while the house was quiet."

"I'm not disturbing you, am I?" Harry sat down before he could reply.

"Not at all," Oliver replied edgily. "But I do have an appointment in town soon." He pulled out his pocket watch as if to emphasise the point.

"I thought we might use this opportunity to talk," said Harry. "We rarely have a moment to ourselves, and it's time we caught up with things." He noticed the hunted look in Oliver's eyes, the way he fiddled with the watch, then unnecessarily resorted to tidying his desk. "I'm here to listen as well," he added. "Come on, Ollie. Tell me what troubles you."

"I'm not a boy any more," Oliver blustered. "I do not need to confide in my big brother."

"Why not? A problem shared is a problem halved, and even if we can't resolve it, at least you won't bear its full burden."

"Clichés and platitudes are all very well," muttered Oliver, "but they solve nothing. The problems I once shared with you were the worries of a boy — easily dealt with."

Harry saw the bruising of sleepless nights under his brother's eyes, noted the trembling in his fingers as he plucked at the paperwork on his desk and knew his brother was closer to the edge than he'd thought. "What's happened, Ollie?"

There was a long silence, broken only by the buzzing of a fly as it batted against the window. Oliver rose from his chair, went to a cupboard and pulled out a bottle of whisky and two glasses. "Drink?"

"You know I don't," he replied, "and neither should you. It's barely eleven o'clock."

"It helps," Oliver muttered, as he slumped into his chair. He took a drink and watched the sun catch the crystal as he twirled the glass. "Whisky is a panacea for all ills," he murmured. "It numbs the mind, so I don't have to think." He turned his gaze to his brother. "I know you disapprove, as do Amelia and Gertie, but at times this is my only friend."

Harry was so shocked he spoke without thinking. "That's dangerous talk, Ollie. It's not your friend but your worst enemy. Whisky makes you a slave as much as opium, and far from being a panacea, it offers only temporary escape from reality. That reality is your wife and son. Don't you love them enough to stop?"

Oliver drained the glass. "I can stop any time I want," he said defiantly. "As for loving my wife and son, what kind of question is that? Of course I do, and I take objection to your accusation."

"I was harsh because I care," Harry said flatly. "I saw our father drink himself into madness, and it frightens me to see you going down the same path."

"Our father's madness had little to do with his drinking."

"It didn't help."

The unspoken words lay heavily between them. Harry wondered if Oliver was remembering their mother's bruised face, the black eyes and the sound of her tears in the night, wondered if he thought of the debts their father, Edward, had left and the tangled web of intrigue and dark deeds that were his legacy to his

144

widow and sons. He hoped he did, for that was the reality of drinking to excess and gambling with his family's future.

"Let's not argue," he said. "I came to offer help, listen and try to find a solution to your worries, but I can't do that if you won't confide in me."

Oliver eyed the empty glass and pushed it aside. "I need a thousand pounds for the railway venture," he said flatly. "Do you have that kind of money, Harry?"

"A thousand pounds? I'd be lucky to scrape together three hundred."

"Then you cannot help."

"Why such an amount? I thought all the finances were in place?"

"The cost of importing the steel was higher than anticipated. Coupled with that, the labour costs are going through the roof and Niall refuses to renegotiate. One of the syndicate members has withdrawn his support, the government refuses to help, and the bank has turned down my application for another loan. Without Niall's investment, I am a thousand pounds short of my pledge to the syndicate, and if I don't find it within the week, I will not only lose my place in the company, but everything I have already put in."

"God," groaned Harry. "What a mess."

"That's putting it mildly."

Harry thought for a moment. "It seems the only answer is to find another investor. Surely there must be plenty who want to be part of such a scheme?"

"This is the country of the land rich and cash poor," muttered Oliver. "The entrepreneurs who might have backed us are already heavily involved in the railways being built in Melbourne, Adelaide, Perth and Van Diemen's Land."

Harry pursed his lips. "Why did the syndicate member leave? Could he not be persuaded to return?"

"There was a clash of personalities," muttered Oliver. "He wanted more say in the running of the Sydney Railway Company. I doubt he'll be persuaded to return: there were harsh words at the last board meeting."

"I suppose I could lend you a hundred pounds," said Harry, with reluctance, "but I would have to speak to Lavinia first."

Oliver raised an eyebrow. "Your wife holds the purse strings?"

"Yes. She has a good head for commerce and I trust her judgement entirely." He grinned. "Don't look so shocked, Ollie. Some women are more astute than any man when it comes to business, and I think it's a disgrace to waste all that talent by barring them from commerce."

"I dread to think what a mess Amelia would make of things if she was let loose with my money. She has enough trouble coping with her allowance."

"But Gertie handles the housekeeping admirably," Harry reminded him. "Given the chance, I suspect she could run any enterprise, for she has a keen eye and a firm grip on financial matters." He sighed. "But I digress. Think about my offer, Ollie, and don't dismiss it out of hand."

Oliver gazed at the empty glass with longing. "Thank you, but a hundred pounds is a drop in the ocean."

"Not if we can find nine other investors. Think about it, Oliver. It's a small amount to risk and yet the return on that investment promises much once the railway is finished." He could see his brother wavering and pressed his point. "The board could offer hundred-pound shares to the first ten investors. After that the price goes up to a hundred guineas. There are bound to be takers, for this is a land of gamblers, and everyone likes the chance to turn a quick profit."

"I will certainly put it to the board," said Oliver. He smiled for the first time that morning. "You never used to have an eye for business opportunities. I'm impressed."

"I've had to learn," Harry said gruffly. "Running the estates and keeping out of debt has been my life's work since I was twenty-one."

"Having a title must help."

"Not really. People assume the title is accompanied by wealth, and a certain standard of living is expected among our peers as well as our employees." He smiled. "But then you know that — look at how you live. This house, your wife's jewellery and the horses in the stable are all stage-dressing to impress would-be business colleagues and investors, and yet here you are, in need of a thousand pounds."

"If I had your title, I wouldn't need to go cap in hand for anything," muttered Oliver. "It's amazing how many doors would open to me if I was an earl instead of plain Oliver Cadwallader, esquire." He heaved a sigh.

"But fortune didn't smile on me, and I've had to work to achieve all this, not be handed it on a plate, like some."

Harry was stung. "That remark is not worthy of you, Oliver. Fortune didn't smile on Charles either. He died, remember? Shot by our father who was so drunk he could barely stand. I had no wish to inherit the title, especially under those circumstances."

Oliver had the grace to look ashamed, but Harry was not going to let him get away with his accusation. "The estates were run-down, the farms and fishing villages unkempt and disorganised when I inherited them. I might not have had your vision, but I rolled up my sleeves and got stuck in. The title meant nothing, and still doesn't — it will never make me rich or replace the feeling that I've achieved what I have through toil and sweat and the knowledge others depend upon me to succeed."

"The allowance from the whaling fleet and wholesale businesses must have helped," said Oliver sourly, "and they don't run themselves, you know."

The bitterness was clear, and Harry was hurt and dismayed by it. "George left those businesses to you on the understanding that a third of the profits would come to me. You were given this house, and the one Mamma and George lived in, to do with as you pleased. I think you got the best of it, Oliver, and I'm amazed you feel otherwise."

"I didn't inherit an estate with land, mines, farms and villages, and a host of people to work them. I didn't inherit a title that would open doors to business opportunities. What I did inherit had to be shared with you, only you don't have the responsibility of looking after our sister, or Amelia's — you provide nothing towards their keep."

"I didn't realise how resentful you were," said Harry sadly.

Oliver defiantly poured another whisky and downed it in one. "You don't know the half of it," he retorted. His bleary gaze took in the fine coat and pristine shirt. "Life in England must be pleasant. Judging by your attire, I would guess you aren't short of a few pounds despite your denials to the contrary."

"Hmph." Harry glanced down at his coat. "This is at least six years old, but yes, it was made by a good tailor, so it has lasted." He leant forward. "Oliver, this is not about tailors and a seat in the House of Lords; this is about two brothers who should be working together to solve this problem — not arguing about something neither of us can change."

Oliver twirled his glass, deliberately evading eye contact, his mouth petulant.

Harry realised his brother would not be swayed from his jaundiced opinion, and despaired that it should have come to this. He'd only wanted to help, but all he'd done was stir Oliver's sleeping rancour. "The offer of a hundred pounds is still on the table," he said quietly. "Find another nine investors and you will have what you need. I'm sorry I cannot offer more, and if you doubt my word, you may check with my bank in London."

Oliver remained silent.

"If Gertrude agrees, and Lavinia approves, then I will gladly take our half-sister back to England when we leave," he said. "A change of scene might improve her temperament, and if so, I have little doubt I will be able to find her a husband. Amelia's sister is really not my concern, and I suggest you obtain her a divorce and find her another husband."

"No one wants a divorced woman," muttered Oliver.

"You'd be surprised," retorted Harry. "The men outnumber the women here by at least twenty to one, and they aren't as choosy as they might be anywhere else." He gave a sigh. "As for Freddy, he is to come to England anyway, and I will pay a portion of the school fees." He regarded his brother, who was staring out of the window. "But if I am to do all this, then I will have to keep my share of the income from George's businesses. Gertie's annuity comes from George's estate, and that must also be transferred into my keeping. The income will improve her chances of finding a husband, and as I have two daughters approaching marriageable age, I must guard my own income to provide them with decent dowries."

"So you give with one hand and take with the other."

Harry clenched his fists. "It's the best I can do in the circumstances."

The two men eyed one another, and in that moment Harry realised they could never recapture the boyhood closeness that had once sustained them, for the years had led them down very different paths and they no longer understood one another.

★ ★ ★

"Do you have the mark of the Cadwalladers?" asked Charlie.

"What mark?" Freddy was engrossed in the maps and not really listening.

"The birthmark of red teardrops," said Charlie impatiently. "Father told me about it, but as he doesn't have it, I have never seen it." He snatched the maps from Freddy and held them behind his back. "You'll have these when you've answered me properly."

Freddy sighed. "Why do you want to know?"

"Because I do. Do you have it or not?"

"Yes."

"I don't see it."

Freddy yanked at the neck of his shirt to reveal the red droplets that ran across his collarbone. "Satisfied? Now can I have those maps back?"

"Not yet." Charlie pursed his lips, his expression thoughtful. "I am the heir to the title," he said finally, "and by rights should have that mark."

"Didn't your father explain that not all Cadwalladers carry it? Our uncle Charles had it, but of course he's dead, which is why you are the heir." Freddy made a grab for the maps, but Charlie held them out of reach. "Your sisters may have the mark — have you asked them?"

"Yes, but they deny it."

Freddy shrugged. "They're probably lying. You know what girls are like when it comes to their looks."

Charlie nodded and handed back the maps. "Girls can be awfully prim about such things, I agree, but to have the mark would be an honour."

"I don't see why." Freddy folded the maps and stored them in the saddlebag. "Girls don't inherit, so having the mark would make little difference to them other than to their vanity. Our grandfather Edward's was on his temple, so I suppose I'm lucky mine's out of sight. It would be awful to be teased about it at school."

Charlie seemed to lose interest in the topic and began to dig about in the trunk. "Let's have a duel," he said, as he lifted out the box of pistols.

Freddy liked that idea. It was much more interesting than birthmarks. He chose his weapon and stood back to back with Charlie before they counted the three paces. It was quite a large tree house, but not really big enough to have a proper duel and he would have preferred it if they could have taken the pistols outside, but that would risk getting caught with them, which was why neither of them suggested it.

"What are you boys doing up there?"

With guilty starts the boys hid the pistols behind their backs. "Nothing, Aunt Gertrude," Freddy replied, his voice quavering.

"Which means you're definitely up to something. Show yourselves immediately or I shall come up there."

Freddy shot a horrified glance at Charlie, and they quickly stuffed the pistols into the box and shut the trunk's lid.

"What was that you hid?" Gertrude was at the top of the ladder.

Freddy stared at his aunt in horror. Old women weren't supposed to climb up to tree houses. "Just some maps and things," he muttered.

152

"Then you won't mind showing them to me." Lifting the hem of her skirt, she entered the tree house and perched on a low chair as she dabbed her face with a handkerchief. "Bring that over here."

Freddy glanced at Charlie. There was no ignoring the order. They dragged the trunk across the floor and reluctantly lifted the lid.

Gertrude opened the box, saw the pistols, then gingerly lifted them out.

The sweat trickled down Freddy's spine as she coldly regarded him and Charlie. "Where did you get these?"

"We found them," said Freddy hurriedly. He shot his cousin a warning glance and hoped he understood to keep quiet about the attic crawl-space.

"Where?"

"They were buried behind the stables," he replied, not daring to look her in the eye.

"And I suppose this also was buried?" Gertrude drew out the military sword and scabbard. "They look in remarkably good condition," she said dryly. Her penetrating gaze settled on each of them in turn.

"We spent ages cleaning them," Freddy replied truthfully. "Look, there are the rags, and we borrowed the paste from the kitchen — ask Cook if you don't believe me."

Gertrude barely glanced at them. "Your fathers will hear of this," she snapped. "How *dare* you play with such things when you know how greatly they are detested in this house?"

Freddy had heard the stories of his mad grandfather and knew why guns weren't permitted. He shivered at

153

the thought of his father's anger. "Please, Aunt Gertrude," he begged, "don't tell Father. We promise not to play with them again."

She ignored him and rummaged in the trunk. "What else have you got hidden in here?"

"Just maps, a saddlebag, a spyglass and a couple of books," said Freddy sullenly.

Gertrude finally closed the lid. "You will help me down and then wait in your rooms until your fathers call for you," she ordered.

They raced for the house the moment Gertrude reached the bottom of the ladder. They were for it now, and neither of them expected to get away with less than a good tanning.

Harry was on the point of leaving Oliver to his whisky when there was a sharp rap on the door. Before either man could answer, their sister had barged in and dropped the ebony box and sword with a clatter on the desk.

"I found the boys playing with these," she informed them, arms folded tightly across her narrow chest. "They have been sent to their rooms until you are ready to deal with them, and I have ordered Cook to withhold their supper."

"Good grief," gasped Harry, as he lifted the sword and the pistols. "These were Father's. Where on earth did they find them?"

The blue eyes glinted with anger. "They *said* they were buried behind the stables, but I believe they have compounded their deception with a lie."

154

"You go too far, Gertrude," remonstrated Harry. "My son is not a liar."

"Maybe not," Gertrude sniffed, "but the pair of them looked as guilty as sin when I caught them up in the tree house, and Frederick is always up to some kind of mischief. They are hiding something, I just know it."

Harry wanted to smile at the thought of his prim sister clambering into a tree house, but knew that to do so would cause even more frostiness. "We will talk to the boys," he said calmly. "Thank you, Gertrude."

"I will take these and burn them," she said, reaching for the offending weapons.

Oliver quickly stayed her hand. "You will leave them where they are, Gertrude," he said firmly. "As much as I dislike weapons of any kind, these are valuable family heirlooms."

Harry could see his point, but the presence of his father's duelling pistols and sword were tangible reminders of a man possessed with violence, of how swiftly such weapons could be abused, and the shadows of the past seemed to crowd in. "Send the boys down, Gertrude," he ordered quietly. He waited until the less than mollified Gertrude left the room, and as the door slammed behind her, he looked at his brother. "What will you do with those?"

"Sell them. They are of no use to me, and I could do with the money." He sheathed the sword and stroked the polished ivory handle on one of the pistols. "They should fetch a pretty price, and I know just the man who might buy them."

"Good. The sooner they are out of the house, the better, but I wonder where the boys really found them and what else was with them. They certainly don't appear to have been buried for forty years."

The hesitant tap on the door silenced further discussion, and Harry turned as two fearful boys crept into the study. They looked sufficiently contrite, with downcast eyes and shuffling feet, their hands tightly grasped behind their backs; but had they fully understood the seriousness of their crime? "What have you to say for yourself, Charles?"

"I'm sorry, sir," the boy stammered, his face reddening.

"Sorry for getting caught, or sorry for lying about where you found them?" Harry watched his son's face and saw the conspiratorial glance he shot at Freddy. "Speak up," he barked. "And I will have the truth."

"I found them, sir," interrupted Freddy. "They were in the old nursery, up in the attic."

"Is that so, Charles?"

He nodded, his gaze firmly on his feet.

"So you did lie to your aunt?" growled Oliver.

Freddy muttered an affirmative. "I'm sorry, sir, but she frightened the life out of us and it was the first thing I thought of."

Harry had to bite the inside of his cheek to stop the smile. Gertrude would frighten most people, and in the boys' position, he would probably have done the same. "What else did you find in the attic?"

"Maps and things, and a spyglass."

156

"I should like to see them." Oliver rounded his desk and picked up the thin switch he kept on the bookshelf. "You can show me after you've had your punishment."

"I don't think they need further chastisement," interceded Harry quietly. He had never believed in corporal punishment as a way of teaching obedience. "No harm has been done, and as long as we discover the full extent of their treasure trove, we can rest assured there will be no repeat of today's events." He eyed the boys, who nodded their compliance.

Oliver replaced the switch and slumped back into his chair. "I have no appetite for beating the boys," he admitted, "but Gertrude will never let me hear the last of it unless I do something."

Harry suspected their half-sister had her ear firmly pressed to the door. He looked at the boys and kept his voice low, his expression stern. "I want your word you will not lie again, and that should you discover anything else, you will bring it to us immediately."

They nodded eagerly.

"But lying is not acceptable, so I propose the tutor is recalled and you spend four hours of each day at your studies. I will be watching your progress closely, so mind you keep out of mischief from now on and earn good reports at the end of each month."

He saw their reluctant nods and turned back to Oliver. "Hand me the switch."

It was passed to him with a questioning look. Harry pressed a finger to his lips before dealing five hefty blows to a cushion. He paused, dealt five more and handed it back. "Consider yourselves suitably punished." He leant towards the boys, his voice barely above a whisper. "And remember, your backsides should be stinging by now, so you can take the newspaper out of your trousers."

"Thank you, sir." Their relief was tinged with bashfulness as they removed the wads of paper and hobbled dramatically out of the room. They were in such a hurry they nearly knocked over their aunt, who hadn't been quick enough to move from her listening post.

"Come, Oliver, let us discover what it is those two rascals have got hidden."

"You go," replied Oliver. "I'm not built for climbing trees, and I want to take these into town and get them valued."

"I should say this ill wind has done you some good, Oliver. Those will fetch more than enough to keep you in the syndicate, and probably leave you with a nice little nest egg."

"I suppose you want a share in the proceeds?"

Harry saw the challenge in his eyes. "I want nothing to do with it, but I would appreciate your permission to withdraw from my offer of a hundred pounds."

"If I sell them, then you are released from your promise," Oliver muttered.

Harry left him with his spoils, and as he ran down the steps into the garden, he noticed Gertrude watching from behind a downstairs curtain. Poor Gertrude, what little sense of humour she had once possessed seemed to have deserted her — and yet she'd been quite right to confiscate the weapons, for they were dangerous in the hands of careless boys.

He had to bend double to gain entrance to the tree-house hideaway. Slumping to the floor, he leant against the door frame and mopped his brow as he cursed the passing years. There had been a time when he could have made this climb with ease, but now he was hot and slightly out of breath. And yet, as he sat there with his feet dangling into space, he realised the view was magnificent, stretching above the trees to the shoreline and clifftops. No wonder the boys spent so many hours up here.

The trunk was an old one of George's. Harry recognised it from when they had travelled to Cornwall all those years ago, and as he lifted the lid, he felt an overwhelming sadness that his stepfather was no longer with them. How he would have loved to join his grandsons in the games of pirates and renegades, to hide away up here from the women, the duties of father and husband, and all the responsibilities that came with adulthood, for George had always had a lively, enquiring mind and had never quite lost his youthful exuberance.

Harry sifted through the seashells, half-eaten apples, bits of paper and string, masks made of papier mâché, wooden swords, eyepatches and boxes of dubious remains of long-dead creatures. It was reminiscent of his childhood hoards, and nothing to provoke interest.

He'd left the saddlebag until last, and when he opened it, he found numerous maps and notebooks hidden in a leather pouch. Riffling through them, he realised they were detailed notes of his father's campaign against the natives. He stuffed them back. Just touching them made him feel tainted by the blood Edward had spilt during that time, and he prayed the boys hadn't perused them too closely.

Harry grimaced as he made his way back down the ladder. He had no need to read about his father's heinous exploits, for his mother had told him most of it, and now they were destined for the fire, where the shame and dishonour Edward had brought upon the House of Kernow could be purged once and for all.

Freddy watched from an upstairs window as Harry threw the maps and notebooks on the bonfire. The loss of the pistols and sword were nothing compared to the relief at not having been beaten, and this was enhanced by the knowledge that he had saved the hidden journal from the flames that now devoured his other treasures.

Charlie's silence had somehow approved of that small deceit, and it had brought them to a closer understanding now they shared the secret of the hidden niche in the nursery wall. Even so, shared secrets had a habit of being revealed, and although he trusted his cousin, and looked on him as a brother, he wondered if it might be wise to retrieve the journal and find another hiding place.

★ ★ ★

Beyond the Blue Mountains, December 1849

They reached the end of the track in the dark, and the relief was tangible as they watered the horses and oxen, set up camp and waited for Duncan. Kumali decided she liked her horse, and after she had tied the hobbles the way Ruby had shown her, she stroked the animal's neck and let him snuffle her. His whiskers tickled and she giggled in delight.

"Kumali, can you get me some water?" called Ruby, as she skinned the wallaby Fergal had shot that morning.

Kumali picked up the heavy cooking pot and happily made her way through the trees to the nearby stream. It was a warm, starlit night, she had survived the walk down the mountain, and soon there would be tasty tucker to fill her belly.

Wading into the water, she stood for a moment and looked up at the sky, remembering how, long ago, the Elders had told her about the Ancestor Spirits who lived there. With a sniff of derision, she dipped the pot in the water. The Spirits were supposed to protect her and watch over her, but she didn't believe it — not after what she'd been through — and she'd come to the conclusion that her fate lay in her own hands. She lifted the pot, now even heavier with water, and balanced it on her hip. The blaze of the campfire was her guide, and she headed towards it.

The hand was over her mouth before she could scream. His arm went round her waist, pulling her so tightly to him she could hardly breathe. The pot fell to

161

the ground as she lashed out, her fingers clawing to gouge his eyes.

His breath was foul as his lips traced her cheek, his voice a low growl. "Struggle all yer like, bitch. I've waited long enough for this, and I mean to 'ave yer."

Kumali wriggled, kicked and grabbed his beard, pulling as hard as she could. She sank her teeth into his hand, biting down until she tasted blood. His grip loosened as he cursed and she rammed her elbow into his midriff. Regular food and exercise had made her strong, and as he made another grab for her, she kneed him in the balls and gave him a shove.

He stumbled back, fury in his eyes. Then his foot became entangled with the fallen pot, and as he tried to regain his balance, his other foot slid into a crevice. There was a loud crack as his ankle twisted, and with a yelp of pain he fell heavily to the ground. His skull split like ripe fruit against a boulder and then he was suddenly still.

Kumali began to scream. The sound echoed through the bush and rang in her head as Bert's blood seeped across the boulder and pooled on the riverbank shale.

Ruby heard the screams and knew immediately what had happened. She'd already left the campfire, worried that Kumali had taken too long to fetch the water and that Bert seemed to have disappeared. James and the others were right behind her as she reached the girl. The sight that greeted them brought them to a stunned halt.

Kumali was hysterical. Bert was obviously dead.

162

"See to Kumali and get her to shut up," ordered James.

Ruby gathered a trembling incoherent Kumali into her arms while James examined Bert.

James ran his hands through his hair, his expression grim. "God, what a mess. What are we going to do now?"

"Bury him," replied Ruby. "No one will miss him."

"I can't condone murder by burying him," James snapped. "We'll have to inform the authorities." He began to pace as he tugged at his hair. "I told you she'd be trouble. Why the *hell* don't you ever listen to me?"

"Kumali no kill boss. 'Im break head on rock. Bert try jig-jig. Kumali no like, but no alonga kill 'im."

Ruby was furious with James. "I am always listening to you," she retorted, "and I do not appreciate being shouted at." She glanced at Fergal and Wally. "It's obvious what happened," she raged. "He tried to rape her, she defended herself, and he hit his head on that rock. Kumali didn't kill him — it was an accident."

"So she says." James looked mulish.

"Don't be ridiculous," she said scornfully. "Look at the wound, and the broken ankle. He fell."

"Accident or not, Bert's dead. She's black, Ruby, and blacks aren't allowed to kill whites."

"Black, white, what the hell does it matter?" she yelled, her temper well and truly roused. "He got what he deserved."

"It is a kind of justice," muttered Fergal.

"See! Even Fergal agrees with me," she stormed. "What about you, Wally? Do you think we should go to the authorities?"

"I ain't got nothing to do with this," he muttered, taking a step back.

"Only because Bert got there first," she spat. "I've seen you watching her. You just want to thank God that's not you lying there with blood pouring out of your head."

"All right, Ruby, calm down."

"Don't patronise me, James. I know what's right, and if you go to the authorities, then . . . then . . ." She fell silent, unable to think of a suitable threat.

"Ruby, you're not thinking straight," he said impatiently. "Bert was assigned to us by the Prison Service. They keep track of these men, and it's our duty to report his death — especially if a gin is involved."

Ruby was incensed by his lack of understanding and his insensitive language. "We could tell them he's run off."

"Do that and we'll be starting our new life with a lie," he protested. His gaze was fierce, but Ruby would not be cowed. "For heaven's sake, Ruby," he snapped, "be sensible."

"I am being sensible," she retorted, hands on hips. "Bury him, James. No one will look for him. The authorities have got too many convicts to worry about, and they're always running off. I can almost guarantee they won't come to check on him." He was wavering and she pressed her advantage. "Come on, James," she coaxed. "You can see it was an accident. Inform the

164

authorities and Kumali will be thrown in gaol and probably hanged. She won't get justice in a white court. Let it go."

The long silence was broken by Fergal. "I'm thinking it's right what Ruby says, James. Let's bury the man and have done with it."

"What do you say, Wally?"

Wally's gnarled hands twisted his hat as he eyed the lifeless Bert. "I ain't one for getting the authorities involved," he muttered. "I spent too many years in the clink, and this kinda thing ain't gunna keep me out. Bury 'im I say."

With a sigh James relented. As the men returned to the camp to fetch spades, Ruby put her arm round Kumali. "Come on," she said softly, "it's over. No one but us will know what happened tonight. And don't be frightened of Wally — he wouldn't dare step out of line now."

As she comforted Kumali, put ointment on the scratches and tried to mend her torn dress, Ruby gently teased the story out of her. She was relieved Kumali hadn't actually been raped, but it had been a damned near thing and she blamed herself. Her soft heart and stubbornness had brought the girl into danger, and she'd been forced to accept that James's mistrust and dislike of the natives would never change. Perhaps it would have been better to heed his advice after all, but it was too late for regrets. She would give Kumali a knife to carry.

Duncan arrived with the sheep as the last spadeful of earth fell on Bert's grave. He listened as James told him what had happened, then scowled and spat. "Always trouble with women about," he said under his breath, "but sounds like he deserved it. Good riddance I say." He strode off into the darkness and settled down with his dogs and sheep within the calico pen.

When they woke the following morning, there was no sign of Wally. The bedroll and saddle were gone, as were one of the horses and a bundle of supplies. The loss of yet another horse and more supplies was a blow, the loss of another pair of hands inconvenient, but none of them was surprised that Wally had decided to take his chances on the run.

CHAPTER
SIX

Lawrence Creek, Hunter Valley, December 1849

The children had been overexcited all morning, and as it was the final day of school before the Christmas holidays, and she wanted to prepare for that night's party, Jessie had let them go home early. She stood on the steps of the schoolhouse, watched the twenty-four children saddle up and waved until they were out of sight.

With a sigh of contentment, she went back indoors and began to tidy up. Christmas was only days away, and the past week had been spent making presents. The older boys had carved wooden toys, and the more capable girls had sewn rag dolls and aprons and knitted potholders. The little ones had made brightly decorated calendars. Each one had been engrossed, their heads bent over their work as she'd read to them, guided thread through needles and helped untangle wool.

With the last of the material scraps returned to the linen bag hanging on the back of the door, and the wood shavings swept outside, she sat and relished the silence. A trickle of perspiration ran down her ribs, and she dabbed the dew from her top lip with her handkerchief. It felt strange to be celebrating Christmas in this heat. There should be snow on the ground, a nip in the air and frost tingling her toes and fingers, but as she gazed out of the window, she saw only a cloudless sky of the deepest blue, the haze of heat making the distant trees look as if they were standing in water.

She wondered if it was the same for her brothers. Were they thinking of her, of the Christmases they'd spent in Cornwall when their mother and grandmother had been alive? Did they look at the same clear sky, feel the heat of this southern December and long for them to be together again? She gave a deep sigh. She hadn't heard from them, but then she'd only been here a matter of weeks and the mail took months to get through. She hoped they had found the same contentment in their new lives.

Jessie realised she shouldn't be idling while Hilda was cooking for the party, but time ticked away as her gaze lingered on the bright pictures of robins, snowmen and mistletoe the children had pinned to the wall. They were incongruous in this climate, but were dearly held images handed down from parents and grandparents who'd experienced the festive season in much colder climes.

Her gaze drifted to the empty pegs and rows of vacant desks. The number of children had seemed daunting that first day, and although they ranged from six years old to thirteen, they had proved easy to teach. The older boys had tested her at first by showing off, but had soon learnt she wasn't impressed and had settled down, shyly bringing her gifts of apples or a comb of honey.

The children had listened that first morning as she'd described her life in Cornwall and her arrival in Sydney, and had laughed with her when she had recounted how frightened she'd been by the dragon lizard. Then it had been her turn to listen, and she had been struck by the thread of determination that ran through their stories. Unlike the downtrodden urchins of England, these children weren't cowed by poverty and squalid housing, or threatened by the workhouse system that was the end of the line for most — these children would battle against all odds, overcome hardships and the elements to carve out a life here and make a success of it.

She opened the window, leaning out to enjoy the cool shadows of the overhanging trees. The valley spread before her, golden in the sun, the lines of dark vines spreading away into the distance. There was wealth in the valley, but it lay in those vines and in the land. Only a few of the children wore boots, preferring the freedom of bare feet, which had been hardened by running about on the heat-baked earth.

This third or even fourth generation of Australian children bore little resemblance to their whey-faced, puny English cousins, for beneath the grime and ragged clothing they were sturdy and clear-skinned, with gleaming hair and eyes bright with curiosity. Their limbs were long and straight, their physical strength honed from working on their parents' vineyards and from riding their shaggy ponies everywhere. The clear

169

skin came from the abundance of fruit, fresh vegetables and sunshine to be had in the valley, but their eagerness to learn was inbuilt, for these were the children of pioneers and were therefore instilled with a thirst for knowledge of what lay beyond their valley home.

Feeling she was being unfair to Hilda, Jessie cast a final, approving glance over the neat classroom, grabbed her bonnet and went outside.

"I could do with some help and no mistake," panted Hilda, as she peered through the steam and mopped her scarlet face. "These puddings should be done by now. Grab that cloth and we'll get them out."

The plum puddings were each wrapped in calico and tied firmly to a long pole. There were six in all, and they weighed a ton — or so it felt. Struggling to keep them out of the dirt, they carried them away from the enormous cauldron of boiling water and set them carefully on a nearby table. "Too hot to touch yet," muttered Hilda. "We'll leave 'em there for now and get on with stirring the cake mixture."

Jessie breathed in the wonderful aromas of dried fruit and spices. It had been a rare occasion when they could afford such luxury at home and her mouth watered. "Do you always have plum pudding at Christmas?"

Hilda nodded, her sturdy arms working to mix the heavy ingredients that smelt so enticingly of fruit, sugar and brandy. "Wouldn't be a proper Christmas without plum pudding, and a nice fat goose."

Jessie grimaced at the thought of all that food in this heat, but if she was to enter into the spirit of an Australian Christmas, she would have to find an

170

appetite. "You seem to have made a lot of puddings," she said, when she'd done her share of mixing.

"Two are for us, one is to be kept for next year, and the others are for tonight." Hilda eyed her sharply. "Have you decided what to wear?"

"I don't really have much choice," she replied. "It's either this" — she plucked at her plain brown dress — "my best dress or the skirt and blouse."

"I've got a nice cameo brooch that would look a treat with your blouse," said Hilda, as she spooned the cake mixture into a vast tin and set it in the centre of the pot-bellied camp oven. Slamming the door on it, she took a deep breath and mopped her brow. "With your grandma's shawl you'll look as pretty as a picture."

"What about you? Won't you need the brooch?"

"I've got a lovely row of jet beads with a pair of earrings to match. That'll be enough for an old crone like me." She nudged Jessie. "There won't be no Mr Abel Cruickshank or his like making eyes at me, my girl — those days are long gone."

Jessie blushed and ducked her head. There had been no sign of Mr Cruickshank since her arrival, and she couldn't help wondering if he would be there tonight.

Mr Lawrence kept them busy all afternoon. Hilda was ordered to press and brush his black suit, and polish his top hat and shoes. Jessie was sent back and forth with armfuls of things that had to be loaded into the carriage, stopping only to join him for a late luncheon.

She was in a fever of impatience as the clock ticked and he slowly ate the cold collation and sipped numerous cups of tea. Barely able to contain her frustration, she eyed the clock, realised they had less than an hour before departure and despaired as he deliberately cut into a slab of cheese and settled down to munch. "If you will excuse me," she said, unable to sit any longer. "I have many things still to do."

He peered at her through the monocle. "As this will be your first real introduction to the local inhabitants, I hope you conduct yourself with suitable sobriety," he said, through a mouthful of cheese. "You will accompany Mrs Blake and help her with the food, and when your duties are fulfilled, you will remain at my side for the rest of the evening."

She held his gaze, aware her heart was thudding, her face flushed. Surely he didn't really mean for her to take no part?

He pulled out his pocket watch, checked the time against the clock and snapped it shut. "We will leave in precisely forty-five minutes. You are excused."

When Jessie emerged from her room forty minutes later, she knew she looked well. The skirt and blouse had been set aside in favour of her best dress. The sprigged cotton billowed into a full skirt from the narrow waist, the neckline covering her shoulders to hide her birthmark, the décolletage made less daring with a froth of lace into which she had pinned Hilda's brooch. She had brushed her hair from a centre parting and had twisted it into two heavy plaits, which she had coiled over her ears and finished off with blue and yellow ribbons. With the beautiful shawl around her shoulders, she felt like a princess — even though her

172

boots were worn, she had no other jewellery, and the hated corset pinched.

"My, my, don't you look a treat?" Hilda was magnificent in black bombazine, her jet earrings and necklace glittering in the late afternoon sun.

Mr Lawrence's eyes widened as Jessie clambered into the carriage. "Cover yourself," he hissed, his gaze flitting to her shoulders. "If we weren't already late, I would demand you changed. That is most unsuitable attire for a schoolmistress."

Jessie pulled the shawl closer, her cheeks reddening, the pleasure of the moment dashed by his criticism.

"I think she looks lovely," snapped Hilda.

He slapped the reins over the horse's rump, his bearing making it plain he disapproved of them both.

Jessie soon forgot his disapproval as the countryside opened out before them. This was a new part of the valley to her, and it was interesting to see the subtle differences. Several of the houses were very grand, with red-tiled roofs and whitewashed walls, others more like bark huts, dotted in among the lines of vines, some of which had been planted in terraces on the surrounding hills. As she took in the scene, she wondered where Abel Cruickshank lived, and if he still remembered her.

The sounds of the party drifted to them as they approached a particularly grand house and made their way up the long, tree-lined driveway. There were carriages parked to one side of the drive, and through the trees Jessie could see horses grazing in a nearby paddock. Wagons had been hauled into a field, and she

173

waved back in delight as she recognised several of the children who were playing around them.

"There is our host," muttered Mr Lawrence.

Jessie saw the handsome, fair-haired man standing on the steps next to an older woman. "He looks very young to own such a splendid vineyard," she replied.

"His parents came from Germany and founded the place about forty years ago. Gerhardt has taken over since his father died. That is his mother, Frieda von Schmidt. She is a doyenne of local society and a generous benefactress to my charities, so I expect you to make a good impression."

He handed her down from the carriage and Jessie smoothed the creases in her dress as Gerhardt came to greet them.

"Miss Searle." He clicked his heels and kissed the air above her fingers as she bobbed a curtsy. "It is an honour to meet you at last."

She saw the depth of blue in his eyes and the way the sun glinted on his golden hair. He was tall and broad-shouldered, with lightly tanned skin and a fine moustache. Her heart did a little flutter. His mother was tall and elegant, her expression patrician above the high neck of her black lace gown. Jessie bobbed another curtsy.

Frieda eyed her through a lorgnette as she leant on her walking cane, then smiled. It was as if the years had been swept away to reveal a hint of the beauty she must have once been. "Very pretty," she said, her gnarled finger tipping Jessie's chin. "An admirable addition to

174

our little community. Welcome to our party, my dear. I hope you enjoy it."

"Miss Searle is not here to enjoy herself," said Zephaniah Lawrence tightly. "She is here to help Mrs Blake and get acquainted with some of the parents of her pupils."

"You know, Zephaniah, you can be awfully pompous at times." The faded blue eyes were coolly appraising as she eyed the minister. "For a man of God, you seem to have little charity in your heart for a young girl who must be homesick."

Jessie watched with amusement as he squirmed and tried to explain himself, thereby tying himself in knots beneath her unforgiving glare.

"I will have the servants take the food to the barn," said Gerhardt. "Please, let me escort you ladies to the party."

Hilda winked at Jessie and took his proffered arm, and together they walked through the immaculate gardens, which had fountains and arbours and was filled with the heady scent of blossom. Jessie gazed in awe as Hilda prattled to their host, for this was grander than any park in England.

The barn was set some distance away, and the bustle of activity was accompanied by the sounds of fiddlers tuning their instruments and children calling to one another as their parents chatted and caught up with gossip.

"You must allow me to have a dance later on," said Gerhardt, as he guided them towards tables that were already groaning with food.

Jessie dipped her chin. "Thank you, sir, but I will be too occupied to dance."

The blue eyes twinkled. "It is my party and my right to claim at least one dance from the prettiest girl here."

Jessie blushed furiously as he bowed and left them.

"Goodness, you don't let the grass grow under your feet, do you?" giggled Hilda, as she tied a vast apron over the bombazine. "You've made quite an impression there, my girl."

Jessie tied her own apron and hoped she didn't appear too flustered by Gerhardt's attentions. "I'm here to work, not dance."

"We'll see," muttered Hilda.

The noise rose as more people arrived and the musicians began to play. The fiddle and drum was accompanied by the penny whistle, banjo and squeeze-box, and the heat increased in the barn as the dancers took to the floor. Jessie couldn't resist tapping her foot as she stood beside Hilda, but as the dancing brought an even greater demand for cool lemonade and beer, she had little time to regret not being able to join in.

"Will you have this dance, Miss Searle?"

She looked up at the tow-headed youth who stood before her, his fingers nervously twisting his hat. He was the elder brother of one of her pupils. She was all too aware of Mr Lawrence's beady gaze and knew he was waiting to find fault. "I'm sorry, but no, I am too busy," she said, with an apologetic smile.

176

He reddened and swallowed, obviously not quite sure what to do next, but before he could make up his mind, he was joined by four other young men, who jostled him out of the way. "Come on, Miss Searle, dance with us. You cannot be busy all evening."

She looked to Hilda for help as the group surrounded her, but Hilda was deep in conversation with their employer, her hand firmly on his arm as she steered him to the far corner of the barn, where a knot of elderly ladies had gathered. "I'm sorry," she said, "but I am not permitted to dance."

"Not permitted? By who? Not that old curmudgeon Zephaniah? Come on, Miss Searle, you're far too pretty to be a wallflower."

Jessie backed away. They meant no harm, were merely being somewhat overenthusiastic, but she didn't know how to avoid causing offence.

"Excuse me, Miss Searle. It is my dance, I think." Her apron was untied and tossed to a nearby youth, and without waiting for a response Gerhardt pulled her from the mêlée and whirled her into the centre of the dance floor. "I could see you needed rescuing."

She returned his smile, but was all too aware of Mr Lawrence watching from the shadows. "You will earn me a reprimand," she said nervously. "Mr Lawrence has expressly forbidden me to dance."

"Then I must make sure your evening is memorable enough to warrant any reprimand, Miss Searle."

He bowed over her hand as the music came to an end and gave a nod to the knot of young men who had been watching them. His eyes were bright with mischief

177

as he looked down at her. "Enjoy the party, Miss Searle."

Before he had moved a step she was surrounded again. The music began and she was whisked into a lively polka by a beaming young farmer who had two left feet. As the evening progressed, the heat became almost unbearable and the music and noise grew louder. Jessie was kept on the dance floor until she was quite giddy, but she had long since ceased to care what Mr Lawrence would say — she was having too much fun. Even so, she needed to rest and get her breath back. She thanked her latest partner and was about to return to Hilda when she saw Abel Cruickshank standing in the doorway. Their eyes met and he smiled and tipped his hat in acknowledgement. Jessie felt a flutter of expectation as he moved from the doorway. He was going to ask her to dance.

"My turn again, I think."

Before she could protest, Gerhardt had led her back on to the centre of the floor and, as the music began, guided her into the simple square dance. A glance towards the doorway confirmed that Abel was watching, his expression unreadable as he followed their progress around the floor.

"You really are pretty," said Gerhardt, as they drew close and swayed together before separating again.

She glanced towards the doorway. Abel had turned away — he was leaving.

"Will you permit me to escort you to supper, Miss Searle?"

She tried to smile through her disappointment. "I would be honoured, sir," she replied, "but Hilda and I will be busy serving."

"There are plenty of other women to do that," he said imperiously, as he swung her round. "You are my guest and I wish to have supper with you."

They parted and changed places with another couple, and as they held hands and formed an arch for the others to go through, she realised she could not refuse. "Thank you, sir," she said above the noise. "It would be a pleasure."

"The pleasure is mine, Miss Searle."

His blue eyes were looking down at her with an intensity she found rather unsettling, and as the music stopped, she dipped a curtsy. "I must rest," she said breathlessly.

He kept hold of her hand. "I am delighted you have come to live in the valley," he said, as he led her off the floor. "My mother has taken a great liking to you." He smiled. "And so have I."

"Thank you," she replied, her gaze darting around the room for sight of Abel.

He clicked his heels as his lips hovered above her gloved hand.

"That is quite enough of that," stormed Mr Lawrence, as he roughly grabbed Jessie's arm. "Go about your duties, Miss Searle."

Gerhardt placed himself between them, his gaze arctic. "You seem to forget yourself, Lawrence. You have no right to manhandle the lady in such a way."

"Manhandle?" Zephaniah Lawrence sounded as if he was being strangled as he released his grasp. "Miss Searle is my employee, and it is strictly forbidden for her to conduct herself in such a wanton manner — even if it is with her host."

"Dancing isn't wanton," retorted Gerhardt. "It's just a way of having fun and getting to know people."

"Not if she wants to remain in my employ, sir. Come, Miss Searle, you will sit with me for the rest of the evening."

"My mother has expressly asked that Miss Searle accompanies us for supper." Gerhardt turned to Jessie. "I will return for you in an hour."

"Disgraceful behaviour," hissed Mr Lawrence, as he again grabbed her arm. "I should have known you were unsuitable for the post, and I will be writing to the Board in the strongest terms."

Jessie glared at him. "Unhand me, sir."

He reddened as the monocle dropped and bounced on its ribbon.

Free of his grasp, Jessie felt the heat flood through her as she realised everyone had witnessed that sorry little scene. She crossed the floor with as much dignity as she could muster and decided that she too would write to the Church Board and clarify her position. She found the darkest corner and looked for Abel.

"He's gone home," said Hilda, as she sat down next to her and mopped her brow. "I suppose he realised he couldn't compete with our host." She patted Jessie's hand. "Never mind, my duck. Gerhardt is certainly the finer catch, and he's obviously smitten."

180

Jessie tried to appear unfazed by Hilda's words, but the thought that Abel had left the party under the mistaken assumption her head had been turned by their host sharpened her disappointment. It had been an evening of lost opportunity, and as Gerhardt crossed the floor some time later to claim her, she couldn't help but wish it was Abel she would accompany to supper.

Beyond the Blue Mountains, December 1849

"There it is," said James, as he took off his hat and squinted into the sun.

Ruby stared in delight at the sweeping pastures, undulating hills, meandering rivers and stands of shade-giving trees. The grass gently rippled in the light breeze. The sky was the clearest blue, the sun gilding the tops of the trees. "It's an Eden," she breathed.

"Then that's what we'll call it," said James. "Eden Valley."

"I like that," she agreed. "Or Edenvale? It's less of a mouthful."

James squashed his hat back on, his expression sour. "Your father paid for it, so I suppose by rights you should name it. I'm surprised you don't want to call it Rubyvale, or Niallvale, or something Irish like Donnyvale."

Ruby gnawed her lip. She'd heard the scorn and hadn't realised her father's gift was such a bone of contention, for until today the ownership of the land had been scarcely discussed. She eyed her husband, unwilling to accept she knew so little about him, unwilling to believe he could be so short-tempered and moody. His manner had changed since the loss of horses and supplies, and after the attack on Kumali, she knew he hadn't slept well. His dreams had plagued him with images of soldiers coming to arrest him for hiding the dead convict, his moods darkened by the fear that this new life of theirs would be for ever overshadowed by what had happened. They had been in constant peril of bickering, and because Ruby loved him, she'd come to realise compromise was the only solution.

"Father bought this land, yes, but he has leased it to both of us," she reminded him. "You have as much say in the naming of it as I — please don't be cross," she coaxed.

"I'm not cross," he snapped, "merely sick of being contradicted and ordered about by a wife who should learn to keep her tongue still."

Ruby's anger flared, but she held it in. To yield to his goading would merely cause another argument and she didn't want to spoil what should have been a special moment. They had come so far, had endured so much, and she was made of sterner stuff than to give in to his moods and abandon their plans by returning home.

"Eden Valley it is, then." He climbed into the saddle. "I'm off to find the best place to set up camp before it gets dark. Duncan and the others are way behind us, so stay here until I get back." He kicked his horse into a gallop and was soon a speck in the distance.

Ruby led the horses into the rich pastureland. The swish of grass against her legs and the rising scents of warm earth and crushed wild flowers did nothing to

182

ease her concerns. This Promised Land was all she could have hoped for, but their new life together, and the joy she should have felt, had been tainted not only by her husband's resentment, but by their experiences on the long journey here. Would their love wither as the resentment simmered and the isolation and struggle for survival took their toll, or would the belief in their union and the shared dreams for their future hold fast? She could only pray they would.

"Boss no happy. Kumali t'ink cossa me."

"He's just tired and hungry. He'll be better once we've made camp and had a good night's sleep."

Kumali frowned. "Him no like black-fella woman. Kumali betta away, away."

Ruby sighed. In hindsight, it would have been better if she hadn't insisted upon Kumali travelling with them, but the decision was made. Kumali was not to blame, and sooner or later James would have to come to terms with it. Her presence did make things difficult, though, for Kumali followed her everywhere and insisted upon sleeping as close to her as possible — allowing little intimacy with James — which was probably the main reason for his disgruntlement.

"Missus Ruby?"

"You'll stay with us," she said. "James and I will need everyone to help settle and build and tend the flock, and once you've shown him how useful you are, he'll come out of his black mood."

Kumali's brow furrowed as she struggled to understand. Then her expression softened and she smiled. "Kumali cook tucka, good, good. Build *gunyah*,

183

catch fishes and find honey. Boss like alonga Kumali soon, soon."

"Let's hope so," muttered Ruby.

The horses and oxen had been hobbled and were grazing, their tails and ears flicking at worrisome flies. Fergal was stretched out in the shade of a tree, his hat over his face as he snored, and Duncan was sitting in the deep shadow cast by the dray, his attention focused on the book of poetry he always carried. The dogs panted in the late afternoon heat, but their attention never strayed from their duties as they watched the flock.

Ruby sat on a fallen branch and observed Kumali stoke the fire beneath the smoke-blackened billycan. The smell of cooking meat rose into the valley, attracting even more flies, and Ruby wondered if mosquitoes would take their place at dusk, for there was plenty of marsh water about.

The sound of galloping hoofs brought them to their feet, and as Ruby shielded her eyes against the sun, she realised it was James.

"I've found the perfect place," he panted, as he swung from the saddle. "Well away from stagnant water, but close enough to the river so we can water the stock. It's about five miles that way," he said, jerking a thumb over his shoulder.

"Is there shade for the beasts, and enough flat land to build on?"

"Ruby," he groaned, "I do know what I'm doing. Of course there is."

Duly chastened, Ruby turned to Kumali. "Let's have that cuppa before we set off again. We'll eat when we get there."

Tin mugs of fragrant, steaming tea were handed around and sipped as quickly as possible, while James extolled the virtues of the place he'd found and the plans he had for it. Fergal and Duncan had many questions, and as James answered, Ruby noticed how he turned his back on her, tacitly denying her any part in the conversation.

She was thoughtful as she and Kumali hauled the cooked wallaby from the ashes, sliced it into chunks and wrapped it carefully in oiled paper. James's reaction to her innocent question had not gone unnoticed by the others, and she'd seen the flash of sympathy in Fergal's eyes, the confusion in Kumali's. She had to learn to keep her mouth shut, to read her husband's moods and try to understand and work with them until his nightmares ceased and he could forget the unfortunate beginning to their adventure and return to his usual sunny disposition.

The fire was doused and raked through, the surrounding stones left to contain any spark after they had gone. With the oxen harnessed, the extra horses on leading reins and the sheep in a tight bunch, they set off.

As the sun sank and cast streaks of orange, red and yellow across the sky, James called a halt. Lorikeets, parrots and cockatiels of every hue squawked and circled as they headed for their night roosts. The pink-breasted galahs squabbled in the tree branches,

185

and wheeling flocks of bright green and yellow budgerigars darted and swooped.

Ruby stood beside James and looked out at the land that would be their home. The valley floor was sheltered by a quarter-circle of low, heavily timbered hills. A river meandered to the west, and although the pasture would need clearing of box and ironbark, there was good, rich soil and plenty of grass. A waratah blazed with scarlet blossom, and a line of red gums and she-oaks followed the river's path through the valley.

"It's perfect," she breathed. "Well done, James."

He seemed to have shrugged off his earlier ill temper, and now he smiled as he put his arm across her shoulders. "I propose we build on the higher ground just beneath the summit of that arc of hills. It's above the flood plain and will give shade during the day."

She nodded in delight, eager to keep him in this good mood. "I can't wait to get started on building our first home."

He grinned and shoved back his hat, once more the familiar easygoing James she had fallen in love with. "I reckon we'll have to leave that until first light," he said softly into her ear. "But I can think of other ways to celebrate this homecoming."

She shot a glance over her shoulder, but the others seemed occupied. With a soft nudge in his ribs, she smiled back at him. "I thought you were tired," she teased.

"Never too tired to show my wife how much I love her," he murmured, as he nuzzled her cheek. He glanced back as he took her hand. "Just going to show

Ruby where I want to site the homestead," he called to the others. "Get the animals sorted, and we'll be back soon."

Kumali dropped the saddlebag and would have followed if Duncan's hand hadn't stilled her. She whirled to face him, knowing her fear showed in her face.

"Leave 'em be, lassie," he muttered. "There's plenty of work tae do here, and they'll come back soon enough."

Kumali didn't understand. She shook her head, fearful of his intentions as she tried to free her arm. "Alonga Ruby," she gabbled.

"Nay, lassie," he said firmly, his grip unrelenting. "Ruby is James's wife and they need some time together — alone."

At last Kumali understood. She looked up at the Scotsman, saw no threat in his expression and noted for the first time that he wasn't ugly and fierce, but probably quite young under that beard hair. As his grip relaxed, so did she. "Kumali alonga you push sheeps?"

"Aye, lassie," he said softly, a rare smile tweaking his lips. "I'll let you push sheep, as long as you don't talk too much and you do as I tell you."

Kumali nodded. "Alonga you till the missus back."

Duncan eyed her thoughtfully as he scratched his beard. "I think it might be better if you stay with me for a while and nae go bothering newly-wed folk." He must have seen Kumali tense, for he hastened to add, "Just until James and Ruby are settled in their house."

"Alonga you?" Kumali wasn't at all sure about this strange man, or what he wanted from her. "No beat 'im? No jig-jig?"

"Hmph. Jig-jig, indeed. You're no more than a bairn — what kinda man dae ye think I be?" His expression softened. "Look, Kumali, I am asking you tae help me with the sheep and offering you shelter at night — nothing more. I will not beat you, touch you or even talk tae ye if that's what you prefer. Do you ken?"

Duncan the sheep man was strange, but she was no longer wary of him. "Kumali alonga you push sheeps."

"Right," he muttered. "Now that's settled, let's get these beasts into a fold before we have the dingoes after them. Come, lassie, let me show you how tae string out the calico."

Ruby giggled as James led her through the trees and up the gentle slope of the sheltering hill. "They know exactly what we're up to."

"I don't care," he said, as he picked her up and ran with her through the trees and up the steepest part of the slope.

Ruby laughed and clung to his neck, revelling in his strength and determination.

Panting, he reached a plateau that was sheltered from view by gum trees and placed her back on her feet. His arms encircled her, and as his pulse slowed, he kissed her. "This is our honeymoon, remember?"

"How could I forget?" She could feel the drum of his heart beneath her fingers and the urgency of his need as he drew her closer. "Oh, James," she sighed, "I do so love you."

He kissed her again, his lips rousing her own need to hold him and be held — to feel his hands on her body, his flesh on her flesh. They sank to the ground, lost in their own world as they came together. Their bed was a mattress of eucalyptus leaves, their roof a star-studded sky, but this was home, and the act of love that bound them to one another and to this wilderness was more precious to Ruby than any jewel.

Eden Valley, New Year's Day 1850

The bark hut was perched on the broad, flat area that ran a third of the way along the hill. Its frame had been fashioned from the ironbark trees they had chopped down, the thick slabs of overlapping paperbark acting as walls where they were nailed to the uprights. The roof was made of wooden tiles, tightly lashed with vines and roughly thatched with dried grass. The hill behind the hut had been burrowed into and formed the fourth wall, providing a cool, dark storeroom for their precious food, grain and seed. A sheet of canvas acted as a door, and crudely fashioned shutters covered the single window to keep out insects.

The furniture was a mixture of bush carpentry and pieces she had brought from home. Grandmother Nell's patchwork quilt adorned the bed, her shawl was draped over a chair, and on the wall, lined up on shelves, were her precious pieces of china that had survived the long journey unscathed. There were few luxuries in this bush hut, but it was home and Ruby hummed contentedly as she crossed the earthen floor and took the bowl of dirty water outside to water the fledgling vegetable garden.

She stood admiring the tiny green shoots that were already pushing through the dark earth, then looked beyond the garden into the valley. They had worked hard in the past couple of weeks, and the result of their labours could be seen not only in this crude little hut, but in the animal folds, the partially cleared paddock and the outside kitchen, where a rough table and five chairs now took pride of place.

The camp oven stood pot-bellied above the blazing fire Kumali was tending, the sturdy pots and pans her father had forged hanging from hooks nearby. Duncan had built a lean-to byre for his breeding ewes, the chooks they'd purchased from a passing trader were pecking contentedly in their sturdy run, and the horses and oxen grazed alongside the sheep. Fergal had slung a makeshift canvas shelter between two trees down by the river, so he could go fishing, and she could see him now, sitting on the bank, the line in the water as he dozed.

"Happy New Year, Ruby."

She turned and smiled as James took her in his arms. "Our first in our new home," she breathed. "It couldn't be happier."

He drew back, plucked a stray curl from her damp cheek and tucked it behind her ear. "Not too lonely for you after all those family celebrations in Parramatta?"

190

"I miss them, yes," she replied honestly, "and it would have been lovely to see them again, but this is our dream and I am content."

He put his arm round her as they looked out upon the valley. "I get a feeling of great satisfaction to see what we've achieved in such a short time," he said. "Just think, Ruby, we are the first white people to settle in this valley, and for thousands of years it has just been sitting here waiting for us. It makes a man feel humble."

"Humble? You?" She giggled and dug him in the ribs. "That's like saying I'm a quiet, shy little thing who wouldn't say boo to a goose."

"Yeah, all right," he conceded bashfully. "But you know what I mean."

She nodded, thinking how Grandma Nell and Aunt Alice must have felt the same when confronted by miles of emptiness and the years of labour that lay ahead. Yet the thought didn't daunt her — it excited her.

"Time for presents," said James.

"It's not Christmas," she laughed.

"Just because we missed Christmas doesn't mean I can't give you presents," he replied as he led her back into the bark hut.

There were parcels on the bed, each tied with ribbon. "Where did these come from?" she asked delightedly, as she tore open the first.

"I had to hide them in my saddlebag for weeks. I hope they're not damaged after going through that river."

191

There was a beautifully sewn nightdress from her mother, a new pair of boots from her father, some riding gloves and a hat from her siblings, and a warm shawl from her aunt Sarah. Uncle Walter had sent two gold coins, which were swiftly added to her tin box and hidden behind the sacks of grain.

"This is from me," he said, his eyes gleaming with suppressed excitement.

She gasped as she drew back the brown paper to reveal a silver locket. "It's beautiful," she breathed.

"I bought it before we left Parramatta." He fastened the chain round her neck. "Your mother helped me choose it. I hope you like it."

"I love it." She kissed him passionately before pulling him out of the hut. "Come and see what I've got for you."

Racing down the hill, she came to a halt by a startled Duncan, who had been engrossed in his book. "Let him see," she said excitedly.

Duncan drew back the calico, his usually dour expression lightened by the hint of a smile.

The cow stood calmly chewing cud, her liquid brown eyes studying them with a certain air of curiosity as her calf nudged her udders and flicked its tiny tail.

James stroked the gleaming brown-and-white hide. "Where did she come from, and how did you get her here without me knowing?"

"Duncan fetched her from the Lathams when he went last week, and we kept her hidden in the eastern pasture until this morning." The Latham family had the nearest farm, which was about forty miles away.

James frowned. "She's of good stock, and the calf's a bonus, but how on earth did you pay for her?"

Ruby nervously licked her lips. "Papa gave me a little money before we left. I used some of that."

James eyed her, his thoughts unreadable. "How much did he give you, and why didn't you tell me about it?"

Ruby's happiness ebbed. "It was a wedding present to me," she said quietly. "I didn't realise . . ."

"No, you never do," he said bitterly.

Ruby noticed how Duncan had moved away, probably embarrassed by the exchange. "I wanted to surprise you," she persisted. "Please, James, don't be cross — not on such a special day."

"You've spent money we can ill afford on something we don't need," he muttered. "Money I had no knowledge of. What other secrets are you keeping from me, Ruby?" His tone was flat with suppressed anger.

This wasn't how she'd imagined it would be. She was bewildered by his attitude, unsure how to placate him. She'd waited days for this moment, had rehearsed what she would say and daydreamed about his reaction — now it was spoilt. "I do have one other secret," she confessed, "but I don't want to tell you when you're so cross."

He shoved his hands in his pockets, the shadow of his hat-brim not quite masking the angry expression. "Get on with it, Ruby."

Ruby took a deep breath. "I had a very good reason for buying the cow," she said, lifting her chin in defiance, "and in the months ahead she will prove more than her worth."

"I can't see how."

"Pregnant women need milk."

His eyes widened with shock. "You're pregnant?"

She nodded, the moment ruined. "I think it's due in June."

He took off his hat and ran his fingers through his hair. "We can't afford a baby, not yet," he muttered. "There's so much work to do, so many things we need."

Ruby fought the onset of tears. "A baby doesn't take much money to keep," she said defensively, "and I can work right up until it's born."

He saw the welling tears and must have realised how thoughtless he was being, for a hesitant smile softened his expression as he drew her into his arms. "Are you sure?"

She nodded, hope rising that at last he could share her joy.

He kissed the top of her head. "Oh, Ruby," he sighed, "the timing's all wrong, and you're going to find it tough with a baby, but you've given me the best present ever."

Ruby nestled into his embrace and listened to his soft endearments, but her heart was heavy. James was speaking the words she'd been longing to hear, but they didn't ring true after his initial reaction, and she knew that the baby she carried would change things between them for ever.

★ ★ ★

The flames flickered before their faces as they sat round the fire that night, and Kumali listened as the men tried to outdo each other with tales of their adventures. She had noticed Ruby was strangely quiet and guessed she and James had had some kind of argument. Kumali wondered what it was that had made Ruby so sad, but she was heavy-lidded with sleep, sated by the roasted vegetables and chicken they had eaten earlier, and her thoughts drifted.

The plum pudding had been delicious, and she licked her lips, savouring the stickiness that still lingered. There was lots of wine and rum to be had, for James had bought it from a dray that had come up from Melbourne on its way to Five Mile Creek, but her head felt strangely light after drinking so much and all she wanted to do was curl up in the possum blanket and sleep.

She moved closer to the fire and snuggled down, letting the warmth wash over her as the talk continued. Despite their isolation, Ruby and the others had come to know most of their far-flung neighbours, and they had been joined by some of them for this special occasion, each bringing something to eke out the feast. There were two local squatters, sons of Englishmen who'd come out here to seek their fortunes, an itinerant shepherd and two cattle drovers who were on their way east to a new job. Kumali had seen them stare at her, had known from their expressions they didn't approve of her, and had kept close to Duncan all evening.

"Why don't you stay here?" said James. "There is work enough for a hundred more like you."

The elder of the two drovers grimaced. "We go where the money is," he muttered. "They pay better out east and it ain't so isolated."

"You're free to choose, of course," said one of the Englishmen. "It's a pity there aren't still convicts about to do the work, as they were less fussy, and there's little point in trying to get the blacks to work — they're a bone-idle lot and run off as soon as you've fed them. I don't know how we'll cope now we have the spring lambs to contend with."

Kumali shrank further into the possum blanket as the man's scornful words sent a shiver of fear through her. It seemed her people would never be accepted and understood, but she had no right to defend them, or herself — better to pretend she hadn't heard.

The two Englishmen talked of England as home, despite having lived out here for over fifteen years.

"Bloody immigrants," snorted Fergal, who was sprawled on his back unable to sit after all the wine he'd had. "You come out here and still feel the need for Queen Victoria's apron strings. If you liked it so much, why did you leave in the first place?"

"The adventure, old chap, that's why. It's just a pity no one warned us of how primitive it all was."

The shepherds bemoaned the sheep-stealing, the threat of dingoes and Aboriginal attacks, and then the drovers complained about poddy-dodging — the theft of unbranded calves, which had become endemic throughout the region. Duncan talked of sickness among the beasts that could wipe out a flock within days and of the lack of help, which meant shepherds, drovers and squatters had to spend their days on horseback to watch over their animals. "We live like gypsies," he grumbled, "sleeping under trees at night and never in the same place two days running."

"Have another drink," said James, "and let's forget about our problems for tonight. We are supposed to be celebrating."

As the flames flickered and died and the talking ceased, they wrapped themselves in coats and fur cloaks to ward off the night chill and were soon snoring.

Kumali, who had dozed for a while, lay on her back and looked up. The stars were so bright and numerous in the Great White Way that she felt she could reach out and pluck them from the sky. Nestled beneath the pelt of possum, she turned from this celestial display and watched the sleeping Duncan, who lay a few feet away. He had been as good as his word, treating her kindly ever since she had agreed to stay with him, and yet, as she watched him sleep, she wondered what it would be like to crawl beneath the pelts that covered him, to feel his arms round her and share the intimacy of his bed.

In sleep his face became youthful, the lines of care and his usual grumpiness rubbed away. She looked at the strong, capable hands that lay outside the furs, knowing how gentle they were when he birthed a lamb, or tended a sick ewe or dog, saw the strength in his face, the set of his brow and the width of his shoulders. He was a strange man, with his books of poetry and his Jew's harp — sometimes taciturn, wanting his own company, and at others only too happy to tell her about

197

his life in Scotland, where he'd worked for someone called a laird and had tended a vast flock of sheep.

The wanting had begun some time ago, and now Kumali could feel the heat of it rising as she watched the sleeping man. As if her scrutiny had pierced his dreams, Duncan opened his eyes. In silence they stared at one another. Kumali wondered if this was the time to go to him, but as she made to rise, he rolled over and hunched beneath the pelts.

She cupped her cheek in her hand as she watched his shoulders rise and fall with his breath and felt content, for Duncan's eyes had told her more than any words, and when he decided it was time for them to come together, she would go to him willingly.

CHAPTER
SEVEN

Kernow House, Watsons Bay, June 1850

The lamps had been lit to dispel the gloom of a rainy winter's day, and there was a fire glowing in the hearth, but Harry was becoming increasingly irritated by what he was reading in the newspaper. "Utterly ridiculous," he snorted, rustling the paper.

"What is?" Lavinia regarded him with amusement as she put down her needlework.

"Australia's colonial legislature, not London, should hold the power to collect taxes, the revenue arising from the sale of Crown land. It's utter madness that the colony legislators should have to refer all measures of importance, no matter how great the urgency, to an inexperienced, remote and irresponsible department in London. As if those idiots know anything about the needs of this place, or the trouble they are causing by being pig-headed."

"Oh dear," she sighed, "you are out of sorts."

"Well, it's preposterous!" He threw the paper aside and glared out at the rain. "It's all very well giving the power to those who own land and property — there is no aristocracy here — but the majority will not stand for it, mark my words, Lavinia. This is a colony with convict roots and any elitism will be stamped out. It will be impossible to maintain authority here if London holds the whip."

Lavinia poured a cup of tea and handed it to him in silence before pouring one for herself.

Harry nodded his thanks, but his thoughts were far beyond the drawing room. "No one has given proper thought to the sort of constitution needed here — that's the problem. For all their bluff and bluster, these legislative councils have no real experience in local government, and with the wide dispersal of settlement, it will be almost impossible to administer. Then there are the disadvantages of trying to have four colonial parliaments legislating on such things as railways and customs duties. I declare, Lavinia, every one of those blasted railways is run on a different gauge. It's a complete fiasco!"

"Then perhaps it is a good thing we are returning to England at the end of the month," she said, eyeing him over her cup. "As a member of the House of Lords, you will be perfectly suited in experience and knowledge to advise Her Majesty's Government on how to run the colony in a more satisfactory manner."

"By Gad, I will too," he muttered. "Russell's an idiot if he thinks the colony will just sit back and take orders from London. Australia needs to advance, to stand on her own two feet and prove herself to the rest of the world, and she can't do that if she's tied to Queen Victoria's ridiculous rules and regulations. There will be another Boston Tea Party, and I for one would support it."

"Harry!"

"Sorry, my dear, but it makes me hot under the collar."

"So I noticed. Drink your tea, dear. You'll find it will soothe you."

Harry glumly sipped tea and stared out of the window, his thoughts churning over how to approach the prickly problem in the House of Lords — but approach it he would, and tonight, once the house was quiet, he would set out his ideas and commit them to paper.

The sound of a carriage trundling up the driveway brought him back to the present, and he frowned as he saw the unfamiliar vehicle. "Are you or Amelia expecting visitors?"

"Amelia's resting and has made no mention of visitors." Lavinia followed his gaze and watched as the passenger alighted. "Who is that?"

"It's Niall Logan. What on earth does he want?" Harry got to his feet as Niall ran through the rain and up the front steps. The Irishman was ashen-faced, his hands agitatedly tugging at his coat. "Something's wrong. I'll go and talk to him."

"There you are, thank God. It's Oliver," panted Niall.

"Oliver?" Harry felt a chill. "Where is he?"

"In my carriage."

Harry ran down the steps and flung open the carriage door. The sight that greeted him chilled him further, for Oliver was slumped on the seat, his face distorted by violent spasms. His eyes were bulging, and his right arm and leg were twitching in the most alarming manner. "Help me get him into the house," he ordered the coachman.

The rain was teeming as they struggled to get him out of the coach. Oliver was heavy, and the spasms that shook him made it almost impossible to carry him. "We need more help," Harry shouted, but it was already there, as the servants were pouring out of the house at the sound of the commotion.

"What is it? What's happened?" Amelia's shrill voice pierced through the quiet murmurs of the men as they lifted Oliver out of the carriage. "Oliver!" she screamed. "Oliver, no!" She shook off Lavinia's hand and practically threw herself at her husband.

"Calm yourself, Amelia," barked Harry, who was in no mood for her hysterics. "Get her away, Lavinia."

The five men carried Oliver into the house and up the stairs as Amelia wailed. Harry kicked open the bedroom door and they deposited his brother on the large canopied bed. "Have you sent for a doctor?" he asked Niall, as Gertrude quietly took charge and began to loosen Oliver's collar.

"I've sent a runner to the infirmary. He should be here soon."

"You'd have done better to take him straight there," muttered Harry. "I don't like the look of him at all." He wiped the rain from his face.

"Oliver, Oliver, oh my darling, what's happened?" Amelia's face was drained of colour and tear-streaked as she ran into the room, thrust Gertrude aside and threw herself on to the recumbent form. "Speak to me, Oliver. Tell me what's wrong."

Harry hauled her off and held her tightly as she struggled. "I think he's had a seizure," he said, with more composure than he felt. "Throwing yourself at him isn't going to help. Amelia, you must stay calm. Give him air and let Gertrude tend him until the doctor comes."

"He's going to die!" she keened. "I just know it."

"No, you don't," he said sharply. "Stop it, Amelia."

Her blue eyes widened at his tone, but it seemed to have calmed her.

"Papa?"

Harry whirled round, saw the two frightened boys standing in the doorway and thrust Amelia into Lavinia's arms. "Get her out of those wet clothes and keep her quiet," he ordered. "I'll see to the boys." He drew them down the hall to Charlie's room.

"Is Papa dead?" Freddy's voice was very small, his expression bewildered and frightened.

Harry put his hand on the boy's shoulder. "No, but he is very ill, so I want both you boys to be brave." He saw the little face blanch and his heart went out to him. "Come, Freddy," he coaxed. "Your papa is a big strong man — he will pull through, I'm sure of it."

"Do you promise?"

Harry knew he couldn't lie, but the pain of the truth was so great he could barely speak. "I . . . I . . . can only pray that he will," he admitted.

203

"Will the doctor be able to make him well again?" The hope was evident in his eyes.

"I don't know, Freddy. All we can do is wait and see." Harry lapsed into silence. How to find the words to console a small boy when his own fears were raging? It was impossible.

They were still sitting there in an uneasy silence when the swish of Lavinia's skirts heralded her arrival. "You're needed in the other room, Harry," she murmured. "I'll take over here."

Harry looked for some positive sign that his brother would indeed pull through, but he saw only strain in her drawn features and the pessimistic slant of her shoulders. "Amelia?"

"I gave her laudanum and put her to bed. She'll sleep for the rest of the afternoon."

Harry gave a consoling smile to the two boys, wished he could have done more to ease their fears and left them to Lavinia's more tender care.

Oliver's grand bedroom had already taken on the aura of a sickroom, with the shuttered windows and low, flickering lamplight. A fire had been lit in the hearth, but it did little to diffuse the gloom. Niall and the doctor were in consultation at the bedside, while Gertrude administered a cooling cloth to the fevered brow and cruelly distorted face. Harry noted that the awful twitching had ceased, but his brother lay supine and was troublingly still as the leeches on his chest slowly swelled with his blood.

"Sir Harry." The doctor bowed low.

"How is he?" Harry had no time for formalities.

The plump little man pursed his lips, his winged eyebrows drawing together as he assumed a solemn air. "I'm afraid, sir, that your brother has had a seizure."

"I gathered that much," Harry snapped. "What kind of seizure?"

"A seizure of the brain, sir — that is why his face has been drawn down to one side and his right limbs are affected." He sighed and stroked his moustache. "We will not know how severe the seizure was until he awakens from his stupor, but I suspect he will suffer a certain amount of paralysis and might have difficulty with speech."

"Will he get better?"

The delicate, pale hand waved in the air. "We can only apply the leeches and hope they will thin the blood that has clotted in his brain," he replied. "Some patients recover fully, but others are left with permanent disabilities. It all depends on the success of the blood-letting."

"Is there a likelihood of further attacks?" Harry looked down at his brother. Oliver suddenly looked old and shrunken in that vast bed. Where there had once been vitality and strength, now there was only sonorous breathing, and the grotesque mask of a face that bore little resemblance to the man he'd been hours before.

"There is," said the doctor, with a woeful expression. "He must be watched most carefully over the coming weeks, and although I will attend every day, it will be necessary to arrange for a nurse to stay with him. He'll need expert care from now on."

205

"I am perfectly capable of looking after my brother," interrupted Gertrude.

"Of course you are," soothed Harry. "But you cannot do it alone." He turned back to the doctor. "Please have a nurse sent as soon as possible. There is plenty of room here to accommodate her."

"There would be a fee . . ." The doctor looked embarrassed.

"Of course," rasped Harry. "Send your accounts to me."

As the doctor left, Harry turned to Niall. "We need to talk," he said quietly. They went back downstairs, and Harry ordered a fresh pot of tea for himself and a whisky for Niall. "What happened to trigger this?" he asked, when they were settled.

"The Sydney Railway Company has gone bankrupt," the older man said, as he sipped the whisky. "I can't say it comes as any surprise; it was always a possibility when one considered the haphazard way they went about things."

The lilt of the Irishman's voice filled the room, and Harry detected a hint of disapproval in those blue eyes. "You must be relieved you've escaped unscathed," he replied, rather more sharply than intended.

Niall shook his head. "I take no pleasure in another's downfall," he replied.

"I apologise. I didn't mean . . ."

Niall shrugged away the apology and sat forward in his chair. "I did try to warn Oliver that the finances wouldn't be enough, but of course he's not a man to take advice from an ex-convict." His smile was wry.

"The bank has foreclosed and the syndicate has lost everything they invested."

"But surely such an important enterprise will be taken up by the government?"

Niall gave a deep sigh. "It will pick up the pieces because of the need to have the railways opening up the interior, but the original investment is lost."

Harry watched the Irishman finish his whisky. There was no sign of triumph, no feeling that Niall was crowing over the fact his money was safe — the contract to lay the steel and provide the workforce was still in place regardless of who paid the bills. Instead there seemed to be a profound sadness in the man, an understanding of the consequences of today's events.

"I wish my brother had heeded your advice, and that he possessed your business acumen."

The blue gaze was direct in that handsome face. "We are all different, each set on our separate paths to achieve more than the generation before. You cannot blame Oliver for being ambitious." He set the glass aside and stood. "I will take my leave, Sir Harry. Please keep me informed, and if there is anything I can do to help, you have only to ask."

Harry returned the firm handshake and followed him outside. Heedless of the rain, he stood on the steps long after the carriage had gone, his thoughts troubled. His plans to return to England within the month were in tatters, and until he had more idea of how things would turn out, he couldn't make any decisions at all. He looked up at the shuttered windows and, with dread, re-entered the house.

Eden Valley, the next day

Ruby had carried the disappointment with her as the child inside her grew. James had given up pretending he was pleased with the idea of becoming a father, and in the past months had rarely spent a night in the bark hut.

She understood that he and the others had to keep an eye on the increasing flock, and that it was necessary to remain far from the hut if they were to be protected from dingoes and thieving neighbours, and yet she ached for the tenderness they had once shared, longed for the moments of intimacy that had bound them so closely and despaired at his disregard for her well-being. It was as if he didn't love her, and as the months had dragged on, she'd become convinced James resented the coming child — was perhaps even jealous of it.

She put these thoughts firmly aside as she smeared rain from her face and tried to find a more comfortable position in the saddle. She had been riding the boundary, checking the fences since before dawn, and now there was a persistent ache in her back. Sliding from the saddle, she stretched and eased her aching muscles, and decided she would find shelter among the trees. Duncan and Kumali were camping somewhere nearby, and she'd thought she'd seen a wisp of smoke rising through the bush canopy.

With her head bent against the rain, she led the horse into the trees and followed the scent of woodsmoke and cooking fish. Her stomach rumbled at the enticing

208

thought of food. She hadn't eaten since the previous night, and the cup of milk she'd had this morning had not been enough to sustain her through the day.

As she approached the camp, she heard Kumali's laughter, and when she caught a glimpse of them through the trees, she drew back. They were sitting beneath a canvas shelter on a bed of dried ferns, and Duncan's usually dour expression was soft as he tried to teach the Aboriginal girl to read from the simple book Ruby had given her a few months before.

Ruby watched as, unaware of her presence, the black girl and the Scotsman forgot about the reading lesson and gazed into one another's eyes. His hand cupped her cheek, the thumb gently caressing the narrowness of her chin and the arch of her neck. He spoke, and though the words were too soft to hear against the patter of the rain, there was little doubt they were words of endearment.

Ruby felt her tears mingle with the rain as she saw the tenderness of his kiss, and she turned away as Duncan gently took Kumali in his arms and drew her down to that bed of ferns. Feeling like an intruder, Ruby quietly left the glade and found shelter further to the east. As she sat huddled beneath a tree, her voluminous oilskin keeping off the worst of the rain, she began to sob, the disappointment and hurt bursting through the dam she'd so carefully built over the past months. How she longed for such tenderness, how she wished James still looked at her in that way, but here she was, cold, wet and lonely, with a pain in her back that seemed to have shifted and strengthened.

209

The realisation brought an abrupt halt to the tears and she pressed her hands over her swollen belly. It was as taut as a drum, and as the pain tightened its grip, she felt her waters break. She knew then that her baby was about to be born, knew what to expect, for her mother had warned her.

"I must get help," she muttered, as she struggled to her feet, caught up the reins and leant against the mare's neck. "Come on, girl," she coaxed, as she led the horse through the trees.

A few minutes later there was another wave of pain. She gasped at its ferocity and leant, trembling, against the mare's flanks. "Steady, girl," she panted. "Don't spook now or I'll be done for."

As if sensing Ruby's predicament, the mare snuffled her cheek and waited patiently until the pain ebbed. With the decorum of a maiden aunt attending church, she obeyed Ruby's orders and slowly picked her way through the undergrowth, stopping only when Ruby needed to deal with another contraction.

Ruby could smell the campfire now. "Duncan," she called against the rattle of rain on the overhead trees, "Duncan, I need your help."

"What is it, lassie?" He appeared out of the gloom, Kumali close behind him. "Och," he sighed, as he hurried to her side. "Nae need to fret now. We'll take care of you. Do you think ye can make it to my camp? I have shelter there, and it's better to be out of the rain."

Ruby nodded and bit down on a cry as another wave of agony tore through her, and yet, as she released the

210

mare's reins, the world seemed to spin and she would have fallen if Duncan hadn't swept her into his arms.

"Get the horse, Kumali," he ordered.

Ruby felt the softness of bracken beneath her as Duncan carefully lowered her into the canvas shelter. His eyes were concerned as his knowledgeable fingers gently kneaded her swollen belly. "Tisnae right for me to be doing this, lassie," he murmured. "I'll send Kumali to fetch someone."

She grabbed his arm. "There isn't time," she panted, "and you have experience enough with birthing."

He reddened. "Nae this kind," he muttered.

"I don't care," she gasped. "This baby is about to be born and I need your help. Get on with it, Duncan!"

"Aye, well, if you're sure."

Ruby glared at him with such venom he actually looked to Kumali for guidance. Kumali shrugged and dropped a knife into a billycan of boiling water, as Duncan had taught her to do when they birthed lambs. "Go away, Duncan," she said bossily. "I take off her clothes and get the blanket."

"No!" shouted Ruby. "You don't go anywhere."

"Let me get you dry. Then Duncan help alonga you baby."

Ruby eyed the rather stern Kumali and stopped fighting. It seemed the girl and Duncan knew what they were doing and Kumali, bless her, was only trying to protect her dignity. "Hurry, Kumali," she gasped. "The baby is coming."

An hour passed before the wail of the newborn child rose along with the woodsmoke and drifted above the canopy of trees into the grey sky. Duncan cut and tied the cord, and Kumali wrapped the infant in what remained of Ruby's petticoat, placing the precious bundle in Ruby's arms.

"She's beautiful," Ruby sobbed, as she touched the velvety cheek and traced her finger through the damp, dark red hair. "Oh my God, she's a miracle."

"Aye, all babies are miracles, be they sheep or bairns." Duncan smiled as he returned from burying the afterbirth, rested back on his haunches and put an arm round Kumali's shoulders. "She's a bonny wee lassie. Have you and James thought of a name for her?"

Ruby looked up at the Scotsman and knew she couldn't tell him how distant James had been, how he'd refused to accept the idea of a child coming so soon after they had arrived here, much less given thought to naming her. She looked back at her precious child, saw how blue her eyes were and came to a decision.

"I will call her Violet Nell Alice Tyler," she said. "Violet for her eyes, Nell and Alice in memory of two inspirational women. I hope their spirit lives on through her as it does in me." She looked back at Duncan and Kumali. "Thank you both. Now, if you wouldn't mind, I'd like to go home."

James had been erecting fences in a distant pasture for over a week. He returned home finally to discover Ruby digging in her vegetable garden, the baby swaddled in a shawl against her back. "When did this happen?" he asked, as he regarded the baby.

"Five days ago."

"She's very small," he said nervously, as Ruby put her in his arms.

"Her name is Violet Nell Alice Tyler." Ruby watched as he stared at their baby in perplexed wonder. Perhaps now she was here, he would warm to the idea of fatherhood.

"I would have liked to have called her Gladys, after my mother," he said, returning the infant to Ruby, "but it seems the decision is out of my hands."

To Ruby's mind, Gladys was a horrible name — far too ugly for such a beautiful child — but if James was ever to accept their daughter, then some compromise had to be made. "Violet Gladys Nell Alice Tyler is a bit of a mouthful, but I don't see why not," she murmured.

"Gladys Violet is enough," he muttered. He kissed her forehead and grabbed his hat. "I'm taking Fergal off to celebrate. There's a new bush tavern at Five Mile Creek, and the supplies were due to be delivered today. I could do with a drink."

"But you've been away so much, I thought . . ."

"Babies are women's work, Ruby. You don't need me getting under your feet."

Ruby stood in the dark earth of her vegetable garden with the infant in her arms and watched her husband ride away. She doubted she would see him before the end of the week, for the bush-hut taverns were notorious drinking dens. The hurt of his dismissive welcome to their daughter rankled, and as she fought the onset of frustrated tears, she vowed to remain strong.

"Come on, Violet. Let's get on with this, and then we'll start on the laundry. It looks as if your papa has other things on his mind."

Kernow House, Watsons Bay, a few days later

Oliver was propped against a mountain of pillows in the gloomy bedroom. There had been no further seizures, but he had yet to speak and had great difficulty in moving his right limbs, which obviously frustrated him, for although he was helpless, his eyes were alert as he tried to communicate.

Harry was sitting by the bed, the newspaper spread on the covers as he read out interesting snippets. The nurse was asleep upstairs, having sat with him through the night, Lavinia had taken the boys for a ride, and Gertrude was in her usual place at Oliver's side, fussing with a cool cloth.

The door opened and Amelia stood there, surveying the scene. She had been a rare visitor during the previous week, seemingly unable to bear the sight of her husband in such a poor state without bursting into hysterical tears, but today, Harry noted, there was a certain determination in her he hadn't witnessed before.

"Leave that, Gertrude," she said, as she swept into the room. "I will see to my husband."

"You have no experience of a sickroom," retorted Gertrude, as she wrung out the cloth. "It would be better if you stayed away."

214

"Then it is time I learnt." Harry watched in amazement as his sister-in-law snatched the cloth, dumped it in the basin and handed both to Gertrude. "He doesn't need that," she snapped. "Can't you see he's sick of being pawed about?"

"'Pawed about'?" Gertrude was ashen with shock as she rose from the chair. "I'll have you know I'm an expert nurse, and the last thing he needs is you caterwauling over him." She held the basin against her narrow chest, which rose and fell with pent-up fury.

"This is my house, and Oliver is my husband. You seem to have forgotten your place, Gertrude."

"My *place*?" Gertrude squeaked.

Harry busied himself with the newspaper, unwilling to be drawn into this argument, but absolutely fascinated as to the outcome.

Gertrude collected what was left of her dignity. "You were content enough for me to take over the running of your house," she rasped, "and to allow me to nurse your husband this past week, so don't you *dare* talk to me like that."

"I'll talk to you in any way I wish." Amelia's expression was grim. "I let you run things because you took over and made it impossible for me to be mistress of my own home. But you are not the chatelaine."

Gertrude reddened, then snorted in a most unladylike fashion. "You can't manage your clothing allowance, much less organise servants and the day-to-day accounts. I dread to think what would have happened if you'd been left in charge all these years."

Amelia sat in the chair recently vacated by Gertrude and took her husband's hand. "You have succeeded admirably, and I thank you, but I managed very well before your arrival. Now the time has come for me to take charge again."

"You couldn't take charge of a pan of milk," sneered Gertrude.

"I'll thank you to keep a civil tongue, miss," snapped Amelia. "You forget, Gertrude, I am the daughter of an army officer and perfectly capable of running my home and my affairs without interference from a sour spinster."

"How *dare* you?"

"And how dare *you* assume you are indispensable?"

Harry admired this fiery Amelia, but decided things had gone far enough. "Gertie, why don't you go and find us a nice pot of tea? I'm sure we could do with some refreshment."

"I am *not* a servant to be ordered about," she hissed.

Harry gently steered her towards the door. "I know, my dear," he murmured, "but I think it might be wise to let things cool down, don't you?"

She shot a murderous glance at Amelia and left.

"Thank you, Harry." Amelia smiled as she held Oliver's hand and lovingly stroked his hair back from his twisted face. "I'm sorry you had to witness that, but I realised things couldn't go on as they were." She gave a deep sigh. "I've been a fool to allow Gertrude to bully me, and I admit I let her have her way because it was easier than arguing all the time, but Oliver's illness has brought me to my senses. My husband and son need

216

me to be strong, and I am determined not to let them down again."

"Bravo to you," Harry said softly. "Your fire is quite admirable, Amelia, and I commend your new-found determination, but looking after a sick man is not the easiest task, and with Gertie in high dudgeon, you will have the household as well as Freddy to consider."

"The nurse will advise me on what to do, and I am quick to learn." She smiled ruefully. "Freddy has Charlie to occupy him. As for the household, there are more important things to consider, and I hope the servants are loyal enough to get on with what they do best." She kissed Oliver's brow and smiled adoringly into his eyes. "I may appear to be giddy, but my upbringing in army quarters made me much tougher than I let on. I am my father's daughter, Sir Harry, and not easily defeated."

He bent and kissed the soft cheek. "I admire your tenacity, Amelia, and of course Lavinia and I will do everything we can to help you through this."

Amelia gently lifted Oliver's head while he sipped some water. Dabbing his chin with a clean square of linen, she eased him back into the pillows. "Your ship is due to sail at the end of the month, and I understand you have not yet cancelled your passage. I think it might be wise to carry on with your plans."

"I cannot leave while Oliver is so ill, Amelia."

She folded her hands in her lap, her strength of purpose clear in her deportment. "I'm not asking you to," she said. "I'm proposing Lavinia and Gertrude go with the boys. Freddy has already missed far too much schooling and shouldn't be stuck here in this gloomy house." She looked at Oliver. "I think you will agree, my dear," she said softly, "that it would be for the best."

Oliver blinked and his mouth struggled to form words, but his left hand squeezed her fingers as if to confirm his agreement.

"But I can't let Lavinia and Gertie travel all that way alone," protested Harry.

"They are both capable women, and I am sure they understand that my need for your help is greater than theirs. You see, Harry, there are certain things I cannot do, and I will need you to run Oliver's business affairs until he is well again."

Harry doubted Oliver would ever again be strong enough for commerce, but kept silent. As for remaining here without his wife and son; that was a different matter. "Have you asked Gertie if she's willing to go to England?"

Amelia gave a knowing smile. "After today I suspect Gertrude will want to get as far from me as possible."

"So that little scene was part of your plan?" Harry stared at her with admiration and astonishment.

"Gertrude is far too settled here and should think about expanding her horizons," said Amelia rather tartly. Her eyes were bright as she looked at him. "I just gave her a prod in the right direction, that's all."

"I never suspected you of being devious," he replied, with a shake of his head. "Poor Gertie, she never stood a chance, did she?"

"Not really." She cocked her head. "So, Harry, will you stay and help me?"

"I have already neglected my estates for too long, Amelia, and even though I have only given cursory attention to Oliver's business affairs, I can see it will take months — even years — to repair the damage inflicted by the railway fiasco."

It was as if he hadn't spoken. "Lavinia assures me she is perfectly capable of running your estates."

"You have spoken to Lavinia?" Harry was rather startled that his wife had kept this piece of information to herself. Perhaps she hadn't taken Amelia's proposal seriously. Until today none of them had suspected her hidden steel.

Amelia nodded. "She is amenable to the idea and assures me her papa will be on hand to advise her should a problem arise."

"I cannot expect my father-in-law and my wife to oversee the estates for what could turn out to be years," he protested. "You ask too much, Amelia."

"I ask only what is my right," she replied, her gaze steady. "I do not really expect you to remain here for years — that would be too selfish — but as a man of honour, surely you must see that your duty lies with your brother? He needs you, Harry, just as I do." She looked up at him, the determination squaring her shoulders and lifting her chin. "So, will you help us?"

He realised she had him cornered, and although he admired this new-found strength of purpose in Amelia, he didn't appreciate being railroaded into making decisions of such importance without giving them due thought. "If Lavinia agrees, then I will stay, but the situation is to be reviewed every six months, and should there be a crisis at home, then . . ."

"Thank you," she sighed. "That is a great weight off my mind. Now I can concentrate on my husband's needs."

Harry looked down at Oliver, saw the gratitude in that distorted face and felt the weight of his responsibilities press down on him. "I must find Lavinia," he muttered. "There is a great deal to discuss if she is to leave by the end of the month."

Lawrence Creek, Hunter Valley, the same day

The rain's thunder on the tin roof made her ears ring. Jessie gave up trying to hear the children recite their times table and wrote a few sums on the board so the younger ones could work individually on their slates. With the older children settled in one corner with their readers, she paced along the lines of desks, making sure each child was fully occupied.

The fire had been lit earlier that morning, and the cheerful blaze took the edge off the chill as the damp coats steamed on the clothes horse in front of it. Kerosene lamps flickered and smoked from their hooks in the ceiling, their feeble light doing little to dispel the gloom. As she passed a window, she looked out at the paddock and the miserable ponies huddled beneath the trees, their coats sodden, necks drooping. It was not a day to be outside, and yet these children had ridden here and would ride home again, regardless of the weather.

She was about to turn from the window when she caught sight of a wagon emerging through the curtain of rain. The driver was huddled in the folds of a hefty coat, his face masked by the brim of his hat as he dug his chin into the collar. Jessie watched the horse plod through the puddles, and as the wagon drew to a halt outside the main house, she felt a surge of pleasure. It was Abel Cruickshank.

"Carry on with your work," she said, as she grabbed her shawl and battered umbrella. "I must attend to our visitor. I won't be more than a few minutes."

She hurried out into the rain, dodging the puddles as she ran across the yard to the veranda. Out of breath, she blushed as his grey eyes met hers and she was forcefully reminded of how very handsome he was. "Mr Lawrence is visiting a sick parishioner with Mrs Blake," she said, as she shook out her umbrella. "He isn't due to return until this evening." She looked up at Abel, blushed again and wished she'd taken a moment to tidy her hair.

"Good afternoon, Miss Searle," he drawled, tipping his hat, his laughing eyes looking down at her. "No worries, I don't need to see him anyway." His gaze held her for a moment before he began to unload the sacks and boxes.

"You have been a stranger these past months, Mr Cruickshank."

"I've been busy," he replied, as he placed a sack on the veranda.

"Did you have a good harvest, Mr Cruickshank?" She was desperately trying to find something to say that would keep him a little longer.

"Good enough."

"Does that mean you can at last make wine?"

His mouth twitched with a smile, the laughing eyes glinting as they swept over her. "It won't be up to much: the vines are still too immature, unlike the vintage the von Schmidts produce. But then you must be familiar with their wines, having been such a frequent guest to Possum Hills."

She reddened. News obviously spread quickly out here. "Frieda von Schmidt is head of the Hunter Valley Ladies' Group. I was honoured to be invited to join such prestigious company, and she has made me very welcome."

"I'm sure she has." The unloading done, he leant against the railings. His coat had fallen open, and where his shirt had become unbuttoned, Jessie could see the tanned flesh of his broad chest.

Jessie hurriedly looked away. "What do you mean by that?"

He shrugged. "It's a well-known fact the old lady wants her son married and producing heirs before she dies, so your arrival here must have cheered her up no end."

"Don't be ridiculous," she blustered.

He raised an eyebrow and folded his arms. "You seemed pretty taken with him at the dance," he drawled.

222

"He was merely making sure I had a pleasant evening."

"Yeah. By monopolising you so no one else got a look-in."

"I danced with lots of people." She lifted her chin, but couldn't quite meet his gaze. "I am a busy woman, Mr Cruickshank," she said rather haughtily, "and as I'm sure you didn't come all this way to discuss my social life, perhaps you'd better tell me why you're really here."

He raised a wry eyebrow and pointed at the stores he'd stacked on the veranda. "And I've brought the mail." He drew a packet of letters from the inside pocket of his oilskin coat, but didn't hand them over. "There's a couple in there for you, and I also picked up the new boots Mr Lawrence ordered." He dangled the boots by their laces.

Her pulse raced with hope that at last she had received a reply from the Church Board.

Abel dumped the boots on top of a sack, but maintained his grip on the packet of letters. "Miss Searle," he said, clearing his throat, his gaze not quite meeting hers, "would you consider . . .?"

Their fingers touched as Jessie reached for the packet, and she was finding it hard to breathe. "Yes, Mr Cruickshank?"

He let go of the letters, yanked his hat-brim and looked away. "Never mind," he muttered.

Jessie could see he was about to leave. "Please," she said breathlessly, "what would you like me to consider?"

"It was a stupid idea. Let's forget it, shall we?"

"Stupid idea or not, I should like to hear it," she persisted, realising this was another moment that could be lost for ever if she didn't do something. "Please, Mr Cruickshank."

The colour rose in his face as he rammed his hands into his coat pockets and refused to look at her. "I reckon I was gunna ask you if you'd like to see my place," he muttered. "But of course you wouldn't be interested, not after being entertained at Possum Hills."

"I would like that very much," she replied.

His grey eyes widened as he looked down at her. "You would?"

She nodded and smiled encouragement, even though doubts were crowding in. If there was no letter from the Church Board, then Mr Lawrence would not give his permission, so how on earth could she make such a promise?

"Don't expect anything grand," he said hastily. "Me and Tumbalong make the best of things, and the house isn't up to much, but I'm a dab hand at cooking, so you won't go hungry."

"Please don't go to any special trouble on my account," she murmured, afraid now that she would have to let him down if Mr Lawrence forbade her from going.

"I can entertain as well as anyone in this valley," he replied mulishly.

"I have no doubt of it."

"So you'll come, then?"

224

She swept aside the doubts and nodded. "But I would have to seek Mr Lawrence's permission."

He eyed her thoughtfully. "He doesn't object to you going over to Possum Hills."

"That's because I'm chaperoned by Mrs von Schmidt."

"Mrs Blake is a good sort. Ask her to come with you."

She dared to look at him and found reasonable thought fled the moment their gazes met. "I'm sure she would be delighted to accompany me — as long as Mr Lawrence agrees."

A slow smile made his eyes twinkle with mischief. "He's going to Newcastle Saturday week. Perhaps that would be a good time to arrange your visit?"

She knew she was playing with fire, but couldn't help it. "That would be perfect," she agreed.

Abel grinned. "I'll come early — then you'll have time to really see the place." He ran down the steps, clambered on to the wagon and, with a wave of his hat, set the horse into a trot.

Jessie watched until he was out of sight. She no longer saw the rain, or felt its chill, for Abel's smile had chased away the gloom. Several minutes passed before she remembered she had a classroom of children waiting for her, and as she ran through the rain, she had to resist the urge to dance in the puddles.

CHAPTER
EIGHT

Kernow House, Watsons Bay, 29 June 1850

Freddy watched the carriage bowl away and turned from the window. Charlie and his mother had gone shopping and would not be back for some time. Aunt Gertrude was closeted with the dressmaker making last-minute alterations to her travelling wardrobe, and Uncle Harry was working his way through the accounts. His mama was in her usual place at Papa's bedside. To all intents and purposes, he had the house to himself.

He stood in the silent drawing room and etched the familiar surroundings into his memory — for this house, and everything in it, was all he'd known, and it would be many years before he would see it again. As he wandered through the dining room and into the entrance hall, he saw the trunks and boxes that would be taken to the docks tomorrow morning. Now the chaos of packing was almost at an end, he felt a sense of finality — there would be no change of heart, no altering of plans. The ship would sail and he would leave for England — far from home, his parents and a way of life he'd thought would never change.

A pang of something akin to fear twisted inside him, and he hurried up the stairs, determined to banish such emotions. His twelfth birthday had been a solemn affair due to his father's illness, and boys his age didn't cry — no matter how scared they were. And yet, as he tiptoed past his parents' bedroom, he had to battle the overwhelming need to throw himself on their mercy and beg to be allowed to stay.

The sanctuary of the old attic nursery welcomed him, and as he lit the lantern, a sense of calm descended. There were the familiar boxes, the jumble of discarded toys and furniture, the sturdy pillars of the chimneys and the dark rafters. He crossed the scarred floor to the rocking horse and stroked the remains of the blond mane, remembering the many races he'd ridden on that faded saddle. Pegasus had once seemed so imposing with his scarlet saddle and flowing mane and tail; now he just looked rather forlorn and moth-eaten, his stirrups black with age, the reins missing. He set it in motion and the rockers creaked as Pegasus's shadow moved on the wall — a reminder of boyhood, of times when things were simple.

He stilled the horse and, with a sigh, turned away. Eyeing the trunks that had been discarded as unsuitable for travelling to England, he half-heartedly rummaged through them as he'd done so many times before. There was the usual collection of old clothes, curtains and linens, and he quickly lost interest. As he was about to close the lid, however, he saw a small tin box he hadn't noticed before. He drew it out and felt a flutter of excitement. The metal hasp glinted in the lamplight, proof it hadn't been stowed away until recently, but as he carefully pulled out the pin and pushed back the lid, he felt sharp disappointment. It was empty.

He sat in the silence, deep in thought. The fact that it was empty didn't really matter, for it was big enough for his needs. He crossed to the hidden niche and pressed the catch. He'd meant to move the book, but had become distracted by other things; now he hoped it was still there.

It was many months since he'd last crawled into this space, and he discovered it was a very tight squeeze. Sweating from his efforts, and mindful of how easy it would be to get stuck, his searching fingers finally found what he was looking for and he breathed a sigh of relief.

The journal had been nibbled at the edges, and the tiny clasp had dropped off, but it didn't appear to have suffered much damage. He placed the journal inside the box. It was a perfect fit, and now it would be protected from mice and possums until he returned from England. Hopefully, by then he would be able to decipher what was written inside. The idea that it was a pirate journal had long since been dismissed as childish, and he suspected it was merely the private diary of some long-dead member of the German side of his family, but his curiosity remained strong and he was determined to solve the mystery.

228

Having placed the box back into the niche, he sighed with satisfaction and left. He would spend the rest of the afternoon with his parents, for after tomorrow he wouldn't see them again until he was eighteen.

Lawrence Creek, Hunter Valley, the same day

The letter from the Church Board had not come, and despite her initial disappointment, Jessie felt relieved. Mr Lawrence would accuse her — quite rightly — of going behind his back, and it could make for a very awkward situation. Then, of course, there was always the possibility the board would agree with Mr Lawrence, and if that was the case, she would have little chance of changing things.

She had come to the conclusion that her hastily penned request had been a mistake. It wasn't as if she'd come all this way to find a husband, and even though Gerhardt von Schmidt was an attentive host — and Abel Cruickshank seemed keen to carry on the friendship they had begun on the journey here — she couldn't honestly claim she was being courted.

Jessie had accepted that things had turned out for the best and had become immersed in her brother Daniel's letters. They had raised her spirits, and she'd read them many times during the past two weeks. His writing was poor, his spelling even weaker, but his efforts were more legible than John's, who had proved an unwilling student when Jessie had suggested they learn to read and write before they left Cornwall.

It was Saturday morning, and she sat in the pre-dawn gloom trying to picture the place called Kapunda. Daniel had been quite descriptive about the mud and stone cottages they shared with the large contingent of Cornishmen and the almost daily influx of Welsh smelting specialists and Irish labourers. The mine was producing over three thousand tons of copper a year, so their jobs were secure, and as the town's population rose, they were amply catered for by the numerous German farmers who'd settled in nearby Bethel.

She drew back from her reverie, noted the sky was lightening and hurried to prepare for the day. Mr Lawrence would be leaving for Newcastle soon, and he had expressly ordered her attendance at his house before he left, but her thoughts were on Mr Cruickshank and the visit to his vineyard later that day.

The magnified eye glared through the monocle. "You seem rather flushed, Miss Searle. I hope you are not sickening for something."

Jessie hadn't realised her excitement was so obvious and attempted a more solemn demeanour. "I am feeling well enough, Mr Lawrence," she replied.

"Good. This conference of Church ministers is vital to the welfare of the community — indeed to the whole country, for it is the chance to air our views before the bishops' conference in Sydney later in the year. The bishop of New South Wales has bestowed a great honour upon me by asking me to speak, and I cannot have you indisposed during my absence. There is much to be done here, and to that end I have made a list." He reached into his coat pocket and pulled out a wad of paper. "These tasks are to be completed by my return on Monday."

Jessie scanned the list, her spirits ebbing. It seemed as endless as the past month's rain, which mercifully had stopped late last night. "I am surprised you wish me to take Sunday school when there will be no church service."

"My absence is no excuse for slacking, Miss Searle. The children must have their religious instruction."

"But they come so far five days a week — surely it wouldn't hurt to let them stay at home with their families this Sunday?"

The monocle fell as he raised his brows in horror. "The Devil makes work for idle hands, Miss Searle, and we must set a good example to the natives. Sunday school will take place as usual and I expect full attendance."

Jessie resisted the temptation to remind him that even God took a day of rest while creating the Earth. Such a remark would only cause further delay.

Mrs Blake emerged from the house and handed him his portmanteau.

"You have your list?" he asked.

Hilda nodded, her hands demurely clasped at her waist, her expression unreadable.

"Then I will take my leave. I must not keep the bishop waiting, and it is a long ride to Newcastle." With studied self-importance, he took the reins from the native boy and climbed into the gig.

231

Jessie and Hilda watched as the horse trotted away, and when it was out of sight, they heaved a sigh of relief.

"Three whole days without him — what bliss," Hilda said.

"But we have our lists, Hilda. We will be occupied fully," Jessie replied with a giggle.

Hilda sniffed as she stuffed her list into her skirt pocket. "I seem to have mislaid it." She laughed and linked arms with Jessie. "Let's have a cuppa before Mr Cruickshank arrives."

The sun was shining from a clear sky when they heard the wagon approach. Jessie quickly tied her bonnet ribbons, ran her hands down the skirt she'd spent so much time ironing the night before and tweaked the frills on her blouse. With a hasty glance in Hilda's mirror, she saw that the heightened colour in her cheeks had lent a sparkle to her eyes and that she looked as well as she ever had.

"G'day, Miss Searle." He swept off his hat and clutched it between nervous fingers as his admiring gaze darted over her.

"Good day, Mr Cruickshank." Jessie noted that he'd had a shave and was wearing a clean shirt and moleskin trousers.

"We'll never get there at this rate," muttered Hilda. "Put this pie somewhere safe and help me up."

Once she was ensconced, Abel turned to Jessie. "I put the cover on the wagon in case it rains again," he murmured, as he helped her climb.

She felt the warmth of his touch long after he'd released her hand and knew she was blushing as he sat next to her. "That was most thoughtful of you," she replied, her voice unsteady, "but it seems we are to have a sunny day at last."

"Sunshine, home-baked apple pie and good company," he said, as he slapped the reins over the horse's back. "What more could a man ask?"

Jessie kept her gaze firmly on the horizon as they left the yard. Hilda had no such inhibitions and kept up a stream of inconsequential chatter as they trundled deeper into the valley.

"There it is," Abel said, as they emerged from the forest. "Beech Tree Vineyard."

Jessie heard the pride in his voice and understood it, for the sight before her was breathtaking.

Abel's vineyard lay within the sheltering curve of mile-high mountains and bronze sandstone cliffs. To the west was the glimmer of water where another beech forest spread from the foot of a mountain right to the far bank. To the east was a rustling crop of tobacco. The tiny house stood in the very heart of the valley, surrounded by regimented lines of dark vines.

"It might not be as grand as some," he said hastily, "but it's all mine."

"It's lovely," breathed Jessie.

"You haven't seen inside the house yet," he muttered, but his pleasure and relief at her reaction was clear in the way he relaxed.

Jessie realised this was far removed from the stately perfection of Possum Hills, but there was a charm

233

about it that touched her profoundly. The house was mud brick and needed a fresh coat of whitewash. The roof had been haphazardly patched, but the door and shutters had been recently painted, and the stone chimney seemed sturdy. There were broken wagon wheels and bits of rusting machinery littering the yard where a coterie of chickens pecked among flourishing weeds. Shirts flapped on a line of string nailed between two trees, and goats bleated from a nearby pen.

There was a sturdy barn, the usual outside lavatory and a lean-to, which housed a copper boiler and camp oven. In the distance, Jessie could see the curl of smoke from the Aborigine camp that was the usual huddle of grass humpies and battered tin shelters.

Tumbalong emerged from the house, tipped his hat and held the horse while everyone alighted. "Boss happy now you come, missus," he said, with a broad smile.

Abel scuffed the ground with his boot. "Yeah, all right, mate," he mumbled.

"Him clean house, make Tumbalong fix roof and paint windows."

"Haven't you got work to do?" Abel glared at him.

"Plenty work, boss."

"Then get on with it."

Tumbalong was still grinning as he unhitched the wagon and led the horse to a fenced paddock.

Abel stomped up the steps to the veranda. "I expect you'd like a drink," he said over his shoulder.

"A cuppa would be most welcome," replied Hilda. "Would you like me to make it?" Without waiting for a reply, she handed him the pie and bustled away.

Abel hesitated in the doorway. "It's a bit basic," he said shyly, as he clutched the plate. "Perhaps you'd prefer to sit outside?"

Jessie took the pie before it slid to the floor and smiled up at him. "I think it might be wise to put this under cover."

He waved away the swarm of flies that had appeared as if from nowhere now the sun was out and it had stopped raining, and led her into the house.

After the brightness outside, it took a moment to adjust to the gloom. She smiled as she noted the tin can stuffed with wild flowers. Abel's simple gesture spoke volumes, and she placed the pie next to it on the scrubbed table. "They are very pretty," she said softly.

He covered the plate with a cloth. "Thought they'd brighten up the place," he muttered.

"They do indeed." A swift glance took in the single room where a narrow iron bed stood against the wall, and a line of pegs acted as a wardrobe. There was a home-made nightstand with a solitary stub of candle in a saucer, and a heap of boots had been tossed into one corner along with bits of riding tack. The floor had been swept, and there was no sign of spider-webs, but there was little comfort to be had in the thin mattress and blanket and the lack of rugs, curtains or pictures.

"I did warn you it wasn't up to much," he said.

Jessie smiled. "You have made it home, and that is enough."

He eyed her thoughtfully; then led her back outside.

Tea was drunk from thick white china, and after a stroll among the vines, and an interesting lesson in the art of making wine and drying the tobacco crop, they were introduced to Tumbalong's family. They ranged from elderly grandparents and uncles to young children. Jessie, who had defied Mr Lawrence's rule about not visiting their own small band of natives, noted that these children suffered from the same weeping eyes and noses and skin sores, and wondered why nothing could be done about them.

She waited until they sat down to eat the rich chicken stew Abel had prepared before she broached the subject.

"They don't like interference from us whites."

"Surely they could be persuaded to bathe their eyes and keep themselves clean?"

"They use water for drinking, not washing, and the kids are always grubbing about in the dirt." He must have seen her concern, for he hurried on, "I've tried telling 'em, but it's not their way. They won't thank you for what they see as meddling."

"Mr Lawrence is of the same opinion," she replied sadly. "It's such a shame, because infection like that causes blindness, and it could so easily be avoided."

"I can see you have given deep thought to the problem, Miss Searle, but I assure you there is nothing you can do."

Jessie finished her meal in silence, and as the plates were cleared away, she realised Abel spoke the truth.

The natives' ways were alien, and although she didn't understand why they refused help and advice, she had to accept it was none of her business.

"Why don't you two go for a walk?" said Hilda, as she settled into the moth-eaten cushions of the veranda chair. "I like a nap after lunch, and it's wonderfully cool here."

"Would you like to see a platypus?" Abel asked. "There's a bunch of 'em down in the river, and we might be lucky enough to catch sight of one, though they're very shy."

"What's a platypus?"

Abel tugged his ear and frowned. "It's got a bill and webbed feet like a duck, fur like an otter and a flat tail like a beaver. You won't see anything like it anywhere else, but they're difficult to spot, so don't be disappointed if we can't find one today."

Jessie wondered if he was teasing, for the creature sounded very strange. "You have intrigued me," she admitted, "and if this creature truly exists, then I should like to see it."

They strolled towards the river, the companionable silence broken only by the swish of the grass against their legs and the occasional screech of a rainbow lorikeet.

"It is beautiful here," said Jessie, as Abel draped a rug over the grass at the tree-lined water's edge. "I can understand why you love it so."

"Is it that obvious?"

She nodded. "Thank you for sharing it with me."

"It's my pleasure," he murmured, as he tugged his hat-brim. "And I made sure there were no dragons about, so you're quite safe."

She giggled. "I must have looked very foolish."

"Oh, I dunno — I rather liked rescuing you."

She saw the smile twitch at the corners of his mouth, knew he was teasing, but couldn't help feel embarrassed at the memory of throwing herself into his arms. "You can rest assured, Mr Cruickshank, that I will not be so foolish as to do it again."

His grey eyes regarded her thoughtfully, then he grinned. "I like your spirit, Miss Searle. Now, let's see if we can find a platypus, but you must keep very still or you'll frighten 'em away."

Jessie hesitated, then cast aside her doubts and followed his example by lying on her stomach so she could look into the shadowy water. It was undignified, but his enthusiasm was infectious, and it was fun to behave like a child again, for it reminded her of when she used to fish for tadpoles in Cornwall.

There was a splash and Abel pointed. Jessie peered into the water, caught a glimpse of something dark moving swiftly through the shallows to disappear beneath the reeds. It had been so fleet she'd barely seen more than a shadow. She was about to express her disappointment when Abel excitedly pointed again, and this time she saw the strange creature more clearly. It was as he'd said, a curiosity created from parts of other beasts.

Entranced, Jessie watched the extraordinary creature scramble along the muddy bank and plop into the

238

water, where it was joined by several others. The game of chase lasted some minutes, and then they were gone. She waited, hoping they would return, but it seemed they had found something to occupy them further downstream.

She sat up and smoothed the creases from her skirt and blouse. "I've never seen anything like them before," she breathed.

His smile was wide. "Glad you liked 'em. We were lucky to find 'em today."

"We'd better get back," she said regretfully. "Hilda will wonder what has happened to us."

"Will you come again?" he asked, as they slowly walked towards the house.

"If I am permitted," she replied softly.

"You'll always be welcome." He took her hand and helped her step over a stream that meandered through the pasture. Gaining the other side, he didn't release his hold, and his expression was unreadable as he looked into her eyes. "I know it might be difficult for you to come again, Miss Searle, but I really would like you to try."

Jessie could feel the heat rise in her face as his fingers clasped hers and they were drawn closer as if by some unseen cord. "Mr Lawrence might not give his permission."

"Then I shall ask for it."

"And if he refuses?"

"Then I will ask again. If he remains stubborn, then your next visit will have to wait until he is out of the valley."

"I have been deceitful enough, Mr Cruickshank, and should he learn of today's visit, then he will have every reason to dismiss me."

"He can't dismiss you for something so . . . so . . ."

She reclaimed her hand. "He has made it very clear that he can."

His expression was mulish. "He gives consent to you visiting von Schmidt."

"I visit his mother, and only because she is patron of the church charities."

"Whereas I'm just a labouring vintner."

She heard the bitterness. "That has nothing to do with it."

His eyes were flint. "I think it does," he replied.

She held his gaze. "Not for me."

"So you will seek his permission?"

"Please don't spoil the day by bullying me — I have enough of that with Mr Lawrence."

He gave a great sigh, slapped his hat against his thigh and tugged it over his head. "Sorry. I didn't mean to sound off like that, but I had hoped you liked the look of me enough to come back. It seems I was mistaken."

"You assume too much, Mr Cruickshank," she scolded softly, "and if you are fishing for compliments, then you will be disappointed."

He grinned down at her. "Fair go, but you can't blame a bloke for trying." His expression became serious. "I may be speaking out of turn, Miss Searle," he began hesitantly, "and if what I say offends you, then I will not talk of it again."

240

Jessie realised he needed to get something off his chest. "Go on," she said slowly.

He reddened and stared into the distance. "I can't compete with von Schmidt, but I hope you enjoyed my company."

Jessie nodded and was about to reply, but Abel seemed determined to finish what he was saying and rushed on. "I have very little money — it's all invested in land and crops. I work for von Schmidt to bring in enough to live on, and tend this place when I can. Tumbalong and his tribe muck in, and although it's frowned upon in some quarters, I regard them as family and look after them as best I can." He paused, clearly hesitating over his next words. "I want you to know who I am before you hear the gossip." He licked his lips, his gaze elusive. "You see, I don't have a particularly honourable background, so I wouldn't blame you if you didn't visit again."

Jessie was intrigued. "How so?"

"My great-grandparents were convicts and so was my father. Nothing too serious," he added hurriedly, "petty theft, forgery and a bit of smuggling, but the convict stain has been passed down to me and probably to my children and grandchildren, and as long as Australia is classed as a convict colony, so the stain will continue."

"But you own this land — you are a free man."

"I might be free, but I'm from convict stock and therefore shackled to my family's past." He talked through her protest. "Men like Gerhardt von Schmidt will always be among the 'exclusives'. His parents came

241

here as free citizens, their money and education making them part of the ruling class. I could have twice as much money and land as he does and still never be fully accepted into his society, even though I was born here."

Jessie ached for this proud man, whose admission had clearly not come easily.

"I'm sorry, Miss Searle, but you needed to know how things are."

"It seems to me it isn't very different from England," she replied softly. "The poor will remain poor, the rich will get richer on their backs, and regardless of how much a man achieves he is still locked within the class of his birth."

"Then you do understand," he said on a sigh. "But it doesn't alter the fact you're a free educated woman, whereas I . . ."

She realised it was time to put him straight. "My grandmother lived with the shame of being born on the wrong side of the blanket," she said flatly. "I was raised in a two-roomed, rented cottage in a backstreet with my widowed grandmother, my parents and two brothers. My father was a fisherman, and by the time I was five I was mending the nets on the quay. He was lost at sea, and my brothers had to go into the tin mines before they were old enough for long trousers." She hurried on before he could interrupt. "My education came from nights of poring over books by the light of a candle-stub and was paid for by working every spare hour at packing herring into salt barrels. I wouldn't be here today if it wasn't for a minister who saw my ability and nurtured it, so don't talk to me of 'exclusives' and 'stains', Mr Cruickshank, for I have battled with both and will continue to do so for as long as I live."

"My goodness," he breathed, "you can be a fierce little thing, can't you?"

Her anger passed as swiftly as it had appeared and she gave a wan smile. "Only when I feel I'm being unfairly judged."

"I'm sorry." A smile touched his lips.

"So am I."

They stood and looked into one another's eyes, unaware they were being watched by a most interested Hilda. "So," he said, breaking the silence, "you'll come here again?"

She smiled. "Should you invite me, then I would be delighted to."

"What about Mr Lawrence?"

"I shall approach him when I think he is at his most amenable," she replied. They were brave words, for her employer was rarely amenable to anything beyond his strict code of conduct.

"If there's any facing up to do, then it is me who should be doing it," he said grimly.

"Don't make things worse," she urged.

He made as if to reach for her hand, changed his mind and ran his fingers through his hair in frustration. "You're a free woman," he rasped. "Why do you let him bully you?"

"It is just his way of asserting his position," she replied, "and I did agree to his terms of employment."

"It's ridiculous," he exploded, as he rammed his hat back on and stuffed his hands in his pockets.

Jessie touched his arm in a gesture of understanding. "Thank you for your support, Mr Cruickshank," she murmured. "I do appreciate it."

"I just wish there was something I could do to help."

She experienced a surge of determination to overcome Mr Lawrence's pettiness once and for all, and drew herself up to her full height. "You have given me the courage to face Mr Lawrence on his return and demand a review of his rules."

"But that could see you out of a job."

"Then I will find another."

"This is the only school for miles. Where would you go?"

Courage ebbed as reality sank in. "I don't know," she admitted. "Perhaps Newcastle?"

"Then you must think carefully before you speak with him." His eyes pleaded with her. "The valley won't be the same without you, and the kids really like you. Besides, Newcastle's a day's ride away, and the people there aren't half as friendly as they are here."

"Then let us hope Mr Lawrence is mellowed by the conference and conducive to persuasion."

"Are you sure you wouldn't like me to have a word with him?"

The fighting spirit burnt in his eyes and she shook her head. "I think it would be better if you left it to me."

He held her gaze, then nodded. "I've never got the hang of diplomacy, so I reckon you'll make a better fist

244

of it." He tentatively took her hand, his gaze seeming to travel deep into her core. "Good luck, Miss Searle."

Jessie could scarcely breathe, mesmerised by his gaze, all too aware of the hammering of her heart at his touch. "Thank you," she managed.

They reluctantly broke contact and slowly walked towards the waiting Hilda. Jessie wondered if he too was loath to see the end of what had been a wonderful day.

Sydney Harbour, the next day

Harry could all too clearly remember the anguish of being forced to finish his education in England and take up the earldom, so he understood Freddy's despair. The boy was trying hard to appear adult, but his eyes were haunted and there was a vulnerability about him that made Harry wish he could do or say something to ease his fears. And yet Harry knew there were no cures, for the loneliness would remain with the boy — as it had with him — for many months. The uncertainty over his father's health was an added burden, and Harry admired the way the youngster was conducting himself.

He put his arm round Freddy's shoulders as they stood on the quayside, and tried to convey his understanding. Amelia had rightly decided not to come, and the boy had made a tearful farewell to his parents, clinging to his mother at the last minute in a desperate attempt to prolong their time together. Now, despite the determined bearing, his wan face and reddened eyes bore witness to his inner turmoil.

"The time will fly," he consoled him. "I know you don't believe me, Freddy, but you'll soon be far too busy to give us much thought, and before you know it, school will be over and you'll be back home."

"You will look after Mama and Papa, won't you?"

"You have my promise." Harry looked into the trusting brown eyes. "And I want you to promise to look after Lavinia. She will need help while I'm away."

"You have it, sir." The boy drew from the embrace, shook his hand and wandered off to stare out at the water, his shoulders determinedly rigid.

"Don't worry, Harry," murmured Lavinia. "I will care for him as if he was my own." She stepped into his embrace, heedless of the milling crowd and curious glances, and kissed his cheek.

He felt the lump grow in his throat as he held her close, but knew he must show no sign of weakness — not now — for they had already said their goodbyes in private, and the time for tears had passed. "I will come home as soon as I can," he promised. "God speed, my love."

"All aboard. The ship will sail in ten minutes." The sailor's cry was accompanied by the enthusiastic ringing of a bell, and the crowd surged forward.

Harry and Lavinia drew apart, but their gaze held, speaking far more than any words as the crowd eddied around them. The knot of tears in his throat swelled as he held his son. "Look after your mother, Charlie, and kiss your sisters for me."

"We must go," said Gertrude. "They are about to haul up the gangplank."

Charlie gave him a watery smile, then took his mother's arm and led her towards the ship.

"Goodbye, Harry," murmured Gertrude.

Harry kissed her cheek, gave her a hug and managed to smile. Her dour expression had lightened, and there was colour in her cheeks and a sparkle to her eyes again. Even her clothes were more cheerful, her bonnet prettily decorated with silk ribbons. It seemed this enforced exile had renewed the lust for life she had once possessed and brought back the beauty she'd tried to hide. "Safe journey, Gertie," he said, "and don't worry about us here. You have looked after everyone splendidly; now it is time to find someone to look after you. Good luck."

He stood on the quayside, his gaze fixed to the beloved figures high above him on the deck. Impervious to the noise and the jostling crowd, he kept them in sight while the anchor was raised and the rowboats drew the *Miniver* slowly from the quay.

He raised his hand in farewell as the sails unfurled and caught the wind, and the *Miniver* began to turn her bow towards the harbour entrance. The figures were smaller now, indistinguishable among those who swarmed the decks to catch their last glimpse of Sydney before the ship rounded the headland.

Harry watched until the sails became a speck on the horizon, and as that speck disappeared to leave an empty stretch of water, he finally succumbed to the awful loneliness that he knew would remain with him until his family were together again.

Lawrence Creek, Hunter Valley, 1 July 1850

Jessie discovered she couldn't keep her mind on anything but Mr Lawrence's return. The children sensed her distraction, and played up accordingly.

"Be quiet," she snapped, as the chatter grew. "Take out your readers and concentrate on page eight."

The children eyed her warily and Jessie immediately regretted being so sharp. It wasn't their fault she was on edge. As they settled down to reading, she paced back and forth, her gaze flitting repeatedly to the window for sight of his gig, and yet dreading its appearance. It was all very well being brave in her thoughts, but the reality was, she feared Mr Lawrence's reaction to her demands and, after having confided in Hilda, was having serious doubts over the wisdom of approaching him at all.

As the clock ticked towards eleven, she sighed and sent the children outside for an early lunch break. She had no appetite, but her mouth was dry as she headed for the outside cooking area to make a cup of tea. She was sipping the strong, sweet brew when she heard the sound of an approaching horse. Stepping out from the lean-to, she flinched as the animal skidded to a halt within inches of her boots.

"Mr Cruickshank, *really!*"

Abel swung down, took off his hat and apologised. "Is Zephaniah back yet?"

She led him out of earshot of their curious young audience. "He is due very soon," she said urgently. "You must go."

"I just wanted to say good luck."

"You said that on Saturday," she reminded him.

"Yeah, I know," he replied bashfully, "but a bit more wouldn't hurt, would it?"

She looked into his grey eyes and was lost. "No," she murmured. "I don't suppose it would."

"No worries, then." His expression became cheerful as he replaced his hat. "You'll be right, Miss Searle. Old Zephaniah won't stand a chance once you turn on the charm."

She was unnerved by his overwhelming faith and determined optimism. If only things were that easy, she thought. "Please go, Mr Cruickshank," she urged. "I have my responsibilities to attend to."

"Righto."

She watched him swing into the saddle to be soon lost in a plume of dust. With a smile she returned to her duties, but she couldn't quite dismiss the idea that Mr Cruickshank would have made a good knight — even if his armour was moleskin and cotton, and his steed a scruffy stock horse.

The children were leaving for home, their shaggy ponies trotting eagerly into the dwindling light of a winter evening. Jessie stood on the schoolhouse step and watched until they were out of sight. As she turned towards the door, she noticed the gig emerge from between the trees. Mr Lawrence was almost home.

She darted into her room, tidied her hair and snatched up her grandmother's shawl. Its warm familiarity brought comfort and bolstered her courage as she hurried to join Hilda on the veranda.

"Let's hope he's in good spirits," muttered Hilda. She turned to look at Jessie. "Will you speak to him tonight, or have you changed your mind?"

"I will gauge his mood and then decide."

"Rather you than me."

Jessie kept her thoughts to herself as the gig approached and the Aboriginal children came scampering from their camp to help with the horse.

"Please think carefully, Jessie," the older woman urged. "It would be awful if you were dismissed."

"Let us hope it will not come to that," she replied, her attention focused on the gig.

It came to a halt beside the steps and the time for private conversation was past. Zephaniah clambered down and threw the reins to one of the Aboriginal boys. "Mind you rub the horse down properly and give him a good feed, and don't scratch the gig when you put it in the barn." He watched the gaggle of children race towards the barn, their excited chatter ringing in the hush of evening, before turning to the veranda. "Good evening, ladies," he boomed.

"I take it you had a successful trip, sir?" Jessie bobbed a curtsy as Hilda took charge of his portmanteau.

"Indeed I have," he replied, his chest puffed out like a pigeon's. "Most successful. Come, ladies, and I will tell all over supper."

Jessie and Hilda exchanged glances as they followed him into the house. He was in an ebullient mood, which augured well, but Jessie felt no lessening of the tension as she helped Hilda to serve.

As he tucked into cold mutton and mashed potato, he regaled them with his news. "The bishop was most gracious in his praise for my speech, and although I am a modest man, I confess it was one of my best." He took a long draught of wine, smacked his lips in relish and returned to his food.

Jessie found she couldn't taste anything, but knew it would cause comment if she left it. She let his words wash over her and kept up the pretence of interest, but her thoughts were on the speech she had been practising since Saturday night.

"The accommodation was poor and rather cramped, but my days were so filled with activity I hardly noticed. It was quite exhilarating to meet such a diversity of ministers, and although I am but a humble country parson, I never once felt overshadowed by such a worthy gathering." He paused to drink, waited for Hilda to clear the plates and serve pudding. "Ah, apple pie," he sighed, "my favourite. You do know how to spoil me, Mrs Blake."

"It's to welcome you home, sir," she replied, her gaze firmly averted from Jessie.

The interminable meal went on from dessert to cheese and port as Zephaniah extolled his admiration of the bishop and regaled them with his opinion on the Catholics, Presbyterians and Benedictine brothers who'd attended. "He is a far-seeing man and realises

251

that the Church, in all its variety of teachings, must continue to police the morals of its flock. There is a great following for the Temperance Movement, and I am persuaded that sobriety must be encouraged, especially among the lower classes, where depravity has reached alarming proportions."

Jessie smothered a smile as he lifted his glass of wine to his lips. Mr Lawrence was obviously not going to practise what he preached — but then he rarely did.

"I realise my sermons will fall on deaf ears in this valley of vines, but it is the native we must protect, and those whose lax constitutions cannot withstand the effects of alcohol." He seemed pleased with this little speech and polished his monocle. "I take it things have run smoothly in my absence?"

Jessie clasped her hands in her lap, for they were trembling. "Yes, sir, and all the tasks on your list have been completed."

"Good, good," he murmured. "I knew I could rely on you and Mrs Blake. Do you have the list of Sunday School attendance?" He scanned the list Jessie produced from her pocket and nodded his approval. "The six absences can be explained?"

"The native children are sick with a chest infection. Their coughs are quite alarming, and I wondered . . ."

He grimaced. "A common occurrence brought about no doubt by their lack of clothing." With a heavy sigh he threw down his napkin. "I try my best to instil moral fortitude into those people, but still they live like naked, filthy savages. I despair." He must have noticed Jessie's sad expression, for he eyed her sternly. "Your pity is

252

wasted on them, Miss Searle, and we will have no more talk of it. Now we have finished our repast, I wish to discuss my future plans."

She was startled by the way he suddenly left his chair and began to pace, for Mr Lawrence usually sat at the table when he wanted to pontificate.

"The bishop has offered me the great honour of a seat on the Church Council in Brisbane. It will mean much travelling and prolonged absences from my important work here, but I feel it is my duty to accept." He stopped pacing and frowned. "You both seem rather taken aback. I was hoping you would be delighted at my news, for it is a great advancement."

They uttered hasty congratulations as they exchanged worried glances.

"Thank you." His smile was self-satisfied, his chest puffed in pride as he clasped his hands behind his back. "I see it as an endorsement of the sacrifice and hardships I've borne to bring God to this benighted corner of Australia. It is most gratifying that my small efforts have not gone unnoticed."

Jessie's thoughts were in a whirl. "What of the school, sir?"

"Despite your age and inexperience, you have proved capable of running the school. I trust I can rely on you to continue?"

"Of course, sir." She felt relieved, for, as ironic as it was, she'd feared her job was in jeopardy.

"The bishop has appointed a curate to oversee the pastoral duties of this parish, but of course I will continue to offer my guidance and support whenever I am able."

"What of me, sir?" Hilda's face had become ashen, her eyes wide with dread.

He glanced at his pocket watch. "You will continue to keep house for the new incumbent, and I expect you to maintain your excellent standards." He closed the watch with a snap. "I wish to discuss the matter of household finances, Mrs Blake. Miss Searle, you are dismissed."

She rose from her chair. "When are you expected in Brisbane, sir?"

"In the new year. Good night."

Jessie closed the door and wondered if Hilda was experiencing the same heady hope that at last things would change. She pulled her grandmother's shawl around her to ward off the chill, and smiled at the thought of how Mr Cruickshank would greet her news.

CHAPTER
NINE

Lawrence Creek, Hunter Valley, September 1850

The rain had returned several weeks ago, with devastating effect, and as Jessie stared out of the window, she wondered how Abel was coping. She had yet to tell him about Zephaniah's planned departure, but with the rain had come the struggle for survival among the vintners, and the chances of him calling on her faded with each drenching day.

She coughed and blew her nose. The cold had started three days ago and didn't seem to be improving — in fact her throat felt as if she'd swallowed a packet of needles, and the cough hurt her chest. She pulled the shawl more firmly round her shoulders and shivered. The chill lingered in the schoolroom despite the cheerful blaze in the hearth, and the grey skies matched her mood as she watched the endless rain obliterate the view.

The children hadn't come to school in over two weeks, for the country tracks were flooded, the rivers running too swiftly to cross, and she suspected they were needed at home to help salvage what they could before everything was washed away. Her thoughts meandered as her gaze drifted towards the native camp. She hadn't seen smoke for several days, and she hoped they had found better shelter than their grass humpies. She tapped her foot in agitation, fretting over the bewitching children who always greeted her with big brown eyes and cheeky grins. They had so little and yet seemed happy, coming to Sunday School, helping with the horse and wagon, playing hide and seek among the trees as they watched the vintners' children in the schoolyard.

"They must be cold," she said under her breath. "Hungry too. I wish there was something I could do to help."

Another coughing fit seized her, and when it was over, she closed her eyes and tried to ignore the hammer of rain on the tin roof, but it beat in her head and would not be denied. Realising she had to keep occupied if she was not to be driven mad by the noise and the claustrophobia of the schoolhouse, she donned her oldest and most faded dress, tied an apron round her waist and set to scrubbing the floor.

"Miss Searle! Miss Searle!"

Jessie dropped the scrubbing bush into the bucket, pushed away a stray lock of hair and eased her back. "Now what?" she muttered crossly. Getting to her feet, she sneezed and blew her nose as she went to the door.

Mr Lawrence was huddled beneath a dripping hat and large oilskin coat. He looked as miserable as his horse. "Miss Searle, you must make haste. The river has broken its banks and the water is rising. We need to save the books and anything else of value before it is too late."

A swift glance took in the swirling water that rose almost to the animal's hocks and lapped at the bottom step. Another took in the river that now raced down the track. Without a word she hurried back into the schoolroom.

Working in silence, they packed up the precious books and Bibles, along with the children's sewing, slates and chalks. The fire was damped down; then they stacked the benches and desks on the dais and perched her upholstered chair on top.

"I will take these boxes to the house while you pack," Mr Lawrence instructed. "You and Mrs Blake will share the spare room in my house until this is over."

Jessie grabbed the carpet bag and quickly packed her clothes, the writing case and shawl. Tossing in her second pair of boots and her brush and comb, she turned to what was left and, between coughing fits, stripped the bed. Once the bedding was firmly rolled, she clambered on to the chair and carefully wedged it between the rafters. The mattress proved unwieldy until she found a length of string to tie it in a tight bundle, and this was also shoved out of harm's way. The iron bed was too heavy to shift, so she dragged the nightstand and chair across and placed them on top. The chest of drawers would have to stay where it was.

"Miss Searle? We must go."

With a hasty glance around the room in case she'd forgotten anything, she picked up the carpet bag and umbrella, and hurried outside.

The bottom step was now under water, and as she hesitated, Zephaniah lost his patience. "Give me the bag and put that umbrella down. It won't do you an ounce of good, and I cannot sit here while you dither."

She did as she was told and took his proffered hand. With a foot in the stirrup, she was hoisted into the saddle. The rain beat down, plastering down her hair, and she blinked against the onslaught.

"Hold on to me," he ordered.

Jessie tentatively clutched his coat as the horse began to splash through the water. Her grip tightened as it became clear the animal was having difficulty against the swift, rising flow, and although the distance was short between school and house, the journey seemed to take hours.

Sodden and bedraggled, Jessie almost fell into Hilda's arms as Zephaniah handed her down. Retrieving her precious bag, she went indoors. "I didn't realise it had become so bad," she said, dabbing her sore nose and trying to control another coughing fit.

"Never mind, pet," soothed Hilda. "Let's get you out of those wet things, and then we'll have a cuppa." She opened the bedroom door to reveal two narrow beds surrounded by numerous boxes and cases. "You and me will be sharing for a while," she said. "There isn't any sign of this weather changing."

"Have you heard how everyone else is doing?" Jessie's teeth were chattering and she was having trouble getting her numb fingers to undo the wet laces of her bodice.

258

Hilda shook her head as she helped Jessie undress and dry off. "There's been no news. No one's come this way in days, but I suspect they're in the same situation as us — especially the ones living close to the river." She must have read the concern in Jessie's eyes, for her smile was warm and consoling. "Abel's a strong, healthy man. He's survived worse, I'm sure, so there's no need to fret."

Jessie felt slightly warmer now she was dry, and she used the towel to conceal her face as she rubbed her hair. "I'm not fretting over Mr Cruickshank," she said defensively. "I'm merely concerned about my pupils and their families."

"Of course you are, ducks."

Jessie shot her a suspicious glance, but Hilda seemed occupied with gathering up the sodden clothes. "I'll wring these out and hang them in front of the fire. Come into the parlour — it's warm in there and supper's almost ready."

Jessie eyed the bed with longing. Her head was throbbing, her body ached, and all she really wanted was to curl up and go to sleep. Turning her back on the tempting sight of fresh, crisp sheets and soft pillows, she blew her nose and prepared for a long evening.

"We are lucky my parents had the foresight to build so high off the ground," said Zephaniah, as they sat by the fire after supper. "I have never known the house to flood, so we shall be quite safe."

It was a blessing not to have to shout above the thunder of rain, for the tiled roof seemed to deaden the sound, but Jessie was finding it hard to concentrate through the headache that seemed to tighten in a band behind her eyes. "What of the natives, sir? They have little shelter and their camp must be awash by now."

He shrugged. "They make their own arrangements."

Jessie frowned. "How?"

"I don't know," he snapped, his monocle plopping on to his chest. "They go off somewhere — higher ground probably. They are not my concern."

Jessie was on the point of telling him they should be when Hilda came back into the room and announced she'd just seen Zephaniah's horse jump over the paddock fence and head through the trees towards the hills. "And that's not all," she added grimly. "Your buggy just floated out of the barn along with everything else and is probably halfway to Brisbane by now."

With a cluck of annoyance, he hurried to the window and Jessie, smothering another cough, took the opportunity to make her apologies and escape to bed. The fact he seemed more concerned over his horse and buggy than the plight of the Aborigines made her so angry she couldn't bear being in the same room as him.

She fell asleep almost immediately, but her dreams were confused and brightly coloured, so when she was shaken awake some time later, she felt a stab of fear as she opened her eyes to see a ghostly lamplight.

"It's only me." Hilda raised the lamp and tugged back the bedclothes. "The water's in the house, Jessie. We've got to move."

Confused and disorientated, she stared at Hilda. "Water? In the house?"

"Get out of bed and you'll find it's up to your ankles." Hilda was grabbing boxes and cases, and piling them on her bed as she spoke. "Hurry, Jessie. Save what you can and get in the dining room."

Jessie frowned, moved her aching limbs and gasped as her bare feet sank into icy water. Shivering uncontrollably, she sat on the bed and pulled on the dry clothes she'd mercifully left hanging on the back of the door. It seemed to take a great deal of effort.

"Here, let me help." Hilda's efficient hands worked on buttons and laces, and when Jessie was finally dressed, she threw a large cape around her shoulders. "There you are ducks," she murmured. "That should keep the cold out."

"My bag. Where's my bag?"

"I've got it safe — don't fret. Now come on."

Jessie had the presence of mind to lift her skirt as she waded after Hilda, but the fever that raged through her was making everything dream-like, and she wondered if she was still asleep after all. The bobbing lantern light led the way, and she was vaguely aware of how its gleam caught in the ripples stirred by their feet, but nothing was as strange as the sight of Mr Lawrence, who was perched cross-legged on the dining-room table looking for all the world like a Jewish tailor.

"Don't just stand there," he barked. "You'll catch your deaths."

Jessie burst out laughing. "You do look funny," she spluttered. "Are you sewing a suit, or perhaps a new jacket?"

His voice was as arctic as his glare. "Mrs Blake, kindly assist Miss Searle and keep an eye on her. I have enough to contend with without having to deal with hysterical females."

Jessie frowned as Hilda helped her climb on to the table. She was having a very strange dream, but then, if it was a dream, why was she cold one minute and hot the next? It was all very odd, and she wished Hilda would light the fire, for it was chilly in here. She leant against Hilda's motherly shoulder, her eyelids drooping with weariness, the yearning to sleep too great to resist.

She was dreaming she was back on the ship, her bunk swaying with the roll and dip as the vessel ploughed through the gentler waters of the Indian Ocean. And yet, even as she dreamt, she knew she couldn't be, for Mr Lawrence and Hilda had not accompanied her from Cornwall and she could hear them talking.

"If the water gets much higher, we'll have to swim out of here," said Hilda.

"I think you are dramatising the situation, Mrs Blake. The rain will stop soon, and at least we are safe and dry, if not all that comfortable."

"And if it doesn't stop? What then?"

"Your pessimism is not helping. If you have nothing useful to say, please remain silent."

Jessie drifted in and out of her dreams, the rocking of the boat and the gentle slap of water like a lullaby.

"Jessie, you've got to wake up. Come on, pet. Sit up and open your eyes."

She blinked and tried to focus, but Hilda's face seemed blurred. "Let me sleep," she murmured.

"No, Jessie. You have to wake up."

Jessie's eyes flew open as she was roughly shaken. Clarity came with startling swiftness as she realised the rocking was not from any boat, but from the dining-room table, which was floating about the room.

"Listen, Jessie, we have to steer the table out of the door while we still have the chance. The water is rising fast and soon we'll be trapped. Do you understand?"

Jessie nodded as it all finally made sense.

"Good girl." Hilda handed her a cooking pan. "Use that as a paddle, and when we get outside, make a grab for the veranda post."

She frowned, wondering why she should do such a strange thing, but as Hilda seemed so determined, she dutifully began to paddle. Despite the seriousness of their situation, it was fun dipping the pan in the water so the table floated across the room and out into the hall. It reminded her of childhood, and the times she'd had with her brothers in the harbour, and she couldn't help but smile as they sailed towards the front door.

"It's a good thing it opens inwards," muttered Zephaniah, as he grabbed the handle, which was already under water, and tugged.

The rush of incoming water sent them back up the hall to crash against the study door. The table juddered and swayed and they clung to its sides as it threatened to capsize.

"Paddle now," he ordered, "and don't forget to grab the veranda post or we'll be washed downstream."

263

Sobered by the coldness of the water, and now fully aware of the danger they were in, Jessie began to paddle. As they shot through the front door, she dropped the pan and made a lunge for the nearest post. The force of the deluge tore the table from beneath her and she clung to the post, gasping for breath.

The river had become a torrent, and as it threatened to carry her away, she had to battle to get a foothold on the railings. Inch by inch she managed to counter the increasing weight of her sodden clothing and the tug of the tide, and drag herself up until she was standing on the rail. Pushing her hair from her face and blinking against the battering rain, she looked for the others.

Zephaniah and Hilda were clinging to the post on the other side of the steps. "We must climb on to the roof," he shouted. "It is our only hope."

Jessie saw the fear in Hilda's eyes and knew she wouldn't make it without help. "You go first," she called back, "and I'll follow. Then we can both help Hilda."

He nodded and, with quite startling agility for an overweight, middle-aged man, began to clamber up the post to the ornate iron trellis-work that hung below the veranda roof. Pausing for a moment, he then reached up, grasped the guttering and hauled himself on to the tiles.

Jessie nodded assurance to Hilda and followed suit. It was easy to climb the post, easy to grab the guttering, but the weight of her sodden clothes was dragging her down, and for a moment she doubted she had the strength in her arms to haul herself up. Strong hands pulled her to safety, and she lay there in the teeming rain too exhausted to thank him.

"Come, Miss Searle, we must help Mrs Blake."

Unable to speak, and still trembling from the effort it had taken to climb up here, she followed his example and crawled back to the edge of the roof and lay on her stomach. Hilda, being the tallest of the three, had managed to grasp the trellis-work quite easily, but as she stretched up, grabbed the guttering and let her feet swing, there was an awful sound of groaning metal. The guttering, already weakened by being used as a handhold, couldn't stand her weight, and as nails and screws were loosened, it began to come away from its moorings.

Hilda screamed and thrashed her legs.

"Keep still, woman. You're making it worse." Zephaniah stretched and tried to reach her hands. "Help me, for goodness' sake, or we'll lose her."

Jessie leant down as far as she dare. Her fingers brushed Hilda's, but she was still out of reach.

"You've got to let go," Zephaniah shouted. "One hand. Let go. I'll catch you."

"No, no, no," Hilda moaned.

"Just do it," he yelled.

Hilda shook her head. Her fingers desperately clawed over the guttering, which was slowly buckling.

"Trust him, Hilda," shouted Jessie. "It's your only chance."

Hilda stilled, and Jessie and Zephaniah inched forward. With a cry of anguish she let go. Her flailing hand waved inches from Zephaniah's fingers. Then he had her wrist in his grasp.

"Let go the other hand," he roared, his face red with exertion. "And hurry up. I can't hold on much longer."

Jessie made a grab for Hilda's wrist as she let go. She was heavy and Jessie's arms were almost torn from their sockets as the older woman was slowly hauled up on to the roof. They collapsed against the tiles and fought to regain their breath as Hilda burst into noisy tears.

The thick cape provided little protection now, as it was soaked through, and when Jessie finally sat up and surveyed the scene, she realised they could die on this roof, for everywhere she looked there was a sea of brown, swirling water. Barrels and tree branches hurtled past, along with dead kangaroos, wagon wheels and even an outside lavatory — still intact, right down to the mahogany seat.

She began to tremble as the fires of her fever returned. There was no sign of life, and it seemed they were doomed to remain here until the water subsided — and that could take days, maybe even weeks.

Jessie had lost all sense of time, drifting in and out of consciousness, her dreams vivid. Her fever was raging, making her almost unbearably hot, yet she shivered with cold, which was only emphasised by the misery of the endless, battering rain.

She was aware of the others as they huddled close to the chimney, aware of grey daylight and the profound dark of night, but despite their encouragement and attempts to shield her from the rain, she no longer cared what happened to her. Abel hadn't come, and she'd lost her carpet bag, and therefore her most treasured possession — her grandmother's shawl.

"Jessie, look — someone's coming. We're going to be rescued at last."

She opened heavy lids and peered into the twilight, hope rising that it might be Abel, but as the figures approached in the rowing boat, she saw Gerhardt von Schmidt's blond head, heard his shout and knew Abel had forgotten her. Her eyes closed again, and she was only dimly aware of Gerhardt's strong arms around her as the rock of the boat and creak of oars carried her away.

Eden Valley, October 1850

Ruby woke to a strange silence. She lay next to James, confused by what it could mean, and then she realised and gave him a nudge. "It's stopped raining," she shouted, flinging back the blankets and leaping out of bed. "And look at the sky — it's blue again."

Woken by her shout, the others joined her at the doorway. "Praise be," muttered Fergal, scratching his beard. "I was thinkin' we'd be stuck here for ever."

"So was I," grumbled James, as he hastily pulled trousers over his woollen combinations. "Come on, you two, let's get out of here and check the stock."

There was a bustle of movement as Duncan and Fergal searched for shirts, hats, trousers and coats, and started to dress.

Violet, disturbed from her sleep, began to whimper. Ruby picked her up, glanced across at the heavily pregnant Kumali and frowned. "Are you going with them?"

Kumali nodded.

"You'd better not drop that kid while we're out there," said James flatly. "We'll have enough on our hands rounding up the mob."

"I'll look after her, dinnae you fret," said Duncan with a glower.

"Make sure you do," he retorted.

The friction had grown over the past weeks, as James had made it plain he didn't like sharing his home with a native, and certainly didn't approve of her pregnancy. The only reason it hadn't come to blows was Duncan's mild temper and implacability on the subject of his woman's safety.

Ruby supposed she should be thankful Duncan didn't feel quite so strongly about his dogs, for they had been banished to a nearby shelter of entwined willow branches. She quickly changed the topic. "Don't you want breakfast?"

"We'll eat on the way," James replied, tying his bootlaces. "I've been stuck in this blasted hut for weeks and need space, and" — he glared at Kumali — "fresh air away from the stink in here." He grabbed the mutton from the meat safe and the damper bread from the table, and stuffed them into his saddlebag along with a packet of tea, a tin of syrup and a billy can. With a dismissive peck on Ruby's cheek he was out of the door almost at a run.

268

Ruby held the wriggling Violet as she watched the others follow him. There was a chorus of excited barking from the kennel. Kumali smiled at her as she passed, then waddled off happily in Duncan's wake. She looked incongruous with her cotton dress, wallaby-skin cape and bare feet, but seemed as relieved as all of them to be outside again.

The horses had been hobbled so they wouldn't run off, and they were skittish and overexcited when they were finally released. Ruby heard them ride away, but was transfixed by the view before her. It was depressing to say the least, and she thanked goodness Duncan had insisted upon getting the animals into the hills so quickly, and that their hut was perched high enough to be out of harm's way. The river had broken its banks, flooding the valley, and although the water seemed to be ebbing at last, there were still vast lakes lying where there had once been pastures. Trees had been washed away, mud lay where the wheat had been starting to shoot, and her vegetable garden was in ruins.

The outside kitchen remained flooded, and it would be a while before she could check on the damage to the camp stove. Luckily, she'd had the presence of mind to bring the cooking pots up to the makeshift canvas shelter outside the hut, where she and Kumali had fed everyone by cooking over a stone-ringed fire-pit.

Violet was getting impatient, her wriggling and whining more urgent. Ruby changed her napkin and added it to the pile in the corner before she put her to her breast. It was no wonder they couldn't wait to escape, she thought, as the baby suckled. The hut

reeked of unwashed napkins and bodies — of damp
and mould, and the lingering reminder of cooked
meals, woodsmoke and tobacco. It had been hard
enough to feed everyone, but washing was impossible,
and because of the lack of privacy, they had rarely
changed their clothes.

She wrinkled her nose at her own sour smell, thought
longingly of a hot bath and had to accept her ablutions
would be carried out, as usual, with cold water and
hard soap, as it would take too long to heat up enough
water over the open fire, and her first priority was to do
the washing and scrub out the hut.

Kumali had grown accustomed to riding horses and
liked the sense of freedom it gave her, but this morning
was different, and as the horse broke into a trot, she
could feel the baby inside her squirm at the rough
treatment. She tried to slow the animal, but it pranced
about and yanked on the reins in frustration. Kumali
clung on as it executed a tight circle and tried to buck
her off. If she fell, she would hurt the baby, and it
didn't matter how scared she was, the baby's survival
was more important.

"Are you all right, lassie?"

Kumali nodded, relieved Duncan had seen her
plight, and that his strong hand was now firmly
gripping the bridle.

"Perhaps it might be better if you went home," he
said, his concern mirrored in his expression.

She shot a wary glance at James, who was watching
them with a frown. "You go. I follow soon."

270

"Ye dinnae have to, Kumali. I can manage."

Now the horse had ceased its dancing, Kumali felt more relaxed. She smiled at the man she loved and once more took charge of the reins. "Kumali dinnae have to," she replied in the strong Scottish accent she was starting to pick up, "but Kumali come anyway."

"That's ma wee bonny lass." His grin was broad as he gently cupped her cheek with his gnarled hand. "Away wi' you, then. I'll follow in case you need me."

"When you've *quite* finished," snarled James, as they caught up with him, "there's work to be done, and I don't pay you to be idle."

Duncan glared and James kicked his horse into a gallop. "Dinnae be minding him, lassie. I ken his measure."

Kumali smiled, but felt uneasy. She always did when James was about, for it was obvious he didn't like her, and she suspected that if it wasn't for Duncan, he'd have thrown her off the property a long time ago. The past few weeks of being cooped up with him had been torture, for his cold eyes had seemed to follow her, his sneer ever present.

Yet she had the sense that James was angry not only with her, but with the restrictions of life in the valley. He was rude to Ruby, hardly took any notice of Violet, who he insisted on calling Gladys, and had paced the hut like a caged dingo as the rain thundered on the roof. Perhaps now the rains had gone, he would leave for the bush tavern and peace would return to Eden Valley, but it was a selfish hope, for despite the tears she tried to hide, Ruby loved him.

Kumali set aside her thoughts and concentrated on the task ahead. They had reached the upper slopes of the hills, and there, dotted like white clouds against the green, were the sheep. The oxen had been hobbled, as had the cow and calf, and they were grazing contentedly within the boundary fences she had helped to erect. They looked sleek and well fed, and regarded the riders with an air of surprise as they approached.

"We'll leave the cattle here until we're sure the rain's over," said James, tipping back his hat. "Duncan, get your dogs to work. We'll need to check the numbers and make sure they're healthy."

At Duncan's whistle the eager dogs set off, delighted to be free after so many weeks of idleness. He gave Kumali the reins of his horse, climbed down and followed his dogs, crook in hand, the half-trained pups kept in order with quiet words as they trotted at his heels.

She felt a warm glow as she watched his gentle handling of the pregnant ewes. She'd been so fortunate to find him, so blessed to be carrying his child. Looking up at the clear blue sky, she wondered if the Elders had been right and that the Ancestor Spirits were indeed watching over her, for they had given her a sign and she had followed it — leading her to this man. Now she was finally at peace.

Possum Hills, Hunter Valley, November 1850

Jessie opened her eyes and was immediately blinded by the light streaming between the sprigged curtains. She turned away, her confusion growing as she noted the fine mahogany furniture, the thick rug and ornately framed pictures on the wall. Dragging herself up the pillows, she plucked at the lace edging on the fine linen and traced the embroidery on the delicate muslin nightdress. "Where on earth . . .?"

The door opened and Gerhardt's smiling face appeared. "Good morning, Miss Searle. I see you are awake at last." He strode into the room, bringing the scent of the outdoors with him. "I hope you are feeling better?"

Jessie slid down the pillows, pulling the sheet to her chin. "Where am I?"

He was still smiling as he sat in a chair by the bed. "You are at Possum Hills, Miss Searle. My mother and I have been most concerned, but it seems the doctor we brought from Newcastle has earned his keep and you are at last on the mend."

Jessie digested this, but it still didn't make sense. Then she remembered the flood, the climb to the roof and the interminable wait to be rescued. "How are Mrs Blake and Mr Lawrence? Did you rescue them too?"

"They are well and returned some time ago to clean up the mission."

"How long have I been here?" She slid further beneath the sheet, intimidated by his presence in this unfamiliar bedchamber.

His expression sobered. "Almost five weeks."

"Five weeks?" she gasped. She clutched the sheet and scrambled to the other side of the bed. "I must get back to the school," she gabbled. "Mr Lawrence will need my help, and I have neglected my duties long enough."

"Stay where you are," he ordered. "You have been very ill, and Mr Lawrence is fully aware that you will be unable to return for some time."

"But . . ."

His expression softened. "I admire your determination to return to your duties, Miss Searle, but as one who has survived a most pernicious attack of pneumonia, I doubt you will have the strength to leave your bed just yet." He made as if to pat her hand, thought better of it and toyed with his pocket watch instead. "The new minister has arrived to help Mr Lawrence run the school, so all you have to do is concentrate on getting stronger."

Jessie rested against the pillows, her short burst of energy suddenly depleted. "You're right," she admitted. "I feel as weak as a kitten."

"Rest now and I will get someone to bring you food. You must be hungry."

Surprised to discover that she was, she nodded her thanks. "Tell me," she said, as he was about to leave, "what is the new minister like?"

"Peter Ripley is an energetic widower of middle age with a true Christian heart." His blue eyes twinkled. "He is the very opposite of Mr Lawrence, and I think you will find him a most agreeable employer."

"Good," she breathed, very weary now. Her eyelids fluttered as sleep beckoned. "But for all his faults, Mr Lawrence was very brave. We wouldn't have survived without him." She was asleep before he had closed the door.

When she next opened her eyes, the room was softly lit with lamps, and there, in the chair Gerhardt had vacated, was Frieda. "Hello. Good sleep?"

"Thank you, yes." Jessie sat up with a vast yawn. "I didn't realise I was so tired."

"It's only to be expected," said the old lady, her soft palm resting on Jessie's forehead. "But it appears your temperature is down, so you are finally on the mend." She sat forward, her expression concerned as she took Jessie's hands. "We were afraid we would lose you, my dear. It came very close on several occasions, and I can't express my happiness and relief that you have pulled through."

Jessie could remember only terrible pains in her chest and back, coughing fits that threatened to choke her and blinding headaches. Her dreams had been confused and vivid, and she suspected reality and imagination had become so interwoven it would be impossible to define which was which. "You've been so kind," she murmured. "How can I ever thank you?"

Frieda rose from the chair and planted a soft kiss on her forehead. "There's no need," she murmured. "Your return to health is thanks enough." She became businesslike and tugged at the bell pull. "I will order a fresh bowl of chicken soup," she said. "We must build up your strength and put some flesh back on your bones."

"Has anyone called to ask after me?" She tried to sound matter-of-fact.

"Mr Lawrence sent his best wishes, as do your pupils and their parents. Mrs Blake has called once a week, and the new minister is praying for you."

"Oh."

The intelligent eyes sharpened. "You sound disappointed."

"Not at all," she lied. "I just regret not being awake to speak to Hilda."

"Mrs Blake is due to return on Sunday," she soothed. "Now stop fretting and enjoy being spoilt. You have many friends in the valley, and once you are fully recovered, we will have a party to celebrate."

"What day is it today?"

"Tuesday."

Jessie fell silent. Only five days to go before she could learn what had become of Abel.

With each new day she felt stronger, but when she insisted upon getting out of bed to sit by the window, she found she tired quickly. Frieda was a calm, quiet presence, often sitting by the bed with her sewing, or reading out in her deep contralto from a book of poetry.

Gerhardt, on the other hand, exhausted her with his enthusiastic cheerfulness and his chatter about the happenings on the vineyard. He never sat and read to her, or talked quietly, but would pace about the room moving things, flicking at the curtains and opening and shutting books. She appreciated his intentions to jolly her along, but soon realised he felt awkward in such intimate surroundings, and she suspected he was as

276

relieved as she when it was time for him to leave. She was being unkind, she knew, for he meant well, but she just wasn't strong enough to cope with all that energy.

Sunday came at last, and once the maid had helped her wash and change into a fresh nightgown and feather-down shawl, she sat by the window and brushed her hair. She could see the long gravel driveway from here, and waited eagerly for sight of Hilda.

The clock in the hall was striking two when the gig appeared at the gates and came up the drive. It disappeared round the corner to the front of the house, and Jessie could barely stand the wait as Hilda talked at length with Frieda in the corridor before tapping on the door.

"Hello, ducks. My, my, don't you look a picture?"

The beaming smile and boot-button eyes were so wonderfully familiar that Jessie was close to tears. Hilda swamped her in a matronly embrace.

"I've missed you so," Jessie sniffed, as they drew apart. "I don't need to ask how you fare, for you appear as well as ever. How is Mr Lawrence?"

Hilda plumped down into a nearby chair and pulled a face. "The same as usual," she said dismissively. Then her eyes sparkled and a smile lightened her features. "But I think his nose has been put out of joint by the new minister. Such a nice man, and so easy to please too — it's a pleasure to look after him."

"Was there much damage?"

"I'll say. There was mud up the walls, and every stick of furniture was ruined. The outside lav disappeared, along with my kitchen, and Zephaniah had to send a large order to replace everything, right down to books and slates. He's also brought in men from Newcastle to do repairs and make new furniture."

"Why from Newcastle? I'd have thought it was easier to employ locals."

Hilda shook her head. "The lower-lying part of the valley was almost destroyed. Local men are too busy salvaging their own places to seek other work." She stood suddenly and rushed to the door. "I have a surprise for you. Wait one moment."

Jessie's heart was pounding so fast she could hardly breathe. Had Hilda brought Abel to visit her? Was he her surprise?

"Look what I found," she said, as she reappeared in the doorway.

Jessie's heart sank when she saw Hilda was alone, but her disappointment was soon swept aside. "My bag!" she gasped. "My precious bag. But how . . .? Where . . .?"

Hilda's grin was wide as she handed it over. "I'd put it up on the top of the dresser in the dining room. It was about the only thing in the house that escaped the flood water."

Jessie delved into the bag and pulled out the writing case and shawl. "Oh, Hilda," she breathed, clutching them to her heart, "I thought I would never see them again."

"That's all right, ducks," she replied comfortably.

Jessie carefully stowed the writing case back into the bag and replaced Frieda's shawl with her grandmother's. "Now I know I shall get better." She looked at Hilda and frowned as the older woman refused to meet her gaze. "What is it, Hilda? What are you not telling me?"

Hilda shook her head and stared out of the window. "Nothing, ducks."

Jessie touched her arm, fearful now of what she might learn, but needing desperately to know what it was that Hilda was keeping secret. "Is it about Abel?" she whispered.

Hilda still refused to look at her. "I brought one of my apple pies," she said. "Thought it might cheer you up."

"Hilda, please don't change the subject. What's happened to Abel?"

At last she looked at her. "Nothing for you to worry about," she said, her fingers twisting in her lap.

"But something's happened. Tell me or I shall go and find out for myself."

Hilda sighed and looked down at her hands. "No need for that, ducks — he ain't there."

Jessie stared at her, unwilling to voice her fears but knowing she had to. "He's not . . . not dead?"

Hilda grabbed her hands. "He's alive and well. I saw him only three weeks ago."

"Then why hasn't he called or written? He must know I've been ill."

"He probably felt a bit intimidated by all this." Her gaze swept the luxurious room. She gave another sigh. "I didn't want to tell you any of this, not until you were on your feet again."

"Please, Hilda, you can't . . ."

"I know, ducks." She paused and wet her lips. "He came to see me once the water subsided enough to get through. He was looking for you, and I told him you'd been brought here and were being well cared for."

"Then you must persuade him to visit. I'm much stronger now, and Frieda won't object . . ." She fell silent as she noted Hilda's sorrowful expression.

"He won't be coming, Jessie. He's left the valley."

She felt as if the breath had been punched from her. "But he loves this valley," she whispered. "Why would he leave?"

"The river broke its banks and the flood water rose higher than anyone could have imagined. He lost everything, Jessie. He and Tumbalong's family managed to get away with the horses and the rest of the animals, and they camped in the hills until they could go back to assess the damage. He realised then he would have to start again, but he's lost heart in it and I doubt he'll come back."

"But he has to. What about the land? It's his — he owns it. He can't just leave, not without saying goodbye."

"He said to wish you good health and good luck, but seemed determined to start again elsewhere."

"Where?"

Hilda shrugged. "He was heading for the mines in Newcastle, but he also spoke of Brisbane and Sydney. He has relatives there, I believe."

"Then he is truly gone?" Jessie drew the precious shawl closer and tried to garner comfort from its familiarity, but all she could see were his grey eyes and smiling mouth, and the way the muscles flexed beneath that tanned skin. She had fallen in love with him — she realised that now — but it was too late and he would never know. Yet a small part of her refused to believe she would never see him again, and she clung to that hope as she burst into tears.

PART TWO

Gold Rush

CHAPTER
TEN

Kernow House, Watsons Bay, 15 May 1851

"Put those in the small drawing room and take the trunks up to the old nursery," ordered Harry. "The maid will show you the way." He watched the carters unload the delicate desk and box, along with the heavy trunks, and carry them inside. His mood was sombre, for these were the last tangible memories of his mother and George Collinson. There was bitter irony in the fact they had been returned to this house — the house his mother had despised.

"Is that the last of it?" Niall Logan emerged from the drawing room.

"It is," replied Harry. He eyed the sprightly older man, who'd become a close friend over the past six months, and gave a wry smile. "As you see, I have kept Mother's desk and sewing box, but the rest of the furniture has been sold. The new tenants will move in tomorrow."

"You've done the right thing, Harry. Amelia's sister has made a good match and she'll be comfortable in Port Stephens." Niall settled into a chair. "I know how hard you must have found today, but the feeling will pass."

Harry remained silent as he poured the tea and passed a cup to Niall. Before today he'd managed to avoid the house where his mother and George had settled after their marriage — not because it held bad memories, but because he'd known it wouldn't feel the same without them. "It seemed much smaller than I remembered," he said on a sigh. "With the furniture gone and the rooms emptied, it's as if I have erased their presence. I feel like a traitor."

"You're low because you're missing your family," said Niall, "but it is just a house, and they would have condoned your decision." He took a sip of tea. "Now there is no need to pay the annuity to Amelia's sister, the rent from the house is added income." His blue eyes regarded Harry over the teacup. "And that's what's important now."

Harry stared into the hearth, where a few lacklustre flames hissed over damp logs. "There's still a long way to go," he murmured, "and I know Oliver resents what I'm doing. Yet I have no other option, and in his heart I think Oliver knows that."

He took a cigar from the humidor and snipped the end before lighting it. "Selling that ridiculous office building in the city cleared some of his debts, but with the number of servants more than halved, and the horses and spare carriage sold, I feel I'm destroying everything my brother has striven for. You have no idea how deeply that hurts."

"I'm sure it does," murmured Niall, "but I think the hurt was more profound when you discovered he'd been consistently cheating you out of your inheritance."

Harry closed his eyes. He'd once considered his share of the whaling and warehouse income to be fair, but the accounts had been all too clear, the rows of figures proving beyond doubt it should have been three times greater. He hadn't wanted to believe it, but the facts were indisputable, and Harry still felt the sick plunge of despair every time he thought of it.

"I wanted to have it out with him, to demand an explanation," he replied, "but of course he was far too ill, and what was the point? What's done is done."

"I wouldn't waste time on regrets, Harry. You have more than proved your loyalty in the way you've handled things since. Oliver's kingdom was built on sand, but you've shored it up and put it on firmer footing. Instead of resenting your help, he should thank God for it." He put down the teacup and stood. "Enough of this gloomy talk," he said forcefully. "I have news that will assuredly brighten your day."

Harry dredged up a smile. "The banks are wiping out all debts and giving money away?"

Niall laughed. "That would be a fantasy. But there is something afoot, and it promises wealth beyond our dreams if you agree to cut a deal with me." He closed the door.

Harry's dour mood was dispelled. "You have me intrigued," he admitted.

"A man called Hargraves has found gold."

"Gold? Where?" Harry was on the edge of his seat.

"In a tributary off the Macquarie River, just outside Bathurst." Niall's eyes were shining as he perched on the arm of his chair.

Harry's pulse raced. "But how do you know this? There has been nothing in the newspapers and —"

Niall laughed. "Hargraves might have been thought a fool by some, but you know me, Harry — I recognise fire in a man and, after hearing him expound his theories, knew his experience in the California rush of 1849 could prove profitable." He rose, clearly unable to remain still. "It cost me very little to have my nephew Finn follow him and the bushman, Lister, up river to Guyong. Finn remained at the inn until their return a week later from the bush-country. It was clear from Hargraves's excitement that he was on to something." He grinned. "Hargraves wrote a letter that night to Thomson, the colonial secretary. Finn offered to deliver it."

"And brought it to you first," Harry finished. Niall's excitement was catching, and for the first time in months Harry felt the weight of responsibility lighten. "How much gold did he find? Rumours of other strikes came to nothing. Who's to say this will be any different?"

"Hargraves went about things scientifically. Having noted the geography of the Californian strike, he compared it with that near his home in New South Wales and concluded there had to be gold in Australia. It took him less than a week to find it, and he writes of vast quantities lying underfoot, just waiting to be taken."

Harry and Niall grinned at one another like schoolboys. "We're on the verge of a gold rush," breathed Niall, "and we are the only people in Sydney to know about it."

"I am most flattered that you wish to share this bounty with me, Niall."

He waved the thanks away. "You have become my friend and confidant, and I know I can trust you to cut a fair deal."

Harry was warmed by the other man's sincerity. "What of your nephew? Can he be trusted not to speak?"

Niall nodded. "Finn and his brothers are already on their way back to Ophir to seek their fortune. I will have the letter to Thomson delivered on the fourteenth. That will give us seven days to prepare before the news is released to the press. To be forewarned is to be forearmed. Once word is out, the madness will begin. This is our chance, Harry, and we must grasp it with both hands."

Despite his initial excitement, Harry sobered as doubts flooded in. "We're a bit long in the tooth for camping in the bush and digging about in icy rivers, and I for one don't know the first thing about prospecting. Besides, Oliver's health has deteriorated since his second attack, and I can't leave Amelia to cope on her own."

"But you don't need to, Harry — that's the beauty of it." Niall positively radiated energy as he paced. "We can make our fortunes here, and to that end I've already set things in motion."

"How, if the gold is in Bathurst?"

"By supplying the thousands who will go in search of their pot of gold," he said softly. "Think, Harry. Once word gets out, there will be a stampede for Bathurst, and every last one of them will be wanting wagons, tools, provisions, clothes, tents, mules and horses. Our fortunes will be made from supply and demand, and believe me, Harry, the demand will grow with every ship that docks here."

Realisation hit and Harry leapt to his feet. "Our warehouses are fully stocked with tea, salt, sugar, flour and lamp oil, and the latest consignment of canvas and rope was delivered yesterday, along with dozens of bolts of cloth and a thousand pairs of boots."

"I know, I checked." Niall chuckled. "The timing couldn't be more perfect."

Harry's head was reeling and his pulse raced. "If what you believe comes to fruition, then there is indeed a fortune to be made. Let us hope there is enough gold in Ophir to keep the prospectors coming."

"Oh, there will be," replied Niall confidently, "and you can be sure that other strikes will follow, for the geography around Bathurst is not dissimilar to that north of Melbourne."

"How on *earth* do you know that?"

"I made it my business to find out and procured maps of the interior, which I studied thoroughly last night." He tweaked his moustache. "My four sons are already heading that way, and I don't expect it will be long before I have good news."

"You're an astute old devil."

"Takes one to know one, and less of the old — I'm only ten years your senior." His eyes twinkled with merriment as he poured a glass of whisky.

"Actually, it's twelve, but who's counting?" Harry raised his teacup and proposed a toast. "Here's to a golden future." They drank deeply of their preferred tipples, exchanged delighted grins, then got down to discussing the best strategy for meeting the demand for their goods.

Port Jackson, 29 May 1851

The whaler *Sprite* had come out of Tahiti, and after six months of hunting in the icy Southern Ocean, Hina Timanu was as impatient as the others to reach Port Jackson. News of the gold strike had quickly spread from ship to ship, and *Sprite's* crew eagerly awaited their first glimpse of Sydney.

Hina was now thirty years old, and he'd been forced to continue working on *Sprite* because Puaiti's father had refused his suit, insisting he needed a greater wedding gift than he could possibly afford. He strode along the deck, his bare feet making little noise on the planking, and stood in the rain, ready to drop anchor. This would be his first sight of Sydney, for *Sprite* usually docked in Melbourne's Port Philip. From his vantage point at the bow, he regarded the bustling harbour and the city that sprawled against the backdrop of hills as they were slowly towed into shallower water.

What he saw made him long for Tahiti, for there were no volcanoes rearing towards a tropical sky, no emerald ferns, or beaches of black sand with dug-out canoes and smiling *wahinis* to welcome him — merely a curtain of rain that swept over a landscape of gloomy buildings and slender, drooping, grey trees.

"D'ya reckon there really is gold here?" His friend and shipmate Bones came to stand at his side.

Hina smeared the rain from his face, gazed at the vast number of ships already at anchor and the mass of people jostling on the quayside. "I don't know, but if there is, I mean to find it, though it looks as if I won't be the only one."

Captain Jarvis shouted and they paid out the anchor. "Mind if I come with you?" Bones asked. "Only I've 'eard from them Americans it can get rough on the diggin's and no one picks a fight with a bloke your size."

Hina smiled at the irony of this statement. Far from being a deterrent, his size seemed to provoke a certain kind of man into challenging him and he'd spent most of his adult life fending off such aggression. "You can come if you want, Bones," he said quietly. "I'd be glad of your company and we can share the cost of supplies."

"And the gold we find," Bones replied, the stumps of his remaining teeth revealed in a grin.

Hina was about to join the rest of the crew, who were preparing to unload the cargo, when a shout for permission to board came from a painter that had been rowed alongside. At the captain's nod, he unfurled the rope ladder and watched in amazement as a finely dressed gentleman made his precarious way up.

Curious as to why such a man was in a hurry to board *Sprite*, Hina was further astounded to see the captain embrace him before they fell into animated conversation. There was little doubt they were old friends, and Hina wondered if this was the owner of *Sprite*, but the noise around him made it impossible to eavesdrop.

"We have sold the cargo, so start unloading," shouted Captain Jarvis. "It will be taken immediately to the Collinson-Cadwallader warehouse, and Mr Cadwallader has promised each man a bonus if it can be done in under two hours."

Hina realised this was not the owner, but a merchant in a hurry to see the cargo ashore as quickly as possible. His pulse began to race as he hauled on the ropes and the first barrel rose from the hold. The man's haste proved there was indeed a fever on shore — not only for gold, but for the supplies needed to seek it out. The rumours were true, and soon he would be on his way to discover the fortune needed to secure Puaiti's hand in marriage.

The last barrel was unloaded and Hina eased his aching muscles and caught his breath. It had been the swiftest unloading he'd ever witnessed, and the impatience of the crew was almost tangible as they milled about waiting for their wages.

"Crew to starboard!"

"I wonder how much our cut is and how big the bonus will be," muttered Bones, after elbowing his way to the paymaster's table.

"I think it will be good," replied Hina, who stood firm as a man-mountain at the front, thereby forcing the others to eddy round him. "The merchant must have paid well for the cap'n not to auction the cargo."

"Right, you scabrous rabble," yelled the captain, "I'm offering double pay to any man who is on board when we sail again. You have two months ashore — plenty of time to cool your fever and return to your senses. What do you say?"

"I'd rather find gold and make me fortune," yelled one of the crew.

"Yeah, it's the rich life for me, cap'n."

"You're all bloody fools," he yelled above the shouts. "We secured a high price today and will be able to demand more on our next trip. This is where you'll find your gold — in the holds."

"It ain't ours," yelled a seaman. "It belongs to *Sprite*'s owner."

"Yeah, that's right."

A dark mutter swept through the crew, and the captain angrily signalled to the paymaster, who began doling out the wages.

Hina took his pay and eyed the coins in his hand. It was more than he'd ever earned before. Naturally cautious, he carefully knotted them into the tail of his shirt and tucked it firmly under the broad belt.

"Can I at least rely on *you* to return at the end of shore leave?"

Hina felt uneasy at having to disappoint him. "My family is poor, captain, so if there is gold, then I must at least try and find it."

294

"Have I not paid you well this trip, Hina Timanu? Do you reject my promise of double pay for the questionable lure of gold?"

The coins beneath his belt pressed against his skin, making it even harder to deny the man who had employed him for over fifteen years. "You have paid me well," he admitted, "but when a chance comes like this, it would be foolish to ignore it."

The captain scratched his stubbly chin. "Aye, you're right," he sighed. He looked out at the rapidly clearing decks. "But it looks as if I'll be stuck here with no crew. There'll be no profit for me or the owner until everyone returns to their senses."

"Then why don't you come with me and Bones?"

The brown eyes regarded him thoughtfully. "I been a seafaring man all me days," he muttered. "What do I know of prospecting?"

"About as much as any of us," replied Hina, with a smile.

Captain Jarvis took off his salt-bleached cap and scratched his scalp as he gave this some thought. "I can't sail without a crew, but neither can I leave *Sprite* unattended." His weathered face creased into wrinkles as he grinned and tugged the cap back over his greying hair. "Clear off, the pair of you, and find your gold. I'll see you back here at the end of your shore leave, by which time you'll probably have had enough of digging."

★   ★   ★

Eden Valley, 1 June 1851

Ruby was sitting in the hut, listening to the rain drum on the roof as she suckled her hungry baby. Nathaniel Logan Tyler had been born a week before, and his father had yet to see him. Ruby could only pray that James would be delighted with his son, and that his welcome would be warmer than he'd given his daughter.

The rocking chair creaked on the earthen floor as she marvelled at her son's beauty. From the fine, pale hair to the peachy softness of his tiny cheeks he was perfect, and although she gave thanks for his safe arrival, and her heart swelled with love, her weariness made her eyelids droop and her shoulders sag.

The past nine months had been gruelling, coming so soon after Violet, and had been definite proof that breastfeeding didn't stop another baby. It had happened during the long weeks of the flood, and having James home for such a length of time had brought her an uneasy contentment, for his grumpy moods and barely veiled dislike of Kumali had shown her a James she didn't like.

Then disaster had struck. She'd waited until she was certain before telling him she was with child again, dreading his reaction, knowing it was too soon, and yet hoping that this time he would be pleased. James had said very little, had merely packed his bedroll, saddled his horse and gone off with Fergal to drink in the Five Mile Creek Tavern. His visits home had become increasingly rare, and although she knew that some of the time he'd been forced to patrol the distant pastures, she had resented his absence, and the few days they had actually spent together in the past months could be counted on one hand.

She woke from her doze, realised Nathaniel had fallen asleep and gently laid him in the wooden cradle her father had sent up from Parramatta when Violet had been born. With a vast yawn, she stood in the doorway and stared out at the heavy rain. It had been falling intermittently for almost two months. There had been precious little work done, and her vegetable plot was again so sodden the crop was rotting. Yet she had little enough energy for her children, let alone chores, and she thanked God for the rain and the respite it gave.

She looked longingly at the bed and wondered if she dared snatch a few moments' rest before Violet woke from her afternoon sleep, but she was already stirring and Ruby steeled herself for the coming tantrum: at just under a year, Violet was demanding.

Violet screamed as Ruby tried to change her napkin, her angry cries making Ruby's head ring. "Hush, Violet. I'm going as fast as I can, and if you would only keep still, it would make things much easier."

Violet kicked out, rolled on her stomach and crawled away, the tears replaced by a crow of victory.

Ruby sighed and let her go. "To hell with it," she muttered. "What does it matter if she's half naked?"

"Missus Ruby, I take Vi. You sleep. Make strong. Give plenty milk."

"I didn't hear you come in, Kumali."

"No one hear not'ing when baby shout," she replied, as she padded across the room and sank on to the bed. A coughing fit overtook her and it was a moment before she could speak again. "Dat Vi make big noise — alonga make head bang."

"It sounds like you need rest more than me," said Ruby, eyeing the swollen belly and the sleeping baby she had in a sling over her wheezing chest.

Kumali put baby Natjik in the cradle with Nathaniel and made a grab for the wriggling Violet. "My Natjik good black-fella. Get plenty sleep."

"Where's Duncan?"

"Away with sheep up rivva. Big watta maybe come again, but he back soon."

"I'll be glad of your company," Ruby said, as she leant into the pillows and watched Kumali wrestle with Violet and finally get the napkin pinned. "There's no doubt about it, Kumali," she murmured sleepily, "you're an expert at handling my daughter."

"Vi ken who boss," laughed Kumali, as she gave the child a hug.

Ruby's gaze drifted to the two babies in the cot. They looked so peaceful, curled up together, Natjik's coffee-coloured limbs perfectly complementing the pale pink of her son's. There were just seven months between them, and though Kumali's son was small and less robust, he seemed to be thriving.

Ruby's eyelids drooped and the sound of Kumali's singsong voice and Violet's chuckles faded as sleep finally claimed her.

★ ★ ★

The sound of heavy footsteps woke her with a start. "Who's there?"

"It's me. Why? Who else were you expecting?" A match flared and the oil lamp flickered into life.

"James!" Ruby scrambled off the bed, ran into his arms and smothered his face with kisses. "Oh, James, it's so lovely to see you. Where've you been? What've you been doing? It's been so long, and I've missed you."

"Whoa there, Ruby, let a man get his breath." James laughed and swung her round before kissing her. "It's good to be home," he said, as he held her at arm's length and looked down at her. "I'd forgotten how lovely you are," he said softly, "but you look tired."

"There's a reason for that," she breathed. "Come and meet your son." She grabbed his hand before he could comment and tugged him towards the cradle. "This is Nathaniel Logan Tyler, and he's already a week old."

James's awed expression made her pulse race as he peered into the cradle and put a grubby finger against his son's cheek. "My word," he breathed.

"So you're pleased with him?" She didn't like the desperate need that had crept into her voice, but it was so important he loved their baby.

James gently lifted the baby and held him in the crook of his arm. "My son," he murmured. He looked at Ruby, eyes shining. "How could I not be pleased with him? He's a bonzer little boy. Nathaniel means 'God's gift', you know."

299

Ruby could only nod, for she was close to tears as she watched him count the tiny fingers and toes, and caress the soft, pale hair. His look of wonder said it all. At last, at last, she thought. Perhaps now he would stay close to home and they could be a real family.

She glanced at Kumali, who was having a coughing fit and trying to keep a tight hold of a squirming Violet. Natjik must have woken earlier, for he was once more cocooned in the sling. "I'll take her," she said softly. "You rest." She turned back to James. "Say hello to Gladys," she said, stumbling over the unfamiliar name with which he'd saddled their daughter.

But James wasn't listening. "What are you doing here?" he barked at Kumali. "Why aren't you with Duncan?"

Ruby flinched at his tone and hastened to explain. "Duncan's taken the sheep up to drier pastures. Kumali's here because she's heavily pregnant and still nursing Natjik."

"You know I don't like her in the house," he snarled.

Ruby's anger sparked. "Kumali's my friend," she retorted, "my only friend, and when you and Duncan are away, she helps me with the chores."

He put Nathaniel back in the cradle, his expression stony. "Get out, Kumali, and take your piccaninny with you."

"James!" Ruby snapped. "Don't talk to her like that."

"I'll talk to her any way I want."

"Kumali's done you no harm. Surely you don't begrudge me another woman's company?"

300

"You'd be wise to choose your friends more carefully," he replied, as he poured water into a bowl and began to wash, "because when we're rich, there won't be a place for people like her."

Ruby exchanged bewildered looks with Kumali, who hovered in the doorway, and tried to appease James with a more gentle tone. "You can't really mean for her to go out on such a night? The only shelter is the lambing *gunyah*, and Kumali has a nasty cough."

"She's black — she'll survive." His glare had Kumali slink out into the rain.

Stung by his words, Ruby threw a scrap of towel at him and eased Violet on to her other hip. "Why do you hate her so? She's done nothing wrong."

"She's no business to be living in this house, spreading her germs everywhere. She's caused us nothing but trouble since we took her in, and I have to think of my son," he muttered, as he dried himself. "She's always got something wrong with her and I don't want him catching anything."

"Violet is healthy enough," she countered.

He shot a glance at the little girl on Ruby's hip and tossed the towel on to the table. "Her name is Gladys," he retorted, "and she's obviously lucky. But Nathaniel is different and I don't want Kumali or her brat anywhere near him."

"Why do you dismiss our daughter so easily?"

"She's a girl — of no use to me."

Ruby was stung by his coldness, and the love that had once burnt so brightly dimmed even further. Her husband had become a stranger. "There was a time when you would have given shelter to Kumali."

"Yes," he snapped, "and look where that got us — a dead convict, the loss of stores, a horse and saddle, and of another pair of hands. We're lucky we haven't had the police banging on our door looking for that dead convict."

"I know you still fret over that, but it was a long time ago, and Kumali was not to blame. Surely you can't still think they would be looking for him?"

He ignored her. "It's because of her that we're two men down. There just aren't enough of us to keep this place going."

Her anger rose at this unfair accusation. "If you and Fergal stayed more than a couple of days at a time, there wouldn't be a problem," she snapped. "You've been gone almost six months, James, and yet you come in here and start throwing your weight about without a thought of what I might have had to cope with in your absence."

"This is my house and you're my wife. I'll do and say as I see fit."

She lifted her chin, determined not to be cowed, determined to hold her temper. "So where have you been?"

"I had business to attend to."

"What business?"

"My own blasted business!" he roared.

Violet flinched and let out a wail, thereby waking Nathaniel, who began to cry.

"For God's sake, Ruby!" he yelled above the cacophony. "How can a man think with all this caterwauling?"

Ruby took the sobbing baby from the cradle. "You started it by shouting," she said crossly, as she jiggled Nathaniel on her shoulder and tried to soothe Violet.

"Then you shouldn't question me," he retorted. He pulled out a chair and sat down. "This isn't exactly the warmest homecoming. You can hardly blame me for shouting. Sort Gladys and Nathaniel out and get me something to eat. I'm starving."

Ruby was sorely tempted to tell him to feed himself, but knew it would only cause further argument. She swiftly changed Nathaniel's napkin and put him back into the cradle. Once Violet was placated with a crust of bread and straddling her hip, she quickly dished up the last bowlful of stew, added chunks of freshly made damper and put it on the table.

"Is that it?" He poked a spoon through the watery mess, took a mouthful and grimaced. "Where's the meat, and what about vegetables?"

"I've no ammunition for the rifle, so I've had to rely on the traps. There was rabbit in there at one time. As for the vegetables, they're rotting in the ground."

He frowned. "How long has this been going on?"

She held his gaze. "For about three months."

He pushed the bowl away. "You should have cleared the vegetable patch when the rain first started, and Duncan should have made sure there was plenty of fresh meat in the cold store before he left."

She'd had enough of placating him. "And *you* should have been here instead of leaving your responsibilities to others." Her stomach rumbled. "Are you going to eat that?"

"I wouldn't insult my stomach."

Ruby glared at him and snatched up the spoon. "You wouldn't be so fussy if this was all that was on offer every day for weeks on end," she said through a mouthful. "Beggars can't be choosers, James, and you want to thank God there's even this much in the house."

James had the grace to look ashamed as Ruby shared the meagre meal with Violet. "I didn't realise," he murmured. He pushed the last piece of damper across the table. "Sorry, Ruby, but I hadn't meant to be away so long, and I wouldn't have if I'd known the situation here, but me and Fergal got sidetracked."

Ruby could just imagine the female who'd caused this sidetracking, for she suspected James was unfaithful during his long absences. She had no proof, but she feared that one day he would be distracted enough not to come home at all. Realising there was little profit in voicing her suspicions, she ignored her gnawing hunger, wiped the bowl with the last of the damper bread and fed it to Violet.

"Aren't you curious as to what I've been doing?"

"Of course, but you've already made it plain it's none of my business," she said tartly.

He gave a wry smile and scratched his chin. "I asked for that."

304

Indeed he had, but his tentative apology didn't appease her.

"Fergal and I have been to Sydney."

She stared at him, dumbfounded.

"I thought that would surprise you." He leant back in his chair with a broad grin. "But there's more to come, and that's why I had to see you before I leave for Bathurst."

She went cold. "Bathurst? But that's miles away. What's in Bathurst?"

"Gold, Ruby. Lots and lots of gold." He pushed back his chair and stood over her, the excitement clear in his handsome face. "Fergal and I have bought everything we'll need, and we leave first light tomorrow."

Ruby was so shocked she could barely digest his words. "You're leaving tomorrow? But where did you get the money to buy . . .? What about me and the children? How long will you be gone, and how do you know this isn't just another rumour?"

"It's no rumour," he said impatiently. "As for the money" — his gaze slid away — "I borrowed against this year's wool-clip."

Ruby opened her mouth to protest, but he hurried on, "It's a gamble worth taking, and I won't be gone for long. Word is, there's gold lying about waiting to be picked up."

She stood, Violet clutched to her chest. "You gambled our wool-clip? But what if there's no gold? What will happen to us then?"

"But there *is* gold. We're going to be rich, Ruby. Rich enough for you to dress in silks and diamonds and never have to consort with blacks or eat slop like that again. So rich my son will never have to grub in the dirt or be grateful for handouts from his father-in-law."

"You're mad." She took a step back, frightened by the wild look in his eyes.

"Not mad, Ruby — just sick of having nothing to call my own. This place will never really be ours, and I want my son to hold his head high and be the master of his own destiny."

"But this *will* be his in time."

"Why should my son slave for a wool cheque? I have the chance to make my fortune, to ensure he has the finest education so he can achieve something worthwhile, and I *will* do it, Ruby. Just watch me."

Her tears were making it hard to see. "This talk of golden fortunes is nothing but a dream, a madness. As for Eden Valley, it *is* ours: Papa promised to sign over the deeds on our tenth wedding anniversary."

"I'm not prepared to wait ten back-breaking years only for him to change his mind once I've made something of it. I'm off to look for gold, and when I find it, I'll build a grand house in the city and we'll take our rightful place in society."

"Our place in society? But you're a tenant farmer's son, and I'm the daughter of a former convict. This is as good as it gets, James."

"No it isn't," he snapped. "You have no ambition, Ruby, that's your problem. My father never owned a thing in his life — even his cottage was tied to the job, and it's only because my brothers took over that he didn't end up in the workhouse. Do you really think

I'm content to be stuck out here in the middle of nowhere in a house I don't own, with only labourers and blacks for company and damn few prospects?" His eyes flashed and she stared at him in dumb horror. "Well? Do you?"

"But you always wanted a farm — it was your dream, just as it was mine. Papa knew you could never afford a place this size; that's why he leased it to us. He wanted us to have something we could hand down to our children, and he will never break his promise. Please, James, you're not thinking straight."

"My thinking is clearer than ever. I will do this, Ruby, and no one can stop me."

Ruby deposited Violet on the bed and covered her with a blanket. She stood beside her, tears threatening, pulse racing at the thought of the bartered wool cheque and the months of worry and loneliness ahead.

He came up behind her and gathered her to him. "This is our chance, Ruby," he said into her hair, "and I want you to trust me. I know what I'm doing."

She turned and rested her cheek on his chest. "Don't leave me," she begged. "Please don't go."

He kissed the top of her head. "You've managed so well up to now, and I do understand how hard it must have been, but if you can hang on just a while longer, we can live in comfort and be together for the rest of our lives."

Ruby heard the rapid beat of his heart, knew it was the promise of gold that made it race and felt only despair.

★　★　★

Kumali reached the *gunyah*, scrambled in and tried to catch her breath, but the cough wracked her chest and it was some time before she could attend Natjik. As the baby suckled, she took stock of her surroundings. Duncan had built this *gunyah* to shelter the lambing ewes, and the smell of them was strong in the damp straw and earthen floor. The leafy branches that formed the walls and roof had withered, and there were several gaping holes where they'd simply collapsed beneath the weight of the rain.

She shivered, for she was soaked and the night air was chilly. Drying herself with the flour-sack sling, she drew Natjik closer to keep him warm. The baby in her belly was squirming, unsettled by her run through the rain, and there was a throbbing in her head.

Kumali listened to the rain battering the surrounding trees and huddled into the driest corner. If only Duncan was here, if only the boss hadn't come home . . . at least she was warm in the hut, and Natjik could lie in the soft blankets of the cradle. She grimaced. The boss always caused trouble and made Missus Ruby sad, but Kumali had noticed more troubling changes in him since the babies had come, and she suspected it wouldn't be long before he left again never to return.

"It would be good if the boss leaves," she muttered. "I could be in the hut with Missus Ruby and keep dry."

Another hacking cough woke Natjik with a cry of alarm. She tried to soothe him, but he wriggled and squirmed, and as the pain in her head increased, she lost patience. Wrapping him in the sacking sling, she put him on the straw and tried to shut out the sound of his wailing by putting her hands over her ears.

Her tears were warm as she rocked back and forth. She missed Duncan and wished she could have gone with him, for there would be proper shelter, soft wallaby skins and good tucka. If only the rain would stop, she could go and find him. But Duncan had ordered her to stay with Ruby until he returned, and because she relied on him even more since Natjik's birth, she couldn't disobey.

Feeling cold, miserable and unwell, Kumali curled up on the filthy straw next to Natjik, closed her eyes and prepared for the long wait until morning.

Dawn was dismal in the teeming rain as Ruby made her way from the byre with a pail of milk. The weather reflected her mood, for the night had been restless, their farewells hasty before Fergal had rapped on the door. Setting the pail on the table, she wrapped the shawl round her shoulders and stood in the doorway to watch the two men load the mules they'd brought from Sydney.

James had put flour, tea, sugar and tins of syrup in the store at the back of the house. There were oats for porridge, two tins of kerosene, a supply of candles, oil and wicks for the lamps and several boxes of ammunition, and yet Ruby would gladly have exchanged all of it for James to change his mind. He remained impervious to her every attempt to make him forget this foolishness. When gold fever struck, it struck with a force that would not be denied.

309

With the mules laden, the men gathered up the leading reins and swung into the saddle. James blew her a kiss. "I'll be back as soon as I can," he called. "Wish me luck." Not waiting for a response, he nudged the horse into a trot.

Ruby stepped from the doorway into the deserted clearing and watched until they were out of sight. She had never felt so lonely or so frightened for the future, and as her tears mingled with the rain, she looked up at the leaden sky and prayed for courage.

A whisper seemed to come on the rain, and as the breeze rippled the grass like the passage of unseen footsteps, she knew she was not alone.

Ruby wiped away the tears. The rain no longer seemed so chill, or the future as bleak, for her grandmother's love was warm and life-giving, and as she went to find Kumali, she knew Nell would always walk beside her.

Lawrence Creek, Hunter Valley, September 1851

Jessie eased her aching back and wiped the sweat from her face. The copper boiler was bubbling on the roaring fire, the steam making it hard to see. The weather wasn't helping, for it was unseasonably warm for September, and as she prodded the linen with the long wooden stick, she felt hampered by her winter dress.

"You should rest, Miss Searle."

"I'll rest when we've beaten this measles epidemic," she replied. "But I would be grateful if you could feed this sheet through the mangle."

310

The middle-aged minister hurried to guide the sheet into the tin bathtub, and Jessie smiled at him through the steam. Peter Ripley was indeed the antithesis of Zephaniah Lawrence, not only in his jolly appearance, but in his genuine love for others and his concern for the natives; a concern that had been put to the test when measles had swept through the valley, causing devastation among the blacks.

There had been little rest for either of them, and as the weeks had gone on and the deaths mounted in the native camps, she had witnessed his very real pain at the loss of life, and his untiring belief that if he could get them to trust him, he might just make a difference to their wretched circumstances.

"Where's Hilda?"

Jessie was wrestling with the last sheet. "She's gone over to Abel's old place with chicken soup and fresh bread for the native camp. Tumbalong's little boy is still very weak, but it looks as if he'll pull through."

Peter Ripley drew the steaming sheet through the mangle and dropped it in the bathtub. "Thank God," he said fervently. "That poor man has lost three children as well as his aunt and grandparents, and although he puts a brave face on things, I know he's suffering."

"It seems unfair that our children recover so quickly from these illnesses when the natives have so little strength to fight them."

Peter carried the heavy tin bath to the washing line. "I have been in correspondence with my father. He's a medical man and most interested in the effects of our

311

commonplace illnesses on the indigenous people. His theory is, they have never been exposed to such things and therefore have no resistance. He equates this with the white men suffering recurring bouts of malaria in Africa, whereas the natives there seem to have built up immunity to the mosquito."

"All I know is we have lost too many," she said on a sigh, "and Abel will be shocked and saddened by what he finds when he comes back."

"So you still believe he will return?"

Jessie tucked damp tendrils of hair back into the untidy bun and tried to maintain a semblance of dignity as a wave of longing swept through her. "There is always hope."

"Indeed there is, but one must guard against false hope and have the courage to face reality. It has been nearly a year, Miss Searle."

She heard the gentleness in his voice, and knew he was trying to make her see sense. Peter Ripley had become a friend and confidant, yet how could she explain the hope that remained with her no matter how hard she tried to banish it?

"I know," she admitted, "and if the rumours are true, he's no doubt too busy digging for gold to think about us."

"With the strikes in Ballarat and Bendigo following so swiftly after the one in Ophir, it is possible he's gone further afield." His dark eyes were compassionate. "Don't you think you should set aside the past and begin to think of your future? Gerhardt Schmidt is in love with you, Miss Searle, and you are not being fair to him."

Jessie covered her loss of composure by carrying the tin bath back to the outdoor kitchen. She missed Abel, but Peter had a point. She hadn't considered her future at all once he'd gone — filling each day with chores until she fell exhausted into bed. Perhaps she *was* wasting her life in yearning for the unattainable, when the chance of happiness was right under her nose.

She dumped the heavy smoothing irons on the range to heat them through and turned to the stack of clean laundry. Her thoughts were legion, her emotions in turmoil. Abel had cared so little he hadn't bothered to write or send a message — for all he knew she could be dead — and here she was, pretending he would come back. Peter was right, she admitted silently. She was being unfair to herself, and to Gerhardt.

As the sheets became smooth and crisp, she thought about Gerhardt's courtship. There was little doubt he admired her, for he'd been a regular, attentive escort, never once overstepping the mark of familiarity, but making it plain he wished to further their friendship.

Frieda too had encouraged her to visit Possum Hills on the pretence that she needed her at the Hunter Valley Ladies' Group meetings, or to collect clothing and food to give to the poor — she'd even gone so far as to seek her advice on how to prepare bush turkey eggs. Jessie had seen through these excuses but went along with them because she enjoyed her company and, after living so many weeks under her roof, had come to think of her as a staunch friend. She had tactfully let

313

Frieda know she didn't plan on getting married, but had kept all mention of Abel to herself. Frieda of course would have none of it, refusing to believe that one so young should wither into spinsterhood. To that end she made sure Jessie was invited to every party, and that Gerhardt was her escort.

Jessie smiled as she ironed. Frieda was a mainstay of the community, a tireless fund-raiser and absolutely unique. It would have been churlish to refuse her invitations and, she had to admit, she was enjoying her social life — even though Frieda insisted upon lending her dresses that were far too grand for country dances and tea parties.

"What has made you smile?"

"The memory of Frieda bullying me into wearing that dress to her party the other month. She's a difficult woman to refuse."

"That she is, but I'm grateful for her patronage. We could never have afforded the medicines for Tumbalong's family otherwise." He eyed her through the steam. "And may I say you looked very well in that dress. Quite the belle of the ball, as my dear late wife would say."

She blushed and dipped her chin. "That's what Gerhardt said." She had a sudden memory of his fair hair glinting in the candlelight, of his hand at her waist as they danced and of the fine figure he cut in his dark suit.

"So you are not completely immune to his overtures?"

314

"He is charming, and good company." She looked at him. "I've been foolish to treat him so badly, haven't I?"

"Oh, I think he'll forgive you," laughed Peter. He glanced over her shoulder. "If you will excuse me, I have duties to attend. I'll leave you to welcome our visitor."

"Visitor?" She turned and became flustered. "Gerhardt, you have caught me unprepared." Her fingers flew to her hair, aware she must look a fright.

"You look lovely," he said, climbing from his horse. His clothes were immaculate as ever, his shining boots only lightly veiled in dust. He kissed the air above her fingers. "I apologise for my unannounced arrival, but Mother sent me to ask you . . ." He fell silent.

Jessie frowned. "What is it, Gerhardt?"

"I can no longer use my mother as an excuse," he said irritably. "I am a grown man, and it is time I spoke for myself." He took a deep breath. "Miss Searle, Jessie, will you do me the honour of accompanying me on a Sunday-afternoon carriage ride? We will be chaperoned," he added hastily. "Mrs Blake has agreed to come with us."

Jessie realised this was the moment her life could change — that her love for Abel was in reality the romantic whim of a naïve girl, and she could no longer prolong the fantasy. She dipped a curtsy. "I would be delighted," she murmured.

She was rewarded with a smile that brought a deepening of blue to his eyes, and she was once more reminded of how handsome he was.

CHAPTER
ELEVEN

Kernow House, Watsons Bay, February 1852

Harry steeled himself before he went into the room, for his brother's helplessness brought his spirits low. The shutters were closed against the glare of summer, the only light a flickering lamp. Oliver was slumped in the bath chair, staring into an empty hearth. Despite the stifling heat, there was a blanket over his useless legs, and a few wisps of grey hair had escaped from beneath the richly embroidered Egyptian cap. His pasty complexion, distorted face and diminished girth emphasised his frailty.

Harry dismissed the nurse, who'd been reading to his brother, and, with a sinking heart, stood by the hearth. Oliver's health remained a constant worry, and since the second attack, he had lost the use of all his limbs and was blind in his left eye. It was the lingering, wasting destruction of a once robust man, and Harry wondered if he could comprehend the ruination, for the spark of intelligence was all but extinguished, and Oliver seemed to have given up the fight. The doctor had insisted Oliver could hear and understand, and that was the reason the nurse read to him, and the reason for the one-sided conversation Harry was about to embark upon.

"I've just come from Sydney Town," he began. "Things have settled down a little now the clerks, domestic servants and more timid men have realised the digger's life is not for them. They're leaving the gold fields to the adventurers and men of brawn, and are returning in their droves. It's a huge relief to the farmers, who can now get on with the season's shearing, and it is hoped there will be enough labour to bring in the March harvest."

Oliver's drooping, sightless eye was watering and Harry mopped the tears with a handkerchief. "Looking for gold, it seems, is a matter of chance, and those who expect to find it with minimum labour are usually disappointed. It is the well-equipped man willing to work like a dog for months who has success."

There was silence from Oliver, and Harry drew up a chair. "The madness continues, however, and even the more staid of Sydney's matrons are parading about in silk dresses and elaborate bonnets. They are quite a sight, but not as startling as the horses shod with gold and the men sitting in the taverns with a pint of gin in one hand and a wad of cash in the other buying drinks for all and sundry." He smiled. "There are still shuttered shops and offices, but I think Melbourne is suffering more. It is said the city is all but deserted in the rush for Ballarat and Bendigo."

He leant back and, because he couldn't bear to witness Oliver's helplessness, looked towards the dusty beams of sunlight that pierced the shutters. "There are over a hundred deserted ships in Sydney Harbour, and migrants of every colour and creed fight to purchase equipment. Our storekeepers are hard-pressed to keep pace with the demand, and the pavements along the main thoroughfares are stacked with picks, pans, pots and Virginia cradles. The price for everything has skyrocketed, with flour at thirty-five pounds a ton, and bread at eight pence a pound. The flour mill I had built last October is working twenty-four hours a day now we have the wheat concession from the old Collinson farm and more labour."

Oliver regarded him, and Harry looked away — hating the silence — shamefully repulsed by the deadness of that awful eye. "Niall and I have set up stores in Ophir and Ballarat to meet the demand, and his sons and nephews will run them and take their cut of the profits, which, I have to say, are proving most satisfactory."

The silence was as oppressive as the heat, and he hurried on, "All this commerce has served us extremely well. I have managed to keep our warehouses fully stocked by bartering with the captain of every ship entering port, and of course our whaling fleet is supplying us, not only with tea, but with oil and meat. The gold assayer I hired has proved his worth, for he is as sharp as a tack in the current competitive market and keeps the exchange rate just high enough to maintain the flow of business and still provide us with a healthy profit."

Oliver seemed to be listening, for his singular gaze remained steady.

318

Harry gently took the withered hand. "But I bring the best news of all, Oliver. Your debts are wiped out, the future is secure, and you and Amelia need never worry again."

"Can it really be true?"

Harry looked up. Amelia was in the doorway. "There has been a fortune made these past months, and I see no end to it as long as there is gold and men willing to search for it."

Her skirts rustled as she sat down. "But it is your fortune, Harry. You were the one who —"

"I made a promise, Amelia, and Fate smiled upon me in a way I could never have foretold. The riches I've accumulated were for all of us, and they'll be shared equally."

Amelia was tearful. "How can we ever thank you?"

"There's no need," he said gruffly. "Through Niall's foresight and friendship, I have more than one man could spend in a lifetime. It is enough to know I have provided for the family and that future generations of Cadwalladers will not have to fret over every farthing."

Amelia took her husband's hand. "We are saved, Oliver," she murmured. "Now you must concentrate on getting well so we can enjoy our new prosperity."

Harry caught her eye and saw that, despite the positive note in her voice, she shared his doubts for Oliver's recovery. Unable to bear the heartbreak in her expression, he busied himself by lighting a cigar and changed the subject. "Now that things are on an even keel, I feel ready to return home," he said, puffing clouds of smoke into the room.

Amelia looked stricken.

"It's time I went," he said. "Twenty months is a long absence, and I miss my wife and children."

"I suppose it was inevitable," she said sadly, "but we will be sad to see you go. I have come to rely upon your good company and wise advice, and the house will not be the same without you."

"It was never a permanent arrangement," he gently reminded her.

"I know, and I can understand you wanting to return home — it's just that I've got so used to you being here." She lifted her chin. "I am being selfish. When do you plan to leave?"

"There is some business to attend to with Niall, and certain legal documents to be finalised and signed to ensure the continuity of income into the estates, but it shouldn't take long. I'm hoping to sail by the end of the month."

"So soon?" Amelia sank back into the chair. "But there are very few ships now the sailors have gone in search of gold — how can you be assured a berth?"

"I have spoken to the captain of our whaling fleet. The *Constant* will take me to Batavia, and I will make other arrangements from there." He could see she was still fretting at the thought of being left alone with a sick husband, and hurried to reassure her. "Niall has promised to keep you informed of the accounts and promises to remain on hand should you need him." He saw her doubt and was angered by it. "He *can* be trusted. You have my word."

320

"If you're sure," she muttered, obviously not convinced.

"Niall has proved a loyal and honest friend," he snapped. "If it hadn't been for him, you would still be scratching for every penny." He saw her redden at his angry tone and, without apologising for his sharpness, quickly carried on, "I've finally had a chance to go through those trunks from Mama and George's house," he said, exhaling cigar smoke.

Amelia's expression brightened. "Was there anything of interest? I love rummaging. One never knows what one might find."

"It was mostly old clothes and souvenirs of their travels, but there was also a trunk of bills of lading, receipts, letters, sea diaries and legal documents. It took me a while to get through it all, for some documents related to our stepfather George's property in America, as well as for both houses here."

The light of avarice glinted. "Property in America? What happened to it?"

"His old sea captain Samuel Varney willed him a try-works, thirty cottages and five whaling ships in Nantucket. George sold all but the whalers after he'd set up the try-works station in Van Diemen's Land."

Her disappointment was clear, but she forced a smile. "I hope you kept the sea diaries. Frederick would love them, and I am sure they will be educational."

"Indeed I have, along with some of the more exotic mementoes of George's time on the whaling ships." He paused and considered his next words carefully. "There were bundles of personal letters, which I destroyed after glancing through them, but there was also a particular packet of rather startling correspondence that I have decided to keep."

Amelia was clearly excited. "What was in them? Something scandalous? A family skeleton? Do tell."

It was at moments like these he wished Oliver was mentally alert, for discussing such a subject with a woman — especially one like Amelia — only encouraged her thirst for scandal. "There were a number of letters," he began, "and I had to put them in chronological order to make sense of them."

"Who were they from?" Amelia's cheeks were flushed with expectation.

"They were mostly from Ann, the countess of Glamorgan, to George's mother, Susan Collinson."

Amelia frowned. "How on *earth* did Susan Collinson know a countess? She was just a rather lowly preacher's wife."

"That preacher was Ezra Collinson, the youngest of three sons by the earl of Glamorgan. Ezra's brother, Gilbert, Australia's first judge advocate, was married to Ann and inherited the earldom when the eldest brother died without male heirs."

"Good heavens. I never realised the Collinsons were quite so grand, and of course we're almost related because of George. How exciting — I must arrange a dinner party."

He could almost see her mind working on a seating plan. "George's side of the family are modest people interested only in their farm at Hawks Head. They don't do the social rounds." He noted the determined

322

glint in her eye and his impatience spilled over. "I would like you to concentrate on what I am about to say, Amelia, because it is important."

Amelia looked startled at his brusqueness, but again he didn't apologise, for Amelia had to be made to listen. "The letters Ann wrote to Susan were the usual mixture of local gossip, their day-to-day life and social news, but within that seemingly innocent prattle I detected something else."

Amelia sat forward. The fit of pique over, he had her full attention.

"I realised there was a pattern. It began with the mention of a baby being fostered by a middle-aged couple, and over the years that child was mentioned regularly in Ann's correspondence. It may only have been a line or two, and wouldn't have caused comment from a casual reader, but being in possession of all those letters, I began to see that her life was carefully documented from cradle to marriage."

"Almost like a code," Amelia breathed.

Harry nodded. "My suspicions were taking shape, and when I read a hastily penned warning from Ann to Susan in 1804, I knew I was on the right track. Confirmation came in 1832. The letter had been written years before and the solicitor was charged with delivering it only if Susan and Ezra were dead. George, their only surviving son, was the recipient."

"What did it say?" Her eyes were wide, her expression rapt.

"I will give it to you to read, but it must be returned and, Amelia, this must never be discussed outside this

323

room." He looked at her sternly, hoping it was warning enough to hold her gossiping tongue. "I mean it, Amelia," he said darkly. "Not a word. For this reflects not only on the Collinsons, but the Cadwalladers." He maintained the glare as she pouted. "Do I have your promise?"

She nodded and sighed resignedly. "I promise."

Satisfied, he carried on, "George's mother, Susan, had an affair, and unknown to her lover, there was a child, Rose. She entrusted her to Ann before they both left for Australia with the First Fleet. Ann had placed Rose with a couple in Somerset and, when she returned to England, kept Susan informed of the child's progress."

"Who was the father?"

"My grandfather Jonathan Cadwallader."

Amelia paled and Oliver made a strangled noise in his throat.

"So you do understand?" Harry squatted before him, delighted at this turn of events. "Oh, Ollie, I wish you could speak. I do so need you to advise me on what to do."

"*Do?*" Amelia looked at him in horror. "That child is probably long dead by now, and anyway, she's not . . . not . . . *legitimate*." The last word was a whisper.

Harry had some difficulty in keeping his impatience under control. He turned back to Oliver. "Did George say anything to you?"

There was the suggestion of a shift in that one clear eye, but Harry realised that even if George had confided in him, that confidence had been lost for ever in Oliver's affliction. "No matter," he soothed. "George was evidently intrigued enough to do some digging, and he managed to unearth a church register recording the birth of Rose's daughter, Fanny, which I found in the trunk. On my return to England, I mean to continue the search."

"You surely cannot wish to become *familiar* with this person?" Amelia's nose was in the air. "After all, she will hardly be your class, and her sort is not averse to blackmail. You must remember your position, Harry, and think carefully before you do anything foolish."

He eyed her coolly. "Rose was my father and stepfather's half-sister and therefore a Cadwallader — it is my duty to discover what happened to her family."

"And after finding these people, what if there is a challenge to the title? Think of the scandal it would cause." She shivered, but Harry suspected it was more from pleasurable anticipation than horror.

"Rose's heirs have no legitimate claim to the earldom," he replied stiffly, "so you can rest assured the ascendancy is secure."

"Let us hope you are right," she sniffed.

Harry ignored her quip. "It seems that Grandfather Jonathan didn't know of Rose's existence for many years, but when he uncovered the truth, he secretly arranged for her and her family to move counties to a more comfortable cottage in Cornwall, with guaranteed work for her husband. He might have had a reputation as a roué, but he possessed a sense of honour when it came to family."

Amelia was staring at him as if he'd lost his wits, but Oliver's gaze remained steady.

Encouraged by this silent approbation, Harry continued, "Our grandfather died in New South Wales," he explained to Amelia. "He was riding out to the Collinsons' farm at Hawks Head — I suspect to see Susan and tell her of his discovery — when his horse stumbled. He was thrown and killed. He planned to set up a trust for Rose and her heirs, though I believe this died with him, for the papers were never signed, and these were what I found. It is my intention to seek out the family and carry out my grandfather's wishes."

Ophir Gold Fields, February 1852

The shanty town was populated by bearded, unkempt men from all walks of life. The adventurous son of a duke found himself working alongside shearers, labourers, doctors, sailors and office clerks, but the hunt for gold was a great leveller, and life on the Ophir fields had a way of erasing any class distinction.

There were a few hardy wives who did the cooking, minded the children and helped their men by pushing barrows from the diggings to the river, but they soon tired of the rough conditions and returned home. The woman who could survive the raw, uncouth life was rare, and those who stayed were coarsened by their experiences and soon lost any vestige of their femininity as they donned trousers and shirts, and equalled the men in their colourful language and tireless toil.

The clearing by the river consisted of a sea of tents, primitive bark huts and sheets of calico slung between poles. A few of the sturdier dwellings belonged to the licensed merchants, who had to compete with the sly grog-sellers and prostitutes who melted into the bush every time the police came on inspection. Law and order was maintained as, with common single-mindedness, the diggers worked from sunrise to sundown, their summary justice meted out only when there was a theft of gold or water. Religious instruction on the Sabbath came from the bearded parson as he stood on a tree stump and led them with fiery speeches into rousing hymns.

Nights were filled with the raucous laughter of those who'd fared well and the drunken wails of those less fortunate as the grog shops and whores did a roaring trade. Death was an ever-present spectre — from falling trees and collapsing holes to apoplexy, blood poisoning and the severing of limbs by the careless sweep of an axe. Heat shimmered on the horizon, dazzled in the river and seemed to vibrate in the earth as flies swarmed and the stench of the encampment rose.

Hina was used to heat, but there was no soft Tahitian breeze in the middle of this unforgiving country — no cooling sea, but a tepid, slow-moving river and the cloying sweat that soaked him and made him itch. He regarded his reflection in the mirror he'd wedged in a tree and carefully ran the blade over his chin. Unlike the majority, he didn't sport a beard, because he hated feeling dirty. After almost nine months his twice-daily

327

ablutions in the river still caused comment — albeit good-natured teasing from which he took no offence.

The hurtful jibes over his brown skin, blue eyes and long hair were more difficult to ignore, however, and he'd had to maintain a will of iron to hold his temper — for despite repeated denials, and one or two scuffles, a belligerent few seemed determined to believe he was Chinese.

He narrowed his eyes against the glare of the rising sun and wondered at their ignorance. The few Chinese who worked the diggings were of diminutive size, their eyes dark and slanted, their skin more yellow than Hina's honeyed bronze. They seemed to realise they were unwelcome and kept their distance, heads bowed beneath traditional hats as, pigtails swinging, they fossicked in the waste heaps. To others, they were a strange sight, with their long shoulder poles and baskets, inscrutable expressions and unintelligible language, but Hina was familiar with the Hakka Chinese of Tahiti and could speak their tongue — a skill he'd kept secret, knowing it would only arouse further suspicion.

"These blasted flies are driving me mad," grumbled Bones, as he crawled out of the tent. "If they ain't sittin' on yer, they're stingin' yer. I never knowed such torture."

"It's not the flies that sting," corrected Hina, who had finished shaving and now began to cook the chops and steak over the campfire outside the tent. "It's those big flying bugs." He slapped his arm where one such creature perched. It flew off, only to return a second later.

"I've seen men driven mad — runnin' naked and screamin' into the river to tear at their flesh — and I've got damned near doin' the same meself." Bones pulled down the sleeves of his checked shirt and buttoned it to the neck before clamping on the broad-brimmed hat. "Blasted things," he muttered. "It seems no matter how much you cover up, they find somethin' to sit on."

The steaks, chops and damper bread were eaten quickly, for it was a race against the flies that crawled over every morsel. With breakfast over and refreshed with hot, sweet tea, they set about the daily routine.

Hina grabbed the shovel, jumped into the hole and began to dig. As the pile at the side of the hole grew, Bones loaded the wheelbarrow and took the earth to the river, where it was scooped into sieves and washed until only the largest pieces of sediment were left. Hina, because of his strength and endurance, saw little of this process, for his days were spent underground. Fortunately, the gold that glistened in that sieve was shared equally and, at three pounds an ounce, he had a tidy sum tucked away.

He emerged at noon and stripped off his shirt. His golden torso gleamed with sweat, and after dowsing himself in the river, he went to see what Bones had found.

"It's slow goin'," muttered Bones. "There's a ton of earth to shift, and I've only found about an ounce and a half."

"You're getting greedy," said Hina, as he stretched his back. "There are some who find nothing. But I agree it is slow going; perhaps we should consider getting others to join us." He eyed the bustling activity at the riverbank. Most of the diggers worked in teams of four or six, but that didn't guarantee success. "But who can we trust?"

"There's the rub," groaned Bones, as he mopped his sunburnt brow. "I wouldn't trust most of 'em as far as I could throw 'em."

"I'm beginning to think it's time we —" Hina was interrupted by a shout.

"Look out!"

They turned and saw their recently arrived neighbour fighting to keep control of a terrified mule. The animal was rearing up, fighting the traces of the overladen cart and the tight hold the man had on the bridle. The cart fell with a crash over the hole, effectively trapping anyone inside. He cut the animal free and it raced off into the river, scattering pans, cradles and people in its mad dash to escape.

"God darn it," he rasped, slapping his thigh with his California hat before trying to move the wagon. He looked across at Hina and Bones. "Y'all come and help me? I can't shift this on my own."

Bones picked up the sieve and tried to look busy, and Hina realised he wouldn't be of much use anyway and, after telling Bones to catch the mule, hurried across. He put his shoulder to the wagon, and together they managed to get it upright.

"I got two buddies down there," drawled the American. "We're gonna need a hand."

"Cave-in!" Hina shouted. "Two men buried!" Bones ran over and was swiftly joined by others.

The silence was ominous as they forwent the use of picks and shovels and began to dig furiously with their hands. A cave-in was a regular occurrence and usually fatal. They had all witnessed it before and knew they had but minutes to find the men and get them out.

They had been clawing at the earth for what felt like hours when Hina's fingers touched something. It was a hand. "Here," he gasped, renewing his efforts.

There was silent desperation in the way they gouged at the earth and Hina's awesome strength and stamina were pushed to the limit. When the man's arms were finally revealed, Hina grabbed them and began to pull, while the others dug frantically to release the slowly emerging torso.

The earth finally gave him up. Hina saw he was barely breathing as he was carried away. But there was no time to stop: there was still another man to find.

"I see a shirt. Look." The American was scrabbling furiously either side of a patch of red-and-blue check.

Hina grabbed the shirt, but it ripped in his hand. More digging revealed buttons, a neck and then — at last — a bearded jaw and bloodless face. The eyes were closed, there was little sign of life, and the open mouth was filled with earth. Hina used the last of his strength to haul him out, but he feared he was too late.

The American fell to his knees and cleared the dirt from the man's mouth and nose. The man lay still, the open mouth and slack jaw mocking his efforts. "Come on, breathe, God dammit." He sat him up, poured water down his throat and slapped him hard on the back.

There was a jerk in the man's torso, the eyes opened, and a great gasp of air was taken before he was violently sick. A sigh of relief swept through the onlookers, and then they were gone. The drama was over, no one had died, and there was gold to be found — little point in wasting daylight.

"What the hell happened?" The man, still groggy, spat out the last of the dirt and sat up to drink greedily from the American's waterbag.

"That dumb-assed mule got stung by a bug. The wagon knocked the pile and shed its load, which plugged up the hole."

"Where's . . .?"

"He's being looked after." He inclined his head towards the knot of gaudily dressed whores. "I wouldn't mind bettin' a cent to a dollar we won't see him for the rest of the day."

Hina eyed the women and suspected he was right, for over the months he'd noticed that man regularly visiting their tent. "Better to lose an afternoon's work than your life," he murmured. "You can't blame him for wanting to celebrate."

The American's smile creased the corners of his eyes into a network of fine lines as he dusted his hands on his trousers and replaced his strange, high-crowned, broad-brimmed hat over his tangled hair. "I guess we owe y'all a thank-you," he drawled in a resonant bass. "The name's Howard Repton the Third."

Hina's hand was pumped enthusiastically by the American as he introduced himself.

Howard helped his friend to his feet. "This here's Fergal Molony, and the ladies' man over there's his buddy James Tyler."

The day proceeded without further interruption, and once the sun went down, Hina walked to the river for his ritual bath. It felt good to wash away the grime and sweat of the day, to wallow in tepid water, which ran like silk over his body. All he needed now was Puaiti to comb his hair, oil his torso and take away the aches of the day by loving him.

With a groan of frustration he finished his ablutions and pulled on the wet canvas trousers he'd washed earlier. He had never partaken of the dubious delights James Tyler indulged in, and it did him no good to think of home and the beautiful Puaiti. He was here to find the gold that would make her father agree to their marriage. She had promised to wait for him, but neither of them had suspected it would be for so long, and with each passing day he fretted more, for Puaiti had her pick of suitors.

Determined to put all thoughts of her aside, he snatched up the freshly washed shirt and muddy boots, and returned to camp. Bones would have sold their gold to the merchant by now, and he wanted to count his share. It was time to go home.

As he drew near, he saw the American and his friends lounging by the fire and knew he would have to wait before he could tell Bones of his decision. He draped his sodden shirt over a nearby branch and sat down. Howard Repton the Third was talking, his deep, lazy drawl carrying into the night air as Bones cooked supper.

"It might have been rough in 1849 back in the Californian fields, what with the lynch mobs an' all, but at least we didn't have these pesky critters eatin' at us all darn day." He slapped his hat at a swarm of mosquitoes to little avail.

The American fascinated Hina, and he let the talk flow around him as he studied him more closely.

Howard was a tall, angular man, with piercing eyes and an almost indolent way of moving, which Hina suspected masked an energy that could be called upon at a moment's notice. His face above the neat, pointed beard and drooping moustache was weathered, making him appear older than perhaps he was, and the tangled mass of brown hair reached his collar.

He wore dark blue twill trousers and a checked shirt, over which was a fancy waistcoat with the chain of a pocket watch anchored to the top button. At his waist was a finely tooled belt buckled with silver and inset with a stone the colour of Tahitian waters. The same stone glinted in the heavy ring he wore on the small finger of his left hand, and there was the skin of a snake encircling the crown of his curious hat. Hina eyed the tooled boots with their stubby heels, wondered how he managed to walk in them and decided the man was a mystery, and a rather exotic one at that. He turned his attention back to the conversation, over which Howard was still holding forth.

"I remember back in 1849 how the little ladies would come out in their buggies to entertain us. They were classy compared to the ones here, and Lucy Culpepper kept them in good order, I recall. That ol' gal knew her way around a rifle and soon put a stop to any kind'a shenanigans as quick as a blink. One shot and we knew we were in trouble, 'cos she was known to take the heart out of a coin at forty paces." He smiled and shook his head. "There ain't nothing like good ol' American hospitality."

"Oh, I dunno," muttered Fergal. "You should be in a Galway tavern on a Saturday night — now that's hospitality."

"Yeah, I guess. I've met some of your countrymen, and they sure know how to have a good time. But our beer is better, colder too."

Fergal snorted. "Looks and tastes like piss from what I hear," he responded. "You obviously never experienced the nectar of a creamy-headed Guinness."

Howard looked thoughtful. "I guess I prefer rye whisky — now that's what I call a *man's* drink." Before Fergal could retort, he turned to Hina. "I met Fergal and James upriver about three months back," he explained. "We're always arguing about somethin', so don't pay it no mind." He paused to light a cheroot. "Y'all a long ways from home, Hina. How come?"

"I jumped ship with Bones, here," he replied. "But we've not come as far as you or your English friends."

"I'm an Irishman," muttered Fergal, dark eyes flashing. "There's not a bone nor a drop of blood in me that's English, that's for sure."

"I apologise," said Hina immediately. In his ignorance he'd obviously insulted him, and he had no wish to make an enemy of this sour man.

There was a tense silence, before Fergal shrugged. "You weren't to know," he said grudgingly.

"I'm English," said James, "but I came to Australia some years ago and settled, on a parcel of land west of here."

"You have family there?"

James nodded. "My son was born just before me and Fergal left for Bathurst." A faraway look came into his eyes. "Nathaniel must be about eight months old by now."

"You've got a wife and daughter too," Fergal reminded him.

"So? What's it to you?"

Fergal shrugged.

Bones, who had six children and a wife who nagged constantly when he did pluck up the courage to go home, broke into the awkward silence. "It's always hard to leave kinfolk behind. I suspect you'll soon be off to see 'em again."

James shook his head. "I haven't found enough gold yet. But when I do, I'll go back so fast you won't see me for dust."

This statement was a familiar one, and each of them recognised it as having come from a man who would never be satisfied until he'd struck the elusive "big one".

"I will," James insisted, as the silence stretched and the others refused to look at him. "You see if I don't. It'll take just one rich seam and I'm out of here for good."

"Sure you will," muttered Howard through a plug of chewing tobacco. He eyed Hina. "I'm guessing y'all from Polynesia, but which island would that be?"

"Tahiti."

"Ah," he sighed. "Tahiti. The island of swaying palms and black sands, of *wahinis*, coconuts and the biggest, darkest pearls." Howard rested back against the log, hands behind his head, long legs stretched in front of him.

Hina's pulse quickened. "You have been to Tahiti?"

"Only in my imagination," he admitted ruefully, "and because of a little something I picked up a few years ago. But I aim to visit one day — perhaps on my way home to Texas." With a slow smile that spoke of pleasure to come, he nodded as if to confirm this plan. Then all talk of Tahiti was forgotten as he reached for his saddlebag and drew out four small sacks. "I brought gifts," he explained. "There's sugar, salt, tea and flour — our way of thanks for helping today."

"Much obliged," said Bones, who snatched up the bags and quickly stowed them in a tin trunk inside the tent. He returned to the fire and the meal he was cooking.

337

"Well," drawled Howard, "I don't know about you fellows, but I could eat the side of a steer. When's supper ready?"

"Right now," Bones muttered, as he doled out an enormous steak, which the American folded inside a lump of damper before taking a mighty bite.

"That's good," he said through the mouthful, "but it don't beat the steaks in America for tenderness."

"At least we've got steak," retorted Bones, who was clearly tired of hearing how everything was bigger, better and tastier in America. "There are some what ain't eaten meat in weeks."

"Yeah, I know." Howard took another mighty bite and began to munch. "The gold is getting harder to find, and now we have to pay one pound ten shillings a month for a licence to dig, it's going to make things even tougher."

"We're still finding several ounces a day," Fergal said, "and if these new licensing laws mean there are less diggers, so much the better."

"I reckon the stump orators will get things sorted," muttered Bones through damper and chop. "There ain't nothin' like a bit of rabble-rousin' on a Sunday afternoon to get the diggers stirred up, and it won't be long before the gov'ment caves in."

"Things have certainly got to change," piped up James. "I'm paying more for the right to dig than I do to farm twenty square miles of pasture. It's not fair we have no say in the laws being passed."

"I'm with you there," mumbled Bones, who was trying to stuff food in his mouth before it was covered by buzzing insects. He spat one out in disgust. "Even the storekeepers are complainin', and no one likes being hauled through the streets by the police because they can't afford the outrageous amount of money we're being charged. Pound for pound, we're workin' for a pittance and frankly I've had enough."

Hina had suspected Bones was tiring of life at Ophir, for it was hard on any man, let alone one of his years. This was the opening he'd been waiting for. "When were you thinking of leaving?"

"At the end of the week," Bones replied, casting the last of the fly-blown food aside. He took a swig from the ever-present bottle of rum. "I've 'ad enough of heat and flies, and I want to feel the rock of a ship beneath me and the smell of salt in me nose." He eyed the bottle and grimaced. "I seem to drink my money as fast as I make it."

"Haven't you saved anything?" Hina was appalled.

"Some," he replied, with an air of defiance. "But I got a right to spend my money the way I want."

Hina was about to say he would go with him when Howard's voice overrode him. "James, Fergal and I are of the opinion that the gold is almost worked out here. We're having to dig deeper by the day, and the pickings are hardly worth the effort, so I reckon we should try our luck in Ballarat or Bendigo."

"I have heard it is a long way to travel," said Hina.

"That it is," drawled the American, taking the watch from his waistcoat pocket. "But if a man is stout of heart and eager for adventure, it will seem short."

Hina noted how the gold casing gleamed, the stone at its centre catching the firelight.

"I see you're admiring my timepiece," said Howard proudly.

"It is very fine," said Hina.

"It sure is. I bought it from a miner down on his luck in 1849. He didn't want to sell it, but I made him an offer he couldn't refuse." He grinned as his large hands caressed the watch. "There's many a man would pay a fortune for this, but it's my lucky charm, and nothing and nobody will part me from it."

Hina caught James's eye as the American snapped open the casing. Perhaps he too was amused that one so masculine could become enamoured of a pocket watch. It was fine, and undoubtedly valuable, but it was only a watch.

Yet, as he was about to leave the campfire for the relative comfort of his blankets, he saw the picture that nestled in the casing. Unable to move or speak, he just stared. It was in that moment he realised he would not be leaving with Bones at the end of the week.

Eden Valley, February 1852

Ruby was struggling with a reluctant ewe, trying to get the stupid creature on its back so she could shear it. Grasping its scruff and woolly backside, she heaved it off its hoofs and dumped it down, its neck held fast between her knees. "Right, you so-and-so," she breathed. "Now see who's boss."

340

With the sweat stinging her eyes and her hair coming loose from its pins, she began to snip away the thick wool. There were over two thousand head of sheep to get through, and only half of them had been done. The sun blazed, the sheep complained, and the dust filled her nose. The heavy shears had once felt unwieldy, but after long practice she could now work at almost the same pace as the others.

With the ewe shorn, she shooed it through the narrow gate and into the dip, where the newest recruit to Eden Valley shoved her under the noxious brew before hauling her out. Ruby paused, wiped the sweat from her face and took a long drink of water as she watched him. Tommy Saddler was sixteen and, despite his coltish leanness, had proved a strong and willing worker. He'd arrived at Eden Valley a month ago looking for work, and Ruby had taken an instant liking to him. He had the openness of a country boy, and the good sense to tell her he knew little about sheep but was eager to learn.

With a glance at the children, who were happily playing within the boundaries of a shaded canvas pen, she took a deep breath and returned to work. They had all had a hand in building the special shearing pens, and although they bore little resemblance to the huge wool shed at Moonrakers, they served their purpose. The holding pen led into the shearing pen, where they were working, which in turn led to the drenching pit and on to the pasture, where the shorn beasts bleated their humiliation. There was no roof, and therefore no shelter from the merciless sun, but Ruby was energised by the knowledge that the numerous spring lambs had thrived, and that the wool cheque to come might be large enough to clear the money James had borrowed against the wool-clip and still have some left to restock once the "killers" had been sold to the mining camps.

The sun was sinking fast as the last of that day's mob went through the drenching pit and skittered off into the grass. Ruby eased her back and took off her hat to let the cooling breeze riffle through her sweat-soaked hair. "That's it," she said, her voice warm with pride for a good day's work. "Come on, we've earned our tucker."

She smiled at Kumali, who was suffering from her usual coughing fit, and put a gentle finger on the crumpled cheek of the sleeping baby nestled in the sling. Mookah was six months old and very small, with a russet mop of hair and pale brown skin. "It looks like someone had a hard day," she said wryly. "But you did well, Kumali. I don't know how you manage to work so fast with Mookah tied to you like that."

Kumali's smile was soft with love. "She nae heavy." She picked up a grizzling Natjik and, with his plump legs dangling, balanced him on her hip. "Not like Natjik," she said with a grimace.

Ruby squatted down and a grubby Violet ran at full tilt into her arms. She would be two in a matter of months, her sturdy body proof she was blessed with her mother's robust health. Ruby was warmed by her kisses, and the tiny arms encircling her neck, for they were more precious than any wool cheque and imbued her with a love so profound she was often awed by it. Gathering up a sleepy Nathaniel, she kissed his dirty face and hugged him close. Violet took her hand, and accompanied by her childish prattle, Ruby set off for home.

The camp oven had miraculously survived the terrible flood two years before, but Ruby had decided not to chance their luck further and had moved the entire outside kitchen to higher ground. The roasted mutton and baked vegetables had been devoured, and after his ritual after-dinner pipe, Duncan took his family home to the shack he'd built among the trees, while Tommy returned to the hill pasture and bedded down beneath his blanket.

Ruby kissed her children and tucked them into bed, revelling in the warm, clean smell of their freshly washed skin and nightgowns. She lingered, watching Violet's eyes flutter as she fought sleep, her tiny fists curled beneath her chin. An overwhelming sadness swept over her as she turned away. Violet never asked where her father had gone, and Nathaniel had been too young even to get to know him. It was as if he didn't exist for his children, and as nine long months had passed and there'd been no word from him, it seemed he'd forgotten them too.

She picked up soap, a towel and her nightgown and left the hut. James was a fool, and so was she to think he had ever loved her. She had proved she could live without him — why waste precious time willing him home? Because he was her husband. Because she had made her vows and meant to keep them. Because she had loved him once and he had given her Nathaniel and Violet.

Refusing to let the latent anger mar the beautiful evening, she headed for the river. She took off her boots and stood on the bank, wriggling her toes with pleasure in the damp, cool grass. She pulled the pins from her hair, letting it tumble down her back, then stripped off the moleskin trousers and shirt she'd taken to wearing and splashed into the moonlit water.

Its chill made her gasp, but she took the plunge, and when she broke the surface, she no longer felt the cold. Having washed her hair and scrubbed herself with coarse soap, she lay in the shallows. The flow tugged her hair until it streamed behind her, and the moon-gilded ripples washed away the last of the sweat and dirt of the day.

She looked up into the night sky, which was awash with stars. The moon was ripe and rounded, and there were no clouds to spoil its perfection. How insignificant she was against such grandeur, how solitary in the great silence that was broken only by the sound of water and the whisper of bats' wings.

Perhaps I should feel lonely and afraid, she thought, but why should I? I am part of all this, and it is part of me — it's where I belong. She smiled up at the moon, knowing that somewhere in that sky her grandmother Nell was smiling too.

"Are you not cold in there?"

Ruby shot up, her hands flying to cover her nakedness at the sound of the strange voice. "Who's there?"

"To be sure 'tis only me." He emerged from the shadows.

"Finnbar Cleary, how dare you!" she yelled. "Turn round this instant."

He was still grinning as he turned away. "Ach," he said, "I've seen you naked before."

"I was six," she stormed. "Things have changed."

"Yeah, I noticed." His voice was shaky with laughter.

Ruby threw the soap at him and felt only slightly appeased when it hit him on the back of the head.

"Ow," he protested. "What did you do that for?"

"Just be thankful I didn't have my throwing knife handy," she muttered, as she hauled on the nightgown and gathered up her clothes.

"Sure that's no welcome after all these years, Ruby. Are you not dressed yet? I'm getting awful tired of looking at these trees."

Instead of being refreshed and invigorated by her wash, she was furious and hot with embarrassment. Stomping up the bank, the bundle clutched to her chest, she jabbed him in the back. "What the *hell* do you mean by turning up unannounced at this time of night and watching people bathing? Explain yourself, Finn Cleary, and it better be good."

He rubbed the spot where she'd prodded him. "You've a powerful strength in that finger to be sure, Ruby. I'd not be surprised if you've broken me ribs."

"I'll break your head if you don't give me a straight answer," she growled.

His eyes still held laughter and his mouth twitched as he regarded her. "I'm sorry I disturbed you, and sorry I gave you a fright."

Ruby wasn't ready to forgive him yet, for he didn't look a bit contrite, and his next words proved it.

"But you did look lovely there in the water like a nymph, with your hair all floatin' and your skin touched with the gold of the moon."

She couldn't meet his eye, and although she wanted to slap him for his insolence, she could feel laughter welling. "Finnbar Cleary, you are *impossible*," she spluttered.

"Ach, Ruby, you're a sight for sore eyes and no mistake, and I promise I didn't look for long."

"I wouldn't take a wager on that." She burst out laughing. "You've still got the blarney, thinking you can get away with anything as long as you smile and flash your eyes. You haven't changed a bit."

"I'll take that as a compliment." He took off his battered hat and executed a bow. "Now we've called an end to hostilities, are you not going to welcome me properly with a cup of tea and something to eat? I've travelled a fearful way and could eat a horse."

"You'll get mutton and like it," she muttered. Unable to resist any longer, she flung an arm round his waist and hugged him. "Oh, Finn," she sighed, "you are a complete pain in the rear end, but I'm so glad to see you."

346

"The feeling is mutual, Ruby. It's been too long. But would you mind not digging your boots into me ribs? I've suffered enough for one night."

She realised her bundle was squashed between them and drew back. "I had no idea you were so delicate," she teased.

He rubbed his midriff and pulled a face. "Only when I'm hungry. Can we eat now?"

"You're as bad as my children," she said fondly. "Let me get dressed. Then I'll feed you, and you can tell me why you're here and all the news from home."

The cold mutton was sliced and put on a plate with beetroot and tomatoes from the garden and some quickly fried potatoes. Finn told her the family news as he ate, his imaginative descriptions painting such bright pictures of birthday parties, Christmas and the weddings of two distant cousins that Ruby felt she had really been there.

A vast mug of tea and a quantity of damper filled any remaining gaps, and he eventually wiped his mouth with the back of his hand and relaxed. "That's better," he murmured, as he filled a pipe.

"I should think it is," she retorted, "you've eaten enough for two."

He ignored her jibe and puffed contentedly on his pipe as he leant back in his chair and stared at the moon's reflection on the river.

Despite her words, Ruby had enjoyed watching him eat. It was lovely to see him after so many years, and as they sat there in companionable silence, she took the opportunity to study him more closely. Finn was thirty-two by her reckoning — still handsome, still the possessor of great charm, with the hard muscle and capable hands of a man used to heavy labour. His black hair was thick and wavy, his eyes darkly lashed and as blue with mischief as ever, and the lines that radiated from the corners spoke not only of laughter, but of many hours in the sun.

No wonder I fell in love with him all those years ago, she mused. She smiled as she remembered how she used to plague him to play with her and carry her about, how she used to gaze up at him in adoration and wish he would notice her, and how patient he'd been with the little girl who was ten years younger and no doubt the bane of his life.

"What's so funny?"

"Nothing." She saw him raise a dark brow, realised he wouldn't let it rest and decided to fib — his ego was big enough. "I was remembering how you danced with Grandma Nell on her last birthday," she said. "You reminded her of Grandpa Billy, you know, and I'm glad she got the chance to dance again before she . . ."

His hand was warm as it covered her fingers. "I loved her too," he said softly, "but I always wondered if she might have lived a while longer if it were not for that waltz."

Ruby rather liked his hand resting on hers, liked the strength in those callused fingers and the affection that simple gesture conveyed. "It was what she wanted," she murmured, "and although they wouldn't let me see her after she'd gone, I always believed she left us with a smile on her face."

Finn squeezed her fingers, his gaze understanding. Then he released her and dug his hands into the pockets of his moleskins, his expression hardening. "Where's your man, Ruby?"

She licked her lips. "Ophir, I think. Looking for gold."

"You think?" His dark brows knotted.

She toyed with her hands, unsure of what to say without putting James in too bad a light. And yet why should she care about his reputation — he was the one who'd earned it? "He's in Ophir," she said firmly. "He'll be back soon."

"How long has he been gone?"

"Just a few weeks." She didn't dare look at him.

"Your father seems to think it is more like nine months, and that's rather more than a few weeks," he retorted. "Has he written or sent money or message in all that time?"

She lifted her chin, determined not to let him know how abandoned she'd been. "He's busy, and it isn't easy to correspond from the gold fields," she said defensively. "Besides," she added, "I'm managing very well with Duncan and Kumali, and the new lad, Tommy, is shaping up well." She held his gaze defiantly. "If you knew how long he's been gone, why ask?"

"Your da sent me. He got reports of your man up in Ophir and was worried about you being on your own. Your letters told him very little."

349

Ruby sighed and dipped her chin, watching her fingers knot the fringe on her shawl. "There's no need for him to fret," she replied. "The children and the sheep are thriving, and I've even managed to do a deal so my killing stock can supply the gold fields. With the coming wool-cheque I should clear the debt and —" She could have cut her tongue out for mentioning James's debt, but it was too late: Finn was already frowning, his eyes boring into her.

"What debt?"

"It's minor," she said with studied indifference. "Nothing for you to worry about."

She went to rise, but Finn's strong hand clamped over her arm, making it impossible. "Your da was worried, and now so am I. I could always tell when you were lying, Ruby, so you will stay there until you tell me everything."

She opened her mouth to deny the accusation, but his glare silenced her. Realising he would no doubt question Duncan and the others in the morning, she accepted she had little choice but to tell him the truth.

When she at last came to the end of the sorry tale, she was surprised by the tremendous sense of relief she felt. She'd obviously been holding on to the anger, hurt and pain for too long, had buried them deep in the endless round of work and the needs of her children. Now she had given them voice, she felt lighter.

"What the hell did you marry that eejit for in the first place, Ruby?"

"I thought I was in love," she confessed through her tears, "and the chance to follow Grandma Nell's

350

pioneering legacy seemed to prove it was all meant to be. I realise now it was just a stupid infatuation, a silly young girl's dream."

Finn gathered her into his arms and kissed the top of her head. "I didn't mean to make you cry, my *mavourneen*," he murmured. "I'm sorry."

Ruby snuggled against his chest, the old Irish endearment making her cry even harder. "I miss Mam and Da," she sobbed, "and I miss Parramatta and Moonrakers, and my brothers and sisters, and . . ."

"Hush, now hush," he soothed. "I've brought letters and gifts from everyone, and now you have me to take care of you, you won't be alone any more."

She drew back and looked at him through her tears, hardly daring to believe what she'd heard. "You're staying?"

He nodded and pulled her back into his arms. "I'm staying."

Port Jackson, Sydney, 28 February 1852

Harry organised the stowing of his trunks and boxes, then went to stand on the deck of the *Constant* to catch a last glimpse of Sydney as the anchor rose. His emotions were mixed as he gazed at the familiar docks and the sprawling town and realised he would probably never see them again. Oliver's health was failing, and there would always be the guilt of leaving him behind, but it wasn't just the thought of his sick brother that stirred the regrets. He was saying goodbye to boyhood memories and would miss this place, would miss the excitement he'd found in making his fortune, and the adventure of knowing he had played a small part in the events that were already changing Australia from the convict colony of shame to perhaps one of the richest nations in the world.

He'd made good friends too — especially Niall — and he wished he could have persuaded him to accompany him, but Niall's refusal had been adamant. Australia was his home now — a home where his family lived and his reputation grew along with his fortune. He had no desire to visit Ireland; it was already beneath his roof, and in the lilt of the voices around him.

Harry's mood lifted as the longing for home was swept away in the knowledge that, in a few short months he would see England's shores and smell the scents of his beloved Cornwall. His pulse raced as he envisioned holding Lavinia again. Her lovely face would light up when he told her their future was secure, and his children would greet him with hugs and kisses, and draw him back into the heart of his family, where he truly belonged.

He smiled as he saw himself walking over his estate, bidding good day to farmhands and fishermen along the way, perhaps eating a hot pasty as he watched the fishing boats unload their catch, the raw wind stinging his eyes as gulls screeched overhead.

The sails swelled as the *Constant* dug her bow into choppy waves and headed for the open sea.

"Oh, yes," he sighed, "home is definitely where the heart is."

CHAPTER
TWELVE

Lawrence Creek, Hunter Valley, September 1852

"Another weekend stretches before us," said Peter, pouring the wine. "And it looks as if the weather will stay fine for tomorrow."

Jessie breathed in the scent of warmed earth and ripening fruit. She never tired of the view from the veranda, and it was a mild evening after the day's heat. "It appears so," she agreed, "and although I prefer it dry, the vintners are desperate for rain."

"They are never satisfied, but that is the way of all farmers." He sipped his wine, then picked up the invitation that had been delivered the previous morning. "I'm looking forward to the race meeting, and there is much talk of who is going to win the Valley Derby. My money's on Buckaroo, but Gerhardt's Wattle Dancer is a close contender." He eyed her quizzically. "Do you think I should bet on both, or would that be considered a flagrant abuse of a country minister's stipend?"

Jessie smiled. Peter Ripley liked a gamble, enjoyed wine, dancing and the company of women. Men liked him too and he'd proved he could ride and shoot as well as any of them. He was the most unusual minister, and she'd often wondered why he'd never remarried.

"It's your money," she replied, "and I'm sure the bookies would be delighted to relieve you of it. Buckaroo has good form, but if the going is too hard, he might find it difficult to keep up the pace. Wattle Dancer, on the other hand, has won the last three of his races, and if it stays like this, he'll be hard to beat. Just remember, Peter, there are twelve horses entered, most of them with unknown form — you could still lose."

He raised a brow. "You surprise me, Jessie. I didn't take you for a racing expert."

She laughed. "I'm not really," she admitted, "but I've picked up a lot of information from Gerhardt."

He looked at her thoughtfully. "How is it one so talented and attractive remains single?"

"Because no one has asked for my hand," she replied rather more sharply than intended. She smiled in apology. "One could ask the same question of you."

"Oh, I'm dedicated to the Church and my work with the natives. I loved and lost the only wife I ever wanted. She can never be replaced." His grin was mischievous. "Besides, why marry again when I have the estimable Hilda to look after me?"

"I'm sure she'll be flattered," she remarked dryly.

Peter didn't seem to hear her riposte, and his expression became serious. "So Gerhardt still hasn't proposed?" He pursed his lips and gazed at the sprawling fields. "I wonder why."

"Perhaps, like you, he does not wish to be saddled with a wife." Her tone was light, but the puzzle had perplexed her over the past year.

"He seemed so keen."

"Frieda champions his courtship," she reminded him, "and perhaps Gerhardt is unable to thwart her. He's an attentive suitor and generous host, but there is little sign that he wishes more from our friendship, despite his mother's encouragement."

"How do you feel about that?"

"I don't know," she admitted. "He's good company, likeable, handsome and rich. When he takes my arm or dances with me, I feel secure in the knowledge he admires me." She paused. "I like him . . ."

"But?"

"I don't know if what I feel is love," she confessed, "or even if it might be reciprocated. His manners are impeccable — perhaps after twelve months of courtship a little too . . ." She hunted for the right word ". . . correct." She hurried to explain. "Not that I'm complaining, and I'm grateful he respects me so highly, but one would have thought . . ."

"So you seek a more intimate relationship?"

Jessie blushed. "Yes. No. Oh, I don't know," she said in exasperation. "One minute I want more from him, the next I shy from it, preferring to remain as we are. But the crux of the matter is, he led me to believe he cared for me as more than a friend, and I foolishly allowed myself to be drawn into this strange courtship."

"Why is it strange?"

She blushed. "He's never tried to kiss me," she admitted, "not even when we are alone. I'm confused."

"I'm not surprised." His brown eyes were questioning. "Does the ghost of Abel still stand between you?"

She felt the familiar surge of longing and stifled it, for although it happened rarely, it had lost none of its power. "Maybe," she replied, "but I do my best not to let it."

"Then perhaps you have your answer," he said softly. "Gerhardt no doubt realises you still hope for Abel's return and that is why he is taking things so slowly."

"Perhaps." She snapped open her fan. "Can we change the subject, Peter?"

"Of course, and I apologise if I have probed too deeply into your personal affairs."

She was about to reply when she heard the thud of hoofs.

"We've got visitors," he said, peering into the twilight, "and just in time for supper. I'd better alert Hilda."

Jessie watched the approaching riders, her heart thudding painfully as the traitorous hope soared once again that it might be Abel, but as they came into the light of the lanterns, her initial disappointment was overcome with delight. "John! Daniel!" Racing down the steps, she flung herself against John, who'd scarcely managed to alight.

"Now that's what I call a welcome." His laughter boomed as he swung her round.

Daniel grabbed her and she was hugged until the breath was squeezed from her.

"Put me down," she gasped, half laughing, half crying.

"I take it these are your brothers," said Peter.

She gazed up at them — so big, so bearded, so wonderfully familiar. "Indeed they are," she replied. "Isn't it marvellous?"

John grinned as he scratched his beard. "We thought we'd come and see how you're faring, but I can see for myself that you're well." He jerked a thumb at Peter. "Is this here your man, Jess?"

"No!" She blushed as she realised how rude that sounded.

Peter laughed. "I took over from Zephaniah Lawrence and am the minister here. Jessie is mistress only of the school." He turned from John's suspicious gaze as Hilda appeared in the doorway. "And this is Mrs Blake, my housekeeper and Jessie's chaperone, so you need have no fear her honour has been compromised."

Daniel wiped his forehead on his sleeve. "I would have thought our Jess would be married by now," he said with a frown. "What's the matter with the men in these here parts they don't appreciate a fine maid?"

"There's nothing wrong with them," she said lightly, "and I'm amazed at your words. You usually glower at any man who comes within a mile of me." She smiled at them. "Anyway, I'm just not ready to settle down. See to your horses and then come and tell me your news. I want to know what you've been doing, where you've been and how much gold you found."

"Supper's almost ready," said Hilda, when they returned from the paddock a short while later. "You're welcome to join us."

"Thank you, missus," said John. "It's been a long ride and we're fair famished."

Hilda wrinkled her nose. "I'll put water on to heat. You'll be wanting a bath."

"Sorry, missus," muttered Daniel, mangling his hat.

"At least wash those hands before you eat," ordered Hilda.

Jessie laughed. "Don't mind Hilda. She always speaks her mind, and to be fair, you are grubby." She pecked his cheek to show she was teasing. "Wash first, then sit and talk to Peter while I help Hilda. After supper we can settle down for a long chat."

The steak and kidney pudding, fresh vegetables and crisp potatoes were delicious, and the two young men devoured every scrap before they demolished lemon pie and thick cream. All this was washed down with ale, and as the meal progressed, it was clear they were almost starving and were unwilling to speak until they had filled their bellies. When at last they sat back from the table, there were deep sighs of satisfaction. Jessie, whose appetite had been ruined by excitement and impatience, began to ply them with questions.

"We found quite a bit of gold at the start," answered John, as he filled his pipe, "but it soon ran out and we had to move further and further along the dry river bed to seek it out. By the end of the year we found we had to dig as deep as thirty feet, but the amount of gold we found was hardly worth the effort. We thought about

358

moving on to Ballarat and Bendigo, but decided we'd had enough."

"Which is why we're going back to Kapunda to see if we can get our old jobs back," explained Daniel. "At least the money's regular and we don't have to live in such terrible conditions."

Jessie noted the colour in her brother's cheeks. "Are you sure that's the only reason?"

"Well" — he squirmed in his chair — "there is a girl I quite like."

Jessie smiled. "What's her name?"

"Franny Harper." He reddened further and earned a dig in the ribs from John.

"I'm sure she's lovely," said Jessie, glad that at least one of her brothers might settle down. "What about you, John?"

"I've had my share of the lasses chasing me," he said airily. "I'm just waiting for one to run fast enough to catch me."

They all laughed, and sheepishly John swiftly changed the subject back to the mining camps in Ophir. He described, in colourful detail, the shanty-town diggings, the mud, the heat, the flies, the rotting food, the Chinese labourers, the police and constant licence checks.

Jessie looked at them in horror as they casually spoke of terrible accidents, of men sent mad with drink and stinging bugs, and of the hopelessness of those who found nothing and lost everything in their search for the elusive gold. It sounded like hell, and she was glad they'd come out of it unscathed.

359

She refused to look at Peter and Hilda as she posed the question that had been on her lips for the past three hours. "Did you come across anyone you knew?"

John eyed her from beneath black brows. "Plenty," he replied. "Anyone in particular you wanted to know about?"

"I was wondering if you had bumped into Mr Cruickshank," she said, holding his gaze. "It was said that he had gone to Ophir."

John chewed on the stem of his pipe as he regarded her. "He was there."

Her pulse quickened and she struggled to appear calm. "Was he well?"

"Aye, well enough."

Peter broke into the ensuing silence. "We are all interested in what happened to him, for he has been gone nearly two years and there has been no word."

"He was one of the lucky ones," John replied. "Hit the mother lode early and got out a rich man."

"I don't suppose you know where he went?"

Jessie blessed Peter for his probing, for she could barely speak in her disappointment that Abel had made his fortune and forgotten about those who waited for him in the valley.

"No idea." John gave a vast yawn and stood. "My apologies, but neither of us have had much sleep over the past few days. Is it all right if we set up camp out the back?"

Peter nodded at Hilda's questioning glance. "You can sleep in the spare room as long as you bathe first," she said. "The linen is fresh on today, so mind you get all that dirt off." At their nods, she told them where they could find hot water, the tin tub, towels and a bar of soap.

Jessie lifted her face for their kisses. "Will you stay for the weekend?" she begged. "There's a picnic race tomorrow," she added, "and as I haven't seen you for so long, it would —"

"We'll stay until Sunday noon," Daniel interrupted. "Peter's been telling us about this chap you've been courting, and John and I want to take a look at him — make sure he's all right."

Jessie glared at Peter as her brothers left the room. "How could you?" she hissed.

Startled by her uncharacteristic vehemence, he frowned. "I didn't realise it was a secret. Sorry, Jessie."

"You have no idea what you've started," she sighed. "My brothers take an instant dislike to any man who so much as glances at me. Look how John glared when I asked about Abel."

"I was more interested in your face when he replied," he said softly. "Oh, Jessie, what a tangled web you're weaving. Please be careful."

Eden Valley, September 1852

Kumali had followed Ruby's example and turned the saddlebags into cocoons for her children so she could take them with her into the pastures. Natjik was nearly two, and Mookah one, and they were too heavy to carry on her back any more, but they seemed to like this way

361

of getting about, crying only when they were hungry or bored.

She had decided after giving birth to Mookah that she couldn't cope with any more children and so had begun to eat the berries that would keep the blood flowing and kill Duncan's seed, but they made her sick, and she was beginning to wonder if there was an easier, more pleasant way of going about it. Deciding she would ask Ruby when she next got her alone, she tugged at the reins and followed Duncan.

They were in the pasture that spread either side of the river. The grass was as high as a sheep's back and full of goodness after the winter rain, and as spring approached, it promised to be yet another good year.

As she watched him catch a pregnant ewe with his crook and separate it from the mob, Kumali hummed a tune Duncan had been teaching her. She helped the dogs round it up and steered it towards the pen, where the other sheep were bleating. They would be released into a different pasture later so that Tommy and Duncan could keep an eye on them and help when they dropped their lambs.

She glanced across at Ruby and felt a stab of jealousy when she saw her laughing with Finn. It wasn't fair to feel the way she did, for she liked Finn, and Ruby was happy again, but she couldn't help wishing he hadn't come. His arrival had changed things, and Kumali didn't like change, was suspicious of it.

"Will you nae keep your mind on what you're doing, lassie? That's the second ewe you've let past, and Tommy cannae do all the work."

362

Kumali quickly apologised to Tommy, who grinned back. She liked the boy, and Duncan praised his work, and although he often made mistakes, he was quick to learn.

"Are you nae feeling well, Kumali? I ken your mind is elsewhere."

"Dat Finn always with Missus Ruby. She not speak with Kumali now she have him."

"Och, Kumali, give the lassie a chance. He's her cousin, y'ken, and it's good to see her smile again."

Kumali would not be shifted from her dark mood. "Dat Finn cause big trouble when boss come back. Dey have big fight."

His hand, soft from years of handling wool, patted her knee. "Och, it's nae our business, lassie, and I doubt we'll be seein' James for a while yet, so there's nae need to be fretting." He swung Natjik out of the saddlebag and perched him on his shoulder, where the little boy crowed with delight. "The sun's high enough, I ken. Let's eat."

When they reached the trees, she slid from the saddle and plucked the screaming Mookah from her cocoon. "Mookah too much like Vi with her screaming. She give Kumali headache." She dumped the child between Duncan's knees and went to fetch the tucker bag.

"Gi'e her something to chew, Kumali. She's peelie-wally with her teeth, poor bairn."

Calmer now, she tore off a piece of damper and gave it to her daughter. She hadn't meant to be cross with her. "Alonga Mama," she crooned, as she tried to soothe her with kisses.

"Och, you're a good mother," Duncan sighed, as he shared his meal with Natjik, "but I wish you'd ken that Ruby needs Finn. He's a bonny lad, and good with the sheep too. Y'ken it must be a great relief to young Ruby to have kinfolk close by."

"Ruby was *my* friend," she muttered, still unappeased. "Finn come, no see Ruby alonga me no more."

"She's still your friend," he soothed, "but she has her own wee bairns to care for, as well as this bonny place." He kissed her cheek. "Dinnae be too hard on her."

Kumali ate the cold chicken and damper as she leant against the tree and watched Ruby. She and Finn were walking through the long grass, the horses following them. Their arms brushed repeatedly, their steps in unison as he bowed his head to listen to her speak. Now they were looking at one another, laughing again, their bodies moving in perfect symmetry.

Her eyes narrowed as he put his arm round Ruby's shoulder and led her into the shadows beneath the far trees. They looked like a family as they settled the children on their laps and shared the food. Kumali shivered. Did Ruby realise she loved Finn more than a cousin should? Did she know how clearly it showed in her face and everything she did? There was trouble ahead, for James would spot it in an instant.

Hunter Valley, September 1852

"Gerhardt, these are my brothers."

Gerhardt clicked his heels and gave a nod.

John and Daniel were wide-eyed as they studied him from his shining boots to his glossy hair, taking in the beautifully cut coat, the pristine shirt and pale trousers. They wiped their hands down their grubby moleskins before shaking his hand, and Jessie saw the flicker of discomfort in Gerhardt's eyes as their steely grip threatened to crush his fingers. Her brothers were acting true to form.

"What kind of name's that?" sneered John.

"It is German," he replied stiffly.

John's expression was almost insolent. "So you're courting our sister? Are your intentions honourable?"

"John, *please*," she hissed. She wrung her hands in agitation. "I'm sorry for my brother's rudeness, Gerhardt. I'm sure he didn't mean —"

"I'll give my own apologies when I see fit," John interrupted, still glaring at the other man. "Well, what you got to say for yourself? Or isn't your tongue as smart as your boots?"

Rigid with resentment, Gerhardt's eyes were cold, and there was a muscle pulsating in his cheek. "I have the highest regard for Miss Searle," he snapped, "and I take objection to your tone."

Daniel's fists curled as he came to stand beside John. The tension was tangible as the three men faced one another.

"Hear that, Daniel?" John sneered. "Pretty boy here objects to my tone." He rolled up his sleeves and raised his enormous fists to within inches of Gerhardt's nose. "Wanna do something about that, mate?"

365

"There are ladies present, otherwise I would be happy to oblige," he replied coldly.

John gave a bark of derisive laugher. "I bet."

"I think it's time we left," said Peter. "Come, Hilda, Jessie, let me help you into the carriage. Gerhardt, would you please assist with the picnic basket?"

John and Daniel sniggered.

Gerhardt remained defiant. "If you insist upon fisticuffs, then we will finish this tonight, Searle. But I warn you, I have prizes for boxing," he hissed. He kept eye contact with John as if to underline his capabilities, then turned from the confrontation, took the basket and stored it under the driving seat along with the blankets.

Peter regarded the two brothers. "I hope that is an end to it," he said quietly. "This is a peaceful place and we are all friends here." He paused as they reluctantly nodded. "As you see, there's not much room in the carriage, so you must follow us on horseback. Bring your camping gear. We shall be staying at Possum Hills overnight."

Jessie saw how they glared as Gerhardt sat beside her and she dreaded the coming day. When her brothers were in this mood, they were just spoiling for trouble, and it appeared Gerhardt was willing to take the bait. "Before you fetch the horses," she said from her perch on the driving seat, "I want your promise there will be no more unpleasantness. Gerhardt is our host, this is my home, and I have a reputation to keep. I do *not* wish for a scene." She eyed her brothers sternly. "If you cannot make that promise, then it would be best if you remained here until our return."

With barely concealed ill-temper they nodded and went to fetch their horses and swags.

Jessie snapped her parasol open. "I'm sorry," she murmured. "Please don't let them spoil the day by letting them goad you. I was so looking forward to it."

Gerhardt took up the reins, but she noticed his smile didn't reach his eyes. "The day is yours, and it will be my pleasure to make it as enjoyable as possible." Without a glance to see if her brothers were following, he stirred the horse into a trot.

"Mama is waiting at the course, and we have had a marquee erected so the food will not spoil and the ladies will be comfortable." His shoulders lost some of their stiffness and now his smile was genuine. "We have invited the owners to dine with us, and I think you will find we have done everything possible to make it a day to remember."

Jessie could only hope her brothers didn't make it memorable for all the wrong reasons.

Possum Hills, the same day

The racecourse had been laid out in a bush clearing on the northern boundaries of Gerhardt's property. The track had been raked and rolled, but the lack of rain meant it was as hard as rock. Fences had been erected to protect the racegoers from runaway horses, and there were several large tents draped with colourful bunting, which fluttered in the warm breeze. Wagons, carriages and gigs were parked to one side, and children darted around getting under everyone's feet. A brass band was entertaining the crowd between the races, and there was a carnival atmosphere as women paraded their best dresses and hats, bookies shouted odds, and the jockeys, many of them Aboriginal, milled about with their horses and took last-minute advice from the owners. The grog tent was doing a roaring trade, and the men in charge of the races strode importantly about organising everyone.

It was time for the Valley Derby, and the crowd was louder now and more excitable as this final race was called. Jessie had put the earlier unpleasantness behind her and was having fun. She and Hilda had won a few shillings, but they hardly compared with Peter's winnings, and as they joined the rest of their party at the paddock fence, they congratulated him on his luck.

"It's not luck," he replied with a wide smile. "It is having an eye for a good horse. Would you like help in choosing the Derby winner?"

Jessie declined as she watched the runners, as she had already placed her bet. The horses had come from all over the valley, and although they were mostly tough little stock ponies, there were one or two that showed superior breeding. She had quickly learnt not to dismiss the stock ponies, for they were swift and full of stamina, but her eye was still caught by Wattle Dancer, and as she regarded him, her gaze travelled to the jockey.

"Tumbalong?"

"G'day, Miss Searle." Tumbalong's face split into a grin as he nudged the horse towards her. "You put money on Dancer? He fine horse, good runner."

"I certainly have," she replied, stroking the chestnut's patrician nose. "I didn't know you rode for Gerhardt," she said, noting the green and gold of his shirt.

"He's been riding for me for some time," said Gerhardt, slapping the chestnut's neck and running his hand lovingly down its chest to the finely muscled foreleg. "Tumbalong exercises my horses when I am busy. He's the best jockey I've seen in a long while, and we've been working towards this day for weeks." He nodded to the Aborigine. "Win this and we'll enter him for the big meet in Brisbane next month."

Jessie took Gerhardt's arm as they made their way to the finishing post. Thankfully there was no sign of her brothers, and she suspected they had found entertainment more to their taste elsewhere. It had been clear from the start they were overwhelmed by the large marquee and the tables with their white linen, fresh flowers and crystal, which Frieda had provided. The party was made up of rich landowners, vintners, businessmen and their families, and after a sip of champagne, John and Daniel had swiftly made their excuses and left for the more familiar lure of the grog tent and bookmakers, where their scruffy clothes and rough manners wouldn't make them stand out.

Jessie felt the heightened expectancy of the crowd as it fell silent and pressed forward. The starter had the dozen runners lined up on the far side of the track. The horses stamped and snorted, jockeys wrestled to

369

control them, and the crowd held their collective breath.

The flag went down. They were off.

Buckaroo and two chestnuts led the charge, with three shaggy stock horses on their tails. The rest of the field were tightly bunched on the rails. As they galloped round the far bend and into the straight, Tumbalong eased Wattle Dancer clear of the pack and held him steady on the outside. He was in fifth place.

The crowd roared encouragement as they thundered past on the first circuit. Jessie could hear the jockeys cursing and the laboured breaths of their steeds, and she jumped up and down with excitement as Tumbalong kept Wattle Dancer in the chase.

Dust billowed in great clouds, almost masking the runners from the crowd as the jockeys lay low in the saddle and urged their horses down the far straight and into the final bend.

"Come on, come on," she muttered. "Don't push him too soon, Tumbalong. Buckaroo's still got lots left in him."

But Wattle Dancer was moving up. He eased past the fourth horse, then the third, and as they came out of the bend, he was neck and neck with the second, a beautiful grey. Caught up in the excitement, Jessie forgot she was supposed to be ladylike and yelled encouragement. With stretched necks and flying hoofs the three leading horses headed down the straight. Buckaroo and Wattle Dancer left the grey behind. Now there was only a matter of yards to the winning post.

The ground vibrated as they flew past, the air resonant with their thunderous passage. Wattle Dancer's nose edged in front, but Buckaroo was still fighting.

To Jessie, the finish was a blur — over in a blink. "Did we win?" She was quite breathless as she looked to Gerhardt for confirmation.

He laughed. "Just. But a nose is as good as a mile in this business."

Peter waved his betting slip. "I'll collect our money. Don't drink all the champagne while I'm gone."

Sundown came with its usual swiftness, plunging the valley into chilly night. The racetrack was quieter now, with only a few hardy drinkers singing in the grog tent. There had been several scuffles, but nothing serious, and as Jessie and the others left for the house in their carriage, she could see the lights from many lanterns and braziers flickering in the darkness. The families would eat and settle down to sleep in the tents or under wagons, and after Peter's service in the marquee tomorrow morning, they would make their long way home.

"Have you enjoyed yourself?" Gerhardt's voice was soft as they reached the house and he handed her down.

"I've had a wonderful time," she replied, smothering a yawn. "I wish it could have gone on and on."

He chuckled. "I'm glad, but I think we've all had enough excitement for one day." He tipped his head towards the carriage. Frieda and Hilda were leaning

371

against Peter, and it was clear they were all asleep. "It almost seems a shame to wake them, doesn't it?"

She was about to reply when they were awakened anyway by the arrival of the other carriages. Gerhardt swiftly took charge, allocating rooms and campsites, and ordering the ostlers to deal with the horses.

Jessie realised she wasn't needed and decided she really couldn't resist her bed any longer. She glanced into the darkness, felt relieved that there was no sign of her brothers and followed Frieda and Hilda upstairs to the west wing.

Once in bed, she fell asleep almost immediately, and when she next opened her eyes, she was startled to find it was still dark. She lay for a moment, wondering what it was that could have woken her, and then, as the remnants of sleep cleared, she heard the raised voices. Frowning, she padded across the room and opened the door.

The voices were coming from Frieda's suite of rooms next door. Jessie hesitated, wondering who and what had got the old lady so angry. Deciding it really wasn't any of her business, she was about to shut the door when she heard something that stayed her hand.

"It's your duty, Gerhardt. You will ask for her hand before tomorrow night."

"Hang duty," he shouted. "I'm sick of being told what to do."

"And I'm sick of you thwarting my plans. You should be married by now, not making excuses."

"I have no wish to be married."

Jessie sighed. At last she knew the truth — and in a way it came as a relief.

"Why?"

"You know why."

There was a long pause, and Jessie frowned. She wasn't in the habit of eavesdropping, but Gerhardt's reply intrigued her, and she waited impatiently for the argument to resume.

"That's just an excuse," Frieda snapped. "You'll get over it."

"You keep saying that and it's becoming tedious. Why won't you listen to me and at least *try* to understand?" His tone held frustration, but it seemed to have little effect on his mother.

"Other than the usual reason, is anything wrong with Jessie?"

"She's sweet and pretty and excellent company, and I like her very much."

"Marry her, then."

"I don't love her, Mother, and I regard her too highly to marry her under false pretences."

"Fiddlesticks. What's love got to do with it? You're past thirty and need an heir. You like Jessie, and she obviously likes you. She would be the perfect wife."

"Why? Because she's young and naïve and wouldn't question things in her marriage, or because she comes from a lowly background and would bend to your wishes?" He didn't wait for an answer. "You know very well how I feel, and regardless of needing an heir, I will *not* bow to your demands."

"Your father said the same thing," Frieda retorted, "but he saw sense and did what was expected of him. I can't say either of us enjoyed the experience, but it was our duty. Now it is your duty to provide an heir, and you will do it, Gerhardt, or I shall —"

"Cut me out of your will? Disinherit me?" His bark of laughter was scornful. "Your threats are empty, Mother. As empty as your marital bed."

Jessie shivered. Had Abel been right when he'd said Frieda offered friendship only in exchange for a loveless marriage to her son and the provision of heirs? Darker suspicions crowded in, but she pushed them away, refusing to countenance them.

"Your father had more sense of duty in his little finger than you have in your whole perverted body," Frieda stormed. "Can't you just for once think of your family? You might find marriage to Jessie will bring you to your senses. Or are you too much of a coward to even try?"

His voice rose to a roar. "The most cowardly thing to do would be to marry Jessie. I will not do it!"

The door was flung open. Gerhardt stormed out — and froze.

Jessie, caught in the beam of light, could only stare at him. With a strangled gasp, Gerhardt fled.

Jessie became aware that Frieda was watching her. They stared at each other as the hall clock ticked and the front door slammed.

"It is unfortunate you were woken, but eavesdroppers rarely hear things they like, or fully understand. I hope I can count on your discretion."

It was a command, not a question, and although Jessie had little understanding of what she'd heard, she nodded.

Frieda imperiously closed the door between them and turned the key.

There was the rustle of petticoats from the other end of the corridor. "Come, Jessie, let's get you dressed. It's time to go home."

She looked at Hilda in bewilderment.

"It's all right," she soothed. "I heard most of that, and probably understand better than you what it was all about." She gave Jessie a swift hug. "Don't fret. You've had a lucky escape."

Eden Valley, the same night

Ruby couldn't sleep, despite the weariness that seemed to have settled in her bones, for when she closed her eyes, she saw Finn's face, his eyes, his smile and the way his dark hair flopped over his brow. Unsettled by these images, she slid out of bed and pulled a wrapper over her nightgown before tiptoeing to the door. It creaked as she opened it and she held her breath, hoping it hadn't disturbed the children, but they slumbered on. She stepped into the moonlight and stared up at the star-studded sky, her mind troubled.

James had been gone for over a year, with no word that he planned to return. The memories she had of their short months together had blurred and begun to fade — like the contours of his features — and now even the happy times they had spent here in Eden

Valley seemed unreal. It was as if they had been experienced by another Ruby in another time, and she didn't know how she should feel about that.

She looked around. Nell's presence was soft in the night's warmth, rustling in the gilded trees and whispering in the chatter of the stream — an affirmation that her grandmother's love lived on in the very air she breathed.

Ruby picked up James's discarded clay pipe and filled it with sweet-smelling tobacco. She rarely smoked, but tonight she felt the need for its familiar ritual. With the smoke drifting, she sat on the edge of the veranda and stared into the past. It was safer there — it made fewer demands and didn't require her to make decisions.

And yet Finn still haunted her, his laughter echoing in her head, his touch — so light — a memory that brought a thrill to her skin. The blue of his eyes when he teased, the curve of his mouth as he smiled, the sound of his voice and the soft Irish endearments that seemed casual but held a promise of deep affection were so clear it was almost as if he sat beside her.

"This is ridiculous," she muttered. "You're not five any more — you're a married woman with two children. Finn would be mortified if he thought I saw him as anything more than a friend."

Scrambling to her feet, she saw the pipe had gone out and put it back in the jar on the veranda table. For all her fine words and best intentions, she knew she was fooling herself. She had loved Finn for as long as she could remember, and the months of working with him, of sharing meals and talking together had reignited something within her that would not be denied. And yet it must: Finn's affection was for a cousin who needed help until it was time to move on, and move on he assuredly would, for her marriage vows tied her to James — and that was an end to it.

She eyed the rumpled bed and the sleeping children and stepped down from the veranda. Walking barefooted through the dewy grass, she headed for her favourite spot by the river. She would sit and let the tranquillity of this outback night soothe her.

Yet as she approached, she heard splashing and realised someone was already there. Thinking it was probably Duncan, who liked to swim at night, she decided to walk in the other direction, but as she turned, she heard the tune he was singing and knew it was no Scotsman taking a bath.

Her heart hammered as she hid behind a sturdy tree and watched him. What she was doing was wrong, but she had no control over her actions. She was drawn to him as surely as wool through a spindle. Finn stood hip deep in the fast flow. He was singing an Irish folk song, oblivious to his audience as he vigorously soaped his hair and face. His strong arms flexed, the moonlight casting gold on his skin as the droplets of water glittered like diamonds on his brows and lashes.

Ruby was transfixed as the lather meandered down his muscled torso, following each sculptured dip, rise and curve like the caressing fingers of a lover. Her gaze drifted to his hands — so brown from the sun, so sturdy and capable — as they rubbed soap over his

377

broad shoulders, across his chest and down the taut, flat belly to the enticing line of dark hair that disappeared beneath the water.

She drew deeper into the shadows as she felt the urgent blossoming of her desire and the almost unbearable yearning to touch him. It had been too long since she'd been loved, and the thought of Finn's body, silken against hers, hands caressing, heartbeat drumming against her breasts made her tremble. Her body was on fire with need, the musky scent rising from her in reply to his siren call.

Finn slid beneath the water, leaving a whirlpool of moonlit suds and ripples. Then he rose up with a gasp of pleasure and shook his head. Jewelled beads of water flew, and as he stretched his arms up to smooth back his hair, his perfection rivalled the alabaster statues that stood in the halls of Government House.

A strangled keening in her throat was swiftly smothered as she sank to the grass behind the tree trunk and watched him wade to the far bank. The water ran down the narrow waist to the swell of firm, rounded buttocks and darkened the hair on his finely sculpted thighs. The longing to touch him, to smell him and feel those arms around her was overwhelming.

He grabbed the towel from a tree branch, paused and looked across the narrow stretch of water. Ruby knew he couldn't possibly see her, for she was cowering in the grass, hidden by the wide trunk of the coolibah, and yet his gaze seemed to find her, pinning her there for what felt like endless seconds before he smiled and looked away.

378

She realised she'd been holding her breath and released it in a sigh as she watched him wrap the towel round his hips and saunter off towards his tent. He was singing again, but louder now, and it was an Irish song about a colleen sitting by a river, waiting for her lover.

Her face burnt as she raced for the bark hut, and when the door was firmly closed behind her, she crept into bed and pulled the blanket over her head. Sleep had been elusive before, but in the light of what she'd just witnessed, it was now impossible.

Lawrence Creek, Hunter Valley, the next morning

Jessie had slept surprisingly well after her return home, and as she finished telling the native children the story of Noah, she looked forward to the luncheon Hilda was cooking. She watched them scamper into the sunlight, chattering as they went, and gave a sigh. They loved listening to stories, but it was obvious they preferred being outside, and she wondered just how much they understood.

She began to stow the roughly hewn wooden animals into the ark Peter had made to illustrate the story and then cleared the circle of chairs so neatness was restored. Her brothers had returned this morning, victorious with their winnings, but sore of head. They had seemed to have forgotten their confrontation with Gerhardt and, after wishing her well, had left to continue their long journey south.

She stood in the church doorway and watched the children career round the yard in a game of tag,

379

evoking memories of similar games with her brothers. She had no idea when she might see them again and had shed tears on their departure; yet there was a sense of relief that they were gone, for their presence could only cause trouble.

Jessie closed the door and strolled towards the house. Peter had returned from the outdoor service some time ago, and as she headed for the veranda, she could see he was in deep conference with Hilda. She could guess what they were discussing, and their immediate silence on her approach was proof she'd been right.

She had thought over the events of last night and had come to the conclusion that although she didn't really understand Gerhardt's vehement reluctance to marry anyone, no real harm had been caused — except maybe to Gerhardt's pride — and that she didn't need to be fussed over or talked about.

"Hilda's told you, then?" she said to Peter.

"I'm sorry, Jessie." Peter's expression was sympathetic, but he looked uneasy.

"I'm not," she replied truthfully. "At least now I know where I stand."

"But to find out in such a way . . ."

"I shouldn't have been listening." She smiled at Hilda, who was tight-lipped and obviously out of sorts. "Don't be angry on my behalf, Hilda. I didn't love him. My heart isn't broken."

"I'm glad to hear it," she muttered, "but he shouldn't have strung you along."

"Perhaps it would have been wiser," she agreed, "but I too am guilty of not speaking out, so must share the blame."

"You've done nothing to be guilty about," snapped Hilda, "and when I see him again, I'll tell him exactly what I think of him." She folded her arms beneath her heaving bosom.

"Please don't," begged Jessie. "The truth is out, and I am happy for it to be so. Should he call again, he is to be made welcome. I insist upon it."

Peter eyed her thoughtfully. "We will do as you ask," he replied, "but I doubt we shall see him for a while. He has left for the Barossa Valley to procure new vine saplings."

Jessie felt an overwhelming sense of relief, for despite her words she knew it would be awkward to see him again. "Then let us hope his journey is profitable," she said without rancour. "Can we please have lunch now? I'm ravenous."

CHAPTER
THIRTEEN

Eden Valley, October 1852

Ruby was working alongside the others as they stacked the precious bales of wool on to the dray. Duncan had advised a spring sheering so they could profit from two wool cheques a year, and it seemed his advice had been well worth taking. The sheep had been pastured over the Australian winter, and their wool had thickened well. Come autumn, their fleeces would again be ready for cutting.

She smeared sweat from her eyes. It was already hot, the sky cloudless with little promise of rain. "It's a good thing we kept the northern pastures clear of beasts throughout the winter," she said to Finn, who was working beside her. "We could be short on grass this summer."

He took a drink from the leather waterbag and dried his mouth with the back of his hand. "We need to start cutting hay and disposing of the unwanted stock as soon as possible. The spring lambs are already arriving, and if we have a hard summer, we won't be able to feed and water them."

Ruby grabbed the heavy bale and swung it towards Tommy, who was perched on the dray. "Duncan's already started cutting them out of the mob," she said. "They'll be ready by the end of the week to be driven over to the slaughterhouse at Nine Mile Creek."

"It's a shame we don't have enough hands to take the mob direct to the mining camps. I can't see the sense in paying a drover and butcher out of the profits."

"We still make enough," she muttered, as she hoisted another bale, "and you know I can't afford to lose anyone for weeks on end — especially at lambing time."

They worked in silence, and Ruby kept her gaze firmly on her task, yet it was hard to resist watching the muscles flex beneath those sun-browned arms, harder still not to look at him when he spoke. But resist she must, for Finn must never know her true feelings.

What a fragile, precious thing love is, she mused, and yet what a burden it became when you entrusted it to someone in the hope they would treasure it. She had given it to James and he'd discarded it; now it had been reignited from the childhood crush she'd had for Finn, though she was afraid to acknowledge it.

"Rider coming," shouted Tommy.

Ruby joined Kumali in the rush to round up the children, for they could hear the thunder of a horse approaching at speed. With Nathaniel on her hip, she took Violet's hand and waited. The thought it might be James brought mixed emotions. In the earlier months she had longed for his return, but now? Now she didn't know what to think or feel. How did you greet a man who had deserted you, and who was to all intents and purposes a stranger? How to smile and welcome him back when he'd not shown the slightest desire to

383

contact her or consider her welfare and that of their children? And how to look him in the eye when the man she really loved stood by her side?

As if Finn had read her thoughts, he squeezed her fingers in reassurance. Ruby was grateful for his concern, but dared not look at him, for she knew her heart was in her eyes.

The rider came to a skidding halt, his horse raising a cloud of dust that stung and caught in the throat. Leaping from the saddle, he strode towards Ruby.

"Fergal?" The relief was intense.

"G'day, missus. Sorry I've been away so long, but I was hoping there might be a chance of having me job back?" His gaze darted from Ruby to Finn and back.

She regarded him with barely concealed contempt. "You've been gone over a year. What makes you think you can just turn up and get a job?"

"I was hoping you'd need another pair of hands," he said lamely, his gaze once more flitting to Finn, who was standing like a rock next to Ruby.

"My needs didn't concern you before," she said coldly, "and as you can see, I have others to help me now." She saw the questions in his eyes as he looked at Finn, but she was not about to enlighten him. "Why should I take you back when you've already proved unreliable?"

He took off his hat and crumpled the brim, his gaze fixed on his boots. "I've done me share of the gold-digging," he muttered, "and had enough adventure. I won't be straying again." He looked at her, desperation in his eyes. "I need the work," he confessed.

Ruby noted the worn, faded clothes and broken boots. It was clear Fergal was down on his luck, and she needed all the help she could get, but could she trust him? Deciding to make him wait for her decision, she changed the subject. "Why isn't James with you?"

"We parted company some time ago." His gaze drifted to Nathaniel, who was nestled against Ruby's shoulder, and his expression softened. "I'm sorry, missus. I have no idea if he'll be back anytime soon."

"I guessed as much." Ruby eyed him sternly. "But that doesn't excuse either of you for leaving me in the lurch."

"James is awful persuasive," he mumbled, "and the strike at Ophir was too good to miss. Neither of us meant to be away so long, but time loses all meaning on the fields." He reddened and continued to mangle his hat. "I asked James why he didn't write or send a message, but he said there was little need and that you'd understand." He clearly realised this excuse didn't wash and hurried on. "I would have sent a message, but I didn't think it was my place."

"No, it wasn't." She regretted being so sharp with him when it was obvious his regret was genuine. With a sigh, she relented. "I'll take you on for six months. If you can prove steadfast, then we'll come to a more permanent arrangement."

The relief on his face said it all. "Thanks, missus. You won't regret it, I promise."

"Let's hope not." She placed Nathaniel on the ground and watched him toddle off to join Violet on the veranda steps before she made the introductions. "This is Finn. He's my cousin and the manager of Eden Valley. You will go to him for your daily instructions and your pay. Tommy works with Duncan, and Kumali and I work where we are needed. Your evenings will be your own and you will have two days off a month except at shearing and lambing time. If you turn up drunk or disappear for longer than the allotted time off, you'll be dismissed. Is that understood?"

He nodded, but it was clear he resented a woman talking to him in such a manner, for he had always taken orders directly from James. Ruby wondered how long it would be before the lure of Five Mile Creek bush tavern became irresistible. She would see how things worked out. Another pair of hands, no matter how unreliable, was a godsend.

"You can start by fetching a new pair of boots from the stores," said Finn. "Once you're kitted out, you can help load the rest of these bales."

Ruby watched as the two men shook hands, eyed each other with suspicion but then confirmed they both had roots in Galway. It seemed their kinship to Ireland would ease their passage towards a good working relationship, and she was grateful for that. The last thing she needed was to upset the convivial order on Eden Valley that, so far, had proved easy to maintain.

"Come to the house when you've finished the bales, Fergal. We need to talk," she said.

★   ★   ★

The four children were asleep on the big bed. It was noon, but they were cooled by the breeze coming in through the window, and protected from the ever-present flies by a swathe of muslin she'd hung from the ceiling. They would sleep for at least an hour, giving her plenty of time to talk to Fergal in peace. She had already sent Kumali off with Duncan to the lambing fold, Finn was cutting the killers from the mob, and Tommy had taken the dray to Nine Mile Creek, where another oxen team would carry the wool down to Sydney.

Ruby experienced an unnerving flutter in her stomach. Did she really need to learn about the life James had been leading since his disappearance and to delve into the reasons for his continued absence? The answer was yes, but she had a nasty feeling she wouldn't like what she heard.

Fergal emerged from the outdoor kitchen with a can of tea and a lump of damper. With only the slightest hesitation, he approached the veranda. "I hope you don't mind," he said, indicating the food, "but I was hungry."

"I never begrudge a man a meal," she said with a smile. "How are the boots?"

He looked down at the sturdy footwear, which still held a gleam of polish beneath the dust. "Me feet have grown accustomed to softer, broken leather, but they'll soon get used to these. Thanks."

"Come, sit down and tell me about Ophir."

She listened as he described the thrill of finding their first nuggets, and the subsequent searches that took them deeper into the unstable earth. His descriptions were vivid, told with the inate skill of an Irish storyteller, and she could picture the shanty town, the bearded miners and the terrible accidents that often befell them.

"But if you found gold, why didn't you come home?"

"It was never enough," he mumbled through a mouthful of damper. "We had to pay thirty bob a month for the licence. Then we had to buy food, and clothes, and replace damaged tools. A few bits of gold don't go far when it's shared three ways."

"Three?"

He nodded. "We hooked up with an American, name of Repton, and for a while our luck changed. Then we had the accident and I knew it was time to get out. No gold is worth a life."

Ruby went cold. "What accident?"

His words conjured up pictures that made her shudder as he explained what had happened.

"Thank God you were both saved," she breathed.

"God had little to do with it," he replied gruffly. "If it wasn't for Hina Timanu and Howard Repton, we'd still be down there." He hurried to explain. "Hina comes from Tahiti and is built like an ox. Strange sort of cove, with blue eyes and hair down to his waist, but he has a fearsome strength and, according to Howard, pulled us out like corks from a bottle."

"You don't seem to have been injured," she said, her glance taking in his wiry frame. "Did James also escape unscathed?"

388

He gave a snort of laughter. "I'll say. Had every woman —" He reddened and fell silent.

Ruby's anger quickened. "You made no mention of women at Ophir."

His reluctance was clear.

"Tell me, Fergal."

He chewed the last of the damper and sipped his tea as if needing time to consider his reply. "Where there are men, there will always be women," he said softly, "a certain kind of woman, if you understand my meaning." He saw her nod and continued. "When James was rescued, they flocked to him and carted him off to their tent. I didn't see him for hours, but that wasn't unusual. They knew him well, and he was in the habit of frequenting their . . . their establishment."

"I often suspected he was unfaithful," she murmured. "All those weeks away . . ." She drew from her musing and faced him squarely. "Is there any woman who is . . . special to him?"

He shook his head. "James believes in spreading his favours wide," he muttered shame-facedly.

"With so many distractions, it is no wonder he is loath to come home." Her tone was bitter, but it was from anger, not heartache.

"It is the gold that distracts him," he replied. "The women are merely solace after a long day's labour." He reddened, aware his words brought little comfort. "He has the fever, as they say, and no find is ever enough. He's convinced Howard and Hina are good luck, which is why he was planning to go with them to Ballarat."

"Ballarat? But that's miles away." Ruby felt overwhelming sadness for a man who could so willingly give up everything for the lure of gold. "Does he ever speak of me or the children, or are we forgotten in this madness?"

Fergal shifted in his chair, clearly uneasy under Ruby's questioning. "His mind is concentrated elsewhere," he admitted, "but I have heard him talk of Nathaniel, and there's no doubt he's proud of his boy."

"But not proud enough to be a part of his childhood." Ruby could feel the anger rise, but determinedly kept control. "He has made his choice, and I must live with it. It's just a pity his children will grow up without knowing him."

"Aye," he sighed, as his gaze flitted over her. "The man's a fool not to see the gold he already has stored here."

She was disconcerted by his comment. This was a very different Fergal to the one who'd left over a year ago. The experiences of Ophir had clearly brought a maturity that had been lacking before and an understanding of what really mattered in life. To bring the conversation to an end, she stood and held out her hand. "It's good to have you back, Fergal, and thank you for being so candid."

"I'm sorry if I've offended you . . ."

"The truth brings no offence. Just prove you can remain loyal and dependable, and then we can all work together to make Eden Valley the best sheep station in the district."

Ballarat Gold Fields, June 1853

The soldiers arrived at the diggings, horses stamping, sabres rattling. Their intention to pursue the licence-dodgers by any means was in no doubt, and those unfortunate enough to be caught without the necessary papers could expect harsh treatment.

La Trobe, the governor of Victoria, had brought in five companies of the Fortieth Regiment the previous October to enforce the licence law. They were to assist the Native Police Force and the recently drafted retired policemen from Van Dieman's Land, and were universally hated on the gold fields for their bullying manner. It was an insult to be questioned by an arrogant, uniformed native on a horse, for they were still regarded as savages, but now they had the power to stop and search, and it was galling to have to comply with their insolent demands.

This was not the only humiliation suffered by the diggers. The penalty for not paying the fee was the shame of being dragged through the streets on the end of a rope while the soldiers jeered. The punishment didn't end there, for the offender was then chained to a tree and left overnight. As most of the diggers were hard-working, law-abiding citizens, they objected to this loss of dignity, and rumblings of discontent grew louder by the week.

The discord had started long before Hina had arrived in Ballarat. Thirty shillings was a bagatelle for the man who regularly made five pounds a day, but to those who worked for weeks and found nothing, it was an impossible amount. Hina sheltered from the driving rain as he leant against the wall of the Bath Hotel and read the leading article in the *Argus*.

The cheap news-sheet extolled the virtues of republican rule, and Hina agreed with the author that bribery and corruption on the fields stretched from the Gold Commissioner to the lowliest policeman. He'd seen other crimes ignored in the pursuit of licence money to boost La Trobe's coffers, and had witnessed the consequences of such wretched law enforcement. The fees were meant to fund decent roads, hospitals and schools, but while the corrupt prospered, the diggers saw little improvement in their lives.

He was deeply immersed in the article when the news-sheet was slashed between his hands. Shocked, he looked up and found the point of a sabre within an inch of his eyes.

"Where's yer licence?" The soldier was stony-faced beneath the dripping helmet.

Hina dug in his pocket and pulled out the precious slip of paper.

The soldier, sat astride his horse, inspected it. "Can you prove you're free from conviction and that you aren't absent from your legal place of work? Chinese labour ain't allowed here."

Hina squared his shoulders. "I am from Tahiti. I came on the whaler *Sprite* two years ago." He reached into his pocket again. "I have my captain's permission to remain ashore."

392

The soldier was clearly disgruntled. Throwing the papers aside, he yanked on the reins and went in search of another victim.

Hina retrieved his papers from the puddle they had landed in and, with his chin deep in his coat collar, headed back to the diggings. He was getting sick of this life — sick of being bullied and sick of the cold and wet — but he'd come so far, endured so much to keep an eye on that pocket watch: he had to stay, for, as the months had rolled by, he'd become convinced it was the watch his grandmother had spoken of.

Howard seemed determined never to let him hold it, let alone sell it to him, and it was only when in his cups he permitted Hina to look at it. The watch remained an enigma, and he longed to be able to study it without hindrance, but Howard wore it every day, and at night it was tucked beneath his pillow. It seemed he would never be able to confirm his suspicions, and if the chance didn't come soon, he would simply have to walk away and forget about it.

"They're doing a search again," he said, as he reached the tent.

"That'll be the third this month," drawled Howard through a plug of chewing tobacco. He glared out at the sleet. "God darn it. This place is getting impossible."

"Who do they think they're dealing with?" James's face was dark with anger. "We're men, not slaves, and we have our pride." He spat into the deep hole they'd spent weeks digging. "We have a county court and general assizes in Buninyong, and enough legal offices in Ballarat to run an entire country. We have ministers of every denomination, a public lending library, a smart new hotel, news-sheets and regular cricket matches in the summer. Despite all that, La Trobe seems determined to treat us like scum."

"There ain't no point in gettin' riled up, James," muttered Howard. "Things ain't gonna change in a minute, and we have men like Lalor, Humffray and Carboni to speak for us."

"Hmph. Lalor's an Irish hothead with an axe to grind, Humffray's a former Welsh Chartist, and Carboni's an Italian troublemaker. Fine examples to represent us to La Trobe." His sarcasm was not lost on the others.

"At least they try to do something about the conditions," Howard reminded him. "If you feel so strongly, why don't y'all round up like-thinking men and join them?"

James broke eye contact. "I'm here for gold, not politics, and I'm sick of this endless argument. I'm going for a drink." He rammed on his hat, pulled up his collar and splashed through the mud.

"That boy's headin' for trouble," mumbled Howard. "He's just itchin' for a fight."

"He's not alone. The unrest grows with each search."

Howard chewed tobacco as he eyed the gathering darkness of a winter's late afternoon. "I sense the same thing," he replied, "and it puts me in mind of the siege at the Alamo." He acknowledged Hina's obvious puzzlement. "It was back in 1836, when Texas was fighting for independence from Mexico. A hundred and eighty men held the Alamo Mission Fort against the

394

Mexican Army for eleven days before the survivors were finally overwhelmed."

"I can't see the similarities," Hina admitted.

"Put men's backs against a wall when their blood is up, or their families are threatened, and they'll come out fighting — and it'll only take one incident to set off this powder keg, mark my words." He stretched and yawned. "I think I'll join James," he muttered. "We ain't gonna get no work done until we've drained that darned hole. Y'all comin'?"

Hina shook his head. He saw no point in wasting precious savings on something he had no taste for, and as Howard loped off, he sat in the roughly hewn chair and looked at his surroundings. The snow-topped hills had been denuded of trees, the timber taken to shore up unstable holes, roof the tunnels and build cabins. He could hear the beat of the cradles, as steady as the march of an army, as men continued to work through the driving sleet, and he could see the lights of lanterns gleam from bark huts, tents and log cabins.

It was a small community and united in its efforts to find gold, keep out of trouble and survive, for when a man spent weeks chasing the lead of a long-dry, buried river bed, burrowing as much as a hundred feet, he settled in for the long wait to reap the benefits of his labour — hence the log cabins and sturdy huts. The transient diggers of the earlier days were gone: back-breaking, deep digging in slimy holes held no interest for those who sought easy pickings.

Unlike Ophir, there was a large population of women in Ballarat. These respectable wives and daughters

395

almost outnumbered the men, and with them came the restraints of order and decency that had been missing from the earlier gold fields. There were few sly grog shops and even fewer prostitutes, but Ballarat had to be the dirtiest place on earth, with its muddy streets, boggy fields and discoloured rivers.

He pulled a blanket over his shoulders as he sipped the last of the billy tea. The fire had long gone out, but the tea was warm enough to bring comfort. The wind cut like a knife through his worn, wet clothes as it made the canvas billow and snap, and the sleet was almost horizontal as it swept past. Hina moodily regarded the lowering sky and wondered if it would snow again. If it did, it would mean yet another day of idleness.

Slumping back into his chair, he let his thoughts drift. The three of them and Fergal had stayed in Ophir long after Bones had left, for they had hit a fairly rich seam and had worked it until it ran out. Then Fergal had left and they had arrived in Ballarat around nine months ago and had begun their search in Peg-Leg Gully, where they'd had some initial success. Counting on their good fortune continuing, they had been planning to stay, but then trouble had broken out. A hundred and fifty Irish diggers, led by a man called Fahey, had rioted against the police. Fahey was killed, and fearing there could be reprisals, Hina, James and Howard had decided to move to the Gravel Pits diggings, near Eureka, until things calmed down.

They had been here for several months and had already found some sizeable nuggets, but after listening to the old hands, they realised it could take even longer before they hit what Howard called "pay dirt". James had been reluctant to continue, for he preferred to find gold with as little labour as possible, but Howard had been persuasive in his argument that the rewards would be well worth the effort, and he'd been proved right, for in January there had been an astonishing find by a group of diggers on Canadian Gully.

The first nugget weighed ninety-three pounds, the second eight-four pounds, and as the diggers reached sixty feet, they found the real monster, which weighed a hundred and thirty-six pounds. With proof like that, James was only too eager to dig — indeed, the promise of such incredible wealth spurred everyone into a frenzy.

Digging so deep was a dangerous enterprise, and Hina shivered at the memory of the flooding tunnel. He'd been fifty feet down when the water had poured in. His boots had sunk into the mud, the water reaching his hips. If he hadn't been so strong, and if Howard and James hadn't been so quick-thinking, he'd have died in the darkness without ever seeing Tahiti and Puaiti again.

Deciding he'd had enough gloom for one day, he went in search of a thicker, drier blanket. Spying one on Howard's truckle-bed, he clambered over the pile of tools on the floor and tugged at it, thereby dislodging the lumpy pillow. The sound of something striking a pick made him frown. Lifting the nearby lantern, he peered down, and there, glinting in the flickering light, was Howard's pocket watch, nestled between the tools.

A furtive backward glance ensured he was alone. He reverently picked it up. It must have been under the pillow, forgotten by Howard, but at last he held it. He could barely breathe from excitement.

His fingers were clumsy as he felt its weight and smoothness, and saw how the diamond glinted in the light. He pressed the tiny catch and the casing flew open to reveal what he'd waited so long to see. There was no longer any doubt that this was the golden gift, for there, fixed in the casing, was the image of a man.

As Hina held it closer to the lantern, he saw it was of a proud European — a man of substance — with teardrop stains on his temple. He looked into those steady blue eyes and recognised them, looked at the teardrops and traced his fingers across his nape as if to confirm this family legacy.

He crouched over the lantern as he looked at the other painting. Lianni was beautiful; no wonder Jon had loved her. She had the dark eyes, golden skin and sensual mouth that was still evident in his mother and grandmother — her beauty living on through the generations. The long, black hair was held back with a hibiscus blossom, like Puaiti wore hers, and seeing this tangible reminder brought him close to tears. Lianni had lost Jon, but he had given her this gift as surely as he'd given her their son, Hina's great-grandfather. He had to find some way of persuading Howard to part with it.

"What y'all doin' with my property?"

Hina spun guiltily to face the two men. "I was getting a blanket," he stuttered. "It fell on the floor. I was just looking."

"Looks a bit suspicious to me." James scowled. "You sure you weren't trying to steal it?"

Howard's large hand scooped up the watch. The eyes were narrowed and piercing. "Y'all weren't plannin' on that, were you?"

Hina stood tall to square up to his accusers. "I am not a thief," he said firmly. "It fell to the floor and I took the chance to look at it."

James sat on the bed as Howard carefully put the watch in his waistcoat pocket and hooked the chain through the buttonhole. Satisfied it was secure, he turned his attention to Hina. "I've showed it to you many a time, and you know I don't like nobody touchin' my things."

Hina realised James was still watching him with suspicion, but he was past caring what he thought, for it was Howard he must convince of his honesty. "You have let me glimpse it, yes, but I have never held it, or been given the chance to really study the paintings inside," he said, with a calm that belied his desperation to be believed. "If you will give me a chance to explain, then perhaps you will understand why it is so important to me and why I would never steal it."

Howard eyed him thoughtfully. "You've been all fired up over this watch since Ophir, and I have to admit your interest intrigues me, so go on, spill the beans."

Hina told him of Jon and Lianni, and how the watch had been exchanged for a trinket, then showed Howard

399

the birthmark beneath his hair. "To steal such a treasure would bring shame to me and to my family, and it would be for ever stained by the mark of theft."

"I never reckoned you for a liar, or a thief," Howard drawled, "and you tell a mighty fine tale." He opened the watch, and the ensuing silence was broken only by the soft patter of snow on the canvas as he studied the two paintings. "I guess by rights this watch does belong to your family."

Hope surged as Howard looked at him.

"But I'm sorry, son. Possession is nine-tenths of the law — it stays with me."

"I have lots of gold. Let me buy it, please. It would mean so much to my family to have it back."

"No amount of gold can pay me for this," replied Howard, "but I tell you what, Hina — should I die, I will leave it to you. How about that? You have James here as a witness, and I will not go back on my word."

"But you are not an old man," Hina gasped. "You may live for many more years."

"I hope so, son, and I ain't countin' on no 'accidents' neither." His brow furrowed. "Get my meaning?"

He was horrified. "You think I would kill you for the watch?"

"Men have been known to murder for less." Howard's face lit up in a smile as he stood. "But I don't think you'd go that far. Shall we shake hands and leave it to fate?"

He took Howard's hand, relieved the American didn't believe him to be a thief, though he was forced to accept that fate had already played a cruel trick, and

400

would no doubt continue to thwart him. Nevertheless he was willing to bide his time, for he strongly believed that he and the watch had been brought together for a purpose, and he was determined to discover what it was.

Lawrence Creek, Hunter Valley, August 1853

Jessie was sewing yet another tear in Peter's shirt. For a middle-aged minister, he was careless with his clothes and with his person. He was always falling off horses or wearing his best jacket to oil harnesses or fix a buggy wheel. This latest rent had come from climbing a tree to retrieve a kite he'd been flying for the Aboriginal children. She had watched in horror as, heedless of life and limb, he'd clambered up and promptly become impaled on a sharp branch. He'd shrugged off her concern, insisting the cut on his arm was of no importance, but when she'd demanded to see it, she'd been shocked at how deep it was.

"It took five stitches to mend his arm," she murmured, "and even more to mend this shirt. The doctor has become inured to treating his wounds, but there are times when I wish Peter would remember he's not as young as he thinks he is."

"Hmm?" Hilda was lost in thought.

Jessie prodded the fire into a more cheerful glow, put the shirt aside and decided to have a little fun with Hilda. "I met an elephant today," she said.

"Did you, ducks? That was nice."

She stifled a giggle. "Yes, it was rather. He was pink and had lovely manners."

"Good, good."

"He asked me to give you his regards."

Hilda frowned, her gaze at last clearing. "Who sent his regards?"

"The elephant."

Hilda looked bemused, then illumination dawned and she joined Jessie in her laughter. "You are a naughty minx," she scolded, "taking advantage of an old woman like that."

"You were miles away, and it was too good an opportunity to miss."

"What was?" Peter came in and narrowly missed being stabbed by the needle as he flung himself on to the couch.

Jessie retrieved the sewing as she explained. Then she turned back to Hilda. "It's not like you to be so pensive. Is something troubling you?" She caught the glance Hilda exchanged with Peter. "Come on, you two, what's going on?"

"Nothing. Not really," she said, flustered.

Jessie raised a brow. "Which means you're hiding something."

"Well . . ." She shot another glance at Peter. "It's just that I heard something today, and I was trying to think of the right way to tell you."

Jessie frowned. Not much happened in the valley, and it was unlike Hilda to keep gossip to herself. "If it's about Gerhardt's engagement, then I already know," she said. "He sent a note this morning."

"It isn't about Gerhardt, and I'm surprised he had the gall to assume you would want to know about this ridiculous arranged marriage."

"We have remained friends," Jessie said softly, "and as his friend, I wish him well."

"It's not von Schmidt who needs the good wishes," she retorted, arms folded beneath her bosom. "That poor girl . . ." She trailed off. "Anyway, this has nothing to do with him, and everything to do with you." She fell silent, clearly unable to continue.

"What Hilda is trying to say —" Peter was interrupted by a heavy rap on the door. "I have an inkling that all explanations can be left to our visitor."

Jessie was even more confused. Peter was being mysterious, and coupled with Hilda's refusal to meet her eye, it was obvious they were keeping something from her. She glanced at Hilda, who still looked shifty, and tried to catch what was being said in the hall. Apart from the deep rumble of men's voices, she discovered, rather irritatingly, that she couldn't make out a word.

Peter poked his head round the door. "Hilda, would you please come into my study? I have something to discuss with you."

Jessie looked on in bewilderment as the elder woman hurried out. "What on earth is going on?" she muttered, as she rose from the couch.

The door swung open, and as she caught sight of the visitor, her knees threatened to buckle with shock.

"G'day, Miss Searle." Abel took off his hat and smiled.

She stared back, unable to speak. His grey eyes were as mesmerising as ever, the lips parted in a smile that became less confident under her scrutiny. His hair had been trimmed, and he wore an expensive suit. He was shod in fine leather, wore a diamond pin in his cravat, and beneath his jacket, she could see a fancy waistcoat. "What on *earth* are you doing here?" she gasped.

"I've come to see you."

Her pulse raced as confusing emotions raged. "Why?"

He shuffled his feet. "I wanted to see you before you heard of my return on the bush telegraph. There's nothing like it for spreading gossip." His previous confidence had ebbed and now he looked more like the Abel she remembered. "Aren't you just a little glad to see me?"

She looked into the sorrowful eyes, saw the jut of his bottom lip and refused to allow her heart to rule her head. "It is rather late for callers, Mr Cruickshank," she said in her iciest tone. "In fact it is nearly three years too late."

"Oh." His shoulders drooped.

"Is that all you've got to say for yourself?" She was doing her best to remain stern, but the sight of his obvious discomfort made her long to fling herself into his arms and tell him how very glad she was to see him again. Determined to keep these treacherous thoughts well and truly buried, she focused on her anger. "I expected at least a message or a note enquiring after my welfare when I was so ill after the flood, but you were obviously too deeply immersed in your own concerns

404

to think of me." She hurried on as he tried to interrupt. "Then I discover you have left the area altogether with not a word to me. Now you come back after nearly three years and expect me to be waiting for you."

"I was hoping you would give me the chance to explain."

"You'll get it soon enough, but I haven't finished speaking." She took a deep breath. "When you left, I waited to hear from you, and when there was no word, I decided to get on with my life and forget about you." Tears threatened and she fell silent.

"It would seem my journey has been wasted, Miss Searle, and I apologise for interrupting your evening."

"You have interrupted nothing," she said hastily. Her anger had subsided and she didn't want him to leave. "I should be delighted to discover what kept you away so long." She stood aside, waited for him to enter the drawing room and then firmly closed the door. He wasn't going anywhere until he'd told her everything.

He stood awkwardly in the centre of the room as she sat and arranged her skirts. When she looked back at him, she saw the twitch of a smile at the corner of his mouth and realised that far from being daunted by her anger, he was amused by it. "I am waiting, Mr Cruickshank," she said coolly.

"I lost everything in the flood," he began, "and when Hilda told me you were staying at Possum Hills, I knew I had to do something drastic to make you notice me. I could never compete with von Schmidt's money and position, and once the old woman had her hooks into you, you'd be lost. So I left in search of my fortune, assuming that if I returned a rich man, I might persuade you to consider my suit."

"You assumed too much, Mr Cruickshank, but then that was only *one* of your failings."

He raised a dark brow. "Only one of many? My goodness, Miss Searle, I hadn't realised I was so far from perfection." The eyes sparkled.

"There is no such thing as the perfect man, Mr Cruickshank." She didn't dare look at him, for fear of laughing.

He chuckled. "I have learnt that is so, Miss Searle, and it is regrettable. How unfortunate we are that we do not have the female genius for always being right." He moved to the fireplace and rested his foot on the fender.

"You were going to tell me the reason you were delayed so long," she reminded him.

"I found my fortune very quickly, and was on the point of returning to the valley when I realised this new wealth must not be squandered. I travelled to Sydney to see my parents, bought them a house and set up an annuity to ensure their comfortable retirement. I then paid off other family debts and saw my brothers and sisters were provided for."

"I commend you, but your responsibilities here were just as important."

He dipped his chin. "I know, and I will never forgive myself for letting Tumbalong and his family down when they most needed me." He looked up, his grey eyes troubled. "I sent money from Sydney with a verbal message explaining my absence and asking for

406

everyone's patience. It wasn't until my return that I learnt neither had arrived, and that Tumbalong and his family had suffered as a consequence. The carrier had proved less honest than I'd hoped."

Jessie felt a lessening of her anger, but was not yet ready to forgive him. "If you could send a message to Tumbalong, then why not to me? A letter would have sufficed, or even a one-line note."

He reddened and looked at his boots. "I didn't know how," he admitted softly. "I never learnt to write."

She saw his shame in that confession, realised platitudes were unnecessary and remained silent. Her heart ached for his loss of pride, and she bitterly regretted her earlier outburst.

As if he understood her pity, he lifted his chin and squared his shoulders in rejection of it. "Wealth is a wonderful thing, Miss Searle, for now I can read *and* write. I had lessons from a retired English tutor in the Rhine Valley."

"You were in Germany?"

He smiled. "I met a fellow vinter in Sydney, a German who was returning home to arrange for his family to join him in the Barossa. We travelled together and I lived with them for almost a year. By the time he'd sold the house I not only had a decent education in my letters, but in the wine business. I was ready to come home and begin again."

Jessie remained silent. Her thoughts were in turmoil.

"I realise you think I abandoned Tumbalong and my responsibilities," he said, "but believe me, Miss Searle, my thoughts were always here — with you."

She found his gaze fixed upon her, and her heart thudded with hope. "Were they?"

He nodded. "I carried the memory of that day we had at my place wherever I went."

"Did you?" She was finding it hard to breathe.

"I did."

"Oh, Mr Cruickshank," she sighed, "why didn't you tell me sooner?"

"Because I had nothing to offer you, and Mr Lawrence seemed determined to keep us apart." He took a step towards her. "I understand von Schmidt is no longer a suitor, but you have a new employer, and I see he is a fine man, a little too old perhaps, but of good education." His glance took in the cosy room and the shirt she'd been mending. "You would be well suited."

"Peter Ripley is content to remain wedded to his church and his missionary work. It is a situation that suits us both."

"Then tell me I am not too late, Miss Searle."

"Not too late for what, Mr Cruickshank?" she breathed.

He paused before taking another step towards her. "For asking permission to court you, Miss Searle."

She stood and smoothed the creases from her skirt with trembling hands, and when she looked up into his eyes, she knew she could resist no longer. "You have my permission, Mr Cruickshank," she whispered.

He took her hands and drew her close. "Then may I kiss you, Miss Searle?"

408

"You may." Her sigh was cut short by the soft touch of his lips and it was as if the world had spun from its axis and had sent her soaring into the stars. She closed her eyes, her whole being encompassed by this singular moment of joyous emotion, and as his arms tightened around her and she clung to him, she had no thought of anything but the feel of his lips, his hands, his chest pressing against hers. Her faith in his return had served her true, his kiss took her to a heightened sense she had never known before, and she knew in that moment that this was love — true love.

Lawrence Creek, Hunter Valley, October 1853

Jessie was singing as she hung out the washing, her thoughts hazy with happiness. She heard the rider approach, and there he was — hat pulled low against the sun, his smile as warm and heart-stopping as ever. "Hello. What are you doing here at this time of the morning?"

He swung down from the horse. "That's not much of a welcome after a whole day without seeing you," he drawled. "I was expecting at least a kiss."

She giggled as she fell into his arms. "It's a good thing there's no school today," she said much later, "otherwise we would have a most interested audience."

"Oh, Jess, my love, my sweet, sweet love," he murmured into her hair.

She drew back and looked into his eyes. "Am I truly your love, Abel?"

"From the moment I first saw you." His lips brushed her cheek and captured her mouth in long, sweet confirmation.

Jessie was drowning in happiness. She wanted the kiss to last forever, to feel his arms always around her and know he would never leave again, for this was her dream — her heart's desire.

They finally drew apart and Abel's fingers traced the contours of her face, his gaze drinking her in as if he'd thirsted for too long. "I reckon we oughta get married, Jess."

"Is that a proposal?" Her voice was unsteady.

"It is."

"Then I accept."

"Yeehah!" Abel gathered her up and swept her round until her skirts flew. Then he kissed her again and, before she could get her breath, swung her into a fast polka that took them between the flapping sheets and across the clearing.

She tried to protest, but she was laughing so much it was impossible, and anyway, she didn't want this to end, for this was the happiest day of her life.

They finally came to a breathless halt in front of the school, and Abel took her hand as they flopped on the step. "I've been dreaming of this day," he said quietly, "and now it's real, I can hardly believe it."

Jessie kissed his cheek. "Neither can I."

"My sweet Jess," he murmured. His lips brushed hers, and when he drew back, the light of adoration shone in his eyes. "I went to Ophir to make my fortune, but the real treasure was here all the time."

410

"You could have all the gold in the world and it wouldn't make me love you more than I do today," she softly replied.

"Then let's find Peter and set a date for the wedding."

Lawrence Creek, Hunter Valley, four weeks later

The country church was alive with the chatter of many voices that November morning, and the scent of flowers greeted Jessie as she stepped through the door. A glance took in the familiar faces, which beamed back at her, and as she walked up the aisle, she knew she glowed with happiness.

Abel looked so handsome, his hair burnished in the sunlight that poured through the window, and she felt such overwhelming love for him she could barely breathe.

"You are beautiful," he whispered, as he took her hand, "and I love you with all my heart."

They stood before Peter Ripley and exchanged their vows, and as Abel placed the gold ring on her finger, she knew it would remain there always. In a daze of joy she heard Peter pronounce them man and wife, and Abel's kiss sealed the moment to perfection.

Hilda signalled to the little native boy to pump the bellows and, after a couple of false starts, played a stirring tune on the new organ Abel had donated. Jessie acknowledged the smiles and nods of the packed assembly. Her brothers had not been able to make the long journey but it seemed the whole valley had come to celebrate with them, and once they'd emerged from the church, they were immediately surrounded.

"Mr and Mrs Cruickshank, may I be the first to congratulate you?" Gerhardt bowed and smiled.

"Thank you." Abel's handshake was firm. "And when our new house is finished, you and your fiancée must be among the first to come to supper. I would like to discuss the new grape that is being developed in the Barossa and get your views on it."

Gerhardt bowed again and moved away to join the rather plain, plump girl he would reluctantly marry on Christmas Day.

Tumbalong pushed through the mêlée. "Good on ya, boss," he said, with a broad grin. "Missus fine lady — you alonga many piccaninnies."

Jessie blushed furiously as laughter greeted this comment, but Abel slapped his friend on the back and laughed with him. "It's good to see you back on form, you old bludger."

Jessie watched the two men and noted the deep affection between them. Abel had been devastated to learn of how cruelly the sickness had affected Tumbalong's family and had vowed to use some of his fortune to pay for a second doctor — one who would be willing to care for the Aboriginals. He had gone to Newcastle and hired such a man, and now he was firmly ensconced as a valuable member of the community.

"Come, Mrs Cruickshank, time we were off." To shouts from the assembled crowd, Abel swept her into his arms and carried her to the waiting coach. They didn't hear the crack of the driver's whip, or feel the jolt of the wheels, for they were oblivious to everything but each other.

CHAPTER
FOURTEEN

Eden Valley, December 1853

Ruby sighed with pleasure as she entered the cool shadows. The sun was blinding, and it seared through her clothes to her skin. Halting her horse, she wiped her sweaty face and drank deeply from the water bottle. With her thirst quenched and the coolness drying her shirt, she followed the winding track in search of the clean-skin scrub cattle as the calls and whistles of the others echoed through the trees.

The herd, which had begun with her gift to James of a cow and calf, had been added to over the years, and now there were over forty beasts to round up, and that didn't include the spring arrivals, which had to be branded before someone else stole them. Poddy-dodging was a favourite pastime, and Ruby knew speed was of the essence.

Her keen eyes caught the pale gleam in the shadows, and she turned towards it. The two cows had been grazing, but on Ruby's approach, both skittered away. Ruby nudged her horse into a trot and began the endless weaving between trees to try and head them towards the clearing. As she reached the perimeter of the bush, she was joined by Fergal, who helped steer the reluctant beasts into the collection pen.

"We could do with a couple of cattle dogs," she said, as she took off her hat and mopped her brow, "but it's not really worth it for the amount of time we'd use them." She gave a sigh and leant on the wooden railings of the pen, watching the milling cattle. "We must have most of them by now, and once we've branded the clean-skins, we'll decide on what to keep and what to sell."

"And what to eat. Sure it's been a while since I had a good beef steak," said Fergal.

Ruby nodded, the thought of it making her mouth water. She watched Duncan and Tommy prepare the fire and branding irons, and wondered what the children were doing. Kumali was back at the house looking after them — it was far too dangerous to have them here — and she hoped the girl had remembered to keep them out of the sun. Violet's pale skin burnt easily, and it was a constant worry.

There was a piercing whistle and they turned towards the bush. "It must be Finn," said Ruby. "Come on, everyone, he needs help."

They mounted up and galloped into the bush, following the sound of Finn's whistles. As they finally caught sight of him, they realised he was trying to flush out a nervous, bad-tempered bull. Ruby signalled to the others to fan out, so the bull would have to run between them.

The bull came to a standstill, eyed them belligerently and bellowed his frustration as Finn's whip cracked the

415

air. He planted his feet wide and dropped his head, pawing the ground and snorting.

"Stay out of his way, Ruby," ordered Finn, "and mind those horns."

She didn't need the warning, for she knew just how dangerous such a beast could be. Keeping her trembling horse at a safe distance, she whistled and flicked her whip to drive the bull forward. It shook its head and, with a roar of fury, began to trot purposefully towards the light at the end of the tunnel of trees. They stayed alongside, whistling and shouting to keep him on the move as Finn brought up the rear.

Just then an emu darted out of the bush, straight into the path of the bull. The bull skidded to a halt and bellowed. The bird, disorientated and fearful, flapped its tail feathers, its alarm call a deep drumming in its throat. Finn's horse reared up as the bull snorted, turned and prepared to charge.

The emu ran in circles, then fled.

Finn's horse was spooked, dancing and rearing as it whinnied in terror.

The bull's head was down, the heavy hoofs thundering on the ground as it raced towards them.

Finn yanked on the reins to turn the horse and evade those cruel horns, but as Ruby struggled to keep her own horse in check, everything seemed to slow into terrifying clarity.

The bull's horn caught Finn's horse in the shoulder. With a mighty roar it shook its head and the horse was flung, screaming in agony, on to its back. Finn was tossed into the air and landed with a thud against the

416

trunk of a tree. He lay as still as a rag doll, but the bull's horns were inches from his legs as it prepared to gore him.

Four whips cracked above its head, as they shouted and closed in.

The bull, thwarted and red-eyed with rage, backed off, glared at them, then charged through the scrub and was gone.

Ruby leapt from her horse and fell to her knees beside the stricken man. "Finn? Finn!" She found the pulse in his neck and gave a sigh of relief. "He's alive," she said, as the others clustered round her. "Put that poor horse out of its misery and then help me get Finn back to the house."

Ruby winced as the rifle-shot echoed through the bush, but at least the animal's awful screams were now silenced. She eyed Finn, her fear for him squirming like a living thing around her heart. His eyes were closed, and she suspected he'd broken his leg and shoulder, for both lay at awkward angles to his body.

Branches were hacked down and lashed with rope. Finn was gently placed on the saddle blanket they'd thrown over this makeshift stretcher, and once they were sure it could carry his weight, they began the long trek home.

There was no doctor within a hundred miles of this valley beyond the blue mountains, so Ruby followed Duncan's instructions and carefully reset the bones and splinted them. Mercifully, Finn remained unconscious throughout this ordeal, but after three days had passed and there was still no sign of him waking, Ruby began to fear the worst.

The others had returned to work, but Ruby stayed at Finn's side while Kumali cared for the children in her own bark hut. Her limbs were heavy with weariness as she sponged his hot face and tried to keep him cool beneath the muslin fly curtain. He lay sprawled beneath a thin sheet, his naked chest beaded with sweat, his chin grizzly with several days' growth.

She ran the cold, wet cloth over his chest and hesitated at his neck, where she could see the pulse beat beneath the skin. Her fingers hovered, feeling his heat and the throb of life that continued so determinedly there. "Oh, Finn," she whispered, "please wake up, my love."

There was no reply, and she brushed the hair from his forehead, her fingers sinking into the thick, dark mane that reached almost to his shoulders. Unable to resist, she softly traced the curve of his cheekbones, the dip in the centre of his chin and the breadth of his brow. She had never thought she would dare do this, had never dreamt that one day he would be lying on her bed half naked, and yet she knew that once he woke, her moment would be gone. Caught up in her need, she kissed his temple, her lips brushing his salty skin with the delicacy of a butterfly wing.

"What are you doing?"

She sprang back and would have fled, but his hand caught her wrist and held her there even though it was clearly causing him pain. "I . . . I was washing you," she stammered. "You're very hot."

418

His dark brow lifted. "Taking liberties, more like," he muttered, wincing as she struggled to break free.

"Don't be ridiculous," she said, reddening.

His grip was surprisingly firm as he gazed up at her. "So you're not one for the liberty-taking, then? You don't watch a man having a bath in the middle of the night, or kiss him when he's asleep and unable to defend himself?"

Ruby could feel the blush creep down her neck. So he had seen her that night after all. "You're imagining things," she said hastily.

His lips twitched. "I don't think so, Ruby. White nightgowns are awful easy to spot in the moonlight." He gave her wrist a tug and she was forced to perch on the side of the bed. "You always were a terrible liar," he said softly. "But aptly named, for you go as red as rubies."

"I didn't know you were there," she blustered, "and I didn't mean to spy on you . . . but . . ."

"And I suppose you didn't mean to kiss me either?" His blue eyes darkened.

She tossed back her auburn curls. "I gave you a peck on the forehead to wish you well, that's all," she said defiantly, "so don't start getting any ideas that you're special."

"Ach, Ruby, you're breaking me heart, you are." He released his hold, and as he shifted on the bed, he gasped with pain. "What the hell have you done to me?" He glanced about him, suddenly taking in where he was. "And how long have I been here?"

Ruby, still flustered and uncomfortably hot, kept herself busy with the bowl of water as she told him what had happened. "You've broken a leg and arm, and dislocated your shoulder. It's been three days," she finished.

"Three days?"

She watched him from beneath her lashes.

Finn eyed the splinted bandage on his arm, his bare chest and the toes peeking from the end of the sheet. His gaze was questioning as he looked back at her.

"Your dignity is intact," she said hurriedly. "Duncan stripped you down to your disreputable underwear." She felt slightly mollified when she saw him redden, and hurried to fetch him something to eat and drink. When he'd quenched his thirst, she held the bowl and spooned him soup, but his appetite was small and he soon gave up.

"I'll leave you to sleep," she said.

"Could you help me with the pillows, Ruby?"

She regarded him sternly and rather forcefully plumped the pillows. "You have one good arm, Finn, and are quite capable of seeing to your own pillows."

He grinned back at her. "I know, but it's so much nicer if you do it."

Ruby felt like throwing the soup at him, but realised she would only have to clear up the mess afterwards. "You're as bad as the children," she scolded. "Is there anything else your lordship would like me to do before I get on with my work?"

Her sarcasm seemed lost on him as he ran his hand over his chin. "Sure I'd love a shave," he said.

420

Ruby folded her arms. "A shave now, is it? And how do you know to trust me with such a sharp instrument when you have tried my patience so?"

"Because you love me."

They stared at one another, the words hanging between them.

"I'll get the razor." Ruby's heart was pounding as she worked up a lather in the bowl and hunted out James's razor and strop. He'd been teasing her, the words coming unbidden and with little thought, but the underlying truth in them had not escaped either of them, and she wondered if he'd known all along.

She refused to look at him as she sharpened the blade, perched on the bed and placed a towel on his chest, but when she dipped the brush in the lather and coated his chin, she found it impossible to avoid his steady gaze. "Close your eyes," she ordered.

"I'd rather watch — 'tis a rare thing to have a sharp blade so close to me neck and I want to be sure your hand is steady."

Her hand was anything but steady as she took up the razor, and she had to take a deep breath before she felt confident enough to begin. His gaze remained fixed on her as she leant above him. The air was charged, drawing them close in the intimacy of the moment as her fingers touched his face and the blade made its first, tentative sweep. She concentrated on his chin, tightening the skin where the hair grew in the cleft, running the blade through the foam above his lip and along his jawbone. Her ragged breath mingled with his as his gaze continued to follow her, and she could see the pulse race in his neck as she scraped away the thick, dark growth.

Her back ached from bending over him, her nerves in shreds. He was still watching her, and as she took the towel and gently wiped away the suds, she found she couldn't look away. His uninjured arm snaked round her waist, drawing her gently to his battered chest. She couldn't resist, and as his hand moved up her back to her nape, her heart began to thud. His fingers delved into her damp curls, and she could feel the pressure of them as he drew her head closer — so close she could see her eyes reflected in his, so close their lips were almost touching. There was an instant of hesitation, an instant when the world stood still and all that existed was the two of them. Then he kissed her.

Ruby was swept up in an explosion of sensual, demanding emotions that were so powerful she could do nothing to quell them. Mindful of his injuries, she dug her hands in his hair and hungrily returned his kiss. The need to hold him, to be with him, to touch and kiss and make love to him was so overwhelming it made her tremble.

Finn's hand cupped her head as his kiss grew more demanding, and Ruby surrendered to the bliss of knowing he desired her. She had waited so long for this, had yearned and dreamt of this moment, that she wanted it to last for ever.

The sound of Violet's piping voice finally brought her to her senses, and she gently resisted Finn and pulled away. The children were outside — what did she think she was doing? Yet her whole being craved him, her body pliant and trembling with need.

He seemed to understand, for his hand was gentle as it cupped her cheek, the thumb edging along her lip and caressing her chin. "'Tis a powerful thing, Ruby," he said, his voice unsteady. "How are we to live apart now we know how it could be?"

"We must," she breathed, "for I am not free."

He sighed. "Neither of us is free — not after today, my Ruby, my darling, my heart, *acushla*."

"Oh, Finn," her voice broke with emotion, "what are we to do?"

He held her with infinite tenderness. "I don't know, my *mochree*. But I promise you this: I will not be leaving you — not now, not ever — unless you order it."

Ruby could hear the drum of his heart and felt an overwhelming sense of the rightness of being with him, and yet she knew they had crossed an invisible line today, and that only heartache would come of it.

Kumali rounded up the children and chivvied them down to her bark hut. Violet, as usual, was running about with no clothes on, and it took a while to persuade the child back into her dress and bonnet, but it wasn't Violet's nakedness that bothered her — it was what she'd witnessed a moment ago between Finn and Ruby.

She doled out bread and soup, and sat down to rest. There was another baby on the way, despite her precautions, and this one was heavy and made her feel sick. She ran her hands over the mound as it squirmed inside her, but her thoughts were on Ruby.

"That's a mighty frown, lassie. What's fretting you?" Duncan came into the hut, filling it with his presence. He sat and let the children swarm over him, but his gaze was fixed on Kumali.

She didn't want to tell him, not in front of the children, for Violet was far too questioning and she missed nothing. Yet she knew she couldn't keep it to herself. "Kumali seen Ruby alonga Finn."

"Aye, well, she's caring for him. I cannae see the problem."

"Ruby, Finn . . ." She puckered her lips and blew a kiss.

Duncan threw back his head and laughed. "Och, is that all? I've been expecting that for a wee while now, as you have, Kumali. There's nae need to look so shocked."

She shook her head. "Big trouble come when boss come back."

"James has been gone two and a half years, Kumali," he reminded her, as he shooed the children out of the hut. "I doubt he'll ever come back now."

"James is Ruby's husband. He come one day and then there be big fight."

"If he's a wise man, he'll stay away. Ruby's father is nae a man to cross, and I ken he's nae best pleased with his son-in-law." He reached across and stroked the swell of her stomach. "That's a lively bairn you've got in there, Kumali. Another son, maybe?"

424

She shrugged, not really caring what it was, just wanting it born so she could feel well again. "Ruby's fatha send Finn look after her. He no like if Ruby alonga baby with Finn. James no like." She looked at Duncan through her lashes. "Fergal no like . . ."

Duncan chewed on a hunk of mutton. "All this talk of bairns is speculation — it may not come to that." He drank some tea and glowered from beneath his bushy brows. "It's certainly none of Fergal's business," he growled, "and neither is it ours. If Ruby and Finn have finally found each other, then it's up to them what they do about it."

Kumali shook her head in frustration. "Fergal see Ruby with Finn. Him tell James."

"Are you sure?" At her nod he frowned. "Aye, well," he sighed, "that could certainly put the fox among the hens. Let us hope for all our sakes that James never returns."

Eden Valley, July 1854

Ruby had been unable to sleep and, despite the winter chill, was sitting in her favourite chair on the veranda. It was not yet light, but the stars were beginning to fade as soft grey leached the black horizon. Nell's presence was all around her, and she drew comfort from it, knowing it would continue to sustain her, for in these lonely hours before dawn they shared the hopes and dreams of women who loved deeply and well, of women who had fallen for the charm of a man with thick, dark hair and laughing eyes. Nell's love for her husband,

Billy Penhalligan, had remained strong right to the end — perhaps even after death — and Ruby was warmed by the thought they might be together up there among the stars.

As she listened to the night sounds and watched the moon, her thoughts turned to the ancient beliefs of the Aboriginals — that the Ancestor Spirits watched over them, guided them and protected them throughout their lives until it was time for them to become Spirits themselves and live among the stars. How sad it was that Kumali held no such beliefs after her brutal encounters with the white man, and that she, the daughter of a convict Irishman, should hold on to the knowledge that the spirit of her long-dead grandmother still walked beside her.

Her thoughts returned to Finn. He filled her every waking moment, came to her in dreams and spoke to her on the wind. His necessary departure for the hospital in Sydney had come within days of their first and only kiss, and it had become obvious to both of them that it was not a minute too soon, for the temptation to follow that kiss with another — to proceed to the natural fulfilment of their hunger, and thereby throw caution to the wind — had become unbearable.

She had been aware of him watching as she moved about the hut, had known she made excuses to be with him and ignored the chores that were piling up, had realised they were heading for perdition if they dared succumb to what was in their hearts. But then they hadn't needed to speak, for their love was in their eyes, in every gesture and smile.

She unfolded the letter that had come from her mother in Sydney a week ago, and although she couldn't read the words in the poor light, she didn't really need to, for she knew them by heart and treasured them as a link to home and those who loved her.

Her mother Amy assured her that Finn's arm was already healed and that the physician had taken his leg out of splints, but the wasted muscles still needed support. He was not the easiest patient, for he refused to remain in bed and was constantly under everyone's feet as he hobbled about on crutches, but as he kept the grandchildren entertained with stories and was the most charming, likeable man, she forgave him.

Amy had gone on to explain how Niall had found a new lease of life with his jovial presence and that the men often sat on the veranda drinking beer and exchanging taller and taller stories throughout the night, thereby disturbing her sleep with their raucous laughter. It was good to have him stay, but it reminded Amy and Niall that their daughter was far from home, and they longed to see her again.

Ruby carefully folded the letter, her imagination bringing the sights and sounds of Parramatta and her family forcefully back to her. Finn was having a fine time, surrounded by his family, being cared for and fed as if he was royalty, while she . . . she sat here waiting for him to come home.

With a sigh of exasperation, she pulled the shawl around her shoulders and went inside. It seemed she was fated to a life of waiting — a solitary life in which she had to keep her emotions tightly reined lest they weaken her resolve and had her scurrying back to Parramatta.

The cool storeroom they had dug out of the hill was the perfect hiding place for her treasures, and the battered tobacco tin had been tucked out of sight behind the grain sacks. She pulled it out and prised open the lid. The silver locket was wrapped in a piece of cloth, and she regarded it unemotionally. James had given it to her that first New Year, but she'd stopped wearing it two years ago, for it had come to represent her marriage — tarnished by neglect, and no longer something she treasured. There were locks of hair folded within brown paper, one dark, the other copper — her children's hair, and far more precious than any tawdry locket. A handful of coins rattled beneath the pack of letters she'd received from her family over the years, and as she tied the ribbon round the latest, she felt the prickle of tears. Her mother was right: she had been apart from them for too long.

Blinking back the tears, she pulled on trousers and shirt. James had left them behind, and she'd adjusted them to fit. Duncan had been clearly horrified, but they were practical and it meant her dresses would last that bit longer.

"Practicalities," she murmured, as she fetched the pail and headed for the byre. "That's what I have to think about now — not feeling sorry for myself, or daydreaming about Finn."

Work was over for the day and Ruby was sitting with Kumali on the veranda having a can of tea as they watched the children play with the puppies that one of Duncan's dogs had recently whelped.

"Duncan's not going to like his pups racing about like that," said Ruby.

"Duncan with sheeps. What he don't see he don't know." Kumali shifted the sleeping baby to a more comfortable position on her lap and sipped the tea.

"He'll know," she replied, "because they'll be the very devil to train now they've been taught to chase and yap at anything that moves."

"Keeps dem kids quiet. Gives us a bit of peace."

Ruby turned her attention to the baby in Kumali's arms. "I have to say, that child has more red hair than me, and the colour is incredible. It must be the Scot in her." She ran her fingers through the shock of ginger curls. "Violet's very miffed."

"Vi always miffed. I just hope Garnday no have same temper."

"Where does that name come from, Kumali? I haven't heard it before."

"Garnday very important woman in Dreamtime. She led her people south to Warang. My mother said she our Ancestor Spirit. I just like de name."

Ruby eyed the sleeping infant, whose skin was the colour of lightly toasted bread. There were freckles across her button nose, the long eyelashes were as gold as her hair, and so far she'd proved sweet-tempered. "Red hair always brings trouble," she murmured. "I remember *my* grandmother saying that."

"You think she up in sky with Spirit People now?"

"I am sure of it."

"I no believe in spirits," Kumali said with a grimace. "Elders say up there, but I don't see 'em. Story for bairns, is all — not real."

Ruby was saddened, for Kumali had a very different upbringing to the Moonraker natives: her Elders had been barred from teaching the young the rituals and rites of their ancient people in the mistaken belief their ways were a barrier to bringing them to a white, Christian God.

She gave a sigh and watched the children. They didn't see the colour of their skins, had little care for their differences, for in their innocence they were all God's children. What would happen once the outside world encroached and opened their eyes to prejudice and the hatred of anything that didn't conform? She could only pray that these early years would shape their future beliefs and keep them strong.

"What on earth is that?" Ruby stood and listened, noting how the children had stopped playing and were looking towards the track. Then the wind carried it to her and she heard it again. It was fiddle music, which could only mean one thing. Grabbing her hat, she flew down the steps and raced into the clearing.

The extraordinary cavalcade was led by a dusty carriage with two high-stepping black horses. Behind this came a group of dishevelled riders and another pair

430

of horses pulling an enormous wagon. The music was louder now, the fiddles accompanied by a drum and squeeze-box.

Ruby laughed and clapped her hands as tears streamed down her face. "It's your grandpa and grandma," she sobbed to the wide-eyed children. "And there's Finn and his two brothers, and . . ." She began to run towards them, and before the driver could bring the carriage to a halt, she had clambered in and flung herself into her parents' arms.

They all talked at once as they kissed and hugged, and it was only when the carriage stopped outside the hut that she remembered the children. "Mam, Da, this is Violet, Nathaniel, Natjik, Mookah and that's Garnday with Kumali."

"Well, I never." Niall handed Amy down from the carriage and eyed the rather solemn children who looked up at him in awe. "I don't suppose any of you would care for a cone of sherbet?"

Ruby laughed as they overcame their shyness in the quest for such a treat and swarmed round him. Even Kumali had come down from the veranda to take her share and was eyeing Niall with a kind of reverence she had never seen before. But then Da was as handsome as ever, with his white hair and neat moustache, and he struck an imposing figure in his well-cut suit and fancy waistcoat, despite the dust and dirt of their long journey.

She slipped her arm round her mother's waist and held her close, breathing in her familiar perfume and revelling in her presence. The red in her hair might be faded and her face might look more careworn than she remembered, but she was Mam and always would be. "I'm so pleased you've come," she murmured. "But you must be exhausted. How long did it take you to get here?"

"An extremely long six weeks," said Amy with a sigh. "Look at me. My clothes are filthy, my hair is a mess, and as for my lovely new hat . . ." She gave a rueful smile. "But what's a bit of discomfort when I have my girl with me again?" Her faded blue eyes regarded Ruby with love and concern. "I've been so worried about you and would have come sooner, but your papa forbade me to travel without him." She smiled. "Now I understand why. We must have travelled over every mountain and valley for hundreds of miles to get here."

As Ruby hugged her mother, she became aware of being watched, and when their embrace was over, she at last dared to look at Finn. Time slowed and the noise around them faded as their eyes met. "Hello, Finn," she murmured.

He smiled the smile that made her heart flutter. "Sure it is good to see you again after so long," he replied. "As you see, I've brought me brothers to help out until I can get about more easily."

It was only then she noticed he was leaning on a walking stick. "I thought . . ."

"Ach, 'tis nothing. I just need it when me leg gets tired, but I'll soon be leaping about again."

"I've brought a gift for you, Ruby," said Niall, as he untangled himself from the clamouring children and took her hand. "I hope you like it."

She plied him with questions as he led her to the covered dray, but he refused to enlighten her. She stood in excited anticipation as the tarpaulin was pulled away. For an instant she couldn't make out what it was; then realised what the sheets of wood, the beams, frames and tiles added up to. "It's a house," she gasped.

"Aye, that it is," he said with a smile. "A proper house with windows, doors and floors, and there are screens to keep the flies out, and some decent chairs to sit on." He hugged her close. "Finn told me how you were living and I wanted to make sure my girl had a few comforts."

"It's perfect," she breathed.

"I had it made in my new factory."

She laughed. "Another new enterprise?"

"Oh, yes, my Ruby. I'll not be settling down to retirement just yet. There's money to be made with people moving further into the bush, and I aim to provide them with a decent house they can put together in a matter of days."

She saw him glance at the bark hut, Duncan's cabin and the makeshift shack that Finn, Fergal and Tommy shared when they returned from their long stints in the pastures. Shame flooded through her as she suddenly saw them for the shabby hovels they really were.

"Never mind, darling," soothed Amy. "We'll soon have this place to rights, and when the other wagon arrives, there will be new housing for everyone."

Ruby burst into tears, overwhelmed by their generosity and love.

CHAPTER
FIFTEEN

Eureka Gold Fields, Victoria, October 1854

There had been a lightening of spirits among the diggers in the past months. Hotham, the new governor of Victoria, had visited and there was a sense things at last might improve. The licence fee still held, but could now be purchased monthly. And yet, as the hot winds blew in from the north, the resentment built against the spies, police and troopers who continued to harass the diggers. The uneasy atmosphere was made all the more dangerous by stories of sick men dying of neglect in the prison, and the influx of yet more troops.

The military camp sat on a hill by the River Yarrowee and overlooked the Gravel Pits diggings and the Eureka diggings. To Hina and the others, the military camp embodied all that was oppressive, for it was inhabited by officials whose high-living and nefarious links with local business interests were manifest to all.

Then the murder of a young Scotsman called James Scobie ignited this powder keg. A man named Bentley, who owned the Eureka Hotel, was accused of Scobie's murder, but it was common knowledge that Bentley had powerful friends, and with their complicity, the investigation was quickly set aside.

It was as if the hot winds had infected the diggings with madness. Next the Irish Catholics became incensed when their priest and his servant were dragged to court and fined for nonpayment of a licence that by law neither of them needed. The Americans and English were also at loggerheads, mainly over claim-jumping — stealing another man's diggings. And all the while Scobie's friends remained furious that his murderer went unpunished.

Hina felt unsettled as he dressed that morning. It was only six o'clock, but the heat was already intense with the promise of an approaching storm. He couldn't shake off the feeling something even darker loomed. The notices of the latest meeting of the diggers from the surrounding fields had been pinned up all over town. There were only two items to debate, but they were the most important ones — the diggers' freedom to work unmolested, and the need to bring Bentley to trial. Although work was usually their first priority, the general feeling was that justice had to prevail if the diggings were not to descend into anarchy.

"It's asking for trouble having it where Scobie was murdered," drawled Howard. "Bentley's sure to have the police and army to protect him, and I wager there'll be violence before the day's out."

"Then we must go prepared." James picked up a shovel and felt its weight.

435

"Let us just hope our voices will be heard," said Hina, "and that justice will be done without resorting to violence."

James crammed on his hat and left the tent, eager for a fight.

"We'd better catch him up before he lands in gaol," muttered Howard.

Hina stared in amazement at the gathering spread around the Eureka Hotel. There had to be ten thousand people standing in the heat to listen to the miners' leader, Hugh Meikle, and he suspected many had come from the nearby towns of Bendigo and Castlemaine in support.

"Commissioner Rede can't be expecting trouble," murmured Howard. "He's only sent the local justice of peace, and Inspector Evans has less than a dozen men with him."

Hina felt a modicum of relief, but with hotheads like James in the crowd, there was no telling what might happen. He slowly moved through the crowd as the speeches went on and, from his vantage point on the perimeter, saw the arrival of about thirty more policemen armed with staves. They quickly entered the Eureka Hotel — no doubt to protect its owner should trouble break out, for Hina could see no sign of Bentley.

It was almost noon and the heat was stifling as the meeting carried on. There were mutterings at the seemingly inconsequential outcome of it all, and the loss of half a day's work. Shade was sought by the

436

buildings on either side of the Eureka Hotel and dry throats quenched with ale.

Hina eyed the stores and the bowling alley that ran down the side of the hotel. The owner of the alley, an American from Boston, was looking anxious as the angry diggers followed Evans and his mounted police on their approach to the hotel — and well he might, thought Hina, for the buildings were wooden, the bowling alley mainly constructed from canvas. It wouldn't take much to burn down.

"Bring out Bentley," the crowd began to shout. "Show yerself, Bentley, or we'll come in there to get you."

Hina saw Bentley scurry out of the back door of the hotel and quickly mount a police horse. Before the crowd could react, he'd fled towards the army camp.

"Cowardly bastard!"

"Murderer!"

A digger struck the hotel with his fist. "I propose this house belongs to us, the diggers."

Fuelled by anger, excitement and alcohol, the crowd roared its approval. A stone was thrown and then another, which smashed an outside lamp. More stones followed; windows were broken; wooden boards were torn from walls. Hina and others of a like mind pleaded for restraint, but the diggers were set on a course of destruction and would not be turned.

Hina was unsure of what to do. He'd lost sight of James and suspected he was among the wreckers, but wasn't prepared to risk his liberty by going in to haul him out.

More soldiers arrived and Commissioner Rede emerged from the nearby police station to order them to protect the hotel. He stood on a windowsill to address the diggers, but his pleas for calm were drowned out. Turning to Green, the justice of the peace, he shouted, "Read the Riot Act, man. Before we are slaughtered."

Green shook his head and backed away — perhaps realising that angry, beleaguered miners would not be quelled by the reading of a piece of paper.

Hina edged further away, so didn't see how the fire started, but as he looked over the heads, he saw the American's bowling alley was ablaze. As the wind blew and the storm came closer, the flames were swiftly fanned into an inferno.

The police tried unsuccessfully to beat it out. The military, who didn't count firefighting among their duties, left the hotel and returned to camp. Within minutes of their departure the Eureka Hotel was ablaze.

Hina watched in bemusement as the diggers sang and danced and laughed at the exploding windows, the crumbling walls and the collapsing roof. It seemed previous jealousies, resentments and arguments had been forgotten as Americans and Englishmen linked arms with Germans, Scots and Irishmen to celebrate the conflagration.

Eggs and rubbish were thrown at Rede as he kept up his pleas for moderation, the jeers drowning out his words. Policemen made half-hearted arrests, but their prisoners were swiftly rescued by their friends, and the shame-faced Rede and his men beat a hasty retreat.

"We've won, me boys. We've won." The cry came from someone in the large Irish contingent known as the Tipperary Mob. "We are lords and masters of these gold fields, and never again shall we be ruled by those cowards."

As if to throw scorn on these words, and to prove that nothing was more powerful than Nature herself, the wind suddenly gathered strength. It whipped up gravel and sand and anything that wasn't tied down as it spun down the streets. It battered roofs and chimneys, picked up carts and barrows, and flung them into the whirling mass as it banged doors and screens, plucked at iron roofs and howled like a banshee. Men forgot their anger, beasts cowered, and women and children dived for cover wherever they could find it.

Hina lay beneath the sturdy veranda of a nearby store and closed his eyes as the dust storm brought a darkness as profound as night. He had little doubt that today's events would bring retribution, and that it would not be the last call for justice, for Bentley had once again escaped, the military and police had been shamed, and the miners' thirst for revenge had not been slaked.

Eureka Gold Fields, Victoria, November 1854

Governor Hotham realised there would be no peace in the Victoria gold fields until the miners' grievances were attended to. Bentley was finally charged with

439

Scobie's murder and sent to trial in Melbourne, where he was sentenced to three years' hard labour.

But the miners now had another grievance. Ten men had been arrested for the burning of the Eureka Hotel — most of whom had proof they were elsewhere at the time. The judge at their trial said it was the first case of lynch law in Australia, but they were still found guilty.

The Ballarat Reform League was fully established at a meeting on Bakery Hill on 29 November, where it was decided it was time to put words into action and there was a ceremonial burning of the hated licences. Lalor, the league's spokesman, then called for a meeting in five days' time at the Adelphi Theatre, which had recently been built on the Eureka diggings, to elect a new central committee and reform the rules and regulations of the league, which, until then, had been largely disorganised.

Hina stood with thousands of others as they pledged to stand united in opposition to the enforcement of sanctions against the unlicensed digger. As the majority of the miners were American, German, Irish, Welsh and Scots, they demanded to be represented by a flag that symbolised their struggle for justice. Ross, a Canadian, was set the task of designing it. With a dark blue wool background, the dun-coloured cross had a star at the end of each arm and one at its heart. He called it the Southern Cross, after the constellation that glittered above them every night.

Despite the unification of the diggers, and the sense of power that the unity instilled in them, Hina woke the next morning to the sound of yet another licence hunt in the nearby Gravel Pits diggings. He and the others dressed hurriedly and rushed to join the Irish protestors who were standing firm and refusing to pay. More police arrived and the Riot Act was read out. Only a few dispersed and the mounted police were brought in, sabres drawn, on the unarmed diggers. Shots were fired, two men received minor injuries, and eight diggers were arrested.

"God darn it," muttered Howard, slapping his hat against his thigh. "We'll never get justice."

"It's time we fought back," snapped James.

Hina remained silent as those around James began to mutter. It seemed the time for talking was over, and as he stood there, he saw miners down tools and surge towards Bakery Hill, which had become the focal point of their struggle. He was as angry as everyone else at the continued injustices, for his very difference marked him out as a target for the incessant routs. Without a thought for the consequences, Hina followed them.

About a thousand men listened as Lalor ordered those without firearms to make pikes, for they had only picks and shovels to defend themselves and the exposed grounds surrounding the Eureka diggings in case the military attacked.

"I can't say I like the look of this," said Howard, as he oiled his rifle and checked the sights, "but I guess we have little choice."

"If only Hotham showed a bit of common sense, we wouldn't be in this position," replied Hina. "Are they so arrogant they can't see we will not be bullied?"

Howard snorted. "Common sense and politics ain't great bedfellows — never have been. And Hotham's arrogance is inbred, like all Englishmen."

Hina nodded. He'd witnessed that arrogance in Tahiti, where the missionaries and officials seemed to think their laws and customs were invincible. "My people have suffered at the hands of such men," he murmured, as he honed the hunting knife, "and it is time they were taught a lesson."

"That's more like it," said James, slapping his back. "A man of your size would make mincemeat of them."

Hina continued sharpening the blade, his thoughts in turmoil. He abhorred violence, and despite his hatred for the regulators, he doubted he could ever use the knife in anger. Yet the very act of following Lalor put him at the heart of this uprising, thereby threatening his freedom. The idea of being incarcerated made him shudder. He'd heard stories of three men sharing one infested blanket, of broiling heat in the tin shack with no windows, and knew he would never survive it. He listened as others talked excitedly of retribution and battle, and wondered if they shared his doubts as to the wisdom of this unequal contest. They might outnumber the troops and police, and have right on their side, but they were poorly armed and untrained.

Lalor returned some time later and ordered them to build a stockade on the Eureka diggings. The miners, eager to be occupied, began to erect a crude fortification of wooden slabs, which were shored up by earth and stones. This fort surrounded an area of about an acre, which encompassed a few miners' tents and a

442

small store in the heart of the Eureka diggings, and when it was done, it stood on a slight incline next to the Melbourne Road, within two hundred yards of the ruins of Bentley's hotel.

"Follow me back to Bakery Hill and we will gather more recruits to help us defend our cause," Lalor shouted when the work was over.

Hina and Howard exchanged glances. They were growing weary of this rabble-rousing and couldn't really see the point in more talk.

"Come on," urged James. "We have pledged an oath to stand united, and Lalor needs our support."

The sun was setting as the Southern Cross was unfurled again on Bakery Hill. Lalor, rifle in hand, mounted the stump and asked all to leave who were not prepared to swear allegiance. It was clear to Hina that the ardour of noon had swiftly waned, for only half their number stood firm.

He watched in thoughtful silence as the bareheaded Lalor knelt beneath the billowing flag and raised his right hand. "We swear by the Southern Cross to stand truly by each other and fight to defend our rights and liberties."

Shouts of "Amen" echoed into the sundown, and the determined, newly armed men marched proudly behind their flag back to the stockade. The oath they had taken was the first on Australian soil to a flag that was not British. It was a heady moment.

With the setting sun came the rain, and Hina huddled miserably in his oilskins as water dripped from his hat. The mood in the stockade was fretful and

443

impatient, and many of the men had left for their own tents and huts, yet it was clear the military were preparing for an attack, and every man in the flimsy stockade knew it wouldn't take much to demolish it. They were prepared to fight for dignity and the right to work unmolested, but as darkness enveloped them, it became apparent they were sitting targets. There was little sleep to be had that night.

Eureka Gold Fields, Victoria, 2 December 1854

As the days wore on and the rain turned the earth to mud, the miners' courage and enthusiasm for their cause was bolstered by the knowledge there had been no further routs by the officials, no one had been arrested, and it looked as if Hotham had finally seen sense.

It was now Saturday, and Hina and the others in the stockade had finished the military drill Lalor insisted upon and were preparing food as Father Smyth tried to persuade the Irish Catholics to lay down their arms. Hina listened as the mild-mannered and much respected priest begged his flock to give deeper thought to their situation, but his pleas fell on deaf ears and he left the stockade a defeated man.

Hina was sent to requisition supplies and returned just as a band of two hundred horsemen arrived. This was the Independent Californian Rangers, led by James McGill, a man well known throughout Victoria. Hina eyed the revolvers and Mexican knives, saw the jubilation among those in the stockade and the

444

welcoming smile of Lalor. He edged forward to listen as Lalor promptly promoted McGill to second in command. The new password, "Vinegar Hill", was circulated.

"That's a foolhardy password to choose," muttered James. "My father-in-law, Niall Logan, fought at Vinegar Hill and it only reminds the Irish who still remember the battles in Ireland and Parramatta of defeat. Don't those idiots know anything?"

Hina didn't know what James was talking about. Yet it seemed that in McGill at last they had someone with military experience to lead them. McGill swiftly set up an efficient sentry system, told the diggers to stand fast and drew up a general order for the night. A spy had told them military reinforcements were coming up from Melbourne, and so McGill and two-thirds of his men planned to leave the Eureka stockade and intercept them.

"That can't be wise," said Hina. "Rede must know about the Americans, and if it's discovered they have left the stockade, they will surely attack."

"Perhaps McGill and Lalor think it unlikely we'll see action at night," muttered Howard through his tobacco plug.

A new moon sailed in a clear sky as they watched McGill and his men leave. When they saw Lalor retire for the night, they followed suit and left for the relative comfort of their own tent, which lay some way outside the stockade. One hundred and twenty diggers remained in the stockade, armed only with pikes or pistols and insufficient ammunition to go round.

445

Eureka Gold Fields, Victoria, 3 December 1854

The silence of dawn was shattered by gunfire — one shot swiftly followed by another.

"The stockade's under attack." James almost fell over Hina and Howard in his eagerness, grabbed a rifle and was gone.

Hina heard a volley of gunfire as he dragged on his trousers and snatched up the rifle Howard had given him that morning. "The reinforcements must have got through," he breathed. "We won't stand a chance."

"Take my horse and find McGill. Tell him to get here pronto." Howard gave him a shove. "Go, and quickly before we're all massacred."

Hina ran out and, with little idea of where McGill might be, kicked the animal into a gallop and set off towards the Melbourne Road. He could hear shouts from the stockade and the fusillade of bullets from the police and military, and as he approached the Melbourne Road, he realised the cavalry were perfectly positioned to cut off escape. Taking evasive action from the bullets being fired from Specimen Hill, Hina rode south in search of McGill.

He caught sight of the Americans five miles from Eureka. They were already turning back towards the stockade, but ambling in such a manner it would take too long to be of any use to the beleaguered miners. "You have to hurry," he shouted, bringing his horse to a slithering standstill. "The stockade has been attacked and our numbers are too few."

The American gave a nod of thanks and led his men at a gallop for Eureka.

Hina turned his horse to follow them, but as he raced to catch up, it stumbled on the rough road and came to a limping halt. Burning with frustration, Hina slid from its back, ran a hand down the trembling leg, which was already swelling, looked into the distance at the cloud of dust raised by the Americans and realised he would have to walk back.

It was after eight in the morning when Hina had his first sight of the ruined stockade. There was no flag flying, the walls had collapsed, and everywhere he looked he could see the dead and dying. The stench of blood mingled with the smoke from gunpowder and burning tents, and throughout it all hung a terrible silence.

Hina could see the soldiers and policemen rounding up the walking wounded, and those who were too numbed by what they'd experienced to flee. They were shackled and herded into the military lock-up, and he knew that if he was seen, that would also be his fate.

He quickly backed away until he reached the outlying bush. From there he took a circuitous route towards the Gravel Pits diggings and his tent. There was no sign of Howard or James — in fact the diggings were too quiet, and it slowly dawned on him that everyone had gone. Hina made a cold compress for his horse's injured leg and wondered what to do.

The decision was made for him as four policemen rushed into the tent. "This one was there — I saw him. Chain him up and put him with the rest."

447

"I wasn't," Hina protested. "I took no part. I was on the Melbourne Road. Ask McGill." But they were too excited to listen and put shackles on his ankles and shoved him into the line of disconsolate prisoners they had rounded up earlier.

A pistol was waved in his face. "One wrong move, yer bastard, and I'll shoot."

Hina had no option but to move on the order, and the line of chained men slowly crossed the fields to the lock-up. The stockade was in ruins, the Southern Cross flag was torn to shreds, their leadership destroyed. It was a bitter defeat.

The lock-up confirmed Hina's fears, for there were over a hundred men in that airless room, and as the day's heat increased, the injured Italian leader Carboni appeared to be growing incoherent.

"Have you seen Howard Repton or James Tyler?" Hina asked the man squashed in beside him.

"Repton's being looked after by the medic," was the reply. "Took a bullet in the temple and a bayonet in the shoulder. They took him to the London Hotel. I've no idea what became of Tyler — probably dead."

Hina recognised most of the men around him, but he couldn't remember seeing half of them in the stockade.

"Carboni's here, but what of Lalor and the other leaders?"

"There's a price on their heads. Lalor took a musket ball and two bullets in the shoulder. His arm was shattered, but he refused to run although he ordered us to do so. He was losing a lot of blood. We hid him in a

448

woodpile. Friends will smuggle him out when it's safe, but he needs urgent medical attention or he'll die."

Hina listened as the carnage of those fifteen minutes was revealed in the desultory talk around him. There were tales of soldiers bayoneting the injured and dying, of police shooting unarmed men and setting fire to tents with women and children still inside. And yet there were tales of heroism too, as miners armed only with flimsy pikes had stood against the onslaught of bullets and sabres as two-thirds of them were slaughtered.

Despite the chill these stories evoked, Hina thought he would suffocate as night fell. The heat in the lock-up was increased by the number of tightly packed bodies. He was close to losing his mind as the images of that slaughter remained and the desperation for space, light and air overwhelmed him.

He had lost all track of time when the door was suddenly opened and they were ordered out. Taking great gulps of fresh air, he tried to clear his head as they were marched into the starlit night to a nearby storehouse. This proved to be large, clean and cool, and Hina sank on to the straw almost weeping in relief.

It was close to ten in the morning when the door opened again. There had been no food or water throughout the night, and Carboni was now raving with delirium. Rede ordered him to be taken to the camp infirmary, then had the prisoners lined up.

Heads were counted and names were taken. There had been rumours throughout the night of the military digging a large pit within the precincts of the camp, and

449

having witnessed the previous day's cruelty, it wasn't hard for the prisoners to conclude that they were destined to be buried alive.

Hina was sweating profusely as the soldiers and police marched officiously up and down the lines. One night in the lock-up had been bad enough, but now the accusation of treason had been made and several men were being yanked out of line — all of them with foreign names. To die in prison was bad enough, but to be buried alive . . . He flinched as a rough hand hauled him to the centre of the clearing.

"That man was not at the stockade. He was on the Melbourne Road, riding away from Eureka and is innocent of treason."

Hina realised it was one of McGill's men who had spoken and he felt quite weak with relief. The policeman unlocked the shackles, told him to pay a thirty-shilling fine and clear off. With a grateful smile at the American, Hina handed over the money and raced down the hill towards the London Hotel, which had been turned into an infirmary.

Hina finally found Howard among the chaos. He was lying on a narrow iron bed, his shoulder and chest heavily bandaged. There was more bandaging round his head, and a line of blood had congealed on his pale cheek. "How is he?" he asked a passing medic.

"He's unconscious," replied the harassed man. "The bayonet wounds should heal, but the head injury is more serious. I've had to dig the bullet out, and it came cleanly enough, but if he doesn't wake soon, then I fear we may still lose him."

450

Hina asked after James.

"I haven't treated him," the man replied, "but then a lot died and had to be buried the same day because of the heat. There's a mass grave just outside Eureka. You might find his name on a marker there."

Hina saw the lines of beds and the harried men and women who tended the wounded. "Is there anything I can do to help?"

The doctor wearily shook his head. "Most of these poor souls are beyond earthly help," he said. "Go back to the living and be thankful you are not among them."

Hina looked down at Howard, wondering if they would ever speak again. He had become a friend and it didn't seem right that he should die in such circumstances. His gaze travelled to his clothes, which had been flung over the end of the bed, and he remembered Howard's pledge. He saw no sign of the pocket watch hanging from the waistcoat and concluded his friend must have left it behind in his rush to get to the stockade.

He left the hotel and returned to the diggings, his mind troubled. If Howard died, then the watch would be his, but a friend's life was more precious than any watch and Hina prayed fervently for Howard's survival.

It was impossible to work the claim on his own now that James had disappeared and Howard was fighting for his life, and he had little enthusiasm anyway. He glanced at the abandoned tools and clothes and the rumpled beds. So much had happened in such few hours. It had been a battle they could never have won.

"It's over," he murmured. "Time I went home." He began to pack. There wasn't much, for most of his clothes were ragged and ingrained with dirt, fit only to burn. He made a cursory search for Howard's watch in the hopes he could give it to the doctor for when Howard awoke, but it was nowhere to be seen. "I'll go back to the hospital," he muttered, "and check it hasn't been stolen."

He strode outside and descended the rope ladder into the hole he'd spent so long digging. Buried behind a clay brick in the wall forty feet down was the tin box where he kept his banking receipts and a few of the smaller nuggets he'd found. He was about to carry it to the surface when the light was blocked.

"Hina Timanu?"

He hastily returned the box, replaced the brick and smeared mud over it. "Yes?"

"I have a warrant for your arrest," boomed the voice. "Come up immediately."

He hesitated, realised he was trapped and slowly climbed the ladder. "I have just been released from all charges," he protested, "and paid my fine."

He was hauled up the final three feet and thrown to the ground. "I'm arresting you for theft," said the policeman.

"I have stolen nothing," Hina shouted. He struggled against the chains being locked round his wrists and ankles, and the hands that searched his pockets. "I am not a thief."

"That's for the judge to decide," was the gruff reply.

He was hauled to his feet. "What am I supposed to have stolen, and who has made this accusation against me?"

"A Mr Thomas Roundhill swears you stole a gold watch belonging to Howard Repton."

Hina was confused. "I have never heard of this Mr Roundhill," he stuttered, "and if I have stolen such a thing, it would be among my things. Please," he begged, "search the tent. You will find no watch."

"We know you've hid it somewhere," he growled, "but it's up to others to find it. Now move yerself."

Hina protested his innocence all the way up the dreaded hill to the claustrophobic lock-up. They shoved him inside and slammed the door, and Hina slumped against the wall in despair. Howard was unconscious and not expected to live. James must have died in the battle, and the watch had disappeared. He had no defence against the charge, no knowledge of his accuser — and no way of proving his innocence.

PART THREE

Legacies

CHAPTER
SIXTEEN

Eden Valley, 31 December 1854

"Will you walk with me, Ruby?"

She smiled and took her father's arm as they headed for the riverbank. "I wish you didn't have to leave."

"Tomorrow's the first day of a new year, and I have things to attend to in Sydney. Even without the loaded dray it will take over a fortnight to get home." He came to a halt. "I would ask you to come home, my darling, but I have the feeling you are already there."

She nodded. "I love Eden Valley," she admitted, "and although it can be hard sometimes, it is where I belong." She smiled up at him. "Grandma Nell's here, so I'm never really alone."

His blue eyes were bright with laughter. "Ach, she was a rare woman, your grandmother, and I'm not surprised her spirit lives on, for such a woman never really dies." He touched her cheek. "You were special to her, as you are to us, and it's good that she's keeping an eye on you."

Her father's acceptance of Nell's presence came as no surprise, for his mind was open to such things. "I thought she terrified you," she teased.

"That she did, especially when I was courting your mam. But it was only her way of protecting Amy from an Irish scallywag, and I soon convinced her I was suitable husband material. She and I understood one another, you see. We were brought to this country in chains and we survived to make something of our lives that wouldn't have been possible in our homelands."

They began to walk again, revelling in the cool shadows of the trees that hung over the river. "Talking of scallywags," he continued, his tone more serious, "what are we to do about James?"

"There is nothing we can do," she replied.

"You could divorce him for desertion."

"Da!" She looked at him in amazement.

Niall's expression darkened. "The man's a scoundrel, and the sooner you're rid of him, the better."

"But it goes against the Church, and every moral code you've taught us to follow."

"I might be Catholic, and in fear for me mortal soul for saying this, but the Church isn't always right." He grinned and carried on walking. "I've lived long enough to know life is too precious to waste in regrets. Divorce him, Ruby, and have done with it. Then you'll be free to marry the man you really love."

She reddened and refused to meet his eyes. "I don't know what you mean."

He stopped and leant on his walking stick. "You've loved young Finn since you could crawl, and seeing the two of you doing your best to ignore one another has amused me and your mam no end these past five months."

458

"Is it that obvious?"

"A blind man could see it — the air positively vibrates when you are together." He smiled. "Why do you think Finn has never married?" he asked softly. "Why do you think he was willing to leave a thriving business in Sydney to come here?"

She couldn't answer him.

"Because he loves you, you silly girl."

"Then why didn't he tell me how he felt before?"

He looked at her as if she was a slow student. "He's ten years older than you and was well aware of your hero-worship." He patted her hot cheek. "He wanted to make his mark in the world and give you time to know your own mind before he spoke to you, but he waited too long, and then James had whisked you away."

"How do you know all this?"

"Finn and I had a long talk the other night."

The silence stretched as they linked arms again and continued their walk. Ruby's thoughts were clamouring. Divorce was a shameful thing and never contemplated before. Did she dare risk excommunication — dare to flout the mores of society in the pursuit of happiness? And yet to live in sin with Finn was also frowned upon. There seemed to be no way out, but oh, how she wished there was, how she yearned for the simplicity of loving and being loved without incurring the wrath of the Church and society, which in turn could blight her children's lives.

"You need time to think," said Niall, as they reached the clearing. "Let me know what you decide, and I will do all I can to help."

"You have already done so much, Da," she said, hugging him. "The house is wonderful, and the children and I have been so spoilt these past few months. What will we do once you've gone back to Parramatta?"

"You'll continue to thrive," he said softly. "Don't worry your head about convention and hectoring priests — follow your heart."

The turkey looked splendid surrounded by pork strips and golden potatoes. Heaps of vegetables steamed in bowls, the table was set on the veranda, and the children were racing round in excitement. Ruby and Kumali were wearing the new dresses they'd received for Christmas, and Finn, Tommy and Fergal had changed into clean shirts and moleskins to honour the special occasion. Even Duncan looked half respectable for once, and Ruby felt her heart swell with love for all of them.

Niall carved as he joined in with the various conversations that flowed round the table, and the women served the vegetables and handed out plates. The food was eaten with gusto, toasts were drunk, and the talk went on hours after the children had fallen asleep.

Ruby had left the table to fetch something from the kitchen, and she paused for a moment to take in the scene. The lanterns had been lit and the warm glow seemed to encompass them, drawing them together in a tableau. Da, as usual, was holding forth, eliciting roars of laughter as he told them how he'd first met Mam on the ill-fated night before the battle of Vinegar Hill. Ruby smiled, but her heart was heavy as she etched the scene into her memory, for it could be many years before she saw her parents again.

The party had finally broken up at one in the morning, and Ruby fell exhausted into bed and was asleep almost immediately.

"Ruby, Ruby, wake up."

She shrugged off the insistent hand and buried her face in the pillow, but the voice continued to harass and the shaking became rougher. She opened her eyes, and before she could cry out, his hand was over her mouth.

"Do you promise not to make a fuss?"

She nodded and he released her. Wiping the taste of him from her lips, she stared up at her husband in bewilderment. "What the *hell* do you mean by scaring me half to death?" she hissed.

"I didn't mean to, but I had to wait until everyone was asleep."

She drew the sheet to her chin as his gaze trawled over her. "How long have you been here, and why wait until we're asleep?"

"We can't talk here," he muttered, glancing towards the sleeping children. "Get dressed and meet me down by the river."

She glared at him in the darkness, tempted to call out for help, but the men would come with guns, and she didn't want him dead. She pulled on trousers and shirt over her nightgown, and swiftly checked the children before she took a deep breath and followed him.

He was in the clearing, and by the grey pre-dawn light she could see the changes wrought in him. His hair was long, greasy and tangled, his chin unshaven. There were dark rings beneath his eyes and hollows in his cheeks, and his ragged clothes hung from him. As she drew nearer, she saw the bloody stain on his jacket. "Are you injured?"

He shook his head. "It's not my jacket."

She should have felt sorry for him, but she didn't. She crossed her arms tightly over her chest. "You wear another man's jacket and creep home like a thief. Why, James?"

"I would have thought it was obvious," he snapped. "Your blasted father's being holding court all evening, and I wasn't going to shame myself by turning up to your fancy dinner looking like a tramp."

"Don't you *dare* call my father names," she snapped. "And since when have you cared what you look like? You were always too busy drinking for that." She eyed him furiously. "If you hadn't been such a coward, you'd have come home like a proper husband and father and faced the music — out in the open."

"I'm not a coward," he snarled, fists clenching.

"Then why hide?" The anger was so great she could barely contain it. "Are you ashamed of your desertion, or have you decided you need us now you've fallen on hard times?"

"I wanted to see you again."

"Don't flatter yourself that I would ever wish to see *you* again, James Tyler."

His expression darkened. "That's no way to talk to your husband," he muttered.

"You haven't been my husband for bloody years, so don't you *dare* criticise the way I speak to you either."

He obviously realised he was making her angrier by the minute and changed tack by shooting her a smile that might have once made her heart flutter. "Come on, Ruby," he cajoled, "can't we just talk a while without having a row?"

"The charm doesn't work any more, James. Say what you want to say and leave."

His eyes flashed. "I'm still your husband. I've got rights."

"You lost those years ago." She regarded him coldly. "You left me with two children, a mob of sheep and a bartered wool-cheque. I haven't had a word from you in years, and yet I've raised your children and kept this place going. How can you talk of rights?"

"I'll talk of anything I want," he retorted. "We're still married and I have the law on my side. I can move back in and there's nothing you can do about it."

"I have men and guns on the property. They'll do my talking for me if you try that."

"So you'll condone yet another murder, would you?" He grunted with disgust. "Nothing changes."

"What do you want exactly?"

"I would have thought it was obvious." His gaze trawled from her head to her feet. "Though I can't say I find you tempting — not in that get-up."

"Touch me and I'll scream the place down." Her voice was low and laced with fury.

He shrugged, clearly deciding this conversation was getting nowhere, and surveyed the new buildings. "I see Daddy's been throwing his money about."

His sneer infuriated her. "My father's generosity is none of your business."

"One whine from you and Daddy provides, eh?"

"He gave us love, support, a decent house for your children and a shoulder to cry on," she returned. "Which is more than you've ever done."

He eyed her almost insolently. "I see Fergal's back, and you've got a couple of other men working for you. Which one keeps you warm at night, Ruby?"

The ringing slap echoed in the clearing.

He rubbed his cheek, his eyes blazing. "You're lucky I didn't hit you back, you bitch."

"And you're lucky I didn't punch your nose into the back of your head."

His expression was belligerent. "You've turned into a hellcat. No wonder no man will bed you."

"My sleeping arrangements are my own business. I warn you, one more remark like that and I'll really let fly. I'm stronger now than I've ever been. Hard work builds muscle, and I'm not afraid to use it."

He took a step back. "Hell, Ruby, I didn't come here to fight."

"Then what did you come for?"

"I wanted to see you and Nathaniel before I headed west for the new gold fields."

464

"I'm glad you're not planning on staying. You aren't welcome."

He looked at her then, the defiance in his expression not quite masking the lost pride. "You've made it obvious you don't need me. It seems you are tougher than I ever could have imagined."

"I've had to learn to be tough — to fight for survival and for my children."

He was silent for a long moment, his gaze fixed to his worn boots. "You can keep this place," he said finally. "There's nothing I want here, not any more, and you've always made it clear that it was never really mine."

"That's rubbish and you know it," she spat. "You were handed this place as a gift — you had your wife and children who would have loved you unquestioningly, but your greed for gold blinded you to everything."

"Yeah, well, the hunt for gold offers more excitement than you and this place ever did."

Ruby felt a shaft of pity. He would continue to drift until death caught up with him. That he had no intention of staying was a relief, but it meant she must safeguard her own future. "You're welcome to a meal, and there are spare clothes in the storehouse."

"I don't want your charity."

"It's not charity. I feed anyone who comes by." She softened her tone, realising he was defeated, his pride in tatters. "You may see the children, but it might be better not to reveal who you are."

"I saw them while they slept," he confessed. "Nathaniel has grown so much I almost didn't recognise him."

She took a deep breath instead of berating him again, for there was little point. "As I will never see you after tonight, I would ask one thing of you."

"What's that?" His gaze was suspicious.

"A divorce."

The silence stretched as the birds began their dawn chorus. James thrust his hands into his pockets, his gaze once more on his boots. "I suppose it was inevitable," he muttered. "But it will cost you."

Her temper was spent; now there was only a hollow iciness in her stomach. "How much do you want?"

He looked up then and took in the new buildings, the neat yard and well-stocked outside kitchen. "Fifty pounds would do it," he muttered. "Looks like you can afford it."

"You have a deal. I'll hand over the money when you give me the letter for the court." Without looking at him again, she hurried to find clothes and fix a meal before the others stirred. Fresh from his bathe in the river, and dressed in clean clothes, he looked more like the James she'd once loved, as he sat at the outdoor table and ploughed his way through breakfast.

She listened to the horrors of what had happened at the Eureka diggings, learnt how he'd escaped capture on the Melbourne Road by stealing a dead man's horse, and recognised the light of excitement in his eyes as he talked about the fields in the west. James had been drawn into a different world — one from which he

466

would never return — and she hoped he would eventually find peace.

With the ink still drying on the court letter, Ruby watched as he loaded the bulging saddlebags with supplies and adjusted the stirrups.

He turned to her at last, his expression defeated. "I'm sorry it's come to this, Ruby," he said. "But you and me . . ."

"I know. But we were happy for a while, weren't we?"

His smile was sad. "I suppose we were. Just for a while." There seemed to be nothing else to say, and he climbed into the saddle and looked down at her. "You're a fine woman — I know that now — but what we had is gone. Look after our son. See he grows into a fine man for me, will you?"

She nodded, the tears threatening despite all that had passed between them.

He tipped his hat, his eyes soft with emotion. "Goodbye, Ruby, and thanks for everything."

She raised her hand in farewell, but he was already galloping away, dust rising behind him in a cloud.

"Are you all right?" Finn came to stand beside her as the others emerged from their rooms.

Ruby nodded, took his hand and smiled. "Do you love me, Finn Cleary?"

"With all my heart, Ruby Logan."

She touched his face and looked into his eyes. "Will you marry me once I get my divorce?"

"Isn't that a question I should be asking?" His eyes were teasing.

"It is, but if I wait until you get round to it, I'll be an old woman." She stepped into his embrace. "So, Finn, are you asking?"

His voice was soft as he held her. "Will you release me from the terrors of sharing the bunkhouse with Fergal and Tommy and make an honest man of me?" He chuckled as she poked him in the ribs and tried to look fierce. Then he drew her closer, his expression serious. "Will you marry me, Ruby, and make me the happiest man in the world?"

"I will." She flung her arms round his neck and gave herself up to his kiss.

It was the first day of 1855, and although her parents would soon be leaving, it was a day to celebrate and look forward with hope. The congratulations had been bashfully accepted and everyone had returned to their work, leaving Ruby to say a private farewell to her parents.

"I'm glad things have been resolved," said Niall. "Now I can go home with an easy mind and see to it that your divorce goes through without a hitch." He patted his pocket where he'd put the letter. "I'll send one of the boys up to let you know when it's done."

Amy came out of Ruby's bedroom looking flustered. "I thought I'd tidy up before I left, and found this under your pillow." She reddened. "I didn't mean to pry, but this looks far too valuable to leave lying around."

Ruby frowned. "It's not mine. James must have left it." She took the watch and opened the casing. "You're

468

right, Mam, it is valuable. I wonder why he didn't take it?"

Niall examined it closely. "'Tis a fine piece of gold to be sure." His expression was thoughtful. "James was clearly down on his luck, but instead of selling this, he chose to leave it with you. Now why is that, do you think?"

"Maybe he wanted to pay Ruby back for all the years he'd left her with nothing," said Amy with asperity.

"It's more likely he stole it." Ruby's words echoed between them.

"Aye, you could be right," muttered Niall. "But the theft of such a thing would cause a hue and cry."

"He couldn't sell it and didn't want to be caught with it, so he left it behind." She looked at her father. "Take it with you, Da, and see if you can discover who it belongs to. I want nothing to do with it."

"He was last at Eureka, you say?" At her nod, Niall took the timepiece outside so he could examine it in a better light. "I have in mind that I knew this man — no, not this man, but one who looked very like him. It is the birthmark on his face . . ."

"What is it, Niall?" Amy touched his shoulder as he paled.

Niall's eyes were haunted as he stared into the past. "It was the day of the Irish uprising," he murmured. "The soldiers came and we were cut down like wheat. I was but a boy, half starved and terrified for me life." He dipped his chin, his voice breaking with emotion. "The dead and dying were all around me, but the soldiers showed no mercy. There was a man, a soldier, with similar marks to these on his face." His voice dropped to a whisper. "I swear he was the Devil himself. He shot the injured, or ran them through with his sword, and laughed as he did it."

Ruby shivered as her father continued. "I ran for me life. I hid in the bracken and crawled on me belly to get away from him, but I could still hear him ride back and forth, slashing at the undergrowth to find me and cut me down."

Ruby's tears streamed as she and her mother clung to him. She had heard some of her father's history, but not in such graphic detail, and she wondered what other horrors he'd suffered as a boy convict. "But he didn't find you," she sobbed. "You fooled him."

Niall closed the watch, his face leached of colour. "I was caught by others and sentenced to a lashing of the cat, and although I never saw him again, I will always remember his face."

"But why should such a man have his portrait painted in a timepiece?"

Niall gently extricated himself and seemed to regain his composure as he tucked the watch into a glove and deposited it in an inside pocket. "That is a riddle I intend to solve," he said, "and I know a man who may have the answer."

Eureka stockade, Victoria, January 1855

Hina had been incarcerated in the lock-up for weeks. The hearing had solved nothing, for Roundhill could not be found, and neither could the watch. He'd pleaded his innocence and begged to be freed, but had been sent back to the lock-up to await the magistrate's decision.

It seemed he'd been forgotten, left to rot in the filth. As the heat drained his energy and the loss of daylight and fresh air weakened his will to fight, Hina gave in to despair. He would never see Puaiti again, never feel the black sand of Tahiti beneath his toes or smell the exotic flowers. Lying on the floor, he closed his eyes and prayed for the end.

"Open this goddamned door now. And be quick about it."

Hina sat up, his heart racing. "Howard? Is that you?"

"Yeah, it darn well is, and I've come to get you out of this hell-hole." Howard strode in like an avenging angel, pulled Hina to his feet and almost carried him into the sunlight. "Hell, boy," he rasped, "there ain't an inch of meat on you. What in the hell have these fellers been feedin' you?"

"Scraps." Hina was unsteady on his feet as he blinked in the sun, closed his eyes and raised his face to its warmth. At last he felt life stir within him again. Tears ran down his face as he asked, "Am I really free, Howard? This isn't a dream?"

Howard spat tobacco. "This ain't a dream, buddy. Come on, let's get you out of here before you fall down. You might have lost weight, but I sure as hell can't carry you."

Hina leant on his friend as they walked down the hill. "Have they found your watch? Is that why I'm free?"

"I'll tell you all about it once you're sweeter-smelling," drawled Howard.

Hina was aware of how filthy he was, for his clothes were in stinking tatters, his boots had been stolen, and what money he'd had in his pockets was gone. The stares were shaming as they walked down the main street, and he was grateful when Howard led him to the back door of the Diggers Hotel, thereby avoiding the public rooms.

"I hired a room upstairs, where you'll find everything you need. Take your time. I ain't goin' nowheres."

Hina tried to thank him, but Howard merely spat tobacco into the nearest spittoon and walked off.

Hina opened the door, saw the steaming bath and soft towels, and began to strip. Sinking into the fragrant water, he gave a sigh of pleasure as the grime and stench of the lock-up floated away.

As he lay there, he surveyed the room with interest, for this was the first time he'd been inside a hotel and he was amazed at how opulent it was. The bed looked wide and soft, with feather pillows and a thick cover. There were curtains, rugs and chairs, and on the nearby table stood a line of covered dishes. A set of clean clothes had been left over the back of a chair, new boots on the floor beside it.

Having scoured with soap, he used the spare bucket of water to rinse himself and climbed out of the bath, wrapped a towel round his waist and inspected the dishes. The smell of roasted meat and thick gravy drifted into the room as he lifted the covers, and he ate until every plate was clean and his belly distended.

Refreshed, sated and dressed, he knocked on Howard's door. Howard was lying on the fancy bed with his boots on, the hat tilted over his eyes. "Come in and pull up a chair, Hina. There's beer if you want it."

Hina took the lemonade instead. He saw the amusement in Howard's eyes and smiled. "I never got used to the taste of beer," he explained. He sat down, took a long drink and eyed his friend. "Thank you," he began.

"It's nothing," said Howard, swinging off the bed. "I'm just sorry I couldn't get you out sooner." He made light of Hina's concern for his health. "I'm fine. Now I want to find the real thief."

"Roundhill, the man who accused me of the theft, seems to have disappeared, so we'll probably never know the truth."

"He never existed," muttered Howard, opening another beer.

"But he must have. He accused me of theft. And I didn't steal the watch, Howard, I swear. I am not a thief."

"I know that, darn it. That's why I was so goddamned mad when I discovered you'd been accused." He took a long pull of the beer, then lit a cigar. "The police gave me a good description of your accuser, Hina. It was James Tyler."

"But he died in the stockade."

Howard shook his head. "I've been asking questions. He was seen by a bunch of miners who'd managed to hide in the bush. Tyler took the jacket off a dead man, stole his horse and made a dash for it on the

Melbourne Road." He moodily stared out of the window. "We were standing side by side when the bullet hit me. I remember him yelling something, and his hands pulling at me, but then I must have passed out."

He turned and Hina saw flint in his eyes. "He must have thought I was dead, for witnesses said he just left me and ran. They hid me, and it was only by chance that a sabre pierced my hiding place and found my shoulder. A couple of Yankee buddies managed to get me to the infirmary, but I have no memory of that."

"What do you plan to do now?"

"Find Tyler, wring his scrawny neck and get my watch back." He chewed on the cigar and eyed Hina. "Fancy coming along for the ride?"

"How do we find him?"

"We'll start at his home, the place he calls Eden Valley."

Eden Valley, July 1855

Kumali looked up at the leaden sky and wished it would rain. The heat was intense, despite the season. The earth was parched and everything was dying. She picked up the fretful Garnday, took Mookah's hand and waded into the depleted river. It was barely trickling over the rocky bed, but it was cool and shaded by trees, the perfect place to sit. She laughed as Mookah splashed and tried to coax a grizzling Garnday to join in the fun. The little girl watched her sister, then stretched her arms to her. Mookah, who was not quite four, balanced her expertly on her hip and made her smile as she drummed her feet in the water.

Kumali rolled on to her belly, her dress floating around her as she revelled in the tranquility of this rare moment. Natjik was with Duncan, Ruby had taken Violet and Nathaniel to Five Mile Creek to buy stores, and the others were out in the pastures. It was good to have the place to herself for a while, and there was plenty of time until she had to see to the evening tucker.

Mookah had found a hole in the riverbank and was poking it with a stick as Garnday sat waist-high in the water and tried to eat a pebble. Kumali took it out of her mouth, and gave her a cuddle so she wouldn't cry again. Her teeth were coming through and she was chewing everything, but she loved her fiercely and couldn't resist smothering her chubby cheeks with kisses.

"Kiss alonga me too," demanded Mookah.

Kumali gathered her up and nuzzled the soft, sweet-smelling neck until the child was squirming and roaring with laughter.

The sound of approaching horses didn't really bother her, but she was a little put out that the men had interrupted this special moment. Deciding they could do without her for a while yet, she carried on playing with her children. Mookah went back to her search of the hole, and Kumali lay back in the water with Garnday lying on her belly.

"Mama!"

Kumali was on her feet in an instant.

Mookah's eyes were wide with fear. "Look, Mama!"

Kumali followed the pointing finger. Her grip tightened on Garnday and she stumbled back. There were eight riders, and another two driving the enclosed iron wagon. They were black, from another tribe, and wore the Native Police uniform.

Kumali reached for Mookah's hand and tucked Garnday under her arm. "Run when I say, Mookah. Like the wind," she murmured, her gaze never leaving the men.

Another horseman appeared. This one was white, with a pock-marked face and cold eyes. "Get over 'ere, you black bitch. You're coming with us," he shouted.

Kumali edged further back. She had recognised him instantly as the man Wally — the convict who had run away after she had killed his friend — and she knew that if he realised who she was, she would be dead. "I belong here," she shouted back defiantly. "My husband will be back soon, and he's a white-fella."

"I've orders to round up all blacks in the area. White husband or not, you'll come when I tell yer." He nudged his horse closer to the water. "You'll obey me, you black bitch, or I'll kill yer piccanninies."

Kumali's heart was thudding and she could barely breathe. She'd been taken before, and would rather die than be taken again, for men like Wally knew no mercy. She glanced at the far bank, swung Mookah on to her hip and began to run. There was a whoop of excitement and she heard the horses slither down the bank and splash in the river behind her.

Garnday was whimpering, Mookah was screaming, and Kumali found her escape hampered by the shifting stones beneath her feet as she struggled to reach the far bank.

The long shadows of the riders danced across the water, and the sound of swords being drawn made her falter. The bank was too far, the men too swift. They surrounded her now, and she sobbed in terror as she clung to her children and pleaded for their lives.

"I'll come with you if you let my babies go free. They're White-fella babies. See?" She pointed to their carroty hair and pale skin and gabbled in anguish, "White-fella babies. Fatha have the same red hair."

Wally peered more closely at her and Kumali froze, terrified that he might recognise her.

Then he looked away and yawned. "Put 'em in the wagon," he ordered.

Kumali screamed as the native rider ripped the children from her arms. "No! Don't take my babies. Leave them for their Fatha. He's white. You can't take white babies." She ran alongside the horseman, beating at his legs, tugging at his trousers in the hope he might let her children go.

The tribesman grinned at her and kicked out. The spur caught her cheek and Kumali was knocked off balance, but she quickly recovered and scrabbled up the bank. As she saw the wagon door open and the man with her children approach it, she began to run.

"No!" she screamed, flying at him, fingers clawing in search of his eyes.

477

A hand grabbed her hair and she was flung into the wagon.

"Take yer piccanninies and keep 'em quiet," snarled the tribesman, as he thrust the screaming, terrified children at her.

Kumali clutched them as she sobbed, "You're a black-fella — why do you take my babies? I'll go with you, cook good tucka, make jig-jig, but don't take my babies. Please!" It was a wail of utter distress as she staggered to her feet and took a step towards the open door.

It slammed shut with a deathly clang.

Eden Valley, 31 August 1855

The hunt for Kumali and the children had consumed their lives over the past eight weeks. Ruby had sent letters to her father, the governor, and the Church Commission in the hope someone might know where they had been taken. There had been no reply.

Repeated trips to Five Mile Creek and the widespread farming communities surrounding Eden Valley had brought little news. The raids had been swift and brutal, and although several of the squatters had tried to protect their natives, it seemed the law was not on their side. New legislation had been passed to remove all blacks and place them in reserves far from white settlement. Children of mixed race were to be rounded up and put in special reserves where they would be trained as cheap labour.

"I don't know what to do," Ruby sighed. "Poor Duncan has hardly spoken a word since they went missing, and I'm worried about him."

Finn reached across the table and took her hand. "There's very little we can do but look after Natjik. Thank God he was with Duncan that day. I don't know what he would have done if all three wains had been taken."

Ruby eyed the slumbering child who lay between Violet and Nathaniel. The poor little mite was as bewildered as the rest of them, but his safety was paramount, for if the Native Police got wind of him, they'd return.

She sat in silence, remembering how Duncan had roared like a lion when he discovered what had happened to Kumali and his children. He had picked up his rifle and ridden off in search of the kidnappers, vowing to kill each and every one.

Finn and Tommy had gone after him, and when they were finally told by the authorities that Kumali had died in a camp much further north and it became obvious to Duncan that he would never find his scattered children, he'd been almost delirious with rage and pain. He had returned to Eden Valley a broken man, wandering like a lost soul among his sheep, seeming to find solace only when he held his son.

"Poor Kumali must have been terrified. She knew what men like that are capable of, and how it would be for her little girls. What in God's name is happening to our world, Finn, when defenceless women and children are treated like stock?"

"I don't know," he murmured, "but your father would. He was brought here as a child in chains, treated like a slave and lived to tell the tale and turn his nose up at authority. Maybe Kumali's children will do the same."

Ruby burst into tears, and Finn held her as she buried her face in his shoulder and gave vent to the wretched pain she'd been controlling for too long.

The rap on the window startled them, and Ruby knuckled away her tears as she opened the door. The sight that greeted her was so extraordinary she could only stare.

The taller of the two men took off his high-crowned hat. "I'm sorry to disturb you so late, ma'am," he drawled, "but we were looking for Mr James Tyler."

Ruby heard the Yankee accent, saw the other man's tawny skin and long, dark hair and realised they were Fergal's friends from Ophir. "James isn't here, but Fergal's outside somewhere." She gave them a watery smile and shook their hands. "You must be Howard and Hina."

"That we are, ma'am." They followed her inside and were introduced to Finn. "I take it you are Mrs Tyler?"

"Not for much longer," she replied. "We are about to be divorced."

"Have we called at a bad time, ma'am? Only I sense you're troubled."

"We are in mourning," she replied, and went on to explain about the raid as she fixed them food and beer.

"My condolences," drawled the American. "It seems politics and human kindness remain enemies, as Hina and I have learnt to our cost."

"James told me about Eureka."

"Then he did come here?"

"He didn't stay more than a few hours."

"You don't happen to know where he was heading? Only Hina and I have some unfinished business with him."

Ruby saw how the eyes hardened and the smile disappeared. "What did James do to warrant you coming so far?"

"He stole from me, ma'am, and bore false witness against Hina."

"What did he steal?"

"A gold watch," said Hina, speaking for the first time. "A fine gold watch with two pictures inside — one of a man with marks on his face, the other of a Tahitian woman."

"James has gone west to the gold fields, but the watch is not with him. He left it here, and my father took it to Sydney to try and find the true owner. We suspected it was stolen, and I wanted nothing to do with it."

"Then that is where we will go," said the Tahitian in his quiet voice. "We thank you for your hospitality and will not trouble you further."

"It's late and the journey to Parramatta is long. You're welcome to stay in the bunkhouse and have breakfast before you leave. I will write a letter to my

481

father as introduction and give you directions to his property in the morning."

They accepted gratefully, but the sun had barely breached the horizon when they rode away the following morning, and Ruby wondered why two such diverse characters should feel so strongly about a pocket watch.

Broken Hill, New South Wales, September 1855

The heat inside the metal wagon was unbearable, and despite the chains round her ankles, Kumali had fought her way through the crush of bodies so she could sit near the barred window. The slit in the wall was too high to see through, but now and again a draught of dust-laden air filtered down and brought temporary relief. It was the only source of air and light, and therefore valuable, and she had to remain on her guard in case someone stole her place. But she was becoming weaker and didn't know how long she could defend it.

The wagon had been on the move for weeks, stopping only at night, or sometimes just for a few minutes to pick up more prisoners or leave some behind. They were fed thin porridge each morning, drank as much water as they could and had to last until the day's end to get more. The floor of the wagon was covered with their stinking waste, and it was impossible to avoid sitting in it.

She had no idea where she was. The children were so hungry and frightened they could no longer cry, and she was struggling to hold them as the wagon jolted and rocked over stony ground and threatened to fling them from her arms and into the filth.

There were other black-fella women in the wagon, some men and boys with tribal markings she didn't recognise, and several children who seemed to be on their own. These children had lighter skins and reddish hair, and Kumali found she couldn't look at them, for their bewildered faces and hungry eyes seemed to devour her.

Garnday moved listlessly in her arms, searching for her nipple, but she had no milk to give her. She pressed her dry lips to her head and the young child looked back at her with such an expression of resignation it broke her heart. With a gentle smile to Mookah, who clung to her side, she tried to give her courage, yet Kumali feared for them all — feared the next stop and the one after that — for it seemed the events of her childhood were about to be repeated, and sooner or later their fate would be revealed.

As night fell and the wagon came to a halt, there was a sigh of relief. The door was opened and they almost fell out, gasping for fresh air and water.

"No food until you've cleaned out yer shit," yelled Wally, who was still in charge. "Filthy bastards." He aimed a kick at Kumali, which thudded into her hip. "Gaaarn, yer black bitch, move yerself."

Kumali scuttled away. He had yet to recognise her, and for once in her life she was thankful that white men thought they all looked alike. Eyes downcast, she sat the children with the others under a koolibah tree, and hurried with the other women to fetch buckets of water

483

from the horse trough, the chains clanking with every step.

As the men swept out the wagon and she returned to refill the bucket, she quickly took in her surroundings. They had come to a small town, with a few dusty wooden buildings on either side of a broad dirt road lined with trees. It was a white town, for she could see them watching from the verandas and windows, staring out at her as if she was some kind of curiosity, but then she'd become used to that — it was the same in every town they had passed through.

They were made to walk down the road as bystanders pelted them with rubbish and jeered. The clearing was on the edge of town, where they were given stale bread and tough mutton. The river provided their drinking water, but it flowed too swiftly to risk washing in it, hampered as they were by the chains.

Kumali wrapped her arms round her children as she lay on the ground and stared up at the heavens. The Great Ancestor Spirit was a lie, and so were all the other things the Elders had told her. She was on her own, fighting for her life and that of her children. She turned her back on the stars and closed her eyes, the first of the night's tears rolling down her face.

She was woken with a kick. "Gerrup and make breakfast."

Kumali kissed the children, settled them with the others and headed for the camp kitchen. The other women were already busy boiling water for tea and cooking thick slices of bacon in a heavy pan. Her mouth watered and she tried to ignore the squirm in her belly, for the food was not for her and the others, but for the policemen.

She had served the men and eaten the porridge, giving most of it to Mookah and Garnday, when they were ordered back to the wagon. "Bucks first," shouted one of the policemen.

Kumali waited as they climbed on board, saw her place by the window taken and knew she didn't have the strength to fight for it.

"Gins next."

This order had become routine, but Kumali didn't trust it. She handed Garnday to a little girl of about ten who stood by Mookah. A poke in the back sent her stumbling towards the wagon and she was shoved inside.

"Now you, piccanninies."

Kumali watched as they swarmed towards the wagon, her gaze fixed to her children's faces, willing them to hurry.

The door was slammed. The bolts fastened.

"They're taking the children!"

"Mookah! Garnday!" Kumali screamed as she pummelled the iron door. Her keening wail rose with that of the other women as the wagon began to move.

But no one was listening.

CHAPTER
SEVENTEEN

Parramatta, December 1855

Howard and Hina had arrived that morning and were pleasantly surprised to find the two-storey home, with ornate balconies and white shutters, in a leafy suburb. A gravel drive meandered through trees and shrubs, past well-tended gardens to the imposing front door. There was a stable yard, an orchard and a curious ramshackle building off to one side.

A servant took their letter of introduction and showed them into the study. It was a quiet room, shaded from the sun by the veranda, lined with books and furnished with a large desk and comfortable chairs. It was a man's room, musky with cigar smoke, whisky and leather.

"Mr Niall Logan has done well," muttered Hina. "Did you notice how many stores and factories in town bear his name?"

Howard eyed the bookcases. "That I did," he drawled, "but I wonder what that old shack's doing in his garden, and why he possesses so many books. Such a busy man could never find the time to read them all."

"That is where you are wrong, Mr Repton." Niall came in, shook hands and sat down. "Every book you see has been read many times." He laid his ornate walking stick on the desk. "The shack was my first forge, and is a permanent reminder not to get too big for my boots."

Hina was embarrassed they'd been overheard, but Mr Logan seemed unfazed and was smiling.

"I understand from my daughter's letter that you are the rightful owner of the pocket watch, Mr Repton."

Howard told him how he'd purchased the watch and had it stolen at Eureka.

"Your story confirms what I learnt in Ballarat. But what is your interest, Mr Timanu?"

The blue eyes were piercing, but not unfriendly as Hina told him the family legend.

"So there is a conflict of interest?"

"No. Howard bought it honestly. I came because I wish to see the watch returned to him before I leave for Tahiti."

Niall Logan regarded him in silence, and Hina felt a little uneasy, for it was as if he could see the inner pain that belied his words.

"I made enquiries as to the provenance of the timepiece and have discovered some interesting facts." Niall sat forward. "I have a friend in England. His name is Harry Cadwallader. Harry's father was Edward Cadwallader, a particularly odious man with whom I had a short and violent acquaintance. He killed himself some years ago, but it is *his* father who holds the key to the watch. His name was Jonathan Cadwallader."

"The man Jon," breathed Hina.

"Just so." Niall leant back and dug his thumb in his waistcoat pocket. "Jonathan sailed on the *Endeavour* with Captain Cook and a party of royal astronomers. They anchored in Tahiti to watch Venus eclipse the sun before departing in search of the rumoured *Terra Australis*. The rest is history, but Jonathan Cadwallader was a part of it, as was his artist friend Sydney Parkinson."

"Those are the initials on the miniatures," said Howard. "Did he paint them?"

"Undoubtedly," said Niall, "which makes the timepiece very valuable, for Parkinson died on the journey home and his work is now regarded as some of the finest of his generation."

"Does Cadwallader want his watch back?" Howard's eyes narrowed.

Niall coolly returned his stare. "Harry's grandfather was a young man on that journey, a youth with passion for adventure and an eye for a pretty girl. From what Hina has told me, the pieces of the puzzle fit well, and there is little doubt the watch was given as a love token to Lianni. As Harry wrote in his letter, it was his grandfather's watch and he was entitled to give it to whom he pleased. He makes no claim on it."

Howard sighed with relief. "Thank you for your trouble, Mr Logan. Will you write to your friend and give him my regards?"

"I will do that."

"Then I'll take the watch and leave you in peace." Howard made to rise when Niall's voice stilled him.

"There is just one more thing. It is important, as it concerns Hina."

Hina's pulse raced. What was it that made Logan look so serious?

"Are you a direct descendant of Lianni and Jonathan?"

Hina nodded, still wary. "My great-grandfather was their son, Tahamma. His name means 'the hammer of the gods'."

"Do you bear the mark of red teardrops?"

Hina frowned. How on earth could Logan know about that? As the silence stretched and the gaze remained steady, Hina drew back his hair and tugged the shirt collar. "I have this. It is the same as my grandfather's and Tahamma's." Hina readjusted his shirt. "But it is strange, for my mother does not bear it."

"Harry says it sometimes misses a generation. That mark is of great significance, for it has been borne by nearly every earl of Kernow since the title was first bestowed."

Howard laughed and slapped his thigh. "Does that mean Hina's a goddamn earl?"

"Unfortunately, no," said Niall, with a smile. "Jonathan and Lianni were never married — not in the legal sense — which made Tahamma illegitimate. Therefore his descendants have no claim. But I thought Hina should know the history, and the reason for the mark."

"Well, I'll be darned," muttered Howard.

"I have no wish for this title," said Hina. "It is enough to know that the legend is true. I thank you, Mr Logan, on behalf of my family, who will be delighted to hear what I have learnt today."

Niall opened a drawer, looked at the watch for the last time and handed it to Howard. "Keep it safe. There's a lot of history in that piece of gold."

Howard's expression was thoughtful as they headed back to Sydney.

Hina left Howard to his pondering as he took in the bustle of the busy port. There were many ships at anchor and it didn't take long to find one that was going east. The *Mimosa* was sailing that night to New Zealand on her way to the island of Vanuatu. From there he would find another to take him to Tahiti. He paid his passage and went to join Howard, who was standing by their hired carriage with his bag.

"The *Queen Victoria* leaves for America in two days, so I'm staying at the hotel." Howard wiped the sweat from his brow. "I won't be sorry to leave," he drawled, "but I sure am grateful for the fortune I've made."

"So am I." Hina reached into the carriage and took down his bag. The gold coins, nuggets and promissory notes from the Bank of England were tucked in a leather purse beneath his clothes. The tin box hidden in the hole had not been discovered during his incarceration, for they had paid their licence for a year and no other digger could work the claim. It had come as an intense relief to know that after all he'd gone through, his fortune was still intact.

490

Howard walked with him to the *Mimosa*. "I guess it's time to say goodbye," he said, as they shook hands. "Maybe I'll call on you one day and take a look at your Tahiti."

"You would be most welcome, and my family would be honoured to entertain you." Hina's heart swelled with affection. "Thank you for your kindness and loyalty, but most of all, thank you for believing in me."

Howard looked embarrassed as he scuffed his bootheel on the cobbles. "There ain't no call for thanks. It's what friends are for." His wrinkled face lit up in a smile. "I wish you well, ol' buddy, and I hope that gal's waiting for you. She'd be a fool otherwise. You're a good man."

Hina picked up his bag, preparing to leave.

"Before you go, I have something for you." He was still looking embarrassed as he dragged a large box from his bag. "I want you to promise you won't open it until you sail."

Hina gave his promise, but was mortified he had no gift for Howard. Howard shrugged off his apology, raised his hand in farewell and was soon lost in the milling crowd.

Hina climbed the gangway and stood on deck. The carriage had gone, and there was no sign of a tall man in heeled boots and a high-crowned hat. He put the box in his bag and went to find his cabin. The least he could do was honour his promise and wait until he was at sea to open it.

★ ★ ★

It was a starlit night as Hina watched the wind billow the sails and felt the dip and roll of the *Mimosa* beneath his feet. He looked towards the distant horizon, and in his excitement he thought he could almost breathe the scent of Tahiti on the wind.

He sat on the foredeck and carefully opened the box. Howard's bowie knife lay beside the turquoise belt buckle, and as he examined them, he realised something lay beneath the bed of tissue paper. He pulled it back and his eyes widened. The watch gleamed in the moonlight, the diamond twinkling, and as he read the accompanying letter, he felt the prickle of tears.

By rights this watch belongs to you, and I know you will take care of it. It has been an honour to call you friend, and I hope that in the future we may meet again.
   Until then, Godspeed, Hina,
   Howard Repton the Third

Hina folded the letter, opened the watch and gazed at the portrait. "We are going home, Lianni, and you shall be with your family again for ever."

Tibooburra, northern New South Wales, February 1856

Kumali had lost all sense of time and no longer cared what happened to her. There were many like her in the camp, which lay far from the settlement called "the Place of Heaps of Rocks", and although they shared the agony of having lost their children, they rarely spoke of it. It was too painful to put what they felt into words, and so they sat for hours every night, staring towards the track that led to where they had been taken, as if by sheer will they could bring their children back.

It was a desolate place, the ground stony and incapable of growing even a blade of grass. The river was a trickle and provided the only drinking water, and the one tree in the compound had been struck by lightning and was as barren as the miles of emptiness surrounding them. A line of tin huts provided dubious shelter within the high wire fence, and without the sound of children's voices, the deathly hush was broken only by the shifting red sand and the mournful cries of crows.

The men who had brought them here were gone, but others guarded them, and they were lined up each dawn and sent to work in the white township that had sprung up around the gold field.

Kumali was assigned to the landlord of the hotel, and she obeyed his orders silently, her gaze lowered in the hope she would not be beaten. He fed her scraps, but it was rarely enough, and as she worked, she wished only to become a shadow and fade to nothing.

When night came, she would sit and stare beyond the white boss's fine house and wonder what had happened to her children. She prayed Duncan had found them, that they were alive and well. At least Natjik had been spared, and she had to hold on to the hope he would stay free in Eden Valley.

She shivered, for the night was cold after the day's inferno, and her thin dress was now so tattered it gave little protection.

"There is a place where you might find your children."

It was a soft voice, the words in an unfamiliar dialect, and Kumali barely glanced at the elderly woman who sat beside her. "My babies are lost. Don't speak of such things."

"I am of the Warumungu," she persisted, "and my people speak of this place in the far north called Karlwekarlwe."

Kumali tensed, for memory stirred, but it was so faint and disjointed it was hard to pin down. "My babies are in Karlwekarlwe? How can you know this, when the white men took them many moons ago down south?"

"Karlwekarlwe special place," she murmured. "Strong Dreaming — Sacred Woman's Dreaming."

"The Dreaming means nothing to me," she retorted in the tribal language she had almost forgotten after the years with the white men.

The Warumungu woman rocked back and forth. "It is hard to live with *gubbas* and keep the Dreaming, but if baby taken, alonga pray to Ancestor Spirits bring back."

"White men took my babies, not Spirits," she snapped. "Go away, old woman."

It was as if she hadn't spoken. "Karlwekarlwe is place of Rainbow Serpent's Eggs. Alonga caves beneath eggs live *kwerreympe* — Spirit People of the Dreaming."

Kumali continued to stare at the horizon, but she was listening, for the fragments of memory were coming together. The Rainbow Serpent was the most Sacred Ancestor of all, for she had roamed the earth at the beginning of time, her vast body making the valleys and mountains and the beds for the rivers and lakes. Her eggs were permanent memorials to mark her passage and give shelter to those who followed.

"They look like us, but they are really Spirits. My cousin was playing with these Spirit People, and when her family called to her to come back to the fire, she found she couldn't leave. She was very afraid, and the Spirit People say to her, 'Don't leave us, you belong here and we can make you just like us'."

Kumali shivered. "Did they take her?"

"Old people made big ceremony, sing ground and rocks, make *kwerreympe* give back."

"And did they give her back?"

The old woman nodded.

The memories crystallised. She grabbed the skinny arms, begging her to sing the songs, but the old woman said they could only be sung at Karlwekarlwe. "Where is this place Karlwekarlwe? How can I learn the songs? Will you teach me?"

The old woman pointed. "Follow rivva to big watta. Karlwekarlwe north alonga Uluru, south alonga Munga Munga." She gave a deep sigh. "Is far, far, in Never-Never. Take plenty season, much walk." She pointed to Orion's Belt. "See alonga stars? Follow 'im, find Karlwekarlwe."

"You will teach me the songs for this sacred place?"

She shook her head. "Plenty women at Karlwekarlwe sing alonga you. Woman Dreaming place. Plenty *corroborees*."

Kumali rested her chin on her knees as the woman walked away. Her thoughts raced. Did she dare hope? Could she put her faith in something she had sworn never to believe in again? What if she went all that way for nothing? What if she died before she reached the Rainbow Serpent's Eggs? The *gubbas* had taken her children, not the Spirits — did that mean the Spirits could not return them? She stared through the wire, head and heart in battle.

Hope grew as she eyed the compound. The *gubbas* didn't watch the gate, or patrol the fence, for there were miles of desert — the great Never-Never — beyond it, and no sanctuary in Tibooburra. She looked at the stars, then back to the *gubbas'* house. The gate was high, but she could scale it easily. She stood, heart banging. She had nothing to lose — she had to try.

She moved swiftly through the shadows of the huts, stopped, looked at the sky and waited.

As a cloud hid the moon, Kumali began to climb. It was a long way, and just as she was swinging her leg over the top, the moon emerged to flood the landscape with light. She froze, waiting for the shout, the cocking of a rifle.

All was slumbering, the silence of the great Never-Never enfolding her.

Swifter now, her breath coming in shallow gasps, she scrambled down and almost fell in her haste. Knowing that if she hurt herself all would be lost, she took a deep breath and tempered her speed until she reached the bottom. Then she ran, heading for the nearest rock hill, and collapsed behind it. There were no shouts, no rattle of gunfire. She'd done it.

She lay panting as she surveyed the endless sweep of desert. Karlwekarlwe lay far beyond the horizon and she had no idea if she would ever find it. All she could do now was pray she had the strength and courage to survive until she did.

Tahiti, March 1856

Hina waited impatiently on deck as the ship sailed closer to shore. He feasted on the sight before him as his people poured on to the sand and into their dug-out canoes. The sound of music drifted across the water, and he could smell the flowers and the smoke of the cooking fires. He was home at last.

As the canoes reached the side of the ship and the men and women clambered aboard, he searched eagerly for Puaiti. And there she was, as beautiful as ever. He softly called her name and she stilled.

Her almond-shaped eyes widened and her face lit up in a broad smile as she flew into his arms. "Hina! You have come home at last."

Holding her again was like a dream, and he revelled in the smell of her hair, the flower that was tucked behind her ear and the softness of her skin. "It has been too long, my Puaiti. I was so afraid you would not wait for me."

She drew back from the embrace and gazed up at him. "My father has tried to make me marry many of the men he wants to trade with, but I refused them all. He is very angry with me, but I told him I will marry only you, my Hina."

His heart thudded and he drew her closer. He'd lived in dread of finding her married with several children, but now he could breathe easily, for she had proved her love and faith in him were true.

She kissed his lips and sighed as she rested her head against his chest. "But he will not let me marry you if you do not have the promised dowry, Hina. We will have to leave this island if we are to be together, and that will make me sad."

"I have the dowry, Puaiti," he said softly. "We will be married by nightfall."

Her eyes shone as she looked at him. They kissed again: there was no more need for words.

His return to the village was welcomed with much music and singing, and his mother caught and killed a suckling pig in honour of his and Puaiti's wedding. The celebrations went on into the night with eating and dancing, and a great deal of rum. Hina longed to be alone with his bride, but there was one more thing he had to do before the long day was over. "I must speak to my mother and grandmother," he said softly, "and then we will go to the wedding hut."

She pouted prettily, kissed him and let him go.

Hina found the women in their shared hut, drinking the last of the rum and finishing off the pork. "Grandmother, Mother, I have brought you a gift."

"Your return is gift enough, my son," said his mother.

"But this is a special gift, and I give it to you both in the knowledge that you will treasure it." He carefully unwrapped the watch and put it into his grandmother's hand.

The old woman stared down at it, and for a long moment there was silence. When she opened the catch and saw the pictures inside, she gave a trembling sigh, and as she looked back at Hina, her eyes shone with tears. "You have brought Lianni home to us. The circle is closed."

He kissed them both. "The story will never end — not really — for Lianni's spirit lives on in us all, and when Puaiti and I have our first son, we will call him Jon."

The two elderly women nodded, their pride in him clear in their expressions, and he left them to their treasure and went in search of his new wife.

Eden Valley, March 1856

"Is Finn going to be our daddy now?" Violet was three months shy of her sixth birthday, but Ruby wondered at her mature directness.

"One day soon," she murmured, as she tried to get the child to concentrate on her reading book.

"My other daddy's not coming back, then." It was a statement rather than a question, the blue eyes steady as they regarded her.

Ruby hesitated. It was disconcerting to be interrogated like this, but at least it cut through endless explanations and half-truths. She shook her head.

"Good." Violet nudged Nathaniel with a smile of triumph. "Told you so."

"Is my mama coming back?"

She looked into the dark brown, sorrowful eyes and felt a pluck at her heart. Natjik was a quiet child, but then his mother's abduction and Duncan's deep silences probably explained that. "No, darling," she murmured, her hand cupping his cheek, "I don't think she is."

The little boy made no sound as the tears slowly rolled down his face. Ruby gathered him up, her own tears threatening and her heart aching for the lost children and mother, and the bewildered little boy left behind. There had been no news of Garnday and Mookah, despite having repeatedly written to the governor. It seemed they had disappeared, wiped away as easily as chalk from an easel and forgotten.

"It's all right, Natjik," said Violet, who'd become quite soft-hearted since the abduction. "You can share my mummy."

Ruby drew her close and kissed her fiery hair. "Of course he can," she said through the lump in her throat.

She finally managed to stem the tears and distract the children by taking them outside for a nature lesson.

500

She was asking them to name the different birds when Duncan strode towards them. He looked purposeful.

Natjik ran to him, and Duncan's lined face softened. He ruffled the boy's hair. "It is time I took my wee boy home."

"It's early yet and we haven't finished our lessons." She eyed him sharply. "But that's not what you meant, was it?"

He shook his shaggy head. "It isn't safe here, y'ken, and the wee bairn is too often reminded of things in this place."

"You're going back to Scotland?"

"Aye, lassie. There's naught for me here, and I have been away too long from the mists and heathers of the Highlands."

It was pointless to argue, for since Kumali's disappearance things had changed in Eden Valley. It was a change that upset the balance, that left a hollowness in each day, reminding them that nothing was for ever. How much worse it must be for this quiet, gentle man. "I will miss you," she said with a sigh, "miss both of you, but I understand why you must go."

"Wee Tommy's a bonny lad, and he'll tend the beasts well. I have nae fear of leaving him in charge." He looked down at the sheepdog standing beside him and rested his hand on the soft head. "I would ask permission to take Bess. She's a faithful wee dog, and I'm minded she'll pine if I leave her."

"Of course you may." She regarded him thoughtfully. "Do you have enough money, Duncan? The fare is expensive, and you'll have to provide a home for Natjik and feed and clothe yourselves until you find another job."

Duncan's smile was wry. "I'm a Scotsman, lassie, and save what I earn." He patted the stout leather purse under his smock. "There's enough to last until we are settled."

Ruby shook his hand. "We haven't always seen eye to eye, but you're a good man, Duncan Stewart, and I wish you well."

The colour rose in his cheeks. "I have said my goodbyes to the others," he muttered, "so I'll be on my way."

Ruby and the children hugged Natjik for the last time, then watched Duncan hoist him on to his shoulders. He strode towards the dirt track, the faithful Bess at his heels. None of them looked back.

Ruby sighed as they were lost from view. She turned towards the house. Memories of the New Year's Eve dinner were still vivid, but much had happened in the following months and she feared for the future.

A whisper through the trees and a ripple in the grass were accompanied by a breath of warm, comforting air. It told her to keep faith, to hold on to her dreams and walk confidently through the coming years.

The Never-Never, Northern Territories, June 1856

Kumali had soon realised she was unprepared for the hostile desert, and as hot winds whipped up the dust and sent it spiralling across the land, she'd sought

502

shelter on the ninth day, knowing she would not survive.

She had no hunting skills, no knowledge of which leaves and grasses could be eaten, and once the river she had been following meandered away to the west, she had nothing to drink. Her mouth was parched, her lips cracked, and there was a buzzing in her head she couldn't silence. She'd huddled within the rocky shelter, closed her eyes and thought of Duncan and her children as she'd prepared for death.

The Alenjemtarpe people had found her by chance, for this was not their usual route home: the dust storm had forced them to seek shelter off the traditional track. The women gave her water and food, then soothed her feet with sap from leaves they carried in their dilly bags. Their dialect was strange, and Kumali had to use sign language and gestures to communicate.

Kumali had been walking with them for many moons and had learnt enough of their language to chatter with the women and help with their babies. The women had been shocked at her lack of knowledge and had shown her how to conserve water in dried-out emu eggs, how to pull special grasses from the ground and find water in their bulbs, how to hunt the crabs in the Larapinta River and spear a goanna with a sharpened stick.

As they walked, she told them the story of her life and of her snatched children, then of Mandarg, her revered ancestor. She was not surprised they had heard of him and his message of warning about the *gubbas*, for Mandarg had travelled far in his quest to protect his people, and it was said his seed had been sown among many tribes.

The group was small, mostly from one family, and they lived north of Uluru, by a place where water sprung from the ground, grass grew and encouraged good hunting, and trees provided shade. Kumali had asked them about Karlwekarlwe, but they knew little of it, for it was too far north and not a part of their traditional lands. Yet their belief in the Dreamtime and the Ancestor Spirits was steadfast, for they had not known life among the *gubbas*, had not been enslaved, and as Kumali walked with them, she felt the first stirrings of her own faith. The Ancestor Spirits had led them to her, had shown her how life could be in the Never-Never, where the ancient rites and rituals continued, and had brought her closer to the spirituality of her birthright. A birthright she had so far been denied.

As the seductive mountainous curves of Kata Djuta appeared on the horizon, Kumali felt a lightness of heart for the first time in her life. She belonged here, and was free.

Just off the coast of Sydney, December 1856

Frederick Cadwallader stood on the deck of the *London Pride* and searched impatiently for sight of home. The six years in England now felt like a dream, and yet it had seemed to go so slowly at the time, the longing for this moment never lessening.

504

He watched two women negotiate the narrow deck in their crinolines, and smiled as they battled with their voluminous skirts in the wind. The London fashions were quite extraordinary, and he'd been most amused to see ladies lose their dignity as they attempted to board omnibuses or climb country stiles.

He bowed as they staggered past, aware of their flirtatious glances and giggles. At eighteen, he was tall and broad-shouldered, and his mirror told him he was passably handsome, but he'd steered clear of dalliances, for his heart remained in Australia and he wanted no ties to keep him from her.

The letters from Niall and his mother had kept him in touch with home, and he'd learnt of his father's death shortly after Uncle Harry had returned to Cornwall. It had been inevitable, but that hadn't eased his pain, or his anger that he'd been denied the last years of his father's life. Harry had been a stalwart, offering advice and a shoulder to cry on, keeping him occupied by teaching him the rudiments of running the estates. Lavinia had loved and consoled him like a mother, and she would always occupy a special place in his heart. Charlie had become the brother he'd never had, and they had sailed, hunted and fished throughout the holidays, and grown closer with every passing year.

Harry and Lavinia had talked of university, but Frederick didn't see the point. He planned, with Niall's help, to pick up the reins of his father's businesses, and no university could prepare him for that.

As the ship ploughed on towards Sydney Harbour and the sails billowed, Frederick watched the smudge on the horizon take shape. Now he could see towering cliffs, inlets and hills, the sandy beaches and grey-green eucalyptus trees. His pulse raced as he searched for the white house perched above Watsons Bay, and there it was — just as he'd remembered it. He was home at last.

Kernow House, Watsons Bay, the same day

Frederick had hired a carriage, and as it rattled down the gravel driveway, he sat forward with eager anticipation. The tree house looked much smaller than he remembered, and although the trees had grown and the shrubs were more mature, Kernow House looked the same. As he took in the painted shutters and neat verandas, the front door was flung open and his mother, Amelia, ran down the steps to greet him.

Jumping from the carriage, Frederick gathered her up. She was so tiny in his arms that he feared he might squeeze her too tightly, but he could detect the scent of rosewater that was so much a part of her and could feel the energy she'd always exuded.

"How tall you've become, Freddy," she said through her tears, "and how handsome. I cannot believe how grown-up you are."

"Six years will do that to a boy," he said with a smile. He eyed the sparkling jewellery, the flushed cheeks and happy smile. "You look well, Mama."

"There is more grey in my hair than I would wish," she replied, "but yes, I am well, and so very happy to have you home again." She grasped his hand and led him indoors.

His homecoming had proved bitter-sweet, for although his mother had discovered a renewed zest for life and seemed contented in her widowhood, he'd felt the absence of his father in every corner of the house.

"I know you miss him, Freddy," said Amelia, a few days later, "and so do I. But towards the end it was quite pitiful to see him, and I know he was ready to leave us." Her gaze was steady. "It was unfortunate you couldn't be here, but it was for the best. You must remember your father as he was, not what he became, and he couldn't have borne it if you'd seen him during the last few months."

"That's what Uncle Harry said." He gazed out of the window. "He and Aunt Lavinia were very good to me, and I loved being at Trelevean, but this is home, and always has been." He smiled. "I will make Papa proud of me despite my lack of a degree, and I hope I prove worthy of his fortune."

"He was already proud of you," she murmured. "As for the fortune, you will have to wait until you attain your majority, but Mr Logan has proved a trustworthy guardian, and you won't go wrong if you heed his advice."

Through Harry, Frederick was aware of her initial distrust of Niall, and was pleased she'd come to accept him. "I have arranged to meet him in the new year," he said.

"Why wait so long? I thought you were keen to begin your business education?"

"I am, but Niall's visiting his daughter." He was restless and shifted in the chair. "Also I will be going away for a couple of weeks, Mama. There's something I have to do."

She frowned. "But you've only just come home, Freddy. Can't it wait until after Christmas?"

"It's a rather delicate matter," he hedged, "so I'd prefer to deal with it now."

Her expression brightened. "Is it a young lady? Someone you met aboard ship?"

He laughed. "It is something to do with a young lady, but not in the way you think." He saw the familiar petulance and refused to be swayed by it. "I'll tell all once I have concluded my task — until then you must be patient."

Eden Valley, December 1856

Ruby shooed the cow out of the byre and was about to turn back for the milk pail when Finn appeared in the doorway. "Hello," she said softly.

He wrapped his arms round her and drew her into the shadows. "I'm in need of a kiss," he murmured.

His lips were warm and demanding, and she melted into his embrace, the world outside the byre fading to nothing. She trembled with desire as she buried her fingers in his hair and pressed her aching body against him. The yearning to be with him, to love him freely and lie with him was almost unbearable, and as time had rolled on, the urgency had grown.

They drew apart, but she remained in the circle of his arms as they looked at one another. "The waiting is as torturous as the wanting," he sighed. "Oh, Ruby, my darling, when will you be mine?"

"It can't be for much longer," she replied. "Da promised to speed things along, but it seems like for ever."

"I wish —"

She put a fingers to his lips. "So do I," she whispered, "but we must not."

With a groan of frustration he drew her close and kissed the top of her head. "I hate this sneaking around. Everyone knows how we feel — why can't we just be together and to hell with convention?"

"Because I want everything to be perfect." She snuggled closer. "The wait will be worth it, I promise."

Their kiss was interrupted by Violet, who came rushing into the byre, curls flying, eyes bright with excitement. She skidded to a halt and folded her arms as Ruby and Finn hastily drew apart. Her bright blue gaze was accusing. "I saw you kissing," she said, "and that's very naughty."

Ruby actually blushed, but Finn just laughed. "Kissing is not naughty," he said, "not when you love the other person." He ruffled her hair. "Did you want something, or is this just a flying visit to plague us?"

She giggled and tugged at their hands. "Grandpa's come. He told me to fetch you."

509

Ruby looked at Finn and saw the same hope in his eyes as they hurried outside. "Da," she called as they approached him, "is it good news?"

Niall embraced her, his smile broad, his eyes bright with laughter. "It is, it is," he said, "and I have the papers to prove it."

Ruby scanned the document and burst into tears. At last, at last — she was free.

"Now hold on to those tears, Ruby. You can't be getting married with red eyes." Niall passed her a large handkerchief.

"Married? Today? Now?"

"Aye, your mam's inside with the justice of the peace, and no doubt fussing and fretting over the arrangements as we speak."

Ruby stared up at Finn, unable to put into words what she was feeling. She felt the clasp of his hand, read the happiness in his eyes and knew he was as dumbfounded as she.

"There's no time for that. Get on with you, girl, and leave me and Finn to more sensible things like unloading the wine. I just hope the long journey hasn't made it spoil."

Ruby kissed his cheek, and after hugging Finn, she flew up the steps and crashed into the house.

Horatio Withers was middle-aged and portly, and looked rather stunned after the long trip and the turn of events, but as a justice of the peace, he seemed to be taking it all in his stride, and he greeted her with a smile and a firm handshake.

"Right," said Amy, who was resplendent in an ornate hat and billowing dress. "I've laid out your clothes, and there's water to wash. Go and get ready while I organise the children." As Ruby hesitated, she eyed her questioningly. "You do still want to marry him, don't you?"

"Of course," she breathed.

Amy gave her a little push towards the bedroom. "Then hurry up. You've waited long enough for this day — don't dally now."

The dress was the colour of rich cream and fitted perfectly. From the ruffles at the shoulders to the nipped-in waist and full skirt, it rustled as she walked, and as she inspected her reflection in the fly-spotted mirror, she knew she had never looked so beautiful.

Her mother had tears in her eyes as she dressed her hair and added sprigs of blossom to the shining auburn curls. "Your grandma would have been so proud," she murmured, as she kissed her cheek.

Ruby slid her feet into the satin slippers and took the spray of flowers from the bed. "Oh, Mam," she whispered, "I can't believe this is happening."

"I know," Amy murmured, "but you always said you would marry Finn one day, and that day has finally come. Be happy, my darling."

"Aren't you ready yet?" Niall's voice was impatient on the other side of the door, but when Ruby emerged from the bedroom, he was struck dumb. He opened his arms and Ruby went into his embrace. No words were necessary, for he knew what was in her heart.

511

She laughed in delight as Violet showed off her lilac dress and Nathaniel proudly sketched a bow in his suit. Then she took her father's arm and stepped outside.

They were waiting by the river, where a bower had been erected beneath the trees, and ribbons fluttered from every branch. Finn stood beside Fergal and Tommy, his broad smile turning to an awed stare as she approached.

Ruby gazed up at him as he took her hand. She felt amazingly calm, for her certainty was absolute, and she knew Finn felt the same. They listened as the judge began the ceremony and led them into their vows, their gazes dropping only as Finn placed the gold ring on her finger.

"I pronounce you man and wife," said the judge. "You may kiss the bride."

Finn cupped her face and looked deep into her eyes. "I love you with all my heart and will do so until I die."

His kiss was achingly tender, and as Ruby melted into his embrace, she thought she heard Nell's chuckle of glee, but perhaps it was only the river gurgling over its stony bed.

CHAPTER
EIGHTEEN

Hunter Valley, December 1856

Jessie lay within the curve of Abel's body, listened to him breathing and knew this was where she belonged. Still drowsy with sleep, she was warm and pliant in his embrace, the scent of ripening grapes and rich soil drifting in on the cool breeze of pre-dawn.

"Good morning, Mrs Cruickshank," he murmured, kissing her shoulder. "Have I told you how beautiful that little birthmark is, and how it makes me want to ravish you?"

She giggled as he nuzzled her neck. "I thought you were asleep."

"How can I sleep with such temptation lying beside me?" He smiled as she turned in his arms and pressed her body along his. "I love you, Jess, even though you wear me out with all the lovemaking you demand from me."

She dug him in the ribs. "My pleasure," she murmured, already lost in the longing he always roused. His hand moved up her thigh and over her naked hip, and she yielded to his touch, pressing against him. As he cupped her breast and ran his thumb across the nipple, her pulse quickened, and she ran her hands down his hips to the tight swell of his buttocks, urging him to bring this aching need to its glorious conclusion.

"Why, Mrs Cruickshank," he teased, "what impatience." He paused as he looked into her eyes, then slid into her and gathered her close.

Jessie was swept away in the rhythm of their lovemaking, and when her passion was fulfilled, she held him tightly, never wanting to release him.

Their sated slumber was broken by their two-year-old daughter, Jenna, who had little respect for her parents' privacy and wanted breakfast. Jessie quickly donned the discarded nightgown, plucked the baby from the nearby cradle and took them into the kitchen. As Jenna tucked into a boiled egg, Jessie changed Daniel's wet napkins and put him to her breast.

Abel ploughed his way through a bowl of porridge as he discussed the day's work. "The grapes are almost ready," he said between mouthfuls, "and it looks as if this good weather is going to last, so we'll leave them on the vine for another day or so to make sure."

"What about the tobacco? Is that ready to pack?"

"Tumbalong reckons we're about right, so he's gone to round up the others." He put down the spoon with a clatter. "Thank God I still have him and his family. I don't know what I'd have done if they'd been taken."

"I think you and Peter had more to do with it than God," she retorted. "If it had been left to Him, they'd be in some terrible camp."

Abel grinned. "I gave those buggers something to think about, didn't I?" He ignored her look of disapproval at such language in front of Jenna and carried on. "But I know my rights. They can't take our blacks if we can prove they work for us. It's a good thing Gerhardt warned me and Peter about the raids and we got the accounts and necessary paperwork sorted. Those ledgers were what kept them here, 'cos I had every name and wage accounted for, right down to little Jacky-Jack."

She smiled. Jacky-Jack was five years old, but Abel had listed him as an apprentice houseboy earning five bob a year. "It's a shame others don't feel as strongly," she said, as she cleaned Jenna's face and helped her down. "I've heard terrible stories of children being taken from their mothers, and of families being literally torn apart."

Abel's face was grim. "So have I, but if they so much as try that here, I'll set the bloody dogs on them."

The sun was at its zenith, but in the shade by the river, Jessie could relax. The children were having a nap in the house, Tumbalong's niece was busy at the wash-tub, his granddaughter Francie was sweeping the veranda in her usual lacklustre way, and another granddaughter was in the kitchen. She was a lady of leisure until the children woke, so she leant against the tree and regarded her home.

Abel had built four small houses where the native camp had once been, and Tumbalong and his family had moved in as soon as they were finished. The yard had been broadened, there was a sturdy outdoor kitchen for communal use, and a line of impressive barns and fermenting towers stood back from the main clearing.

Abel had extended this clearing too, and overseen the building of the main house so it faced north-south to keep the fierce sun out. It was of lapped timber, painted white, with red roof tiles and pale blue shutters and screens. Standing on a low rise, it was perched on stilts to avoid flooding and termites, and there was an elegant veranda laced with white wrought iron and furnished with daybeds and chairs. Mature trees had been planted to give shade, and a gravel drive ran from the steps to the gate. This gate opened on to the track, which led through miles of lush vines and fields of tobacco to the bitumen road that passed by the schoolhouse and church.

It was far removed from her former life, and although she sometimes helped out at the school and saw Peter and Hilda regularly, she loved being at home. She ran her fingers through Abel's hair. He was lying with his head in her lap, reading to her from a library book. She smiled, for his reading had really come on once he had realised his daughter wanted a story each night.

The sound of an approaching rider stirred them from drowsy contentment, and they shifted grudgingly to see who their visitor might be. "I don't recognise him," mumbled Abel. "I'd better go and see what he wants."

Jessie was in no mood for visitors, but he looked like a gentleman and must be greeted accordingly. "I'll organise refreshments and leave you to it."

"Mr and Mrs Cruickshank?" The young man shook their hands. "I apologise for coming unannounced. My name is Frederick Cadwallader."

Jessie dipped a hesitant curtsy as she noted the rather impertinent way he looked at her. She coolly eyed him back, then made her escape as Abel led him to the veranda.

Having told Francie to bring out some cold beer, she stood by the window and eavesdropped. She learnt little other than that he was newly arrived from Cornwall and his family lived in Watsons Bay, which was near Sydney.

"It is your wife I have come to see," he said. "Would it be possible to speak with her?"

"That depends on what you've got to say," replied Abel.

"It is a little delicate," he confessed, "for it concerns her grandmother."

"What on earth could you know of Jessie's grandmother?" asked Abel. "She's been dead many a year."

Frederick Cadwallader sounded less certain of himself. "As I said, it is delicate."

Jessie was intrigued and went outside. "What of my grandmother, sir?" she asked, taking a seat beside Abel. "You say you are from Cornwall, but I hear no trace of it."

Frederick was clearly uneasy and probably regretting his visit. "I was born in Australia, but have lived in Cornwall these past few years," he explained. "My uncle is the earl of Kernow and wishes me to speak with you on his behalf."

Jessie frowned. "Why should a stranger, an earl, wish such a thing?"

"Oh dear, I'm making a hash of this."

Frederick mopped his brow and looked so ill at ease that Jessie took pity on him. "Why don't you start at the beginning? It's usually best." She smiled encouragement, but it did little to quell her own apprehension.

He took a long drink of beer as if to give himself time to think. "Many years ago," he began, "before Australia was colonised, my great-grandfather fell in love. She was the daughter of a fisherman, and he was soon to become the earl of Kernow. It was not an approved match, and the girl was blackmailed into an arranged marriage with the local parson. My great-grandfather met her again years later, and although he too was now married, they had an affair." His gaze dropped to his hands. "There was a child. Her name was Rose."

Jessie gasped. "Grandma Rose?" she breathed.

He nodded, his relief almost tangible.

"So her stories were true," she muttered. "None of us really believed her, not even when she told me that the mark we shared was proof she was from nobility."

"So you have the birthmark? Then there can be no doubt."

518

Jessie was finding it hard to take in. "What of her mother? Who was she?"

"Her name was Susan Penhalligan."

"I have seen that name somewhere."

"It's the name of the people at Moonrakers," said Abel, taking her trembling hand. "They know my family in Parramatta quite well." He looked at Frederick. "What's the connection?"

"Susan had a brother; it's his family at Moonrakers."

Jessie listened in thrall as he told the story of the ill-fated love affair that had survived decades only to end in a riding accident in the Hawkesbury River wilderness. She sniffed away tears as she heard how Jonathan traced Rose and secretly provided her with a home, and how, after his death, the search for her heirs had continued.

She remained silent as he talked of Susan's marriage to a clergyman named Ezra Collinson, and how it was suspected their daughter had been murdered by Edward Cadwallader — the same man who'd escaped charges of rape — and had killed his own son in a drunken accident — the same man who had married Eloise, this youth's grandmother.

"It is a bloody and shameful history," she said when he at last fell silent.

"My grandfather Edward was a brutal man, but my grandmother Eloise finally found love and happiness with Susan and Ezra's youngest son, George Collinson." He smiled hesitantly. "It is a tangled web, Mrs Cruickshank, and I hope I have not caused you too much distress."

"It is a lot to take in, but I'm glad you told me. My grandmother Rose never knew the full story, or if she did, she kept it to herself." She sighed. "How strange to think I have relatives all over New South Wales, when a moment ago I had only two brothers."

She chewed her lip, her thoughts churning. "Susan and Ezra's children knew nothing of Rose," she murmured, "and as the Collinson-Penhalligan family has found peace with the Cadwalladers through George's marriage to Eloise, then I think this secret should be kept."

"I agree that is wise," he replied, "and I will honour your wishes."

She smiled at him and he visibly relaxed. "There are only two things I must discuss before I take my leave." He reached into his pocket and drew out something in a long velvet box. "My uncle Harry thought you might like this," he said, as he handed it over. "It's rather beautiful, and a bit of a family heirloom, but he wants you to have it to welcome you into the fold, so to speak."

Jessie opened the box and gave a gasp. "I can't possibly accept this. It must be worth a fortune."

"It is our gift to you, and uncle Harry and I would be most hurt if you refuse to take it."

Jessie held the diamond bracelet up to the light and laughed with delight as it caught the sun and sparked fire. "I don't know when I would ever wear it, but thank you. I shall treasure it always."

"I'm glad you like it, although I can see you might feel a bit overdressed on a vineyard."

520

"I'll make sure she has plenty of opportunities to wear it, don't you worry. Thanks. It's very generous of you."

Frederick looked a little disconcerted by Abel's obvious discomfort, and hurriedly changed the subject. "The last thing I need to discuss with you is the endowment uncle Harry has arranged." He smiled at their puzzlement. "He is only following his grandfather's wishes to honour his commitment. He means no offence."

"I don't need money," she said, grasping Abel's hand to silence his protest. "I have all I want right here."

"I can see that," he said hastily, "but if you have no use of it, then it will mount up and who knows, one day your children's children might find it helpful."

She glanced at Abel, saw his agreement in his eyes and smiled. "Then I thank you, but what do I call you? Cousin sounds a bit formal."

"Freddy's what my family call me, so you should too."

"Thank you, Freddy, and you may call me Jessie. Let's drink some of Abel's wine and toast not only my new-found cousin, but the futures of our families."

Karlwekarlwe (the Devil's Marbles), Northern Territories, April 1857

The Rainbow Serpent's Eggs gleamed pale cream against the startling red earth. They sat in jumbled piles among the clumps of grass and spiny plants, some resting precariously upon others, some split in half, others scarred and sculpted by sandstorms, wind and rain.

Kumali had left her friends from the Alenjemtarpe people where the spring bubbled from the ground and had confidently strode north. She was naked but for a belt of hair, and she carried a dilly bag, sharpened stick and an emu egg filled with water. Her belief in the Spirits had strengthened after being with the Alenjemtarpe, and as she approached the sacred Dreaming Place, she thought she could feel Them walk beside her.

She had seen the eggs a whole day before she'd reached them, for they rose from the flat, empty land like a beacon. Yet as she reached the first, which marked the path to the heart of the Dreaming, her footsteps slowed and she shivered. There was something eerie about those eggs.

She sat and ate the last of the lizard she'd caught and cooked that morning, her gaze fixed to the silent, majestic eggs. She had been warned that the Spirits who lived here were not always kind and were quick to anger, but surely they would understand why she had come, and would listen to the songs and return her children.

The silence of the Never-Never wrapped itself around her as she dug a shallow hole in the earth and settled for the night. She would wait until someone came who would know the rituals to appease the Spirits and sing the songs for her.

She waited for many moons, living as her ancestors had done, hunting for food and water, sheltering from the day's heat and the night's cold in a shallow ditch, but as each day had dawned, hope dwindled, and she finally had to accept no one came this way any more.

Gathering her courage, she left the ashes of her cooking fire and made her way through the corridors of towering eggs to the central clearing. She listened nervously to the whispers that came from the caves and cracks. It was probably only the wind, but she suspected it was the *Kwerreympe*, the Spirit People of the Dreaming, who had seen her arrival and were discussing why she was there and what they should do to punish her for intruding.

She dropped the pointed stick and dilly bag, and knelt in supplication, her words coming freely in the dialect of her people. "I honour you, Great Spirit of the Rainbow Serpent. I honour you also, Sacred Earth of this Dreaming Place. I am but a woman who seeks your forgiveness for troubling you, but I beg you, Great Spirit of the Rainbow Serpent, to listen to my humble song."

She let the red sand drift through her fingers. "I sing to you, oh, Sacred Earth, and beg you to hear my voice in this Sacred Woman's Dreaming. And I cry out to you, *Kwerreympe*, as a mother who has lost her children. Bring them back into my arms."

She began to pound the earth, dancing in ever tighter circles until she was so exhausted she fell once more to her knees. "I beg you," she keened. "Bring me my babies."

The whispering was silent now, and as the moon rose, she knew they were watching her from the cracks

523

and crevices. "Please!" she wailed. "Give me back my babies. I do not know the songs. I do not know the dance. I know only that my heart is broken and I cannot live without my children."

She began to wander through the labyrinth of eggs, her entreaties rising in the night's stillness, echoing the cries of the countless women whose children had been torn from their arms.

As the stars began to fade, she knew her pleas would not be answered, for she had not been taught the songs and rituals by the Elders, had not learnt the Ancient Ways of this Sacred Woman's Dreaming because the white man had forbidden it, and her faith had not been strong enough.

She fell to the ground as the sun breached the horizon, and she knew this was where she would fall into endless sleep, her arms for ever empty. The songs to bring back the children had been forgotten. They could never be recalled.

CHAPTER
NINETEEN

Kernow House, Watsons Bay, May 1856

Frederick was sitting in his father's study going through the accounts. The businesses were many and varied, and he admired Niall's ability to keep so much information in his head, for he knew where every penny had come from, what he was owed and what had been spent.

He finally pushed back from the desk, head reeling from endless pages of facts and figures, and was startled to find it was almost dark. He lit the lamp, sat back in the chair and surveyed the room. There was little of his father still here, for Uncle Harry had made it his own during the years he'd taken over, but there were echoes of him in the crystal decanters and glasses, and the expensively bound books.

He smiled as he remembered the day he and Charlie had been summoned here after Gertrude had caught them with the pistols. He recalled how they had almost knocked their aunt to the ground in their haste to leave. Poor Gertrude, she'd been such a sour-faced spinster in those days, and yet the sea voyage had changed her, and he had been astounded by her softened manner and the prettiness in her smiling face. Her marriage to Lavinia's widowed cousin had completed the transformation, and now she was the happy mother of two strapping young boys.

He yawned and stretched. All this sitting about was making him sluggish, and he wished it would stop raining so he could go outside and get some exercise. He picked up the lamp, the memories of childhood lingering as he crossed the hall and climbed the stairs.

It was a shame the sword and pistols had been sold, for he would have liked to have them now, but the things his uncle had retrieved from George's house had compensated a little for their loss, and he'd thoroughly enjoyed reading the sea diaries. "Which reminds me," he muttered, as he reached the landing.

Hurrying past the bedrooms, he opened the door and climbed the stairs to the old attic nursery. It seemed much smaller, but then he'd grown a good eight inches since he'd last come in here. He set down the lamp and looked around him.

The rocking horse looked more moth-eaten than ever, and there were trunks and boxes spilling their contents everywhere. Moving round the clutter, which evoked his lonely childhood and the hours he'd spent poking about up here, he finally turned his attention to the panelling on the far wall. Had his secret cache been found? Was it still there?

He searched for the join in the skirting and pressed it. "Aha!" It flew open, and mindless of the damage to his trousers, he knelt on the dusty floor and reached inside.

His shoulders were too wide, but his arms were much longer than before and his fingers finally found the tin box he'd hidden over six years ago. With a triumphant whoop he pulled it out and took it into the light for a closer examination.

It was dusty and covered in animal droppings, but it opened with a creak to reveal the book. Frederick carefully lifted it out and ran his fingers over the faded leather. He'd had such an imagination as a boy, and he'd long suspected what it really was, but for just a moment he wished it could have been a pirate diary, filled with maps of treasure and instructions on how to find it.

"Come on, Freddy," he muttered, "time you grew up."

Placing the book back in the box, he carried it to his bedroom, eager to read it, confident now he could decipher it. He plumped the pillows and stretched out on the bed. The book looked more ragged than he remembered, and the writing had faded, yet as he opened it and read the fly-leaf, he realised the ink still held enough colour to be legible.

He was not surprised by the name at the front, and although some of the words and phrases were a little old-fashioned, he managed to translate them from the German easily enough after his thorough education in England, and he was soon lost in another world.

When the gong announced dinner, he had reached almost halfway, but the enjoyment and thrill of finally being able to read it had been smothered in the brooding darkness that filled every page — and by the secrets that were revealed.

It was a thoughtful and very troubled Frederick who tucked the book in his pocket and went downstairs.

Parramatta, June 1856

Frederick had finished the diary three weeks before, but the haunting story remained with him. He'd lain awake at night thinking about it, and it niggled at him when he should have been concentrating on other things. He was exhausted, confused and at his wits' end, for the diary had revealed something that could destroy the family and everything it had achieved since that diary had been written.

"Something's troubling you, Freddy. You haven't heard a word I've been saying this past twenty minutes."

He tried to make light of it. "I'm just a little tired," he said. "There's a lot to take in."

Niall rose from his chair and perched on the corner of the desk. "I have the feeling it is more than that," he said quietly. "Why don't you tell me?"

Frederick wondered if he dared. Niall had become a close friend and mentor over the past few months. He was his uncle's trusted friend and business partner, and a man of discretion, but could he reveal what he knew and be certain that Niall would keep it between them? As he looked into the concerned face, he wavered.

"Whatever you have to say will not be repeated beyond this room, Freddy. You have my word."

528

"Even if it is something that . . ." Frederick drifted into silence. If he told Niall, then he would not only betray the author, but everyone he held dear. But not to speak would mean carrying the burden alone, and as the years passed, that burden would grow heavier.

"As you know, Freddy, I am a Catholic, and we believe confession is good for the soul if repentance is honestly given. I cannot imagine what you could have done to cause you such obvious anguish, but surely it is better to share it than let it eat away at you?"

Frederick held his gaze. "I have your promise that what I tell you will not leave this room?"

"I have already given you my word." The blue eyes suddenly lacked their usual warmth. "I am not in the habit of lying."

Freddy swallowed and apologised, for he had never truly doubted Niall's honesty. He took a deep breath and, instead of telling him about the book, talked of the six years he'd lived in England. "My aunt and uncle treated me like their son, and Charlie became my brother, which made life at boarding school a little easier than it might have been. There were so many rules and tacit understandings between the boys and I found them incomprehensible most of the time, but Charlie was always there to help." He had a sharp memory of being bullied and sneered at by the other boys and quickly suppressed it.

"My uncle Harry made a point of spending time with me during the holidays, and we talked of many things, for he understood my homesickness and the struggle I was having to fit in at school. He had experienced the same sense of being different, of speaking with a strange accent, of holding differing views and expectations from my peers. The very word Australia seemed to encourage snide references to convicts and impertinent questions about my ancestry."

"I remember him telling me much the same thing," Niall murmured. "He resented being sent to England and found it very hard to take his place in society, for he looked upon his entitlement as a burden — his time away from Australia as enforced exile."

Frederick nodded. "Harry hated his father. Not only for the murder of his brother, but for the way he treated his mother, Eloise. The title was just another reminder of the man and all he stood for. It was a gift he neither sought nor wanted."

"He feels differently now," said Niall.

Frederick gave a weak smile. "He told me it was his return to Australia that made him see the true value of what he had. You see, he'd spent his entire adult life working to erase all memory of the previous Cadwalladers, especially Edward. It had become an obsession to prove he could run the estates, wipe out the debts and scandal, and rebuild the respect the family had once had. But he did it with anger and resentment, all the while wishing he was here, that he hadn't inherited the title and was free to pursue his own interests like my father."

Niall rose from the desk and poured a glass of whisky. He didn't offer one to Frederick, who, like his uncle, never touched alcohol. "Families are strange, aren't they?" he mused. "Your father resented his duties, and Oliver resented the lack of a title. It seems none of us is satisfied with what has been handed down to us."

"But Harry realised after his visit here that he loved Treleaven House and all it stood for. He was able to step back from it, you see — take a fresh view — and he suddenly realised he cared deeply for his inheritance and for the people who depended upon him. His return to Cornwall brought a renewed energy and lust for life that had been missing for too long. He is proud to be the earl and proud that his son, Charlie, will follow in his footsteps." Frederick fell silent.

Niall didn't speak as he sipped the whisky and stared out of the window. It was as if he understood Frederick needed time to gather his thoughts before he spoke again. As the clock ticked and the sounds within the house echoed distantly, the rain began to fall softly against the window.

"Charlie will make a good earl. It was what he was born to and all he's ever wanted. He turns twenty-one soon, and although he will not inherit until Harry's death, he's already planning to help run the estates and take some of the burden from his father's shoulders." Frederick watched the rain drift across the garden and realised it was time to reveal his secret.

"When Charlie and I were boys, we found some things in the attic."

"Ah, the pistols and swords." Niall smiled.

"You knew about them?"

"There wasn't much Harry didn't tell me. We were close friends and confidants, and we had a good laugh about that particular day."

"But he didn't know about the diary I found at the same time."

Niall's gaze sharpened.

"I never put it in the trunk, so it wasn't found. I hid it away again and retrieved it three weeks ago." He drew the little book from his pocket and placed it on the desk. "I couldn't read it before I left for England, but my education there was solid enough for me to decipher it now. I just wish I had remained in ignorance."

Niall frowned as he picked up the diary. He thumbed through the pages, inspected the edges, where possums had gnawed at them, and put it back on the desk. "So it is this that has given you sleepless nights and broken your concentration?"

Frederick nodded. "It is Eloise Cadwallader's diary, written during her marriage to Edward. She knew that if it was found, it would cause terrible trouble, and she was careful enough to write it in her native German and keep it hidden behind the old nursery wall."

Niall's attention was fixed on Frederick. "Go on," he said quietly.

"Eloise saw that diary as a friend. I don't think she had many, apart from her sisters, but as she poured her heart out to that little book, it was clear she could tell no one else what she was going through."

Frederick took a cigar case from his pocket and, in the ritual of lighting it, gave himself time to gather his emotions and continue. "Edward, the man I am ashamed to call my grandfather, was an evil man," he said coldly. "He didn't care for her, or the children she bore him, and saw them only as possessions to use or discard as he saw fit." Frederick swallowed the lump in his throat. "He raped her, Niall — took her by force and threatened to kill her and my uncles Harry and Charles if she left him."

"Good God," breathed Niall. "I knew he was a monster, but I never realised . . ."

Frederick watched the cigar smoke curl to the ceiling. "My father was the end result of that awful violence, but Eloise was a woman of profound strength and courage, for she was able to write joyfully in her diary that Edward was so stupid he'd insisted upon calling the child Oliver, and as the name meant 'peace', it was proof that some good had come from such evil."

"I'm amazed she didn't leave him," muttered Niall. "It sounds as if she lived in hell."

"She was about to when he attacked her and threatened my uncle Charles's life. He swore he would track her down wherever she hid. She was terrified. Then of course she had my father, Oliver, and all hope of escape was gone."

"Did she say where she was planning to run to?"

"To her lover."

Niall's eyes widened. "Then why didn't that lover rescue her? Surely he must have had some inkling of the nightmare she was living?"

"He knew nothing, not at that stage, and although Eloise was desperate to be with him, she knew their affair had to end. She was protecting not only herself and her children, but her lover too. Edward was a violent, possessive and jealous man given to rages and drunkenness, and she knew that if he discovered her liaison with this man, he would have killed him."

"Who was he?"

"George Collinson."

Niall smiled. "Ah, but she married him in the end. I'm glad. She deserved some happiness."

"That she did," agreed Frederick, "and after the tragic death of her eldest son, Charles, she finally found the courage to leave Edward, who then took his own life. His suicide left her free to marry again." He fell silent and watched the rain as he controlled his emotions. "The love between George and Eloise was as strong as ever, despite the years they'd been forced apart, and although I don't remember either of them clearly, I seem to recall they were sublimely happy."

Niall finished his whisky and put down the glass. "I always like a story with a happy ending." His gaze was piercing. "But I have the feeling that is not the end."

Frederick shook his head. "Uncle Harry is the earl of Kernow, but he has no right to the title or estates." He took a breath and looked at Niall. "He wasn't Edward's son. He was George's."

Niall let out a long, low whistle. "And Eloise told no one about this?"

"Only her diary." He smoked the cigar, the chill of his grandmother's revelations still with him. "She writes of her joy in his birth, of the fear she had that Edward would discover her deception and of the very real danger they were all in if she told George, for George would not stand by and let another man raise his son — especially a man like Edward. He would fight to the death to rescue her and the boy from his clutches."

"Yes," sighed Niall. "George would have reacted before thinking of the consequences. It would have been very dangerous for all concerned."

"After their marriage she contemplated the wisdom of making things clear, but she'd left it too long, and the right moment never seemed to come. Harry took the title, my father seemed content to run George's business, and I suppose she realised it was best for everyone to let things be. Yet the knowledge that she'd cheated my father of his rightful inheritance bothered her and so she ensured he had the lion's share of the business income."

"No wonder you've been elsewhere just lately. What a conundrum."

They fell silent and watched the rain. The clock ticked, the cigar smoke curled, and the household noises faded in their clamouring thoughts.

"Have you come to any conclusions, Freddy?" Niall's gentle voice broke the silence, and his hand rested affectionately on the younger man's shoulder.

"Uncle Harry hated his father and all he stood for. For him to learn that he was in fact not related to him by blood would come as a tremendous relief."

"But?"

"He has made the Treleaven estates his life's work. He has finally found contentment in Cornwall and his place within society. He has earned the respect of his

535

peers, and his estate workers and his opinions are listened to in the House of Lords."

Niall nodded to encourage him to continue.

"His son, Charlie, has been educated and groomed to take over, and from what I have seen of him, I think he will make a fine earl and be a credit to the Cadwallader name."

"But you are the heir."

Frederick stared out at the rain. "Harry took up his responsibilities regardless of his own wishes and has proven worthy of the title. Charlie's already talking of expanding the estates and making improvements in the copper mines. He relishes the prospect of working alongside his father. I have no wish to destroy everything Harry has worked for and sacrificed in his quest to prove there is still honour in the name Cadwallader."

"It sounds as if you have already come to a decision, my boy," said Niall, "but does that decision come from your head or your heart?"

Frederick smiled as he stubbed out the cigar. "My heart and head are firmly here in Australia. I do not wish to live out my days in Cornwall knowing I have besmirched a woman like Eloise's good name and ruined the dreams and expectations of the people I love." He gave a sigh. "My father didn't make a success of his life, but with your help, our family has prospered. Now it is my turn to take up the reins and learn all I can from you so that I will be prepared when it is time to take over."

"Spoken like a true Australian," said Niall with a grin.

"That I am, and always will be," Frederick replied. "This is my country, and I want to be a part of her history." He picked up the diary. "Poor Eloise, she tried so hard to keep her secrets hidden, but the truth always comes out, doesn't it?"

"Not from my lips, and I suspect not from yours. What do you plan to do with that?"

Frederick crossed the room. "Return it to George and Eloise, and keep the secret safe for ever," he replied. He threw the diary into the fire and watched the pages curl and catch light.

"Ashes to ashes, dust to dust. May the Lord give them peace at last."

EPILOGUE

Gallipoli, Turkey, 1916

It had been raining for weeks, and as the exhausted men of the Australian Eleventh Light Horse Regiment tried to find shelter and snatch some much-needed sleep, the trenches were turned into a stinking quagmire. The horses they had been assigned by the British Army were tethered far from the front line, but they stood miserably in the bleak landscape, which bore little resemblance to home. The men who had ridden them to this battlefield were farm boys, drovers and shearers, and like their animals, they knew they had arrived in hell.

The vermin had become increasingly bold, and they ran over the men, stealing scraps of food and sniffing hungrily at the wounded. It was not unknown for a dying man to have his final view of life in the reflection of a rat's eyes as it prepared to feast on his flesh, but this horror was nothing compared to the continuous bombardment that shuddered the earth, cracked the very air the men breathed and rang in their heads. It couldn't be escaped — not even in sleep.

The five youths huddled together, sharing the last of the mouldy bread and hot tea, their talk of home, loved ones and the coming battle. It didn't matter that they were of different ranks, and that one of them was a Pom, for they had survived the landing at Ari Burnu, where they'd been pinned down on the beach by Turkish machine-gun fire, had seen the slaughter of their comrades and knew that after today the number of fatalities would increase. The big push was coming, and they waited only for the signal to go over the top.

They were a strange group, these boys who'd been aged by experience, and whose eyes were glazed from the atrocities they had witnessed and the appalling conditions they had been forced to live in, but they shared a kinship that went deeper than their pride in their country and in their brothers-in-arms, for they were related.

Albert Penhalligan from Parramatta was the eldest at barely twenty-one. Peter Cruickshank from the Hunter Valley was eighteen, as was Billy Logan from Eden Valley. James Cadwallader was a few months past his seventeenth birthday, but because he was the Pommy son of an earl, he'd been swiftly promoted to captain following the deaths of his senior officers. Henry Cadwallader was his cousin. Born and raised in Sydney, he'd managed to fool the recruiting officers by lying about his age and, at fifteen, was the youngest of them all. He had become something of a mascot to this tight-knit little group — a boy to be protected and cherished, a boy whose courage under fire had never faltered despite his youth, a boy they were determined would live to return to his mother.

As the whistles blew and the shouts echoed down the lines and through the trenches, the five came silently together. The letters from home had been read until they fell apart; the photos of their loved ones were faded and besmirched with the mud and blood of the battlefield. Home was on the other side of the world. All they had was each other. There was no need for words, just the solace of another's embrace and the boost of courage it gave to see them through the next few hours.

As the whistles grew louder, they drew apart and prepared to climb the ladders. They were all terrified, but none of them showed it, and as the Australians looked up at the flag of the Southern Cross, which flew defiantly above the trenches, they saluted it with pride.

If death came today, their exploits would be remembered, their stories told, and ultimately Australia would lose the shackles of her convict past and become a nation that could hold her head high. For her youth had shed their blood in these foreign fields, and like the pioneers who had given their lives for this flag — this nation — their sacrifice would not be forgotten.

Also available in ISIS Large Print:

A Kingdom for the Brave

Tamara McKinley

Following the lives of pioneers, warriors and lovers against the backdrop of newly-colonised Australia

Surviving a vicious massacre, the Aboriginal boy Mandawuy is the last of his tribe. He will face the ultimate choice — join with the white man, or rebel alongside his fellow warriors.

When George Collinson meets Eloise it is love at first sight. But Eloise is married to Edward Cadwallader — a man capable of great brutality, who will never let his wife or their son leave him alive . . .

Their husbands are devoted friends but Nell Penhalligan and Alice Quince clash from the moment they meet. However, when tragedy threatens, they will have to overcome their enmity to survive.

Niall Logan is one of many Irish children sent to Sydney in chains. As he struggles to exist in the cruel world of a convict colony, he yearns only for freedom.

ISBN 978-0-7531-8306-9 (hb)
ISBN 978-0-7531-8307-6 (pb)

Lands Beyond the Sea

Tamara McKinley

By the 1700s, the Aborigine had lived in harmony with the land in Australia for 60,000 years. But now ghostships are arriving, and their very existence is threatened by a terrifying white invasion.

When Jonathan Cadwallader leaves Cornwall to sail on the Endeavour, he is forced to abandon his sweetheart, Susan Penhalligan. But an act of brutality will reunite them in the raw and unforgiving penal colony of New South Wales.

Billy Penhalligan has survived transportation and clings to the promise of a new beginning. But there will be more suffering before he or his fellow convicts can regard Australia as home . . .

ISBN 978-0-7531-8038-9 (hb)
ISBN 978-0-7531-8039-6 (pb)